THE LAST POETS

Christine Otten

THE LAST POETS

Translated from the Dutch
by Jonathan Reeder

WORLD EDITIONS
New York, London, Amsterdam

Published in the USA in 2018 by World Editions LLC, New York
Published in the UK in 2015 by World Editions LTD, London

World Editions
New York/London/Amsterdam

Printed by Sheridan, Chelsea, MI, USA

Library of Congress Cataloging in Publication Data is available

ISBN 978-1-64286-003-0

First published as *De laatste dichters* in the Netherlands in 2004 by
Atlas Contact, Amsterdam.

This project has been funded with support from the European
Commission. This publication reflects the views only of the author,
and the Commission cannot be held responsible for any use which
may be made of the information contained herein.

Co-funded by the
Creative Europe Program
of the European Union

This book was published with the support of the Dutch Foundation
for Literature

N ederlands
  letterenfonds
dutch foundation
for literature

Twitter: @WorldEdBooks
Facebook: WorldEditionsInternationalPublishing
www.worldeditions.org

for my son Daniël

The Last Poets are

Jerome Huling / Omar Ben Hassen / Umar Bin Hassan

Felipe Luciano

Gylan Kain

David Nelson

Charles Davis / Abiodun Oyewole

Alafia Pudim / Jalal Nuriddin

Raymond Hurrey / Nilija Obabi

Suliaman El-Hadi

Don Babatunde Eaton

Table of Contents

This was always, and remains
a foreign land. And we are

undoubtedly, the slaves.

There is some music, that shd come on now
With space for human drama, there shd be some memory
that leaves you smiling. That is, night and the way
Her lovely hand, extended. The Star, the star, all night
We loved it
Like ourselves.

THE TIME HAS COME

AUTUMN

Prologue

He remembered the exact day: November 11, 1979. It was a Thursday afternoon. He was in Ameja's place, a swanky apartment on the eighth floor on Columbus Avenue. He looked outside. It was raining gently. He stood in the living room, watching the drops trickle slowly down the window, zigzagging their way over the glass. Outside, the streetlights were already on. He saw the trees in Central Park, the vibrant spectrum of yellow and green and red and rust-brown. The wispy, watery clouds up above and the pale orange-yellow sunlight trying to break through. Even now, twenty years later, he remembered every detail of that depressing view. As if everything stood still. The glossy reflection of his face in the windowpane. The lights of the cars and taxis down below, melting into one long glistening image, a fading flash of light that nestled into his memory. He had never seen New York like this before, the city as an abstract painting, frozen in his gaze. The city as a perfect reflection of his state of mind. He felt calm. His head was clear. He heard the soft hum of the furnace. It was as though he had spent his whole life working toward this moment. Everything he had been through up till now, all the violence, the commotion, the love affairs, the sex, the disappointment, the successes, drained from him and left him empty. That is how he felt: as though he was ready to fall, fall as deep as he could.

Ameja was out. She said she'd be late, that she had to go to Harlem for business and that he should wait for her. The burned, bitter smell of crack cocaine wafted into the living room. Zaid, a prominent Nation of Islam preacher, was in the kitchen. You could always find him at Ameja's. 'Come on, brother Umar, you gotta try this, it's the next level,' he had said, with that whispering, conspiratorial voice of his. 'It's better than sniffing, it's heaven on earth.' Of course, he never said this when Ameja was around. Ameja had forbidden him to smoke the stuff. She would give him as much white powder as he wanted, as long as he didn't smoke it. 'That'll be the end,' she said. 'I'll throw you out.'

He was clean that afternoon. He had shaved and show-ered and put on one of the white silk dress shirts that Ameja had bought him from her cousin on 125th St. Ameja bought everything for him. Brooks Brothers suits, a fedora, shoes, cocaine. And he gave her sex.

He recalled their first encounter, one night a few months back. It was the premiere of *Suspenders*. His first play to be staged. It was about a black and a white man stuck in an elevator in an office building on Wall Street. Larry Fishburne played the lead. There was an after-party and Larry had introduced him to Ameja. Ameja was tall and slender and her hair hung past her shoul-ders. He wondered how she got it to stay so smooth and glossy. Her skin was unblemished and chocolaty.

'So you're the famous poet,' she said, and he heard the irony in her voice. As though she knew he hadn't written a poem in years. He worked as a cook in a diner in SoHo, was married to Malika, and had three children. They lived in a small apartment in Clinton Hills in Brooklyn.

'Good with words. I've got your records at home ...

Haven't played them for years.' As she spoke she measured him up, eyeing him from head to toe. 'Wasn't your name Omar?'

He laughed. 'Umar,' he said. 'Umar Bin Hassan.'

It was as though he escaped from his own life that night. The theater, the applause, the lights, the attention. It was so familiar, so gratifying. Brooklyn seemed light-years away.

'I want to hear your beautiful voice in my ear,' she whispered as she leaned over, offering him a glimpse of her breasts. They went to her apartment. They snorted and screwed until the sun came up.

He watched the clouds slowly dissipate above Central Park. Twilight colored the sky pink and purple. Only now did he really notice the street noise. The agitated honking of the cars, the wail of the sirens, the monotonous roar of the traffic. But the noises remained at a distance, reaching him in waves. He looked down below, saw umbrella-wielding pedestrians hurry along the sidewalk; they were almost like puppets scurrying into the subway. The asphalt glistened under the streetlamps. He saw the row of taxis waiting at a red light; they seemed to jostle like excited children. The longer he observed the tumult on the streets, the further away he felt himself drift. He had no idea what to expect, where he would go, what would happen to him after this afternoon. The only thing he could do was yield; every muscle in his body was relaxed. It was a relief to finally give in to the gnawing, hollow feeling in him, a dark, perplexing desire. As though something was waiting for him. As though he was holding something back. This was the real reason he was hardly ever home. A few weeks back he had taken Malika and the kids to Coney Island. It was a Sunday. An unusually fine day in October. They had picked up his eldest daughter Amina at Queenie's and then went to the beach. It was sunny and warm. The light was white and misty, and from the boardwalk you could barely see where the water stopped and the sky began. The children went on the merry-go-round. They ate ice cream on the beach. He listened to the clear sound of their excited voices, saw how Amina fussed over the little ones. Amina had just turned eight. He looked out to sea, a thin, light-blue ribbon in the distance; he wanted to play with the children, had brought a ball and tennis rackets, but for one reason or another he couldn't get close to them, as though he was observing them, and himself, from a distance. Malika didn't lose sight of him for even a moment.

'Talk to me, Umar,' she said.

'What?'

'You know what I'm talking about. Those suits. The shoes. You can't afford them. What's up?'

'Nothing, not a thing. A little windfall, that's all.'

'You can't snow me with a bit of coke, you know.'

'Is that what I'm trying to do?'

'I don't know.' She looked the other way. He saw her disappointment. He felt like a traitor, but not because he was fooling around with Ameja. Ameja had nothing to do with it. Even when he had sex with her, when he let himself slide along with the warm flush of the cocaine and whispered gentle, sexy things in her ear, drove her crazy with his words and his tongue, even then it was as if he was watching a shadow of himself, an imitation Umar Bin Hassan.

Still, he went back to her apartment every afternoon. He took off his shoes and walked across the deep white wool carpeting that ran through every room. The heat was turned up. He switched on the TV and watched a game show or an old Western. He lay on the floor with a pillow. He forgot all the hustle and yelling and swearing in the diner, the pale fluorescent light by which he made salads, hamburgers, and fries, quick quick, the light that made his eyes sore, the depressing white bathroom tiles and the dirty plates stacked in the dishwashing sink. The hiss of hot oil on the grill. The heat of the subway. Sweat beaded up on his forehead and ran down his back. He always ran that last stretch, from the subway to 79th and Columbus, as fast as he could, as though the devil was nipping at his heels.

He heard a noise from the kitchen. He turned and saw Zaid stagger into the room, flop onto one of the leather sofas, prop his feet on the coffee table, and stare blankly at the enormous lighted aquarium opposite them. It was dark by now, and the aquarium shed a blue glow over the living room.

'Ameja won't be back for a while,' Zaid mumbled.

'Maybe.'

'Poets and preachers have a lot in common, don't you think?' he laughed. His eyes were closed. A blissful smile played around his mouth. 'Both looking for inspiration. Am I right?'

'Get outta here, man. How do you do it? Are they crazy at the Nation? Haven't they got you figured out yet?'

'The first time it's like coming, but, like, with your entire being. A sort of heightened, supernatural orgasm. No pussy even comes close.'

'I know.'

'You don't know nothing. Come with me to the kitchen, Umar. What else are you doing here? You're just like me. Too proud to just give in, but I see what's smoldering in you, man. A little turn-on and a quickie isn't enough for you. What you're looking for, no woman can give you.

Nobody can. Didn't I say poets and priests have a lot in common?'

'You're bullshitting.'

'You know that's not true.'

'What do you want from me?'

'Nothing, brother Umar. I just can't sit here and watch you throw your life away. You belong in the Nation. You know you do. You've got something to say.'

'Bullshit. I don't belong anywhere. No muthafucka's gonna tell me where I belong, you understand me? This is totally insane. Have you seen yourself lately?'

'Come with me to the kitchen.'

'She'll throw me out.'

'So what?'

'Shut up, Zaid.'

'Shhh ... ' Zaid put his index finger over his lips and sank into the sofa. His head flopped back. From one second to the next he had fallen into a deep sleep.

Umar looked at the big orange and red fish in the aquarium. He heard the gentle gurgle of the water pump. A pleasantly restful sound. Zaid started to snore. His mouth hung open. He was as thin as a rake. The way he lay there ... As defenseless as an old man.

He went to the bathroom and took a piss. So many mirrors: he saw himself from all sides. The shiny white dress shirt that hung loosely over his trousers. His round head. His dick in his hand. He shut his eyes. Missed the rim of the toilet. He heard the splatter on the tile floor. If Ameja only knew. He zipped up his fly and wiped the floor with a towel, then threw the towel into a corner. He went back to the living room. Zaid was lying on his side. His knees bent, legs curled up. Umar stood there looking at him, as though watching over a child, waiting until he woke up. Zaid's words had gotten under his skin, they reverberated in his head. He was like the devil, that guy. He'd been badgering him for weeks. Umar had laughed at Zaid's reaction when Ameja read the reviews of *Suspenders* out loud to them both: 'Last Poet Convincing As Playwright,' the critic wrote. In a New York review!

'You're one of them, Umar,' Zaid had jeered. 'What's your next move? Hollywood? Get outta here. You're nothing more than a black mascot for those theater folks, you know that as well as I do.'

It had only taken a few lines of coke to make Umar's euphoria over his success last the whole night. And the next morning he got up at six-thirty and took the A train to the diner. No one there read *The New York Times*.

Sometimes it felt like he was a prisoner of his own thoughts. He had received a letter from a professor at a university in Michigan who taught a class in poetry and the black nationalist movement in the '60s. Wanted permission to include 'Niggers are Scared of Revolution' in a reader for his students. The poem was a classic, the man wrote, it exposed the heart of the problem with which blacks, black men, had been wrestling for years. *Niggers are lovers. Niggers loved to hear Malcolm rap but they didn't love Malcolm. Niggers love anything but themselves.*

He didn't write back. As long he wasn't producing any new poems, he didn't have the nerve to discuss his work. As though he didn't deserve to. He could hardly bring himself to listen to music anymore. He had turned off the record player when Malika put on *Kind of Blue* by Miles one night. It hurt to hear those familiar sounds, the subtle twists and repetitions, the trumpet's warm, sultry whisper, searching for the right tone. Miles was a strange guy, slippery, but his music cut straight to Umar's soul. Behind every note a word was hidden, a mood, an atmosphere, but that night he didn't see a thing, no images, no words; the music blinded and deafened him. He could barely even remember how he himself sounded. As though his poems no longer needed him. They led their own life, independent of him. He saw them: when he hurried through the busy Manhattan streets and saw all those anonymous faces pass by, the lights, the garish neon advertisements, the tall glistening towers, the panhandlers, the hustlers, the junkies, a whirlwind of words and images and sounds that made him wistful.

Zaid rolled onto his other side. Made clicking noises with his tongue.

'Get up, man. She'll be here soon.' Umar gave him a shove in the back. 'Ameja doesn't want any hassle. And she definitely doesn't want your filthy feet on her couch.'

Zaid laughed. He hoisted himself off the sofa and retreated to the kitchen.

But Umar knew he was kidding himself. He knew all along he'd start smoking that shit, sooner or later. He had no choice, really. It was just a question of waiting for the right moment.

So he went into the kitchen. The bright light there blinded him for a second.

'Sit down,' Zaid said. As though hypnotized, he stared at the flame of his lighter as it melted the crack in the spoon. 'There's the pipe.'

Umar picked up the small stone pipe that lay on the table. Zaid drizzled the bubbling mass into its bowl. 'Quick,' he said, 'before it's gone. You have to hold it in as long as you can.'

Umar inhaled, felt the bittersweet smoke burn in his throat, his lungs.

'You feel it?'

Zaid's voice echoed in his head. He closed his eyes.

A warmth flowed through his body; he felt it bend him over backward. It was a gentle, liquid warmth. His cheeks flushed. He felt crackly vibrations in his head, as though he'd just woken up after a long, deep sleep. Everything was red. Red velvet. He wanted to lie down. Got up and walked to the sofa. He saw the fish glide through their viscous water. The bluish-yellow light of the aquarium. The light was clear and crisp and real. He lay down. His fingers tingled; his legs felt heavy and sluggish. The warmth embraced him, caressed him, kissed him. It was like falling into a memory.

'This is only the beginning,' he heard Zaid say in the distance.

He couldn't speak. His yearning melted into the velvety storm that raged through his body. He smiled.

'Everything'll be fine, brother Umar,' Zaid whispered. 'Everything.'

'A.M.' (1990)

That sound … What is that sound? So clean. So fluid.
Emotions so hot in the passing of Summer into Autumn.
The magnificence of awakening to something so rare …
so new. Images dreaming softly in slow dances that wrap
themselves tightly around our doubts.
I touch your face.
You touch mine. He is so tender with our needs.
So strong in our desire to be free. The definitions of his
statement colors the skyline. He wa that one last feeling
of logic before the needle punctured the vein. He was the
music the morning after the resurrection of pain and prayers
in the twisted honor and slight applause of demons and folk
heroes stabbing us in the back.
He was a love Supreme.
He was a love Supreme.

EAST ORANGE, NEW JERSEY, SEPTEMBER 2001

Recollections of Grand Mixer DXT, Greenpoint Studio, Brooklyn, 1991

'There was an abattoir next door to the studio. Every morning, really early, a truck full of chickens drove up, and when the tailgate opened you heard their screeching and wailing. "I don't wanna go. I don't wanna go." Like they knew where they were headed. That high-pitched wail. It always woke me up. And the stench, weekends. On Sunday you smelled the bitter, rancid odor of chicken shit and clotted blood. But we got used to it, right? Once I met the guy who did the slaughtering. Huge guy. He had a sharp knife, and he chopped those chickens' heads off, one by one, and hung them up on hooks. He was merciless. He didn't say a prayer or anything. Just *wham*, head off, that's it, next. Sometimes I miss the studio—don't you, Umar? We were family: you, me, Anton the drummer, and Lane—remember Lane? Young guy. Wonder whatever happened to him. I had lost my house in Los Angeles to the earthquake. Bill Laswell said I could come live above his studio. How'd I know you'd be sleeping there too. Remember the Chinese place across the street? That was really good, the restaurant next door to McDonald's. We didn't have a kitchen. Only a sink and cold water. A shower on the third floor. And a huge wooden table where we sat talking at night. In the winter you had to let the water run or it'd freeze. Later I found an apartment in Harlem, but actually I'd have preferred to stay in Greenpoint. I rode my mountain bike from 132nd St. all the way back to Brooklyn. That studio had something. You know what I mean? You once said I wasted too much time on a beat. Came downstairs at night, muttering that I'd woken you up. But I was totally absorbed in that beat. The rest happened by itself, the sounds, the colors, the dialogues, the chord progressions. I converted it to music. We all had our own rituals. You too. Sometimes you'd vanish all of a sudden, and show up again three days later. Was Bill pissed! You remember? "Go upstairs, go sleep it off." And then you'd start writing again … '

AKRON, OHIO, 1958

Geronimo

'Can you see it?'

Carla Wilson's shrill voice echoed down Howard Street.

Jerome Huling did not budge. He was invisible. The night made him invisible. He thrust his fists deeper into his jacket pockets and saw how the red-to-yellow flicker of the neon lights reflected off Carla's bare thighs. She sat on the low wall behind Roxy's Café. The red turned her thighs gold, yellow turned them silver. With silver you could see her goose bumps. Tiny black dots on the glistening skin.

'C'mere.'

He still didn't realize Carla was talking to him. The longer he looked at her, the less himself he felt, his frozen feet in the canvas sneakers.

'You deaf or what?' She hopped off the wall where she had been sitting in vain for more than half an hour. It was too cold tonight. She tugged her black dress down over her thighs and pulled her thin leather jacket tighter. Then she blew a white cloud into the night.

'It's freezing,' she said in a monotone.

'Aren't you cold?' The words spontaneously escaped from Jerome's thoughts.

'So you do have a voice.' Carla Wilson laughed. Her high cheekbones went up and her eyes became slits. 'Come over here already. Or are you scared?'

Someone opened the door to Roxy's. The gentle, smoky music—until now no more than a muffled background noise—blared down Howard Street. Stridently high saxophone notes, like a scream. An agitated drumbeat. The music descended on them like a warm vapor. Jerome and Carla caught each other's eyes for a moment, then the door closed again.

'You seen Charlie?' Carla asked.

'No,' Jerome lied. A couple of hours earlier Charlie Brown had driven off in his white Pontiac, raising a hand to Jerome, winking. Two women, white women, were in the back seat.

'The bastard,' Carla hissed, as though she read Jerome's mind. 'He was supposed to pick me up. I could just as well have stayed home. What's going on here? Doesn't anybody want to fuck me?'

Jerome looked at Carla's enormous thighs, packed into her tight-fitting, rippled dress. He felt bad for her, the way she stood there waiting, blowing on her hands to warm them up. But he liked Charlie. Charlie was the only pimp in the neighborhood who treated Jerome like a grown-up. Sometimes he took him for rides in his Pontiac and told him things no one else would say. That you shouldn't have sex with white women. 'Let me tell you something, son,' he said. 'You go to bed with a white woman, she'll become your world. But respect her and stay out of her bed, and she'll *show* you the world.' Charlie Brown wore fancy white suits and silk shirts. His skin glistened with oil and his hair smelled like coconut. Even if Jerome didn't send any johns his way, Charlie would sometimes give him a few dollars.

'Maybe he'll still come,' Jerome said.

'Who?'

'Charlie.'

Carla guffawed. Her laugh sounded hollow and ugly in the darkness. 'Who you kidding? How old are you anyway?'

'Twelve,' Jerome Huling lied.

'Twelve,' Carla Wilson said. 'Twelve my ass.'

The music from Roxy's hummed softly and invitingly down the street. It was the only bar that was still open.

'Why don't you go inside?' Jerome asked.

'In that stink hole?'

Jerome knew he should have gone home. He should have gone home hours ago. But as long as Roxy's was open, he had the feeling something might happen. It always went like that. He would hang around long enough to muster up the courage to pick up his shoeshine kit and go inside. Roxy's was a pirate's den. There were men with an eye patch. Jerome once saw a woman without any hair or teeth; she staggered through the bar on matchstick legs. And once, in a corner, there was a man on the floor, bleeding; he had a knife sticking into his belly but nobody paid him any notice. The light in Roxy's was red and smoky. It smelled like liquor and sweet perfume. The music was deafening. Roxy's was like a magnet; he was drawn to it against his will. And never afraid. On the contrary: it was like he was invincible in Roxy's. Like he was flying. And he always earned a few dollars. The later you went, the more work there was. Sometimes the men didn't even seem to realize their shoes were being polished under the table.

'What you standing there like that for?'

She had hoisted herself back up on the wall. She immediately looked prettier in the flickering neon lights.

'Say, what's your name?'

'Geronimo,' answered Jerome.

'Geronimo? What kinda name's that?'

'Just Geronimo.' If she was out to hassle him, she had another thing coming. He was part Indian. The owner of a bar on Exchange Street had given him that name. At first those hillbillies in the bar had just cursed him out: 'You ain't coming in here, nigger.' They spat at him and hit him, but he kept on going there, doing his work. And one night the owner took him aside and asked his name. 'Your name's not Jerome,' he said. 'You're a black Indian. From now on you're Geronimo.' Carla was the first person he told his new name to.

'I'm going in,' Jerome said.

'C'mere now,' Carla said. She sounded friendly for the first time, almost warm.

His hands in his pockets, Jerome sauntered over to her. He looked at the lights and their reflection on Carla's skin. Red, yellow, red, yellow, he said to himself to the rhythm of the neon light. Red, yellow, red, yellow.

'Closer,' Carla whispered.

Red, yellow, red, yellow.

She hiked up her dress and spread her legs.

Jerome saw how the neon light made the enormous patch of hair glisten.

'Feel it,' Carla said. She took his hand and moved it to her crotch. The hairs there felt wiry and hard and warm. Red, yellow, red, yellow, red, yellow. She shoved him down, onto his knees, and pushed his head between her blue-black thighs. He gagged, smelling a pungent, rancid odor that reminded him of fish. He felt her strong hands on his neck, pulling him closer. 'Go on,' she panted. Go on what? He saw thick, swollen lips, wrinkled pieces of purple skin and flesh. 'Mouth open,' she commanded. He opened his mouth, his tongue touched those lips, they were wet and slimy and hot. He tasted the bitter sizzling smell, salty and soft in his mouth. From this close, it wasn't as bad.

Carla arched her back and stretched her body, pushed her groin deeper into Jerome's face, clamping his head between her thighs. He could hardly breathe. All he saw was blackness. 'Higher,' he heard her say, 'higher.' His tongue glided between her lips, from top to bottom, from bottom to top. And again. He felt the blood pound in his temples. His head was empty. His body was on fire. He swallowed her slime, kept on licking. Carla's thighs began to quiver. He pulled his head back and looked up. She smiled at him and shoved him backward. He fell on his ass.

'That's enough,' she said.

Jerome tried to stand up, but was so lightheaded he was afraid he'd fall right back over. The bright flashing lights hurt his eyes.

Carla hopped off the low wall and pulled her dress back down. She stuck out her hand. 'You okay?' she asked.

He nodded and stood up. His throat was shut tight; he couldn't make a sound. He walked over to his kit and picked it up.

'You get yourself home now, Geronimo,' Carla said.

'Geronimo,' it echoed in his head. His head was full of her smell and her taste. He took a deep breath, felt the crisp, cold night air burn in his lungs.

'And you don't have to tell nobody,' she said.

Nobody, he said to himself. He started walking, passing the garbage cans and the half-rotten wooden chairs that stood in front of Roxy's year-round as he left the parking lot. The music accompanied him. The sultry, songlike sound of the saxophone. The muted thud of the bass rhythms. He picked up his pace. He was as light as a feather. He broke into a run. He saw the moon hanging low over Howard Street, coloring the sky silvery and blue. The moon followed him, ran along with him. He ran as hard as he could, and did not look back once.

NEW YORK CITY, SEPTEMBER 2001

Bill Laswell, producer

And so I play I play I play walking to their smiles
Pain uptempo
Sensitivity open to the four winds

I want you to feel this thing I feel when fingers touching
strings
This strange thing that kisses my lips
Whispers in my ears

'Eddie Hazel was a terrific guitarist, very influential, a member of the Funkadelic family. It's a tragic story. Eddie struggled for years with drugs and alcohol. We were supposed to record an album with him. I had helped him get a recording contract and some money; he tried to get clean. He really was on the up and up. Then I had to go to Japan for a few concerts. I postponed the recordings a month. That was in the fall of '92.

I got a call in Tokyo. Bad news. Eddie was dead. Overdose. I was too late. I went back to New York. In the studio I listened to Eddie's material. It was so beautiful. Maybe we should record a tribute to him with all the people he worked with. Bootsy Collins, George Clinton, Pharoah Sanders, Bernie Worrell, Sly Stone.

Umar was living in Greenpoint, Brooklyn at the time, in the space upstairs from my studio, together with DXT and a couple of other musicians. He was making a comeback. Umar was fascinated by Eddie. I think they had a lot in common. One night we listened to one of Eddie's numbers together, a ballad. Right away Umar was on it, he dug into the music. Into Eddie's raucous high licks. I saw it happen: he was totally immersed. Umar is a true musician, even though he can't play a note. His father played trumpet. Music has nothing to do with technique. Absolutely nothing. Being a trumpeter has nothing to do with the trumpet. It's all about the experience of creating. Sometimes you have to wring yourself inside out before something raw and honest emerges. That makes you vulnerable, you become a threat. To create something nobody else does, that's not mainstream. That takes pain, frustration. Drugs can help sometimes. Drugs are cheap.

Umar was gutted when the music stopped. He went upstairs and wrote a poem. "Sacred to the Pain", he called it. We recorded it the next day, over the music. Umar's voice was so strong. He's got a flawless instinct for phrasing, what note to linger on and when to repeat a word. When his voice has to go up, and then up some more. He learned it from Miles and Coltrane. From his father. That searching for the right tone. The recording was perfect in a single take.

Bootsy and George were in the studio that afternoon, and a few other boys from the neighborhood. When the music finished, it was dead quiet. I turned around and saw that not a single one of them had dry eyes, not even George Clinton. Clinton! When you can achieve that with words and music—that's gotta mean something, right?'

Embraces all that I am
This thing called love
Love with no one to receive it
Love with no one to understand it
Love with no one to care for it
Musical discontent in a trance
Eyes rolling back into my head ...
Needs something no not that
My head needs something no not that

AKRON, OHIO, 1953

Grandma Elizabeth

He woke up to the vague sound of voices in the distance. An unintelligible gray murmur that went from high and fast to low and deep and slow. He slipped out of bed, opened the bedroom door, and crept to the landing.

'It's his own fault,' Jerome heard his grandmother say in her high, rasping voice. 'The fool.' He held his arm in front of his face against the bright hallway light. In the downstairs hall, under the large copper hanging lamp, Grandpa Willy, Mama, and Grandma Elizabeth stood in a small circle. Only now did he notice how much bigger his grandmother was than his mother.

'How can you talk like that?' his grandfather said.

Jerome hid behind the banister and peered downstairs.

'How can I talk like that? He never should have come back from Detroit. I'm telling you, he only brings trouble with him. And then I get to look after his brood.'

Jerome did not know who Grandma was talking about, but her words were threatening and ugly. He looked at his mother. Her hands were in her apron pockets, one foot scuffing the wooden floor. She didn't take part in the discussion.

Grandma glared at Grandpa. 'He's no good,' she said.

'He's your son.'

'Not anymore.'

'And what about the children?'

'They can stay till their father's free and then they can all get the hell out of my house. Understand?'

He tiptoed back to the bedroom. His arm accidentally brushed against the door as he passed, making the hinges squeak. He cringed and waited. When he was sure no one had heard him, he dove back into bed and pulled the covers up to his ears. His nose felt as cold as ice. Next to him, by the window, in another bed, Larry lay asleep on his stomach. A stripe of moonlight fell across his face. His mouth hung open and when he inhaled he made a strange rumbling noise. Larry was already six. Larry was a head taller.

Jerome squeezed his eyes shut. The hard words he'd just heard flew in circles inside his head. 'He never should have come back from Detroit.' ... 'He's your son.' ... 'What about the children?' ... 'Till their father's free.' What was up with the father of those children? Grandma was furious. She had stomped off with big, heavy steps. He was glad she hadn't caught him spying.

He rolled over. Larry was restless; more strange noises came out of his mouth. Jerome shut his eyes tight and did his best to fall back to sleep. The words he'd heard banged against the inside of his head like small, muffled hammers. 'They can all get the hell out of my house.' Did he and Larry and the little ones have to go? Where was Daddy? Jerome wouldn't mind leaving Grandma's house, but where to? Why didn't Mama say anything? He tried lying on his back, then on his stomach. No matter how he lay, he was wide awake. He could hear his heart pound in his temples. It was quiet downstairs except for some noises in the kitchen. He'd have liked to get up and go down there, to Mama, but Grandma Elizabeth was always nearby, and she'd send him straight back to bed—'You've got some nerve!'—and maybe she'd even be so mad that she'd yank down his pajamas and spank his bottom. Mama couldn't do anything about it. It was Grandma's house.

In the distance he heard owls calling in the woods. It was like they were talking to each other. First came the deep, dark call of one owl and then, a moment later, another owl answered with sharp, short screeches, and then the first one replied in turn. They must have been talking about something pretty mysterious, because you only heard them when it was pitch-dark outside. The owl's voices became colors in Jerome's head. The call of the first owl was red-brown like the dirt behind the house. The voice of the second owl was silver and as clear as the moonlight. Jerome listened to the strange, distant calls until he drifted off to sleep.

He was nearly five and couldn't say a single word.

'Maybe he's dumb,' he'd heard Grandma say.

'He's not dumb,' Mama said. 'I know he's not dumb.'

'Glad he's not my child.'

He hid from Grandma Elizabeth as much as possible. Fortunately the house was large. It was wooden and had a veranda with a rocking chair and a rickety table. It stood far from the paved road and the civilized world. It was surrounded by meadows. In the summer the grass was dry and yellow and it looked just like a prairie. Jerome would sit for hours staring at the dusty golden field and the sky above that trembled and rippled like water. He had never seen the ocean, but Mama had told him about the Great Lakes and how being there was like being at the ocean, how the lakes looked just as big and blue as the sea and how ships sailed on them. Jerome imagined the golden field blending into the ocean. He looked at the clear blue sky; there was hardly a cloud to be seen, just a few vague, wrinkled white stripes. The white stripes were the foam on the waves. The bright sunlight made the water glisten like silver. He heard the rumble of waves. The boom of a cannon. A ship rose out of the distant mist, a pirate ship with huge, ragged sails. The ship approached, he saw the men wave from the deck, men with long hair and eye patches. The pirates were coming for him, not for Larry. They were coming to rescue him from the big bare house on the prairie.

Jerome did his best to forget the nighttime discussion in the hall between Grandma and Grandpa. But Daddy didn't come back home. Nobody said a word during dinner the next night. They ate their yellow corn soup in silence. Then Grandma Elizabeth served up the roasted pig's feet and the mashed potatoes and the gravy. The gravy glistened in the light of the lamp. Mama winked at Jerome from across the table while she fed baby Billy. Billy made a mess of his food. His face was yellow with soup. He swatted a spoonful of mashed potatoes out of Mama's hand and the potatoes splattered on the wooden floor. Jerome held his breath. He hoped Mama would get up quick and wipe it up before Grandma saw it.

That night in bed he heard Mama and Larry talking. He pretended he was asleep.

'He did it for us, don't you ever forget that,' Mama said.

'Did he have a gun?' Larry asked.

'He had a gun.'

'And a horse?'

'No sweetie,' Mama laughed, 'he didn't have a horse. Your Daddy's not a cowboy.'

'What happened?'

'He wanted to earn money for us. So he could rent us a house.'

'But we live here, don't we?'

'We can't stay here.'

'Why not? I like it here.'

'The little ones tire Grandma out.'

'Uh-uhh.'

'Go to sleep.'

'But what *happened*?'

'What?'

'With Daddy?'

'Your Daddy would never shoot anybody. That's why it went wrong. He's not a robber. He's a musician.'

'Grandma says musicians are no good. She says: "Only thing black musicians do is drink."'

'Your father plays a mean trumpet.'

'I never heard him play.'

'When he gets back I'll ask him to play for you.'

'I don't care if he does.'

'Come on now, Larry.'

'I'm tired.'

'Your father loves you all. And so do I.'

Jerome heard the smacking sound of a kiss.

'Night,' Mama said.

Larry didn't answer.

Then Mama kissed his forehead and left the bedroom. She left the door ajar and a stripe of yellow light from the landing fell exactly between his bed and Larry's.

Grandma had a vegetable patch behind the house. She grew herbs and strawberries and tomatoes and potatoes. No one was allowed in her garden, not even Grandpa Willy. Sometimes, because Jerome couldn't speak, it was as if Grandma forgot he lived there. He would creep outside and spy on her from behind a shrub, and he would watch her as she kneeled, picking herbs or weeding. Her large hands moved as though independently of her body: she was a statue, her back straight and head held high, and she mumbled to herself as though she were praying. Grandma Elizabeth had light-brown, coffee-colored skin, a narrow face, high cheekbones, and a hooked nose. She was half Cherokee. She came from Alabama. That was all Jerome knew about his grandmother. Mama never talked about her. As if it was taboo, as if talking about her was punishable.

'Shouldn't you be playing outside?' Grandpa Willy asked one afternoon.

Jerome was sitting on the windowsill, looking at the sky. The clouds were thick and white and puffy. They looked like cotton balls.

'I saw Larry go to the woods,' Grandpa said.

Jerome could make out a face in one of the clouds. A face with eyes, a nose, and a mouth. It reminded him of Santa Claus.

'Why are you always so serious? Come over here.'

Grandpa sat in the big armchair near the fireplace. A thick Bible lay open on his lap. Grandpa was always reading the Bible, he knew the book inside out.

'I'll tell you something.'

Grandpa seemed small and old, sitting there. His wiry, frizzy hair was almost entirely gray. His broad hands were wrinkly. Jerome stayed put on the windowsill.

'You're a sensitive child, I saw that right away. Not everybody understands that, now do they?'

Jerome nodded. He didn't really understand what Grandpa meant.

'I think you take after your father. Don't let that worry you. Sonny's a good boy.'

Grandpa's words sounded sad and feeble. Jerome wanted him to stop talking like this. He slid off the windowsill and went to the door leading outside.

'I pray to God those white devils don't break him,' he heard Grandpa mumble to himself.

Jerome may not have talked out loud, but there were plenty of words in his head. But as soon as he tried to get the words and sentences to come out, it was as if his tongue was too short and too thick, his throat cramped. All that came out were strange, harsh noises. So he kept quiet.

Sometimes Larry teased him. 'Baby. You're just a baby.'

Jerome let him do it. Even though he was smaller than his brother, he felt like the oldest. Larry never saw what happened to Mama. How Grandma treated her. Grandma acted as though Mama was invisible, and it made Mama look so sad. So he would climb onto her lap, which cheered her up right away.

'Larry's a real Huling,' Grandma Elizabeth said. 'Look how tall he is. Not so round and fat as Jerome. Jerome's a Fuller.' Grandma had it in for his mother's family. She thought the Fullers were hicks. That they made too many children. Grandma never paid his little brother Chris or baby Billy any attention. Grandma said it was shameful that Mama had a fat belly again.

He tried to see Daddy's face. He closed his eyes tight but all he saw was the outline of his hair, a thick round wreath; the face remained blank. Jerome lay on his back in bed. It was already late, everyone was asleep and the house was quiet. He could hear the wood creaking. He wanted to get up and go into the next room where Mama and the little ones slept, but he didn't dare. He tried again. He didn't see anything. He didn't hear anything. His raw throat felt like it was burning. His head was hot, and it pounded. He opened his mouth. 'Dhh,' he tried. Larry turned in his sleep. 'Dhh,' he groaned as quietly as possible. If he could say Daddy's name, maybe he'd be able to visualize him. He pulled the covers over his head. 'Dhh.' He nearly suffocated. From the creaking of the iron bed he could tell that Larry was rolling over. He had to quit now, otherwise he'd wake his brother. He pushed off the covers and heaved a deep sigh. His father evaporated.

AKRON, OHIO, 1955

North Street

Behind the house on North Street was a rocky creek. It was so narrow that Jerome could easily jump over it into a meadow, and beyond that to the woods. When the kitchen window was open he could hear the water gurgling. A nice frothy sound that never stopped.

The house on North Street was a paradise. It was a reddish-brown brick house with four bedrooms, an eat-in kitchen, and a small living room. Everything was different than at Grandma and Grandpa Huling's. They had lots of neighbors. And Mama didn't mind if the other kids in the street came over to play. Mama had had another baby. Sandra. Jerome shared a bedroom with Chris and Billy. Larry stayed behind at Grandma and Grandpa's. Grandma said she could raise her eldest grandchild better than Mama could.

So now he really was the oldest.

He still didn't talk, but Mama said not to worry, now that they had their own house in the Elizabeth Park projects it would come. Sometimes he closed his eyes and the words would reverberate in his head. Creek, kitchen, Daddy, grass, sun, stones, Billy, baby, Mama, house, tree, woods. It drove him crazy. They zoomed around inside him but he couldn't catch them, couldn't grab hold of them. The words became colors and sounds. Creek was translucent white, tree was brown, kitchen was yellow, stones were white, baby was purple, sun was red, and Daddy was white, the white of his eyes and teeth. The colors sparkled in his mind. Daddy was the sound of the trumpet. A thin, humming stammer that rose up from under the house, from the basement. Soft, dark-red sounds that seeped up through the cracks in the floorboards. He could see them, the notes: they were round and glistened like velvet. They looked warm. The highest notes were yellow and jagged, like sunlight at the hottest part of the day. Like crying and screaming. As though Daddy was trying something, trying to get somewhere with his trumpet. He pushed and pushed, higher and higher, and then suddenly out came a muffled, fat, discordant note. Then nothing. Jerome opened his eyes. It was quiet in his head now. He went outside, to the creek, pulled stones out of the ground and threw them in the water. His stones clattered against the rocks beneath the surface.

'You want to see deer?' Daddy asked.
    Jerome nodded.
    'Say it then.'
    He nodded again.
    'Go on.'
    He forced the words against his throat. Thought he would throw up.
    'Easy does it.'
    'De … de … ' His tongue was in the way.
    Sonny Huling squatted down in front of him. Now they were just as tall. 'Deer. You want to see deer.'
    'De—er,' Jerome panted. He was out of breath.
    'Deer. Y'see?'

Sometimes Jerome followed his father.

His hands against the cool window of Jackson's barber shop on Howard Street. The glass is half steamed up, which makes everything inside look all misty. He sees his father. A tall, slender man. His fingers thin and elegant. He sweeps up the hair with a soft broom. Minuscule curls and wisps that together form a small black heap. He opens a hatch in the floor and pushes the heap down it with the broom. Jackson and Daddy chat, they laugh. There's a man in the barber chair, his head hanging back helplessly. Jackson lays a hot white towel on the man's face. Steam wafts off it. Jackson leaves the towel on the man's face while he sharpens his blade on a leather strap, talking to Daddy all the while.

His father's hair is soft and high, it frames his narrow face like a woolly wreath. He likes it that way. He doesn't want to get it cut, even though Mama says a Negro shouldn't wear his hair like that. Not in Akron. Nobody will give him a job this way.

Mama pulled him onto her lap. They were in the kitchen, and a magazine lay open on the flowered plastic tablecloth.

'We're going to read,' Mama said, pulling the magazine closer.

'I'm going to teach you the letters, and if you want you can repeat their name. This is a B.' She circled a B with a pencil. 'Say "B".'

'Bh,' Jerome sighed. He looked at the strange symbols on the paper. If you looked at them long enough they became black stripes.

'A,' his mother said. 'This is an A. You see?'

He nodded. He pressed up against her breast. He smelled soap and flowers.

'An L,' she said. 'And another one.' She wrote the four letters one after the other. 'Ball,' she said, 'this says "ball". Ball.'

She didn't make him talk. He only had to look and listen to how she wrote down and pronounced each word. 'I want you to be able to read when you go to school,' she said.

He listened to her warm, languid voice.

'I throw the ball.'

'The ball is round.'

'I am going home.'

'I am walking down the street.'

He heard the soft smacking sound her tongue made in her mouth. The sentences sounded like a melody. He started singing to himself. I-am-going-home. I-am-walking-down-the-street. I-am-going-to-learn-how-to-talk.

I-am-going-to-learn-how-to-talk.

I-am-going-to-learn-how-to-talk.

I-am-going-to-learn-how-to-talk.

'Jerome?'

'Yeah?'

'Tell Chris to take off that red sweater. I don't want no red in my house.'

Daddy stood in the doorway with his hands on his hips.

'How come?' Jerome sputtered.

'You heard me. I don't want to see that commie color here.'

Jerome looked at Chris, who had heard what his father said. They both shrugged their shoulders and Chris took off the sweater that his mother had bought for him a few days earlier.

Daddy just stood there. As though he was waiting for something. They hardly dared to resume their playing.

'Can we go get ice cream?'

Daddy appeared not to hear.

'Please, Dad?'

'What?'

'Ice cream. It's hot as anything. Can we go get ice cream?'

Jerome looked at his father. It was as though he didn't understand what they said. He gazed past them with a skittish look in his eye. Jerome went up to him and tugged on his arm. 'Daddy.'

'Sure thing, kiddo.' He dug in his jeans pocket and pulled out a few pennies. 'This enough?'

The boys burst out laughing.

'Another fifty cents,' Chris said, nudging him and raising his eyebrows.

'And keep your head held up straight,' Daddy said. 'Look those white motherfuckers right in the eye. They can't take that. Never look down, never. You boys promise me?'

They nodded. Held out their hands so their father could give them the coins.

'Now beat it, you two.'

'But the ice cream money … ' Jerome said.

'Go ask your mother.'

They played on the field beyond the river. Jerome, his brother Chris, his best friend Reggie Watson, and the other kids in the neighborhood. It was summertime. Every morning, older boys and girls from the other side of Akron came to the Elizabeth Park Projects to play with the children and to organize games and competitions. Handball, football, races, hide-and-seek. Sleepy

Johnson was older, about twenty, and towered above everyone else. He was heavyset but when he walked his movements were so supple and light it was as though his body wasn't even touching the ground. Everybody liked Sleepy. He had a low, melodious voice; so low that when he laughed it felt as though the ground was shaking.

One afternoon Sleepy went into the woods to pee. The woods were off limits to the children; they were big, dense, and dark, and in the middle there was a lake they called Mud Bottom because there was mud on the bottom. People had drowned in Mud Bottom. Sucked up by the mud.

When Sleepy Johnson returned from the woods a little while later he lingered at the edge of the field, watching the kids play. He leaned his heavy body against the trunk of a weeping willow, as though hiding from them under its low-hanging branches.

'Hey, Jerome,' he called.

Jerome looked up from his game. They were playing ball and he was behind. Out of the corner of his eye he had kept watch on the spot where Sleepy had gone into the woods.

'I've got something to tell you,' Sleepy said.

Jerome went over to him, pushing away the willow branches as though drawing a curtain.

'Sonny Huling's your father, right?'

'Yeah, so?' he answered, quasi-indifferently.

'He was in the woods. I saw him sitting on the bank of the lake, alone. He's a great player, d'you know that? Real fine jazz. Don't you let anybody say your daddy's crazy, okay? Nobody, you understand?'

Jerome nodded. Sleepy's words made him proud, but at the same time he felt like he'd been caught at something. He thought of the deer. He smelled the warm scent of the pine trees. His father always went to the woods alone. And if anybody spoke to him, he seemed not to hear them, as though he'd forgotten where he was. Then he'd take his trumpet and go out the kitchen door, across the creek and the field, and vanish into the woods. Jerome imagined that he could hear the gentle, fluid tones of the trumpet singing through the trees.

AKRON, OHIO, SEPTEMBER 2001

Barbara Jean Fuller

'Sonny and I knew each other from the Palace on Howard Street. He used to perform there sometimes with a pickup band. He never played loud, it was more lazy and melodious. He had a beautiful voice. "Little Harlem", that's what they called Howard Street, because there were so many clubs and theaters. The Palace, and dance places like the Army, East Market Gardens. Duke Ellington, Ella Fitzgerald, the Count Basie Orchestra, and Billy Eckstine, they all came to the Palace. Sometimes the big bands also played at the East Market Gardens, because it was better for dancing. At the Palace you had to sit in seats. Howard Street was a nice street in those days. The rubber shop was booming and Akron was well off.

One evening I was sitting in the Palace, up close to the stage. I saw Sonny looking at me while he was playing. He was a little older than me, eighteen or nineteen. A handsome guy. At a certain point he got up and walked over with his saxophone. He kept on playing, his eyes glued to me the whole time. I could see the smile on his lips. Back then he just played the sax. The trumpet came later.

My father worked at Goodyear. Thirty-six years he worked there. He came from Macon, Georgia. My mother was from Plantersville, Alabama. We lived on Hickory Street, across from a farm where they had stables. For a few cents you could ride one of their horses down the street. On Fridays my brothers played polo. I was the ninth child, and after me there were three more. I don't know much about my family. There's a street in Akron named after my grandfather, George Washington Fuller. He was an overseer at a cotton plantation in Georgia and came north with a few slaves. He married my grandmother Martha, who had done housekeeping for the plantation owners. She came from Czechoslovakia. That's why some of my children are so light-skinned. I remember my father telling us that he never liked his mother taking him to school. He was ashamed of her because she was white.

Sonny and I got married when I was expecting Larry. I was fifteen. That's when I met Sonny's family. We moved to Detroit because Sonny could get a job there in the Ford factory. On weekends he played in clubs on Hastings Street. We had it good. But one day at work he nearly fell into a melting furnace, y'know, this crucible thing where they melted steel. I don't know exactly what happened, but from that day on Sonny refused to go to the factory. We went back to Akron, moved in with his parents. Jerome was still a baby.

Life at the Hulings was so different than what I was used to. I don't know what it was with Elizabeth Huling; she was very introverted. Maybe things happened in Alabama that we don't know about. That must be it. She never wanted him to play music. It was like she just couldn't allow him to enjoy anything, allow him to be good at anything. She was always yelling at him. "Quit it with that music," she'd say, "you'll never be a musician. Get a job."

His father was a well-educated man. He came from the same town in Georgia as Elijah Muhammed from the Nation of Islam. He talked about him a lot. He wasn't a Muslim, but occasionally he went to the Nation's meetings in Chicago on Saturday. He was no match for Elizabeth.

I think there was something not right in Sonny's head. He never worked anywhere for more than a few days. Later, on North Street, the court had put a restraining order on him. Couldn't come anywhere near the house. Actually Sonny was a good guy, but he had problems. He drank. I don't know for sure.'

Untitled (1957)

Shoeshine shoeshine give your soul a treat
Shoeshine shoeshine can't be beat

AKRON, OHIO, 1960

Dora

'Yo, Jerome, where you going?'

Reggie Watson shouted and waved to him from across Wooster Ave. 'M-m-mammio baked a pie,' he said. 'She says for you come over.'

Jerome shook his head. 'No time, man. Tell her to save me a piece.'

Reggie sauntered across the wide avenue. Hands in his pockets. Head drooping. Reggie always went straight home after school, but now Jerome saw that he was hanging back.

'You in a hurry or something?' Reggie asked when he got closer.

'No, why?'

'I-I-I-I dunno.'

'Daddio will get real mad if you don't get yourself home.'

'Uh-huh,' Reggie mumbled, irritated. He didn't like being fobbed off.

Reggie and he had been pals since the start of first grade. They always walked home together after school. One day Reggie was crossing the street when a shiny blue Cadillac hit him. Jerome saw how Reggie's small body was catapulted about six feet in the air, how his face hit the curb. He lay motionless and limp on the sidewalk. A trickle of blood zigzagged over the gray concrete slabs. Jerome went over to him, but as he approached Reggie leapt up and tore off without a word. The car drove on. Jerome stood stock-still on the sidewalk. He couldn't move. He'd thought Reggie was dead. How could he manage to run off so fast?

The next day at school Reggie had a Band-Aid on his left cheek.

Jerome tried to ignore him, but at recess the boy came up to him.

'Th-thanks,' he said.

It was the first time Jerome heard another child stutter. He laughed. 'You made out of elastic, or what?' he asked.

Only much later did Jerome learn that Reggie had been terrified that his mother would give him a hiding for coming home late. Fear of his mother's open hand had given his wounded body wings. He wasn't allowed to hang around on the street. He lived with his mother, his brother and sister, and his grandparents on Bailey Court, a few blocks from Jerome.

That was how they became friends. Jerome liked going over to Reggie's. Everything about Reggie's home life was the opposite of Jerome's. There was always enough to eat, nobody fought, and Daddio Bellamy helped Reggie with his homework when his mother was at work. Mammio Bellamy told Jerome he was always welcome and could stay as long as he liked. She knew his family.

But recently Jerome's stuttering friend was starting to get on his nerves. Reggie stuck to him like white on rice. He was becoming Jerome's shadow. Jerome had the feeling his friend wanted something from him, but he didn't know what. A while back Reggie had suddenly started in about his father. The whole neighborhood knew George Watson was a drunkard. Why should Jerome care? As though he was supposed to be interested that the bastard left his kid in the lurch yet again. Reggie should just quit his bellyaching.

'I'll see you tomorrow,' Jerome said.

'Can I go with you?'

'You don't want to.'

'Wha-what d'you mean, I don't want to?'

Jerome chortled condescendingly. 'Go on now.' He looked into Reggie's crestfallen face. He hated it when Reggie gave him that look. Should he take him along after all? He could have him stand lookout. But Reggie was such a greenhorn. He'd get the fright of his life. And his mother would give him a real walloping when she found out he'd been hanging around in the city.

'I gotta work, man.'

'You like it?'

'Like what?'

'Wh-what you do.'

Jerome laughed. 'You can come with me another time, okay? See you tomorrow.' And with huge strides, Jerome bolted off.

At home he went to the shed to fetch his shoeshine box, with its brushes, cloths, and polish. He didn't feel like going inside. Through the window he could see the outline of his mother's small frame. She was standing in the middle of the room. He heard the little ones calling and laughing and hollering. He was just about to leave when he heard the high-pitched squeak of the front door. Sandra ambled outside and sat down on the stoop. Her face folded into a frown, she followed his every move.

'Is Daddy inside?' Jerome asked.

She shook her head.

'Tell Mama I'll be back later, will you?'

She nodded.

Jerome was anxious to get moving. He had promised Dora he would be on time. Sandra kept staring at him with her big, questioning eyes.

'Cat got your tongue?'

'Nah,' Sandra said.

'I've got to go. You keep an eye on Mama?'

'You're supposed to stay here,' Sandra said.

'Oh yeah? And who's gonna put food on the table?'

She shrugged her shoulders.

'Okay then.' Jerome planted a kiss on her forehead and hurried off. He went to the end of the street, over the bridge. He heard the water plash against the rocks. The sun was fierce on his neck. His hands in his pockets, he hiked up his trousers and took a deep breath of the hot, dusty, late-summer air. He thought of Dora, saw her long red braids, her pale face full of orange freckles. He had seen her for the first time a few weeks ago, one Saturday afternoon in a bar on Exchange Street where he always went to polish shoes. It was a narrow, smoky joint frequented by real lowlifes. He had never seen any children there except the other shoeshine boys who tried to steal his customers. Dora was sitting on a banquette against the wall. She was small and skinny. She stared blankly into space, aimlessly fiddling with the seam of her faded yellow dress.

He was done working. Out of the corner of his eye he kept looking over at the girl, wondering who her parents were, what she was doing in the bar. He never knew white people allowed their children to hang around in bars like this. When he approached her table she spoke to him.

'What's your name?' Her voice was clear and high.

'Jerome,' he answered.

'Mine's Dora. I'm ten. How old are you?'

'Eleven.' He was surprised by his own honesty. He looked at the girl. She was so pale that you could almost see through her.

'Let's go outside,' Dora said.

'What about your parents?'

She nodded toward a woman who lay with her head on the bar. Asleep, apparently, because her arms hung loosely alongside her body.

'Don't you have a father?'

She pursed her lips and stared at him.

'Okay with me,' Jerome mumbled. He shrugged.

'That's my father.' She pointed to a big, balding man with a red face. He was leaning against the worn wood-paneled wall, a glass of bourbon in his hand, smoking a cigarette. He didn't even notice his daughter pointing at him.

'Well, come on then.' She hopped off her seat and led him outside. It was almost like she was weightless. Her braids bounced upward with every step she took.

'I know a place,' she whispered in his ear.

Outside they blinked against the bright sunlight and crossed a barren field behind the bar. Dora was always a few steps ahead. She started skipping, then broke into a run. Jerome followed, dragging his heavy shoeshine kit. He forgot everything else, kept his eyes fixed on the strange translucent girl darting out ahead of him.

And then she stopped. 'Here it is.' She pointed to a hollow in the ground, surrounded by bushes; further up there was a patch of trees. 'Nice and shady,' she said. She nestled in the hollow. 'Come on.'

Jerome set his kit on the dusty ground and sat down next to her. The girl appeared to know exactly what she was doing.

'I always come here when I want to be alone,' she said.

'Uh-huh,' Jerome said, nodding timidly.

'Nobody except me knows about this place.' She pulled her dress over her head. 'Now you have to take something off.'

'How come?' He tried to avert his eyes from her naked torso, but he couldn't. The white of her skin made him think of ice cream. Her nipples were like two tiny red pinheads. She had goose bumps despite the heat.

'You'll see.' Dora laughed, exposing her beige teeth. She had small, pointy teeth and thin pink lips.

Jerome took off his shirt. 'So what all do you do here?' he asked.

'Just sit. Think.'

'Think?'

'Don't you ever do that? I think all the time. And if I want it to slow down in my head, I come here.' She threw back her head and looked up. Jerome followed her gaze. He saw the thick leafy crown of the trees, the branches and leaves waving gently in the wind. Through the canopy he could see snatches of deep blue and purple sky.

Dora leaned over and kissed Jerome on the lips. Then she held back and stared at him. 'Don't look at me like that,' she snapped. 'Where do you live?'

'In the bottom.'

'The what?'

'The Elizabeth Park Projects.'

'That's only for niggers, isn't it?'

Jerome didn't answer.

'My father hates niggers.' She leaned over again. She pried his lips apart and proceeded to kiss him, pressing her tongue into his mouth and swirling it around in circles.

Jerome felt her hands glide down his chest. He started getting all hot inside.

'You have to take off your pants,' she said.

'Why?'

'Why not?'

Jerome hesitated. He knew what sex was. What all hadn't he seen down on Howard Street. He knew that white men were crazy about black pussies. But what did Dora want? She was so young. She reminded him of the elf from the fairy tales his mother read to him when he was little. An elf in a tree. You could blow her away with just a puff.

'Come on,' she said.

'You gonna keep your panties on?'

'You want me to?'

He shrugged. She started tugging at his belt. He pushed her away and undid his pants.

'Why do you clean those guys' shoes in the bar? They're jerks.'

'Why do you think?'

'Do they pay a lot?'

He shrugged.

'Don't you go to school?'

'Sure I do.' His pants were down around his ankles. He cupped his hands in front of his penis. Dora looked straight into his eyes. Her irises were light green.

'Here, let me.' She pushed his hands aside. She kneeled down in the hollow and took his dick in her hands, caressed it. 'It's so dark.'

'What?'

'Your thing.'

'Well, what'd you expect?' He tried to resist the warm, tingling feeling in his belly. His dick began to stiffen. His balls tightened.

'Now you have to close your eyes,' she whispered.

He did what she said. Something about all this didn't

sit right. But Dora gave him a warm and tingly feeling he had never felt before. It shot through his entire body. It was different from when he played with himself. As though he was sinking into a soft, moist bed. He looked through half-closed eyes. Her small head was bobbing up and down. She licked and sucked on his dick and held his balls firmly in her hand. His thighs began to hurt; all his muscles cramped. The sky and the trees above him started spinning. He closed his eyes again. Dora stopped.

'Like it?' His body felt heavy and strange. He couldn't think straight. He opened his eyes.

'We'll do this again, okay?' Dora asked. She stood up and put on her dress. As if nothing special had happened. 'I'm here every Saturday afternoon, and sometimes after school too. But don't bring anybody with you, all right?'

Jerome hiked up his pants. 'Why not?'

'I picked you, now didn't I?'

He nodded.

'Next week?'

'Okay.'

'Deal,' she said. She clambered out of the hollow and darted back across the bumpy field. Jerome saw how her long red braids floated behind her.

The next two Saturdays they went to Dora's spot. Her parents were always too drunk to notice that they snuck off together. Dora taught him to French kiss, and the second time she sucked him off he came. She licked up and swallowed the white stuff. He almost threw up as he watched her. How could she do something like that? She said it tasted like mushrooms and that he should try it.

'Are you crazy?'

She always took off her dress and sometimes her panties too. Her pussy was a thin straight stripe with no hair on it. Like it was glued shut. He didn't dare touch it. She never asked him to. And he was secretly relieved he didn't have to do anything.

The last Saturday he saw Dora, at the beginning of September, was overcast. Dora wore a blue knitted vest over her pink dress.

'You want to go for a walk?' she asked.

'Where to?'

'Doesn't matter, just for a walk. I'm cold.'

He wanted to put his arm around her but was afraid someone might see them.

They walked across the field and past the hollow. The wind made the leaves rustle. The trees were already starting to turn red and yellow.

'You wanna go into the woods?' Dora asked.

'Fine with me,' Jerome said. He took her hand. There was no one around.

'Will you always be my friend?' Dora asked in a small voice.

Jerome nodded.

'Really? I have to know for sure.'

"Course I will. I'm with you now, aren't I?'

'That doesn't mean anything.'

'Then what do I have to do?'

Dora stopped and looked at him. Her eyes were pallid and watery. 'I don't want to go back.'

'We just got here.'

'I mean: I don't ever want to go back. To my house. It's a pigsty. My mother never does anything. Can I go home with you?'

Jerome laughed. 'What about your father?'

'You have a father too, don't you?'

It was like getting the wind knocked out of him.

Whenever he was with Dora, he forgot all about home. And when he was home and thought of her, he felt himself drift off. He hadn't told a soul about her. If he ever did, that fine feeling would disappear.

'Well?' she said.

'I don't know.' He looked at the ground and dug the toe of his boot into the sand.

'You want to sit down?'

'My father's not all there,' Jerome whispered.

'Not all there,' Dora repeated.

'He steals my money.' He thought of his father. Daddy standing out back smoking a cigarette. Thinking he was alone—but Jerome saw him through the kitchen window, and heard him muttering to himself. Unintelligible gray words and sentences he immediately swallowed back. His tall body hunched forward, as though there was a kink in his spine. Daddy made a strange, high-pitched growling noise that he guessed came from the back of his throat. He sniffed back the snot in his nose. He was crying. Jerome had never seen his father cry before.

'We could run away,' Dora suggested. Her eyes started to glisten. 'You earn money, right?'

'And then what?'

'And then we'd be together forever, and when we get big we'll have babies.'

'What?' Jerome looked at the small white girl in the blue vest. He saw her skinny body. He could reach all the way around her and still have room left over.

'Don't you want to leave too?'

He thought of Chris and Billy and the little ones. Sandra on the stoop in front of the house. 'You have to stay.' Dora cuddled up to him. She traced the outline of his lips with her finger. 'It's like they're drawn on,' she mumbled.

'What are?'

'Your lips.'

He felt her warm breath on his face. Her breath smelled slightly putrid. He stroked her hair. It all seemed unreal, as though they weren't really standing here.

'I'll always be your friend, okay?' he said hastily, hoping she would cheer up soon.

She gave him a shove. Looked at him, laughing. 'The hiding place, come on,' she said. 'Last one there's a rotten egg!' And off she ran.

They had agreed to meet on the field behind the bar at four o'clock. Afraid of being late, Jerome had rushed and was out of breath. His arm was sore from carrying the shoeshine kit. On Exchange Street he already heard the hubbub coming from the bar where Dora's parents always hung out. He darted across the street as inconspicuously as possible and headed straight for the field with the mounds and the holes and the bushes that concealed Dora's hideaway. She wasn't there. He waited for a bit and walked into the woods, calling her name. He heard a vague echo of his own voice in the woods, and the chatter of the birds. He went back to the hollow. No Dora. He ambled back to Exchange Street. He paused in front of the entrance to the bar; he was never able to just walk straight in. He took a deep breath, concentrated, tried to put all thoughts out of his head, shielding himself from the dirty looks and nasty comments from the men in the bar. He shifted his kit from one hand to the other and walked inside. Immediately he saw Dora sitting on the banquette against the wall, where he had seen her for the first time. Next to her was her father.

'Hey, you there, pickaninny. C'mere,' the red-faced man shouted. Dora looked away. Jerome straightened his back and went over to them.

'Gimme a shine,' the man said. 'And then we'll see what you're worth.'

Jerome looked at Dora. Her face looked pale, sallow. She sat with her shoulders hunched up and her eyes glued to the floor, like she was trying to hide inside her own body. He opened his kit and slid under the table. He saw the father's worn-out shoes. He spat on them, took a cloth and started polishing. He'd show that bastard. They all thought their shoes got extra shiny from spit, but only he really knew why he was spitting. After a little while he saw her father's hand appear under the table. A fleshy white hand. The hand rested on Dora's knee, pushed her dress up and started fiddling with her panties. Jerome held his breath. Stopped polishing.

'Hurry it up, will ya?'

He heard the man laugh. A rough, drunkard's laugh. Jerome rubbed the cloth lightly over the shoes as he watched Dora's father's big hand, now inside her panties, nudge her legs open and move slowly back and forth. He felt himself go queasy. It was as though he'd taken a blow to the head. His vision went dark, he tottered on his knees. No wonder Dora knew so much about sex.

'That'll do.' The man pulled his feet back. His hand stayed in his daughter's panties.

Jerome climbed out from under the table, struggled to get up. His head was spinning. He looked at Dora. Her damp cheeks glistened in the smoky yellow light of the bar. She wiped away the tears and smiled at him. He did not smile back. He was numb. He just picked up his kit and turned toward the door without asking for money.

'You're useless,' Dora's father called out after him.

He didn't respond, just headed outside. He was ashamed. Ashamed of that son of a bitch, of himself for walking off without a word. Of Dora. Of her tiny, pale, child's body. He pushed the door open and turned back. Dora saw him looking and smiled again. He forced himself to smile back and went outside, onto the street.

The next day, Reggie was waiting for him after school.

'Want to come over?'

Jerome shrugged.

'M-m-mammio wants to know why you don't come over anymore.'

'Just 'cause.'

'She says sh-sh-she wants to talk to your mother.'

'Is she crazy?'

'Mammio's not crazy.'

'I know that,' he sighed. He kicked a stone. 'Sure, I'll come over.'

They crossed Wooster Avenue without another word.

That morning, everything had seemed all right again. He had slept well and dream-free. His bed was nice and warm. He stretched out in it, enjoying the peace. But it only lasted a couple of seconds. Then it was like a black screen slid down in front of his thoughts. All his muscles tensed and he broke into a sweat. He knew he would never see Dora again. Nor would he ever again set foot on Exchange Street. He shut his eyes tight, but he couldn't get rid of that image of the fleshy white hand crawling up Dora's skinny thigh. It was as though, losing Dora, he'd lost everything: his work, his money, his pride.

Reggie and he were ambling toward Bailey Court.

'Can you keep your mouth shut about something?' Jerome asked.

'Wh-why?'

'Well, can you?'

''Course.'

'I knew this girl,' Jerome began. He already regretted it. It was like he was giving Dora away.

'And?'

'Never mind. I was just thinking … I mean … did you think white girls' skin is cold too? Like an Eskimo's?'

Reggie gaped at him. At least he didn't laugh. Reggie always knew when something was important.

'She was warm. Her blood was warmer than mine.' Jerome was talking more to himself than to his friend.

'Was she pretty?' Reggie asked.

'It's not about that. We were friends. She's gone.'

'Where to?'

'Doesn't matter.' They were in front of Reggie's house. Mammio spotted them from the kitchen and waved. Jerome waved back.

'Nobody knows, right?' Reggie asked as they went in the back door.

Jerome shook his head.

'Good.'

'Homesick' (1993)

We were there at the beginning of trust and faith and respect
behind closed doors we used to speak to each other in the soft
tones of the rainbow smiling through the river's mist cooling
the warmth and passion of time waiting for us to come home.

AKRON, OHIO, 1960

Mud Bottom

He stood on a thick branch, about fifteen feet above the still, black water, naked except for his underwear. He wanted to learn how to swim.

He looked up at the translucent sky ... If I don't come back up, they'll find my clothes, he thought fleetingly.

He crouched, and the branch bent with him. He looked out across the water. Wispy, glistening threads floated in the air. He saw small, shiny insects leap over the water's surface. Wild ferns on the opposite bank, thin stripes of bright green moss between the rocks. It was so quiet and beautiful here. Even the birds and crickets seemed to be holding their breath.

It was his first time here. He thought of his father. It wasn't hard to picture him in this place, sitting on a smooth round boulder at the water's edge. Licking his trumpet's mouthpiece. Rubbing his hands over his thighs, to wipe off the sweat before starting to play. Languid sounds echoing off the still water. The water was black glass. The highest notes evaporated at once. It was hardly a melody, just a string of notes. Who did he play for? Nobody could hear the music except him.

Or did he want Jerome to come listen? Was he afraid to ask?

The water looked deeper and farther away now. The woods were Daddy's. And when he could swim, they would be his. Then it wouldn't be dangerous to come here anymore. Good thing Mama didn't know where he was.

He counted to ten, out loud. One two three four five six seven eight nine ten. He took a deep breath, shut his eyes and jumped.

Jerome heard the wind rush in his ears before he hit the water with a smack.

Eyes wide open. Blackness. The silence dull and deathly. The air in his lungs pressed painfully against his ribs. His throat hurt. He flailed his arms. Felt the slimy clay on his feet. Feet up, quick, quick. If only the water weren't so black and opaque. This must be what being blind is like. Move your arms. That's it. Up. Swim. Come on. Arms up. Toward what looks like a puddle of white floating above.

He pushed the heavy water aside, and suddenly there was light. Air. He spat out the last of his breath. Sucked new, fresh air in. The bright white hurt his eyes. The water felt soft and tepid against his skin. He allowed himself to sink a little, and the water slowly closed above his head. Eyes shut. He waited for a moment before pushing himself back up. Again. He floated. Thought of all those tiny invisible fish and creatures and plants down there in the darkness. The sucking mud at the bottom of the lake. He paddled lazily to the bank. He could hear the soft ripple of the water tingle in his ears. He grabbed hold of a bush and pulled himself out.

'Rhythm Magic' (1996)

Listen

Can't you hear the naked mornings

And the raindrops on the windowpane as the high leaves you

Rhythm magic

The music of the word

Now you hear it

Now you don't

Now you feel it

Now you won't

AKRON, OHIO, 1960

The Hatchet

The puddles in the road disappeared as soon as he got nearer. It wasn't water at all. It hadn't rained in weeks. There was only the reflection of the bright sunlight on the black asphalt, the quivering of the air above it. He trudged further. Western Auto Supply was farther than he thought, a few miles outside of town, along the highway. He had asked Reggie where he could buy a pocketknife.

'Daddio buys his tools at Western Auto.'

'What do I want with tools?'

'They also sell hardware and car parts, that kind of thing. I'll bet they have knives too.'

Reggie didn't ask what Jerome needed a knife for.

Jerome was thirsty. His throat was parched and he tasted dust. Hopefully Western Auto sold Coke too.

The gust of a passing truck nearly knocked him over. He was focused on the green wooden building in the distance and didn't hear it coming. He tried to make out the letters on the sign: it should say 'Western Auto'. He would try to hitchhike back. But not now. He couldn't bring himself to talk to anyone, not before he had his knife.

He paused. Turned his cap backward to shield his neck from the sun. Felt the warm money in his pocket.

Sweat ran down his back. He started walking again. One two three four. One two three four, he counted to himself. He glanced down at his once-white canvas sneakers. The dry, rough grass that crackled under his feet. The monotonous rhythm of his own footsteps relaxed him. He might as well have been out on some everyday errand. An errand for his mother. Although as soon as this thought passed through his mind, he felt his stomach cramp up. Keep on walking, he told himself. Another couple hundred yards. He looked at the green store up ahead, which seemed to swim in the rippling, dusty air.

He had thought long and hard about his decision. Even brought it up with Mama.

'You'll do no such thing,' she said. She just laughed when he announced he was going to kill Daddy.

'He's gotta stop coming around here! What's he good for? He should just beat it!'

'Watch your mouth.'

'How come you put up with it?'

'One day you'll understand.'

'I'm bringing in the money now, aren't I?'

'I know, son. That's already bad enough. But your father can't do any different. Try to remember that. He loves you kids. He's your father.'

'Father,' Jerome repeated. But the word didn't jibe with reality.

He was close. He could read the letters on the enormous sign. Red neon lights with the words 'Western Auto'. But being daytime, the lights were out. The green wood paneling looked more faded from close up; here and there the paint was peeling off. There was a gas pump out in front. A beanpole of a white kid leaned lethargically against the railing of the veranda.

'You lost?'

Jerome shook his head. 'I thought it was closer. I walked.'

The boy laughed, showing his teeth. He was about eighteen, had greased-back black hair, and wore a red bandana around his neck. He looked like a faggot. Jerome wasn't sure if he worked here or was just hanging around.

'I gotta get something to drink.'

'Got any money?'

'Why wouldn't I?'

'Dunno.' The boy shrugged and sauntered over to the store entrance.

'Do you sell jackknives?'

'What?'

'Pocketknives. I need one.'

'You come walking all this way for that?' The boy stopped and turned toward him. 'What do you need a knife for?'

'Boy Scouts. I'm a Boy Scout.'

'I don't think my father's gonna sell you a knife.' The boy stood his ground, legs spread.

'Not just any old knife. A pocketknife.'

'Go in and have a look.'

Jerome took off his cap and wiped the sweat from his forehead. He took the money from his pocket and counted it. Three dollars and fifty-six cents. 'First something to drink,' he mumbled to himself.

'What's that?' the boy asked.

'A drink,' Jerome said, as he stepped onto the veranda and went into the store.

A couple of nights earlier his father had forced his way into the house, yet again. Broke a pane in the front door.

The key still happened to be in the lock.

Mama was in the kitchen, reading. The younger children were already in bed. Jerome was undressing in the bathroom when he heard the breaking glass. He knew right away what was up. He put his pants back on and went out onto the landing. His father stood in the middle of the living room, unaware that his son was watching him. His arms dangled aimlessly along his tall torso, his skittish eyes scanning the room.

'Where are you?' This was how it always started. No answer.

'You can't forbid me coming into my own house. I'm a black man. This is my house.' He went off toward the kitchen. Jerome snuck down the stairs.

'Go away, Sonny,' he heard Mama say. Her voice sounded far too gentle, too weak. 'Think of the children.'

'They're my kids too.' He was in the kitchen. 'What you reading?' Jerome heard a chair scuff against the nonslip linoleum. He sat down on the bottom step.

'Nothin' much.'

'So why you reading it?'

'I like reading. Come on, Sonny. You know what the judge said.'

'Don't fancy yourself getting so smart from all those books of yours. Stupid bitch. I know you think you're better than me, but you're nothin'. Whore.'

The door was open a crack, just enough for Jerome to see inside. His mother took off her glasses, as though to prepare herself for what was to come. She looked calm. Her eyes were deep-set, and her blue-black curls shone in the light of the ceiling lamp. She looked straight at her husband, but Jerome knew she wasn't seeing him, was seeing something else, only he couldn't tell what. She never let on. Like she wasn't real whenever Daddy came home. Like she'd drifted quietly out of her body.

Daddy leaned forward and gave Mama a smack on the jaw. She swayed back but didn't fall over. 'Don't you even feel it?' He got up and walked around the table. With the flat of his hand he slapped her other cheek. He started laughing. 'You like that, don't you? I know what you like.' Jerome's mother sat frozen on the chair, her copy of *Time* magazine still open on the table in front of her. He grabbed her by the arm and dragged her to the floor. He started pounding on her back. Jerome could see his mother shudder to the rhythm of his father's dull blows. She flopped back and forth like a rag doll. She did not cry, made no sound at all. She did exactly what he himself did when Daddy beat him: turn away. Watch his own compact body reflected in the dark glass of the kitchen door. Feel his cheeks burn, swallow back the tears. Just stand there and take the punches. Smile. Breathe calmly. Daddy can't ever see his tears. Can't ever be allowed to see the pain he causes. Jerome held onto the pain with all his might. A dull, burning blackness that pushed against the inside of his skull.

But this stubborn indifference only made Daddy even madder. And Jerome could understand that. He understood why his father beat his mother more and more furiously, desperately. Say something! Feel something! I want to hear you scream. Where are you, goddamn it? Anything's better than nothing.

Suddenly the pounding and ranting stopped. Jerome peered through the crack and saw his father stagger to his feet. His cheeks were wet, but Jerome couldn't tell if it was sweat or tears. The man looked smaller than he had a few minutes ago. He muttered something unintelligible, rubbed his hands on his faded pants. From where he stood, Jerome could smell the pungent eau de cologne-like booze stench that clung to his father. He gagged. He saw his mother move on the yellow linoleum floor. She placed her hands flat on the floor and tried to lift up her body. Jerome didn't know what he should do after Daddy left: he wanted to help his mother, but was ashamed at having witnessed the scene, and he was pretty sure she wouldn't want him to see her in this state.

'I'm leavin',' he heard his father say.

Jerome tiptoed back upstairs. Once he was back in his room he heard the front door slam. One last piece of glass from the windowpane shattered into splinters on the floor.

A small, stout man with a white hat and a face full of burst veins shuffled through the cluttered store. Boxes were stacked everywhere. There was hardly any light in the stuffy place.

'A Coke, please.'

'No Coke,' the man said. He went behind the glass counter and stood with his back to Jerome.

'I'd like something to drink.'

'Faucet's back here, next to the men's room.'

'I'm looking for a jackknife.'

The man didn't respond.

'A jackknife. Do you sell jackknives?' Jerome did his best to sound casual.

The man turned to him. 'You ain't old enough to drive. Whatcha doin' here?'

'I'm in the Boy Scouts and need a pocketknife.'

'Boy Scouts? You?' He laughed.

'Everybody's got one.'

'And you don't.'

Jerome shook his head. His mouth was so dry it was as though he was breathing dust instead of air.

'C'mere.'

Jerome went over to the counter.

'I don't sell no weapons. You get my drift?'

Jerome looked at the scissors and knives and chisels and screwdrivers displayed under the glass countertop. In the middle of all that glistening steel he saw a dull hatchet with a carved wooden handle shaped like an eagle's head. It made him think of Indians.

'I like that one.'

'Three dollars.'

Jerome dug the money out of his pants pocket and laid it on the counter.

'Thought you wanted a jackknife.' The man took the money and slid the hatchet over to him. He turned and fumbled around in the cash register behind the counter. He'd already forgotten Jerome was there.

Jerome felt the weight of the hatchet in his hand. It was heavy for such a small thing. He ran his fingers over the fine woodcarving, over the solid polished steel. It wasn't as sharp as a knife but it had two perfectly honed corners. He pushed his thumb into one of them. It didn't hurt. He pushed harder, kept pushing until he felt his calloused skin break. He put his thumb in his mouth. His blood tasted like iron.

He hid the hatchet under his mattress. He slept deeply, dreamlessly. Every once in a while he took the thing out to admire its fine, light-brown woodcarving. He imagined a proud old Indian with long, lank hair who, wielding a small knife, cut thin lines in the wood, keeping at it until an eagle appeared.

It was as though the hatchet defused his murderous thoughts. The hatchet had nothing to do with death. Death was a big limp rabbit at the side of the road. The smell of rain and rotten leaves. He remembered once poking the animal in its belly with a stick to see if it was still alive. He had lifted up the hind legs, turned the head toward him. The eyes were just like dull marbles. Unseeing. He had held his hand an inch above the wooly gray fur. He didn't dare pet it, but felt its warmth on his skin. As though not all the life had drained from the animal yet. Did rabbits have a soul? Was that what he felt?

One night, a week or two after he had bought the hatchet, Jerome woke up to the rattling of the front door. The broken pane had been boarded up. He heard pounding and shouting. His father's deep, measured voice. 'Let me in. You can't forbid me to see my children.' Even when he was crazy, his voice was still songful and fluid, almost like he was play-acting, like he didn't really mean what he said. But his words were so ugly. 'Filthy whore! You fucking somebody else? I wanna come in. Come on, open the door! Jerome, you there? Jerome!'

Jerome stiffened at the sound of his name. He lay on his back. Chris slept through it all. You could fire off a cannon and Chris wouldn't wake up. Jerome thought back on that time his father came looking for him. It was summertime, late at night. The humid warmth still hung over the streets. He had hidden under the Spring Street bridge and quickly counted his earnings. He heard his father's agitated footsteps. He always walked fast when he was crazy.

'Goddam it, Jerome, where are you? It's 3 a.m.. Have you lost your mind?'

The footsteps got closer. There was no escape now.

His father crouched at the bridge. 'Come on home, Jerome. Your mother's worried.'

Jerome stuffed the dollar bills and coins in his pockets. Looked up at his father. Daddy looked almost timid, as though he were ashamed of something. His glance glided off to one side. 'Come on.' It sounded like pleading. Jerome would rather have Daddy get mad than act like this, so pitiful.

'In a minute. You go ahead.'

'I'm your father.'

'Yeah, I know.'

Sonny Huling laughed to himself. 'I'm not going without you.'

Jerome ambled a distance behind his father. Later, when they got home, the man looked his son straight in the eye. His own eyes were watery and dull. He turned to his wife, Jerome's mother, and said, 'This little nigger is out of his mind. He is one crazy nigger.'

Jerome heard the pride that filtered through his father's pathetic words.

'Lemme in my goddam house!' Daddy's entire body thudded against the front door. Jerome was sliding out of bed before he knew it. Grabbing the hatchet from under his mattress and shooting out of the bedroom on his tiptoes, out onto the landing, his feet hardly touching the soft carpeting; how quickly and nimbly he skipped down the thirteen steps, hid silently next to the front door, just out of his father's sight. His mind was empty. No thoughts except the deep and dark awareness of his mission. It's better this way. Daddy has to die. He can't come around here ever again, not ever. He can't ever beat up on Mama again. He'll kill her.

'I'll bust this door down,' Daddy hollered. Jerome heard the thud of his footsteps on the landing. Mama charged down the stairs, her thin nightgown flapping behind her, like she had wings. She went straight for Jerome. 'I knew it,' she said. 'Give it here.' She yanked the hatchet out of his hand. 'Oh, Jerome,' she whispered. 'Jerome.' She sounded disappointed.

The door swung open. Daddy staggered inside. It looked like his head was balanced loosely atop his torso, the way it trembled and shook. 'Is that why you made me wait so long?' he said, pointing to the hatchet. They gray steel glimmered in the dim glow from the porch light. Mama put it behind her back.

'You think you can get ridda me so easy, you ugly bitch?' He roared with laughter. Mama turned and ran to the kitchen. Daddy followed her, legs wide. He had all the time in the world. From the doorway he turned and looked into the living room. Jerome tried to keep out of sight.

'I know you're there,' he heard his father say. His voice sounded sober and normal. 'Was it your idea?'

Every word Jerome knew drained from him. As though he was mute again. He heard his father laugh. 'I knew you weren't no wimp,' Daddy said, mostly to himself as he opened the kitchen door. The glass rattled in its frame. The door swung shut behind him.

'This is Madness' (1970)

Knock! Knock! Who's there?
It's Rap Brown and if you don't open up I'll strike a light and
burn your house down. And I see Malcolm's spirit his eyes
burning Red Black and Green flames and crying tears of
thunderbird wine that seem to touch my lips and make me
thirsty for a taste of FREEDOM!
Freedom by any means necessary.
It's necessary to have freedom by any means necessary.
And I begin to hate with love and love with hate.
This is Madness!
This is Madness!
This is Madness!

[...]

And during all this time my father was somewhere drowning
his mutant plastic-minded self in a bottle of cheap wine letting
that spiritual catalyst John Coltrane pay celestial homage to
that White God who was riding his main vein.
This is Madness!
This is Madness!
This is Madness!

AKRON, OHIO, SEPTEMBER 2001

Reggie Watson

'One night I'm walking past the athletic field behind our school. Suddenly there's Jerome's voice. "Hey Reggie." I look back. Don't see anyone. It was pitch-dark. No moonlight. "Hey Reggie," I hear again. Like the voice came out of nowhere. Really strange. I hear him laugh. He must have hidden himself. Jerk, I think. Then I see his smile light up. He comes up to me. I see the whites of his eyes. His skin was so dark you couldn't see him from a distance. He dissolved into the night. "You're just like a ghost," I said. A *haint*. "Haint" became "Hank". So from that day onward he was called Hank. I suppose we were about fourteen. Everybody in South High called him Hank.

"Mr. Giovanni?"

"What, Huling?"

"What part of Sicily are your people from?"

"What do you mean?"

Giovanni was our school principal. He wanted to be whiter than the whitest whites, but he looked like us. Thick lips, broad nose. Hank stood facing him in the hallway. "You're from Sicily, aren't you?"

You could see Giovanni getting mad. He held his breath. His cheeks went all purple.

"You got a problem, Huling?"

"No, sir."

"Then cut it out."

"I was only asking what part of Sicily your people come from. Just interested, that's all. Nothing wrong with that?"

I was standing there too. The way Giovanni looked at him, like he could read his mind. *This nigger knows I've got black blood.* He hated us.

"I'm gonna count to three, Huling."

"Okay, okay," Hank said, breaking into a laugh.

"Get into my office."

"What for?"

"Now."

I've forgotten what kind of punishment he got.

'Hank was a constant in my life. There were times when we didn't see each other that much but even then I had the feeling he was close by. He was much freer than I was. In a way he was the head of the household. I never knew exactly what all he got up to. I just wanted to be around him. Even when we were little I had the feeling that somehow or other, he had more know-how about life than I did. Why things were the way they were. Like he had some kind of secret knowledge none of us other kids had. He was himself very early on. A personality. And by hanging around with him I had the sense of becoming more of myself too.

'We had a lot in common. I remember waiting out on the driveway for my father to come pick me up. He'd said he would take me out. It was a Saturday afternoon. Beautiful summer weather. I'd put on my new black sneakers, my jeans, and a tight white dress shirt. My mother said I should come inside, but I sat there stock-still, waiting.

I was convinced he would come get me. Only when it got dark did I go inside. This ritual repeated itself four times. My father was an alcoholic, like Hank's. We felt the same lack of a father, the same pain, the same anger. But Hank wasn't afraid. I remember once a bunch of us hanging around in front of South High. Just messing around, nothing serious. Up comes the police. They tell us to split up, beat it. Hank steps forward and sticks his fist in the air. "Black power! Black power! I'm Stokely Carmichael's cousin." He knew about the Black Panthers. Malcolm X. They arrested him and threw him into the paddy wagon. Only let him free the next day. It was like he was constantly testing himself. How far can I go? And sometimes he tested me too. Once we bought a car together, an old gray Plymouth, for eighty-five dollars. Hank wanted to be the first to drive it. That same night he totaled it. Didn't say a word about it to me. Of course I was mad.

He recently told me that sometimes he picked on me so much that I'd take hold of him and yell, "Stop fucking with me, Hank." Or I'd beat him up. But I can't remember any of that. I must have repressed it. I didn't want to lose his friendship.

He was a good athlete. Colleges were interested in him, wanted to give him a scholarship. But Hank dismissed it. He said, "The minute I break my leg, they'll throw me off the campus." He and Inez Paul were an item. She was his total opposite: popular, well-spoken, nicely dressed, sweet. She came from a good family. Giovanni, the principal, he didn't like it one bit. He was afraid Hank would be a bad influence on her. But Inez was Homecoming Queen and she wanted Hank to be her date. Leave it to Hank to hook a girl like that. He didn't even have to try. And none of the other guys were jealous of him. Jealousy wasn't an issue. We all hated Giovanni. So we got sheets of cardboard and wrote "WE WANT HANK!" in great big letters. We picketed the administration. It was about more than that prom stuff. It was about vindication. And Hank got to be Homecoming King.

I was really tame compared to him. But later, when I was in the service in Germany and Hank had long since left for New York, it was like I assumed his personality. I wasn't afraid anymore. They favored the white guys in the army. Made you feel like you weren't worth beans. But I didn't give a damn. I dealt drugs. Shipped whole packages of hashish to America. Just in the mail. I sucked up to the German dealers and when I had them hooked I'd beat the crap out of them and steal their drugs. I was always high. All that anger came out all at once. Anger at what the whites had done to my parents when they still lived in the South. That they couldn't sit on the same benches. The lynchings. That's what I told myself. I felt like a real Black Panther. One day I beat another soldier on his back so hard that the stick I used broke in two. I stole his dope. The guy was a mess. I'd already been in jail three times. If he pressed charges, I'd be a goner. So I had no choice but to apologize and beg him not to report the incident. He promised not to say anything. Something broke in me then. I thought: maybe I shouldn't hate *all* whites. I was so bitter.

But that was all later. Did I tell you about the Akron riots? The riots changed everything for us. We'd already graduated from high school. Hank and I both worked at Firestone, the tire factory. Wait. Let's go outside, I'll show you where it all started.'

AKRON, OHIO, 1967

Omar Ben Hassen

'I can't bring myself to say it, Jerome,' Mama said. 'Not in my own house.'

'Try.'

'What's it mean?'

'Dunno.'

'So are you a Black Muslim now?'

'Not necessarily.'

'Sure sounds like it.'

'It sounds nice.'

'What does Reggie say?'

'You know Reggie.'

'He wouldn't go changing his name like that. I can just see his mother's face.'

'Huling's a slave name, Mama.'

'And your family name.'

'Daddy's name.'

'Oh, Jerome.'

'Omar.'

'For me you'll always be Jerome.'

CLEVELAND, OHIO, 1968

My Girl

He parked his car on Euclid Avenue, close to the Circle Ballroom. It was around midnight. A halo of light hung over the city. It was the dead of winter, but the air was warmed by the heat and the promise that wafted out of the clubs—the dancing bodies, the smoke, the alcohol, the music. He got out of the car, closed the door, and ran his hand over the red finish. He had smoked a few joints and taken some speed before leaving home. The pills had kicked in as he stood at his bedroom mirror, looking approvingly at the sheen of his silk shirt. Speed mixed with weed provided exactly the feeling he needed on a Saturday night. The energy and exhilaration started in his belly and ran through his limbs; his fingertips vibrated like he'd been given little electric shocks. Meanwhile the weed was making his skin flush and soften, was making the beige of his shirt shimmer hazily like gold. The drive from Akron to Cleveland could last for five minutes or a couple of hours. The view as he approached the city, a real city, the smell of burning steel and sulfur and oil that oozed in through the cracked-open window, the lights in the office towers that stood together in a cluster, the imposing Cleveland Indians stadium ... The road hit an incline, he felt the resistance in the steering wheel, it was as though Cleveland was built on a mountain, which in itself commanded respect.

And then the music in his car. The cassette player he had routinely unscrewed from a parked Pontiac the week before, snipping the wires with his sister's nail clippers. It fit into his Oldsmobile's dashboard like it was made to order. No dealing tonight. Tape in. Tadadam tadadam tadadam. The bass notes vibrated in his stomach. Tadadam tadadam tadadam. The tension that those few low, rolling notes could stir up. Then the guitar coming in— no, wait, once more, rewind to the beginning. Tadadam tadadam tadadam. He snapped his fingers. Now there was no holding it back. The guitar introduced the melody. Lightweight, vibrating notes danced on the thick bass. Pam padadadam pam. *I've got sunshi-hi-hine on a clou-dy day. When it's cold outside ... I've got the month of May.* Shit. Euclid already. He'd have to stay in the car if he wanted to hear the whole song. *I ... guess ... you'd ... say ... What can make me feel this way?* He pulled over to the curb. Took a half-smoked joint from the dashboard ashtray, smoothed it out and lit it. The sweetish odor of the weed filled the car ... *talkin' 'bout my girl* ... His body was too small for what was going on inside him. He felt his blood quiver and itch in his veins. The speed. The sultry violins. The way The Temptations moved in their snug-fitting black suits, supple and self-assured, the understated dancing, their footwork. The hidden messages behind the innocent lyrics. *I don't need no money* ... David Ruffin's voice went higher. The guy had such amazing control; he could even make his whimpers and screams and anger sound like flattery. Like something romantic. *I've got all the riches baby* ... My ass. He laughed out loud. The music was a confirmation of everything he loved. The music was sex, rhythm, glamour, love, speed, pride. Cleveland.

Stop.

'Cognac?'

'Cognac.'

It wasn't busy. A few couples danced at the back of the bar. He followed the movement of their bodies to the fluid music of Al Green. Sipped his Courvoisier. Sucked up the misty smoke and shut his eyes halfway. Squinting into the crowd, he noticed the glittery dress on one of the women. He recognized her at once. Nona Johnson. That dress of hers clung to her body like a second skin, light blue and sequined. It made him think of a snake. Her ass stuck out shamelessly. It was so tight and so big that he was sure her skin wouldn't give an inch, no matter how hard he squeezed. And her breasts, they were the size of little round pomegranates. He liked small breasts. Women with small breasts got wound up quicker. She had cropped hair and bangs. White features but skin so black that her dress was all that seemed to move out on the dance floor. He could pick her scent out of thousands. A sultry, sweet scent. A combination of sandalwood, coconut, and fresh sweat. Her sweat. They had talked last week, although he couldn't remember about what. Nona was a good girl. They'd had a good laugh together. It was nearing dawn. He was as high as anything and her scent did the rest. Like being drugged. It didn't take much effort to imagine how her pussy would smell.

'Hey Nona.'

Her dance partner looked over. Don Cooper from Hough. He didn't recognize him in that shiny white suit. He would offer him something, see how he reacted.

'Nona.' He raised his hand in the air. No reaction. She nestled her head into Cooper's neck and he tightened his grip around her waist. She pushed her pelvis against his groin. He recoiled slightly but was quick to recover and started twisting his hips to the rhythm of the music. Nona smiled. There was jazz on the jukebox, but Omar was still hearing The Temptations. Their high vocals echoed in his head. *I've got a sweeter song than the birds in the trees.* Pa-da-pam pa-da-pam. He could hardly sit still. He tossed back the rest of his cognac and asked for a refill.

Nona either didn't see him, or pretended not to. Cooper whispered something in her ear. Took her by the arm and led her over to the bar. They sat a few seats down from Omar.

'Nona.'

She looked up, held his stare for a second, then resumed her conversation with Cooper. Her expression betrayed nothing. The way she reached for her glass. Her fingers. Long, unvarnished nails. Caressing the glass, playing with it, turning it round and round. Omar tasted the burning, wooden tang of cognac in his mouth. The alcohol warmed his belly. She drank too. Just a sip of syrupy bourbon. Placed the glass carefully back on the bar, as if it might break. He couldn't hear what they were talking about; their conversation dissolved into the buzz of the jazz, in the lazy song of the saxophone. The glitter of her blue dressed was etched onto his retinas. Her neck. The short tufts of hair. He wanted to let his fingers glide over her neck, from top to bottom, feel the soft spot between the neck muscles, just under the skull, press gently. She would relax at once, throw back her head. He saw the thin lines on her throat, the texture of her skin, the endless web of minuscule lines and specks. The taste of her skin, salty on his tongue. Her tongue. She felt so near. In his imagination the barriers between their bodies blurred.

He took his glass, slid off the barstool, and walked

over to Nona. Cooper eyed him furtively, the bastard. Just a few weeks ago they were right here drinking together. He'd arranged a few tape decks for Cooper, at a discount. Cooper liked to act like a big-time hustler. And he was definitely a handsome fellow. Hazel pupils, watery eyes, like he'd just got out of bed. That absent, melancholy look gave Cooper a kind of vulnerable, mysterious air, as though he was in some sort of trouble, and that you could save him just by talking to him. He was never short of women.

Omar said it again: 'Nona.'

She smiled, showing her teeth.

'Let me buy you two a round.'

She looked at her dance partner. Omar repeated the offer.

Nona pointed to her glass. 'With plenty of ice.'

'Ice,' Omar repeated. He smiled with his eyes. She threw him a smirk in return, playful, you'd almost say timid. But he knew full well this shyness was a put-on. Same as his courtesy, which he feigned to hide his anger and desire. But he was enjoying himself. Felt his heart racing. The tingling in his head, like pinpricks.

'You?' he asked Cooper.

The man shook his head, looked into his glass.

Omar slid onto the stool next to Nona's. Got a closer whiff. He felt as though it was pulling him toward her. Her smooth-shaven legs glistened with body oil. He extended his hand to Cooper. 'What's going down, Don?'

'Nothin'.'

Omar signaled to the girl behind the bar to refill their glasses. 'And put something else on.'

The girl pointed to the Wurlitzer at the back of the bar. A proud machine with lighted red and green bands all the way around. But Omar would have to worm his way through the sweating, dancing bodies, pick out a few numbers, put in the coins, wait. It would take too long. Timing is everything. He thought of his red Oldsmobile. Heard the rugged low bass notes. Ruffin's voice as it modulated, about two-thirds of the way through the song. He always waited for it, every time; the whole song revolved around that one moment of release and euphoria. He waited for it while the craziest images whizzed through his mind: the dull gray water of Lake Erie; John Wayne taking off his cowboy hat and wiping the sweat from his forehead. That wound-up kid in his night class at the University of Akron, going on about studying law and his fabulous future. His fake afro. Until Ruffin hit that climax, controlled and sublime. *I don't need no money, fortune, or fame ...* It was a single phrase, a simple inflection of the voice that wiped away all of Omar's thoughts and made his head so empty and clear that it felt like being reborn. Timing was everything. He reached under the bar and slid his hand over the stiff blue sequins of Nona's dress. The curves of her buttocks. He felt her relax. Her body smoldered under that polyester. He pressed harder, squeezed her hip. Nona shifted back and forth with obvious pleasure on her barstool, rocked to his touch while Cooper eyed her, quasi-nonchalant, with that lazy look of his.

'You crazy, or what?' It wasn't clear whether he was talking to Nona or Omar.

Nona pretended not to hear. Omar slid his hand over the fish-scale fabric of her dress until he reached her butt crack. He pressed gently. Felt her pelvis twitch. Tasted her in his mind. The music from the jukebox. Bare, stiff bass notes repeating the same melody over and over. Da-da da-da. Every second note went down and every fourth one went up. Da-da da-da. Da-da da-da. As if the notes too were waiting, expectantly.

'Hard times over in Hough a couple of years ago, huh? Looked like a war zone.' Omar looked Cooper straight in the eye while Nona's heat burned in the palm of his hand. 'Evans wants me to set something up in Akron. Pff. You know Ahmed Evans, right? The nationalist? Sittin' up on the roof last summer, pickin' off as many cops as he could. Were you there?'

Cooper didn't answer. He seemed to be made of ice. His eyes fixed on the smoked-glass mirror behind the bar. The bottles of hard liquor. 'You stay here,' Cooper said to Nona in a monotone. He got up. Walked to the back of the bar, weaving through the dancing couples. Omar followed his every move. And it was as though there were a two-way mirror separating them and the rest of the bar patrons. He saw everyone, no one saw him. Only Nona. She sipped her bourbon. They didn't talk. Listened to the saxophone as it provoked the bass. Soft purple notes wound their way around the earthy sound of the bass. Cool brushes on the drums. Da-da da-da. Da-da da-da. A spellbinding melody. Omar imagined the saxophone player standing above a basket of snakes, trying to charm them, hypnotize them. This wasn't dance music. Those couples out on the dance floor must be hearing something he didn't. They were draped over each other, their movements were gentle and rhythmic and sexy and beautiful. Under the bar, Nona's fingers touched his.

'It's okay, baby,' he whispered in her ear.

'What?' Nona asked, scowling. She jerked around to face him.

'I love you.'

'C'mon, Omar.'

'C'mon Omar what?'

'You been drinking.'

'So?'

'Don'll be back soon.'

'Let's go.'

'Are you crazy?'

'I need you.'

'You need me.'

The way she repeated his words: languid and detached. Guarded.

'I mean it, Nona.'

The sound of their words wafted around the smoky room like bubbles, seeking out the music and its dream-like melodies. Cooper came back without Omar notic-ing. Not till Nona poked him in the ribs. He looked up, right into the muzzle of a double-barreled shotgun.

'Fuck off,' Cooper hissed. 'I'll blow that shiny head o' yours off your body, asshole. Beat it.'

Nona grabbed her bag from the bar and shrank back. Omar reflexively put his hands in the air. He observed his own movements in slow motion. Cooper's grimace. Eyes bugging out of their sockets. 'I'll blow your head off, nigga, you understand?' Cooper's voice echoed in his head. The mirror behind the bar. One sliver of that glass and he could fix that mug of his so his own mother wouldn't recognize him. Omar looked down the barrel of that shotgun, two narrow dark tunnels. He felt Nona's presence behind him. The damp warmth of her breath on the back of his neck. Her fear. His adrenaline rush. The music off in the distance. A busy, chaotic saxophone solo. The bass under it. The same repetitive drone. Da-da da-da. Da-da da-da. The impatience behind the notes. His blood tingled. The veins in his head were ready to explode. He was almost there. It was within reach, that elusive place beyond the crack rush.

'What's buggin' you?' Omar asked.

'I'll kill you.'

'No you won't.'

'Shut your fucking mouth.'

'Shhh.' Omar slowly lowered his hands. Everyone in the bar seemed to be holding their breaths. Somebody had unplugged the jukebox. A glass fell onto the wooden floor. A girl cleared her throat. Not Nona. Omar was alone now. With Cooper standing right in front of him, frozen, his finger still on the trigger of the shotgun.

'You'll go in the slammer for good,' Omar tried.

'You're nothin' but a dirty arrogant nigger.'

'Not worth ruining your life for. Or is it? Take Nona out of here. Come on. You don't want her seeing nasty stuff.'

Omar could see Cooper glance skittishly at Nona.

'You let me go, and you'll never see me again. I swear it.'

'I'm gonna kill you.'

'You just go on home with Nona.'

'Shut up about Nona.'

'You know I'm right.' And as soon as he said those few words, Omar felt Cooper crack.

He lowered the gun. 'Get lost,' he muttered. Omar breathed deeply. Looked around him but saw nothing but a misty golden haze, anonymous, identical faces. He reached for his glass of cognac.

'Beat it, I said,' Cooper whispered.

Omar forgot about the glass and left the Circle Ballroom.

Alone in his car. There was pressure on his temples, like a belt tightening around his head. The silence was a whispering, silvery rustle. The pumping of his heart. The heat of his blood. He closed his eyes. Black. No thoughts. Only a vague sensation of emptiness. A void so silent and dark that he was almost weightless. He couldn't be sure if this was all real. He pushed open the door and got out. Went around to the trunk, opened it, and took out his .38. Got back in the car. His gun on his lap, hidden under the thin silk of his shirt. No music. He waited. He waited and kept his eyes fixed on the brightly lit door to the Circle Ballroom. Time ceased to exist. Just the wait. A drab, empty wait.

Nona came out first. The clatter of her high heels on the sidewalk. Like rushing water in a river. She let her purse dangle playfully from her hand. She wasn't wearing a sweater or jacket over her bare arms. Omar imagined he could see her goose bumps, tiny black bulges on her skin. Then Cooper came out. Didn't he realize how gaudy and ugly that glossy suit of his was? Omar rolled down the window. Pulled out his gun without losing sight of Cooper. Nona was already at their car. She called out something, he couldn't hear what. Omar saw Cooper's movements. Squinted, stretched out his arm, and aimed. The shimmering of the white imitation silk. The coolness of steel in his hand. The play of the trigger under his finger. Don't move. Stop. Don't move. He sucked in the sharp night air and—bam! He recoiled. The dull metal crack hummed in his ears. Cooper lay on the sidewalk in the merciless, bleak neon light that spilled out of the bar. He heard shouting. He had nothing to do with it. It wasn't him. Nobody saw him. Nona hurried on her high heels over to her wounded boyfriend. Omar was afraid she would stumble. He rolled up the window, put the gun in the glove compartment, started the engine, and drove down Euclid Ave.

'A.M.' (1990)

He was a love Supreme

                    a love Supreme

He was a love Supreme

'Epic' (2001)

That possible criminal element
awakens you
to the terror
and loneliness
of running into the silent pain
of someone else
looking to you
for answers.

FLINT, MICHIGAN, SEPTEMBER 2001

Sandra Saint-Claire

'Sometimes Jerome works in my basement. And he's down there, talking and saying his poetry. I hear how his voice changes, low to high, fast, slow. Or just mumbling. I've got a ping-pong table down there, and that's where he used to write. Trying stuff out. I like it when he does that. I like lot of his poetry.

I remember him making ice cream for us from snow in the wintertime. He'd pack the snow down hard and pour fruit syrup over it. Other times he'd bring us crackers and pop in the middle of the night. He was nine. As children we didn't get along. He was so bossy. When we were teenagers, whenever a guy came to the house for my sisters or me, he'd first have to deal with my brother Jerome. He would interrogate them like he was our father. We lived on West Chestnut. But at a certain point my mother couldn't take living with my father anymore and so we moved in with her mother.

So then we lived in a mixed neighborhood for the first time, with Italians and blacks. And anyway, back then white people didn't come into our neighborhoods. Our businesses were black-owned. There weren't even any white kids at school. And believe it or not, it was much better that way. There was more cohesiveness, no confusion. Everybody seemed to get along. My father used to talk about white people. "Don't trust them," he'd say. He grew up in Birmingham, Alabama, and down there you didn't look white people in the eye when you talked to them. My father had some racist ideas, but his ideas gave me self-confidence. I'm very outspoken. Whatever I have to say, I say it. As a matter of fact, some of the kids I went to school with thought I would become a politician rather than a nurse.

I can't remember what started the riots in Akron. I didn't get involved. There was a curfew. We had to stay inside. There were tanks parked on our street. Jerome, he went over to them, gave the military police some lip. My mother called for him to come inside. "Leave those guys alone. They're just doing their job."

You know what did bother me, though? When Martin Luther King got assassinated.

Jerome says this is a blessed house. I think he likes being around me and my kids. The neighborhood is really decayed, but the people are okay. I always tell him he should buy a house here. Invest. At his age. That green house across the street was sold for five thousand dollars. But I don't know what he'll do. I won't be here forever. I've outgrown Flint. I'm thinking about getting back together with my ex-husband, my son Rachet's father. When you get older it's no good being alone. Jerome says he might stay here in the house if I go. He's changed a lot. He takes things more seriously. Even though it does get on my nerves when he spends days in his room just sleeping and watching TV. I think he could do more for himself. But he says he needs it. Sometimes he'll be sitting out here on the porch and suddenly he'll just start saying stuff. I'm pretty sure he just comes up with it on the spot. It's not like he sits down and thinks real hard. It just comes. My daughter gave him a typewriter and he types out his poems later on that.'

◆

You hear that? That deep, dark quiet behind the sounds? That's the difference with New York, Detroit. None of that constant background noise, that drone. Every sound here is individual. The rustling of the leaves on the trees. Killer Joe's dogs barking when his friend feeds them. That guy goes around twice a day, just for the dogs. Killer Joe's too old to take care of them. He's in his seventies, but always well-dressed. I'll bet he was a handsome guy when he was young.

I was sitting out here last night. It was already dark. I dozed off a little. All of a sudden I hear a man singing at the top of his lungs. I look up. An attractive, strong voice, as a matter of fact. I see lights on in the house across the street, the yellow one there. The front door's open and all I see is the silhouette of somebody dancing and jumping. The flickering light is from the television. He's singing along with some rather old song. Must have been drinking. A little later he comes outside. Sees me sitting here, walks over. Tom's his name. Launches into a long story, that he used to live here. Moved back from Arkansas. A musician. He plays in a blues band, he says. And he works in construction now and again to make ends meet. He's planning to fix up that house all by himself.

There's so much talent here.

Before eleven, twelve o'clock in the morning it's dead quiet on the street. Most people are sleeping in. There's practically no work in Flint since the General Motors factories closed down. The quiet suits Sandra fine, 'cause she only does night shifts. Means she can sleep some during the day.

I prefer to sit here after dark.

Calms me down.
Listen.

Are you chilly? Sandra's got a sweater for you.
   It's getting on to fall already.
   Just smell it.

I think I'm gonna to have to find another place if Sandra
moves.

'Redbone' (2000)

You came heavily armed.
And as the Gardenias of Lady Day smiled down on you ...
snatched me from my demons ...

AKRON, OHIO, 1967

The Poet

'Can I have your *Newsweek*? There's something I want to cut out.'

'What?'

'Here, look.'

He held up the magazine, opened to the pages he had just read. Mama put on the glasses that hung from her neck on the gold-colored chain.

'Who's that?' She looked at the picture that went with the article. A small man with bulging eyes and a beard. A bandage around his head, a stream of blood trickling along his forehead, past his eyebrow and over his cheek.

'He's a poet,' Omar said.

'He doesn't look like a poet.'

'He's wounded.'

'I can see that.'

'The dude says some amazing stuff.'

'Like what?'

'Read it, underneath.'

Mama grabbed the magazine from him and held it close to her face.

'What's he doing in *Newsweek*?' She took off her glasses. Looked straight at her son.

'He's right.'

'You think so?'

''Course.'

'That's not why they put his picture in *Newsweek*. And you know it.'

She put the magazine back on the kitchen table. Stood stock-still in front of him, her arms at her side, her glasses resting on her chest. She was wearing a green cotton sleeveless dress. It was summer. Omar looked at her thin, light-brown arms. Her frail figure in the late-afternoon sunlight that shone through the kitchen window. The dust in the air. As though her serenity made everything go quiet. His thoughts. The riot in his head after reading about the wounded black poet from Newark. Omar's eyes glided across the table, the open *Newsweek*. He read, for the umpteenth time, the quote in bold letters under the picture of Amiri Baraka. 'SMASH THOSE JELLY WHITE FACES.'

'D'you remember that poem I wrote for my final exam? That poem about the teachers?'

'It was good.'

'Mr. Giovanni said I should've done it earlier. He said I was too late. That I'd wasted my talents at school. Bullshit.'

'Go on and cut that picture out.'

'It is bullshit, right?'

'You just be careful.'

NEWARK, NEW JERSEY, SEPTEMBER 2001

Amiri Baraka

'I've seen Langston Hughes perform with Charles Mingus. In the '50s I performed with a jazz quartet. Ideally, my poems should be read like music. I still work on them every day, so that a good musician can transform the words into music. The disconnection of poetry from music is a Western notion. Poetry comes out of music, it's music put into words. So a good musician can turn the words into music. Music is not abstract. Emotions are not abstract. Nor is jazz, except maybe for the listener who doesn't understand the concepts behind it. Take Coltrane's piece about the murder of those four black girls in the church in Birmingham, Alabama. It's about the civil rights movement. It's one of the saddest and most touching pieces of music I've ever heard. Trane took regular, popular music as a basis and expanded it with African musical forms, Eastern forms, new breathing techniques. All of it to break out of the prison of commercial music. He could make statements at high speed, and then alter them harmonically, which made the solo much more interesting. It wasn't just about swiftness or virtuosity, oh no, he could play a chord in eight hundred different ways: repeat it backward, inside out, expand it, make use of its invincible power ... plus, Coltrane was very sensitive and political in a completely aesthetic way.

Or take Duke's "Black, Brown and Beige". If you listen to it you'll hear the emotions and the ideas. That's why I can set poetry to his music. Ellington, Monk, Coltrane, those are people whose music I play every day. Their music is part of me. I am that music. Somebody gave me twenty-six volumes of the Duke's music for my birthday. That's the greatest present I've ever had. Well, aside from the forty-five volumes by Lenin I got from my wife. Those are gifts you never get rid of.'

I still hear that
song,
that cry
cries
screams
life exploded
our world exploding us
transformed to niggers

'We had a house like this one, but on the other side of Newark, a big wooden house. In the summer it was hidden behind the thick, full trees. Shady and cool inside. Like here now. We used to call it the "Spirit House". My wife and I lived upstairs with the kids and the theater was downstairs. This was in the mid-'60s. The heyday of the Black Arts Movement. Performances every night. This has always been a rough town. I was born here. I remember my wife and I being in the car one afternoon, discussing how much money we could spend on sneakers for the kids. We had words. A policeman saw us and got out of his patrol car and came over to us. Made me open the door and dragged me out of the car. Beat the crap out of me, because I was supposedly abusing my wife. She couldn't do a thing, just watch until he was done. In '67 people tore the city apart because of police brutality. The whites fled for the suburbs, where they still live. The middle-class Italians had nice houses up north. The more working-class Portuguese lived on the other side. We elected some new people, black leaders. But we found out that skin is thin: racism just changed form, and the corruption stayed the same.

'I come from a lower-middle-class family. My father was a foreman at the postal service and my mother was a social worker. Our neighborhood was where what they called "decent blacks" lived.'

My parents [...] They made me too 'polite', in one sense. Too removed from the rush and crush of blood [...]. I was taught good hair and bad hair. Light-skinned folks in moccasins at picnics was hip. I didn't even really understand the 'war' between my brown grandmother and the cold white boney Miss Banks of the flower committee till years later.

'I wanted to leave Newark to develop my writing skills. I went to the Lower East Side and then to the Village. I performed with Ginsberg and Burroughs and Kerouac. But when Malcolm was murdered I couldn't stay living in a white world anymore. I realized I had to choose. That art had to be politics. But I was married to a white woman, I had two daughters. When Malcolm got murdered I wanted to wage war. Losing my family wasn't easy.'

You arrived, in a brownstone in Harlem. All the Misfits.
Wdbe what? Killers? Agents? Revolutionaries? Black Black Black to the fore.
Black Black Black at the top.
Black Black Black.
You set up housekeeping.

'We had four trucks and every night we drove around the neighborhood giving performances, putting art on the street. Drama here, poetry over here, music somewhere else. We would go to playgrounds, vacant lots, bars; we'd block off streets, and everywhere we went, people crowded to see us. We even got a government subsidy through the anti-poverty program. When they found out what we were doing, they cut it off.

'What is black? Black is a color. Back then they'd shoot each other up over that. Black was Communist, or Muslim, or nationalist, or vegetarian, or reformist. Black was no longer a color. Black was an ideology. That's why I came back to Newark.

'I remember The Last Poets coming to the Spirit House. It was Gylan Kain, Felipe Luciano, and David Nelson; Abiodun Oyewole might have been there too. They asked me what I thought of their work. They were looking for affirmation. They were real young. I gave them a lot of encouragement. I was impressed. These sensitive artists were expressing the most advanced ideas of the political struggle. And at the same time, in their performance they returned to music's oldest form: they used only their voices and the drum.'

AKRON, OHIO, 1968

The Love of Strangers

'Look what that bastard's doing, will you! It just made those motherfuckers' day that all hell's broke loose. Look at that, Reggie. Those crackers were just waiting for this.'

The television was on. Omar opened a can of Budweiser and slid it over to his friend. They were in Reggie's basement. It was nine in the morning.

'I'm gonna go crash,' Reggie said. He was slouched on the enormous white sofa that took up the whole wall of the basement. He took a swig of beer, whipped off his glasses, and rubbed his eyes.

'Just watch,' Omar said. The only light in the low-ceilinged space came from the flickering blue and silver images on the TV screen. Reggie had shut his eyes. Omar kicked him in the shin. 'LA's burning and you're asleep.' On the TV a black policeman used a billy club to beat a black youth lying on the street. Sirens howled in the background. People ran from paramilitaries in dark helmets. The helmets made them unrecognizable and invincible, as though they weren't real people but remote-controlled robots.

Reggie looked up. 'Weird, when the sun's always shining. Makes it look less bad, you know?'

'What do you mean?'

'They've got palm trees in Los Angeles.'

'Yeah, so?'

'I dunno. Even though the whole city's on fire, they've still got the ocean and the beach. I'd dig going to California—you?'

'You're crazy.'

Reggie laughed. He tucked up his legs and stretched out on the sofa. 'We gonna do something tonight?'

'Yeah, right.' Omar got up and switched off the TV. He turned on a lamp, and suddenly the basement looked a whole lot bigger. On the coffee table was a silver candlestick on a floral-patterned cloth. Reggie had put mirrors on the wall above the sofa, and a dark-blue velvet curtain hung in front of the room's only window. There was white wool carpeting and Reggie always made you take off your shoes before you came in. He even had a fancy new brass faucet installed on the hallway sink. The bathroom smelled like soap and flowers. It was like the basement was waiting for a woman to show up. Omar looked over at his friend, who was pretending to sleep. The violent images of the LA riots were etched in his memory. He knew he should go home and rest, that he'd be crazy to do two night shifts in a row without sleep, but he was too wound up. He heard Reggie's breathing become deeper and more regular. There was something endearing about seeing him lie there in the middle of all his fancy stuff. Reggie had refinement. For him, that stuff was like the California palm trees. They protected him. They erased ugliness.

Omar shielded his eyes with his arm. He would always squint as soon as the small steel door slammed behind him, no matter if it was raining or dusky, or if smokestack emissions were the source of the haze. He felt like a mole, cautiously sticking his head above ground, sniffing the cool air, and then ducking back, only to try again later. He couldn't see a thing until his eyes were accustomed to the morning light that cast a surreal glow over the industrial park. The massive gray buildings, the ingenious steel machinery that gurgled and hummed and vibrated and spat out steam. The sky above, light blue from the dust. The heat of the furnace, still burning on his skin. The dust tickled his nose. He heard Papa Snow's languid, wavering voice: 'Come on, Huling, don't go falling asleep again. They'll fire you yet. Show a little respect. You should be grateful.' Grateful. Once outside the gate, when he'd inhaled the thin morning air that smelled like dew and burning rubber, it was like waking up from a bad dream. His life in the factory felt unreal. Firestone was a chimera, something he'd read about in a magazine. Like he'd just arrived in Akron and didn't know his way yet. He shambled down the dusty road, his head becoming clearer with every step. He felt buoyant and high. Everything seemed possible. Maybe it was the night shift that made him feel this way. It didn't matter. These morning walks and the strange blitheness that went with them were the only good things about working at Firestone Tire and Rubber. He never mentioned it to anyone; the optimism he felt at those moments would evaporate the minute he talked about it.

It started to rain. Fine, vertical rain. The street was deserted. In the morning hush he could just hear the raindrops hit the asphalt. A thin, whispering sound. He continued on to Wooster Ave. Caught the fresh scent of wet leaves and grass. The city was asleep. He saw the glistening asphalt. Felt the cool raindrops on his skin. The rain washed away the dust and the fatigue. He tried to retrieve the chaotic images of Los Angeles, the burning cars, the black and white students fleeing the rubber bullets and tear gas, but for one reason or another they eluded him. As though he'd left them back at Reggie's, in the basement where it always felt like night. It irritated him; it felt like something had been taken from him. He walked on. He should have turned left, but he kept on going, without a destination in mind. He just followed the rhythm of his footsteps. The monotony soothed him. As long as he kept moving he didn't feel his restlessness.

'Do you play anything?'

'No.'

'But your father does, right?'

'How'd you know that?'

He stood in Chetta Davis's bedroom. It was about 2 a.m. on Sunday. He had shimmied up a drainpipe, broke open her window with a stone, and climbed inside.

Wearing a lilac-colored nightie, she sat upright in bed, the lamp on the nightstand casting a cozy, soft yellow light. The radio was on. It was as though she'd been expecting him.

'Now what am I gonna do about that window?'

'How'd you know that about my father?'

'My mother mentioned it once. She said he was really good. In the old days, anyway. When she was as girl.'

He looked around. The plaster walls of Chetta's room were painted light green. The carpeting was thick and beige. There was a white vanity table with all sorts of bottles and jars. Dolls and teddy bears filled the top of a hope chest. It was as though he'd wandered into another world. A week ago he and Chetta had danced at the Hi-De-Ho Lounge. She'd worn tight plaid slacks and a sleeveless black sweater. They'd smoked cigarettes and drank port.

'How come you don't play?' she asked.

'I dunno. I'm no good on trumpet. I mean ... I guess I can't carry a tune.'

'How do you know?'

'Just do.'

She turned up the volume. There was a vaguely familiar song playing. A lazy, dreamlike number from an old movie. The music swelled—violins, he figured, but it could just as well have been other instruments. Maybe even a whole orchestra.

He stood at the open window and felt the chill through his T-shirt. Chetta opened the drawer in her nightstand and took out a cigarette and matches. She lit it and inhaled deeply. Held the smoke in her lungs for a bit and then slowly blew it out. Omar watched the wisps of gray smoke spiral elegantly upward until they dissolved in the darkness.

'I love the saxophone,' Chetta said. 'When somebody plays the sax well, you can hear his breathing. Especially the low notes. Just like he's whispering in your ear. A secret. Sometimes I almost can't even listen to it. Like somebody's touching you, with sounds. You follow me?'

'You're a romantic.'

'Why?' Chetta asked.

'Why what?'

'Why am I a romantic?'

'Because you say things like that.'

'How about you? You're crazy to work in that stupid factory.'

'Look who's talking.'

'I know. That's why I said it.'

'Can I sit down?' Omar asked.

'Do I have to give you permission all of a sudden?'

He leaned against the window.

'What'd you come here for?'

'To see you.'

'Oh.'

'Gimme a cigarette,' Omar said.

She shook her head. 'Last one,' she whispered, holding her breath. She'd just taken a drag and held the half-smoked cigarette in the air. She exhaled. 'And you thought: Chetta wants to do it with me. That's what you thought, isn't it?'

He laughed.

'What you doin' here, Omar?'

She was staring back at him, brow furrowed. She had pulled up her knees and leaned her arms on them. She seemed to have forgotten her question. Her thoughts were someplace else. As if it didn't matter that he was standing in her bedroom in the middle of the night.

'You need to go to sleep,' he said.

She laughed. 'D'you know I have an aunt in New York? My mother's big sister. Name's Jo. I only know her from stories. She was just fifteen when she took the bus up north, all on her own. She lived in some backwater in North Carolina. Didn't tell anybody she was pregnant, not even my mother. My mother just cried and cried till her eyes burned and she was out of tears.' Chetta paused. 'I want to go see her in New York sometime. I think my mother only saw her once or twice since. Crazy, isn't it? If you ask me, my mother's still mad at Jo, or maybe jealous.'

She was talking more to herself than to him, but still, her words lessened the distance between them.

Omar sat down on the foot end of her bed. 'Come on,' he said.

'What?'

'Can I kiss you?'

'Sure.'

'And then I'll go.'
'Whatever you want.'
'I like you, Chetta.'
'I like you too.'

He only gave her a quick peck on the cheek. He didn't really know why. There was something in Chetta's demeanor that scared him. He didn't want to hurt her. He got up and went over to the broken window, looked outside, and saw only white. Thick mist hung between the trees and above the lawn and the street. The glow of the streetlamp shone vaguely through it. The mist muted all noise: it was so still that he almost wondered if he'd gone deaf. The world seemed so small. As he climbed back outside he stopped halfway, with one leg outside and one inside. Chetta had already switched off her bedside lamp. She was invisible. He heard only the soft gray hum of the radio as he breathed the cold, damp night air. Imagined he saw clouds instead of mist. The clouds were so thick and firm it was like you could walk on them. His foot felt for the drainpipe and then he slid back down.

He stood in the narrow alley behind their house on West Chestnut. He had no idea how long he'd been walking. His jacket and T-shirt hung heavily on his shoulders, sodden from the fine gray rain. But he didn't want to go inside yet, didn't feel like talking. His grandmother was always home. He leaned against the neighbor's shed and looked into the yard. The branches of the thick old oak tree hung low over the lawn. The grass hadn't been mown for months now; weeds were taking over. At the back of the yard his grandmother grew herbs and strawberries and bell peppers. Billy's rusty bike lay on the stoop by the kitchen door. The garbage can was open, the ground was strewn with leftovers and broken glass: the neighbor's dogs had probably gotten loose again.

He had to go in and sleep. He'd promised Reggie they would go out tonight before work. But he just stood there and felt how tired his limbs were. He hadn't seen Chetta again after that one visit. He'd done his best to avoid her. The way she talked to him, like she knew more about him than he did. 'What you doin' here, Omar?' He was almost embarrassed to think back on that encounter in her bedroom. The thick mist that seemed to swallow everything up. He was the only human being on earth that night; at any moment the cold white clouds might have swallowed him up too.

He pushed off the shed wall with his foot, walked over to the kitchen door, opened the screen door, and went inside.

'Grandma,' he called. No answer. 'Grandma.'

'I'm here,' came the singsong voice from upstairs. 'It's me.'

'There's food for you on the stove,' his grandmother called. She looked down from the top of the stairs. Wisps of scraggly gray hair fell along her round face. He was always surprised that his grandmother had almost no wrinkles. Her eyes sparkled. Sometimes she looked even younger than Mama.

'Somebody came by for you,' she said. 'He left a note. It's on the table.'

'This early?'

'A Mr. Evans. He came all the way from Cleveland. Had a beauty of a car. He was a real gentleman. I made him some coffee.'

Ahmed Evans had left behind a note in elegant, old-fashioned handwriting. *Saturday afternoon, 2 p.m. Antioch*

College, Yellow Springs, Ohio. Let me know if you can be there. Black Arts Festival. You're in charge. Peace, Ahmed.

Fred Ahmed Evans was a black nationalist. Omar had met him at a club in Cleveland about a year back. Evans drank orange juice and water. He wore a black suit with a white dress shirt. He was a small, slightly built man with a suspicious, self-assured look in his eye. Evans had the aura of an intellectual but his hands were large and strong and calloused. He had been a welder in a Cleveland steel factory before deciding to devote himself to the cause.

'Where'd you get that fancy shirt?' Evans had asked him. 'Looks like it's made out of gold.'

'From a neighbor of mine who died. His wife gave it to me. She said it suited me. Why do you ask?'

'Sad.'

'He was sick.'

'I hear you. Sad.'

'What are you doing here? You look lost. That suit and all. You from the Nation or something?'

'I haven't come all this way to be put down again,' Evans snapped.

'Whoa, didn't mean to rile you. Let me buy you a drink.'

Evans made a dismissive gesture. Then extended his hand. 'Evans. I've seen you here before. I hoped we'd get the chance to talk.'

'You're from the cops.'

For the first time Ahmed Evans's stern face broke into a smile. 'You could be doing other things,' he said.

'Like what?'

'For your own people, your own kind ... the way I see it, you're nothin' but a big, stupid, motherfuckin' nigga.'

'Say what?' Omar was surprised that he wasn't even

angry at this slender man with his strange sense of humor.

'All that time you spend on women and hustling. You'd feel better if you did something for your own people. I guarantee it.'

'I feel fine.'

'Really?'

'Why wouldn't I?'

'Because you do exactly what white people expect you to.'

'Fuck off.'

'Why don't you come to one of our meetings.' Evans scribbled an address on the back of a silver foil lining from a pack of Marlboros. 'Tuesday at eight.' Shook his hand, as though to confirm the appointment.

But Omar misplaced the slip of paper with the address of the nationalists.

A few months later he bumped into the man again, at the same club.

'We're looking for someone to handle security,' Evans said. That was after the Cleveland riots.

'Sooner or later the police are going to arrest us, Omar. We've got to be prepared. Protect our wives and children if it comes to that. I don't want to go through that hell again. What do you say?'

Evans rattled on about the right to self-determination and about niggers and Hough and education and the need for discipline, while all Omar thought about was that shiny .38 he'd hidden at the back of the closet in his room after the incident outside the Circle Ballroom. He hadn't touched the weapon again, in an attempt to erase his memories of that cold winter night in Cleveland.

'What do you think, Omar? Can you handle the responsibility?'

It was as though Evans was looking straight through him, giving him a second chance. Omar didn't know if he liked it or not. Evans's tone was self-assured and authoritative, almost arrogant, but at the same time Omar had the feeling that this black activist was actually looking out for him, actually putting his faith in him.

'Yes,' he said.

'Can you change your life?'

He laughed.

Evans wrote down his address again, this time directly onto the inside of Omar's left arm, so he couldn't lose it.

In the kitchen he took a few bites of the catfish his grandmother had fried the night before. He passed over the vegetables and sticky rice. He'd filled up on beer with Reggie. He shook the wet coat off his shoulders, kicked off his boots, and climbed the stairs. He had stuck Evans's note in his back pocket.

Saturday. Antioch College. You're in charge.

That was two days away. He wondered why Evans didn't just phone him. *You're in charge.* He was proud and nervous at the same time. Evans was his mentor. For the past couple of months Omar drove to Hough every Tuesday evening and sat in a stuffy elementary-school classroom listening to the small black man tell about the history of his people, about Marcus Garvey, who long ago had campaigned for the emancipation of the blacks, who believed that blacks could only be free once they had returned to Africa, about Malcolm X and black identity, about black Americans' right to self-defense. But Evans had never put him in charge of security before.

He would take his .38 with him, but that wasn't enough, not for someone in charge.

'What was that about?' His grandmother was waiting at the head of the stairs.

'Nothing.'

'That gentleman drove all the way here from Cleveland for nothing?'

'Uh-huh.'

'Don't mess with me, Jerome. I don't want your mother to worry.'

'You just said that Evans was a gentleman, those were your words.' He put his arm around his grandmother's shoulders. She was a large, powerful woman. Rose Fuller had helped Mama get a job in the hospital's linen room. She had raised the younger children, and for every little scrape or ache she prepared a salve or special tea from the herbs in her garden. She was proud to be a southerner by birth, even though she'd only lived down there as a child. Every day she said how much she missed the wide open space, the heat. The humidity, which was like a second skin. That if it had been up to her she'd never have moved to Akron, Ohio, where it was cold for half the year and where it rained and snowed. 'But your great-grandfather had big plans when he brought us here. He wasn't scared of anything.' She told them about the witches in the swampland. And about her Indian mother, who got medicine and herbs from the witches, which was the only reason, she said, that she and a couple of her siblings survived fever and diarrhea. 'I only realized she was Indian when I went to school and the other kids said so. Until then, as far as I was concerned, she was just black, despite her skin being so light. She talked differently too. Words sounded softer out of her mouth.' The stories were like make believe, like fairy tales. And that's how Grandma told them, too: as though her ancestors were mythical figures from an imaginary land. She had a beautiful voice, Grandma. Omar loved Rose Fuller as much as his own mother.

'I'm going to bed, Grandma.' He felt the letter in his back pocket.

'You're old enough to know what you're doing, aren't you?'

'There's nothing going on. I'm just going to bed. I'm beat.' He opened the door to the room he shared with Chris and Billy. The floor was littered with stuff, old magazines and T-shirts and underwear and socks and empty beer cans, but he didn't care. He flopped onto his bed and closed his eyes. He couldn't move anymore. 'Good night,' he heard his grandmother say in the distance, and he thought of Yellow Springs, Ohio and saw a vast meadow stretched out before him, and cows and trees and cornfields under the clear blue sky. Then he fell asleep.

He saw Don Cooper and Nona walk hand in hand into the Circle Ballroom. Cooper had a dirty bandage tied around his head. 'Hey, Omar,' he said. He didn't let go of Nona's hand. 'Hey, Omar.'

He said something back but they didn't hear him. It was as though he were watching it all from a distance, as though he was seeing himself as well as Nona and Cooper.

'You think you're too good for us? Is that it? Is that why you don't open that mouth o' yours? I said: "Hey, Omar".'

He was outside his own body. He looked at Nona in her glittery blue dress. She teetered on high heels and held for dear life onto Don Cooper's arm. Omar tried to say something to her, something nice, that she looked good, but again his words dissolved into the gray hum of the fan in the middle of the ceiling. She didn't even see him move his mouth. There was no music. There were no other people.

'Come on,' Nina whispered in Cooper's ear. 'Let's go.'

'Bye, Omar,' Cooper said, with a theatrical wink.

'Omar. Wake up.' He heard Reggie's voice from way off. He opened his eyes. He was still lying there on his back on his bed, on top of the covers, fully dressed. He hadn't budged since he fell asleep hours ago. He was cold. His muscles hurt.

'Your grandma said you were here. What's going on? You were supposed to pick me up at six.' Reggie was standing at the foot of the bed.

'What time is it?'

'Seven-thirty. If we're still going to do something ... '

'Easy, man. I ... I ... I ... ' He thought of that note from Evans. 'I have to get something to eat. You go on.'

'What's up?'

'Nothing.'

'We're not going out?'

'I got stuff to do.'

'You look bad, man. Go fix yourself up first.'

'Evans came by.' He propped himself up. 'For a job, Saturday. Sorry.'

'Shit.'

'What?'

'Want me to go with you?'

He shook his head. 'Better not.'

'How come?'

He wasn't sure if it was because he wanted to protect Reggie or just wanted to keep Evans's jobs for himself.

'See you at the factory, okay?'

After Reggie left he put on clean clothes and splashed cold water on his face. He crept downstairs and left the house by the front door.

The keys to Sandra's old vw were still in the ignition. He got in and started the car. He felt in his pocket. Five twenty-dollar bills. It wouldn't be enough for a decent gun but maybe Leo would give him a good deal if he heard that Evans had sent him.

Omar parked halfway up Wooster Ave., got out, and walked to the Hi-De-Ho Lounge. It was getting dark. He looked at the full-leafed lindens lining the street. They grew a little crooked, slanting toward each other; the upper branches and leaves touched but didn't block out the light. It was like he was walking through a tunnel or under a bridge. In a few weeks there would be a thick, porridgy carpet of yellow and red and brown in the road. It was early October, and he could just about catch the sweet-sour scent of autumn. He liked that smell, the smell of earth and wetness and rot. He remembered trudging barefoot through the thick layer of half-decomposed leaves as a child, fantasizing that he was wading upstream through a fast-moving river. A few days later all the mush and mud was gone, the streets clean and new, the trees became bare, and black silhouettes against the sky. As though the earth had been rinsed clean in a single night. How could all those leaves have just disappeared into nothing?

He spotted Leo right away, sitting alone at a corner of the bar. He was pretty much a permanent fixture at the Hi-De-Ho. Always there in that corner. He wore a jogging suit and a baseball cap, which was supposed to make him look younger. But the deep lines in Leo's gaunt face gave away his age. Omar could hardly imagine this man was ever young.

'You're early,' Leo said, with a low, lazy voice.

Omar pulled up a barstool. 'You want to do me a favor?'

'Why would I want to do that?'

Omar took out the rumpled twenties. 'It's for Evans. Evans from Cleveland.'

'When?'

'Tomorrow.'

'Action?'

'Security.'

'Oh la la ... ' Leo sang. Omar wondered if he was being laughed at, but controlled himself. He couldn't afford any nasty business right now. He thought of Evans's note.

'Can I count on you?' Omar asked. He alone heard how formal and official those few words sounded.

'Tomorrow night,' Leo said. 'Same time.'

The Antioch College campus in Yellow Springs, Ohio resembled a vacation resort. The sun gave the proud red-brick academic buildings an extra glow. In the middle of the campus was a large quad. Beyond the faculties and student dorms were meadows and fields and woods and wooden houses. It was a pleasant late-summer day.

Omar checked his watch. One-thirty. That morning he had gone straight home from the factory, slept for two hours, had breakfast, and then driven to Yellow Springs. He felt refreshed, even though he knew that the clear-headedness was mostly thanks to adrenaline. He looked at the black girls with their soft afros and big silver hoop earrings. Girls in halter tops and long flowered skirts. Their satin skin. Boys in brightly colored dashikis. They must be about his age, but they seemed much younger. Everyone appeared so carefree today, laughing and flirting with each other.

He observed, from a short distance, the activity on the quad. His hand glided over the inside pocket of his leather coat; he felt the heaviness of his .38 and the .45 Leo had sold him the previous evening. If those students only knew. Their innocent blitheness had something contagious about it, but at the same time their light-heartedness irritated him. Like this was some kind of party. Evans hadn't asked him to be in charge for nothing: he knew that the event's organizers were being shadowed by the FBI. There was always the danger of provocation, so everyone was patted down at the entrance. He hadn't seen Evans yet—the man probably kept himself at a safe distance.

Omar went over to the auditorium entrance. A young guy in black pants and a black T-shirt was frisking people as they went in. He looked like a bouncer—Omar had seen him before at nationalist meetings—and it looked as though he might burst out of that tight T-shirt any minute, his biceps and torso were so pumped up. He had tried to phone Evans but his number had been disconnected. What did Evans expect him to do? 'You're in charge.' The students thronged inside. The bouncer giggled along with the girls, ran his huge hands lightly over the boys' bodies. Omar turned to look back across the nearly empty quad. The sun reflected off the white and red tiles. He squinted a bit, saw only the bright white light. He heard the excited chatter behind him. He felt invisible. He thought back on the night classes at the University of Akron. He'd gone four times, just to please his mother. He saw the white walls of the classroom, the students chatting at their desks about the courses they were taking, the books they'd read; he saw the satisfied look on their faces, their excitement about the future. They truly believed they were safe within the university's white walls, that it was just a matter of time before they would conquer the world outside those walls. He hated them. It didn't matter if they were black or white. Every time he was on campus he became invisible, crossed an imaginary bridge that led to an island where nothing was real, nothing was tangible, where the buildings were like a reflection of the sky, the air white and rarefied. After class he'd always fled the building to drive over to Howard St. The yellow and red and orange neon lights of the bars and clubs flashed welcomingly at him, as though he had just landed back on earth. The air smelled different on Howard St. He always got a whiff of perfume and dust and alcohol. The hot, rancid, bittersweet smell of sex. Eunice, who smiled at him as soon as he entered the High Hat. The familiarity of that smile, of her perfect blue-black skin. The way she laughed off the grousing of the whores and the pimps. After her shift she usually made out with John behind the bar. He'd never seen a woman so totally surrender herself to a man. Eunice wasn't one to play games. Wasn't afraid of getting hurt. She trusted the half-white, baseball-crazy John. They were a nice couple.

Omar even preferred the sweltering heat of the factory to the vacuity of the university classroom. There, at least, he wasn't kidding himself.

He opened his eyes. Clenched his fists. Music spilled out from the auditorium. He heard conga riffs, brisk Latin rhythms. He squeezed between the students and tapped the bouncer on the shoulder.

'Leave it to me,' he said.

'And who are you?'

'Ben Hassan. I'm in charge.'

'Says who?'

'You know that as well as I do.'

'Don't get bent out of shape, man. Everybody's already inside.'

Omar opened his jacket. Offered the bouncer a glimpse of the gleaming metal.

'What, am I supposed to be afraid now?' He didn't look at Omar, but waved some more students through. 'Go ahead, asshole,' he hissed, and then turned and walked off.

Omar began awkwardly frisking the last few boys. On stage, a small black man with an African cap sat behind two enormous congas. He drummed so fast that you could only see the motion, not his hands themselves. His hands disappeared in the forceful, compelling rhythms that flew off the congas.

A man with a beard and an afro pushed his way in.

'Hey, you!' Omar shouted.

'What?' The man looked back, irritated. He wore a red-and-yellow dashiki. His skin was deep brown.

'Just wait.'

'What for?'

'So I can frisk you.'

'What're you talking about? I'm one of The Last Poets from New York, you fool. I've gotta perform now.'

'I don't care if you're James Brown. I'm in charge of security here. Nobody just walks on through. Otherwise get lost.'

The man raised his hands. 'Can you reach?' he asked condescendingly while Omar's hands patted under his dashiki and along his pant legs. 'That tickles.'

Omar stood at the back of the auditorium, near the exit. He was sweating but couldn't take off his leather jacket because of the guns in his inside pockets. The weight of the metal tugged at his shoulders. For the first time that day, he was relaxed. He watched the drummer on stage. The guy looked like he was in a trance. The complex rhythms seemed completely effortless. Omar leaned against the wall. It was like he was listening to an entire orchestra of drummers—he heard a bassline rhythm and a melody at the same time, but the melody wasn't really being played, it just wafted up from those natural rhythms like a wispy vapor; he caught snippets of soft, mysterious tones that were gone, evaporated, before he even really and truly heard them. He looked at the microphone stands and the speakers on the stage. The students had nestled into their seats, leaning back expectantly. He wished he could go sit with them. He felt superfluous here. He knew he had to stay alert, and that the lazy, relaxed mood could be a forewarning of something else, danger, violence. Evans had explained it to him so often, the principles of security, deterrence, always being a step ahead of your enemy; fear and how to combat it with prayer and weapons, how fear heightened your senses. Omar knew it well. The rules of security didn't differ that much from the rules of the street. He closed his eyes. Fear was the last thing he felt—the complete lack of it, in fact, sometimes worried him. The dull indifference that came over him at the strangest moments. He never told Evans. He didn't want Evans to think he missed the hustling, the drugs, the flashy cars. He was startled out of his reverie by the loud, agitated male voice that came through the loudspeakers. 'They come from Harlem. Their poems are grenades. Give 'em a round of applause: The Last Poets!'

Three men sauntered quasi-nonchalantly up onto the stage. The drummer slowed his rhythm. Omar recognized the man he had just frisked. All eyes were drawn to his brightly colored dashiki. He took the microphone.

'Who's the big talker from security?' he shouted into the auditorium. Snickering from the audience. Omar straightened his back. He didn't give a shit what that nigger from Harlem thought of him.

'This poem's for him and for all the other muthafuckas who think they're ready for the revolution. *When the revolution comes …* ' he chanted, and the other two men joined in at the same pitch. 'When the revolution comes … When the revolution comes … '

The drummer stopped. The audience held its breath. He gave the conga a few cautious slaps, gradually built up the tempo: supple, round beats that seemed to reverberate around the room, faster and faster, becoming a single, drawn-out note that snaked its way around the hall.

The poet moved his head with the rhythm. He appeared to be the youngest of the three. He had a deep, vibrant voice, a forceful, aggressive tone.

When the revolution comes
some of us will catch it on TV
with chicken hanging from our mouths
you'll know it's revolution
because there won't be no commercials
when the revolution comes
preacher pimps are gonna split the scene
with the communion wine …

Omar's attention waned. He couldn't keep his eyes off the attractive Latino who, in the background, kept repeating the poet's words, 'When the revolution comes', like a refrain. He wore tight jeans and his shirt was unbuttoned down to his navel. His mocha-colored skin glistened. He danced. The other poet was older. His skin so black, almost purple in the sharp blue theater lighting. *'When the revolution comes ... '* Omar thought of The Temptations. He imagined them standing on the stage in their chic suits, dancing to the monotone rhythm of this mesmerizing poem. The older poet walked upstage. *'Tell me brother,'* he said, with a husky voice, *'Tell me brother when you first saw yo' child dead son born of a pussy long dead long black yo' son stumblin' in blind rage out past the box ... swollen lips ... '*

The words kept coming out of the black poet's mouth, faster and louder as he gesticulated wildly—faster, louder, angrier. *'Tell me brother ... '* Sweat poured off his forehead. The Latino sang a gentle melody in the background. He had a high, attractive voice. The older poet was like a preacher in church. The poem resembled a sermon. He whipped up his audience with his lofty, solemn voice. *'Tell me brother ... how did you feel when you came out of the wilderness ... screamin' baby ... baby!'*

The words melted into the poet's jagged, gravelly voice. This kind of music was a first for Omar. He felt the bass notes reverberate through his body. His thoughts wandered back to the last day of school at South High, to the poem he had read aloud to the teachers, the applause and laughter from the students, cheering him on, urging him to continue, clearer and faster, how he glowed with exhilaration and triumph. The taut smile on Giovanni's face. He thought of his father, who practiced the trumpet down in their basement, just in case someone invited him to play. No one ever did. Sonny Huling was crazy. Through the melodious violence of the words and rhythms that spattered from the stage he could hear the dreamy, soft tones of his father's trumpet. 'How come you don't play? How come you don't play?' Right in front of him, a girl got up from her seat. She clapped her hands and swung her hips. Her small, round breasts swayed gently along. 'Baby ... baby!' the poet screamed. Omar looked at the girl in the white blouse with the fancy stitching. Her bare, chocolate-colored shoulders. She didn't notice him watching her. He heard the music and the words via her body, saw the sounds in the fluid movements of her hips and hands, her radiant young face. Omar wasn't feeling like himself anymore, wasn't in control of his thoughts. As though someone were pricking needles into his brain. He saw Uncle Jean, Mama's brother. Uncle Jean, dozing on the chair in front of his house, the empty bourbon bottle on the ground next to him. He saw Uncle Jean's yellow Pontiac. He was eleven. He stole the keys from his uncle's threadbare dungaree pocket and opened the driver's door. His head barely reached the top of the steering wheel. He started the car up. The engine drowned out his uncle's snoring. He put his foot on the gas pedal and drove out onto the street and down the hill. The bright sunlight blinded him. Uncle Jean was livid. 'You crashed my car! You coulda got killed!' The beating he got, first from his aunt, then from his mother. The burning sensation on his back and his ass. But—he could drive.

The music stopped. It was like waking up. Applause and cheers for the three poets and the drummer from New York. Omar left the auditorium. A few students were standing in the hallway, chatting and smoking. He ignored their suspicious glances and continued into the open air. Squinted against the misty white October light. He no longer felt the weight of the guns. From the auditorium he could still hear snippets of conga and the melodious voice of the Latino. Unintelligible Spanish words. He heard insects, animals moving in the warm, humid air. Silence. He saw wispy clouds, like feathers drawn on a blue background. It was a pleasant sight. Like seeing the sky for the very first time. He laughed. He knew that lack of sleep was clouding his judgment, that being wound up over Evans's assignment was making him oversensitive, but he didn't care, because after the performance he would go to the poets and ask that arrogant motherfucker in the ugly dashiki for their address in Harlem. And tonight, at home, he would write a new poem. There was bound to be an old notebook stashed in one of his dresser drawers.

Omar drove back to Akron early that evening. It was already beginning to get dark. A thin mist hung above the fields and between the trees. The garish neon lights of the roadside diners beckoned him, but he drove on, concentrating on the gray asphalt in front of him. The endless, monotonous hills zoomed past. In the distance he saw the sparkle of the city lights. He imagined the city was breathing, the lights flickering to the rhythm of its breaths. At Hot Tomatoes, a white hamburger joint on the outskirts of Akron, he ordered chicken wings and beer at the drive-through window. He drove aimlessly into town, eating the wings and taking the occasional sip of lukewarm beer. He felt the grease drip down his chin, a drop splashed on his new green dress shirt. His black leather jacket with the two guns was in the trunk. He drove on, not wanting to stop anywhere. He was enjoying the clarity in his head, the performance of those New York poets still fresh in his mind. Abiodun Oyewole had given him The Last Poets' address on 125th St., in case he was ever in Harlem. He even hugged him when he said he also wanted to be a poet. That nigger was probably just being friendly because their performance was a success; he still came across as an arrogant bastard, but who cared. Omar pressed his foot on the gas pedal. He turned left onto Main Street, stopping halfway at a crosswalk. The street was vacant. He saw the green awning of Hardy's Hardware Store. The post office next door. A few years ago he'd bumped into his grandmother Elizabeth here. He hadn't seen her since they moved in with Grandma Fuller. He was with some friends from South High. Eugene Mitchell gave him a nudge. 'Isn't that your grandma?' He gestured across the street. She was standing in front of the jeweler's, admiring the gold rings, bracelets, earrings, and watches in the window. His stomach clenched. There she was, with her back straight and her gray hair pulled up in a bun. She wore a gray-brown dress till just under her knee. No coat—it was summer, and hot. As he remembered it, the streets were yellow-brown and dusty, like sand in the desert. His grandmother's skin was as dry and cracked as arid earth.

He looked at that rigid back that seemed to radiate nothing but reproach. Nothing had changed. Only now he saw the sad secrets she hid in her rigid body, thick gray knots that made her limbs stiff and wooden. 'Aren't you going to say hi to her?' Eugene asked. Omar shook his head. 'It's your grandma, man.' Eugene shoved him off the sidewalk. Omar crossed the street. Grandma Elizabeth hadn't noticed him yet. Suddenly she turned away from the store window and looked him straight in the eye, as though she knew all the time that he and his friends were talking about her.

'Hi, Grandma.' Omar heard the trepidation in his voice. He was afraid he'd stutter. And again: 'Hi, Grandma.' She gave him a dull, empty look. He could feel her looking right through him and ignoring him at the same time. He remembered the time he was walking down Furnace

St. and had bumped into his uncle and cousins, and everybody was glad to see him, and his uncle put him up on his shoulders. 'Jerome's gonna do the family proud,' Uncle Willy said. 'Jerome won't amount to anything,' his grandmother said. 'Jerome's stupid.' And she pulled him off his uncle's shoulders and gave him the same empty, icy stare she gave him now, on the sidewalk in front of the jeweler's on Main Street. It was a look that erased him, denied his existence. She turned and walked away, her shoulders hunched up. He froze. It was like his feet were cemented to the gray concrete of the sidewalk.

'Fuck you, bitch,' he hissed, loud enough for her to hear him. She did not look back. He watched as the gray-brown back receded. A slowly fading ghost. He almost felt sorry for her. But his own pain was stronger than hers, and he pulled himself together.

'Fuck you, bitch,' he muttered to himself.

At the end of Main St. he turned right and drove to Reggie's place. Hopefully Reggie was still home. It was Saturday night, and Omar didn't feel like scouring the bars for him; he just felt like crashing on the sofa with a few beers down in the basement, watching some TV. Maybe telling Reggie his decision.

Through a gap in the blue velour curtains in the basement window Omar could see a silver-blue stripe of light. He pulled into the driveway and stopped in front of the garage. He wondered where Reggie's Cadillac was. It was an old white rust-speckled tank, but the leather seats felt supple and new. It was like sitting in a limousine. Omar got out and knocked at the cellar door. He heard a muffled grumbling from inside and opened the door. Reggie was lying on the couch, watching an episode of *Thunderbirds*.

'Why d'you watch that garbage, man?' Omar laughed.

'B-b-back already?' Reggie asked. Omar hated it when Reggie asked redundant questions. When he stuttered. Reggie wasted too much time.

'Where's your car?'

'In the shop,' Reggie mumbled.

'Oh.'

'What?'

'How about something to drink?'

'H-h-help yourself.' Reggie nodded at the small refrigerator next to the television. So he was still sore because Omar didn't take him with him to Yellow Springs.

'You didn't miss anything,' Omar said.

Reggie shrugged his shoulders.

'You going out?' Omar asked as he took a can of beer from the refrigerator.

'Nah.'

They watched the action marionettes on the TV.

'Isn't there anything else on?'

No answer.

'You pissed off about something?'

'Not me. Y-you, maybe?'

'Yeah, right,' Omar laughed.

Reggie got up and went out to the hallway bathroom. Omar switched channels. A white woman with an enormous beehive smiled into the camera. Behind her, musicians in black tuxedos. He turned off the sound and flopped onto the sofa. He heard the toilet flush, the water splash in the washbasin. He drank his beer and lay back, closed his eyes and felt sleep take over. His face was flushed, his limbs heavy. He broke into a sweat. He saw Grandma Elizabeth walking down Main Street in the burning sun. He saw an expanse of yellow-brown sand with rocks in the background. Shimmering hot air. Dust.

His grandmother was gone. Reggie put an arm around his shoulder and whispered, 'She can't hurt you anymore, Hank. Don't let her hurt you anymore.' A blind, paralyzing fury shot through his body. 'Fuck off, man.' Everything went black. Black with stars. The stars were clear and bright, their silvery sparkle so brilliant that it hurt to look at them. He closed his eyes. Black.

Off in the distance he heard a mellifluous voice. Unintelligible words that kept getting closer. He heard jazz. Slid comfortably into the warm, clear sound of a saxophone. The music made everything go orange and yellow.

'You asleep?' Reggie jogged his shoulder. 'Wake up.'

Omar opened his eyes. His friend stood in the middle of the room, hands in the pockets of his corduroys.

'What's up with you?'

'What?' His throat was raw, his lips dry, as though he hadn't had a drink in days.

'I don't know. You just don't look good, man. Just look at you sweating.'

Omar propped himself up. In the flickering blue-gray light of the TV Reggie was just a silhouette.

'Just bushed, that's all,' Omar mumbled. His body was being pulled downward. His head throbbed. Reggie's silhouette went all fuzzy. He fell back onto the sofa.

'You should eat something. Mammio made soup.'

The word echoed in Omar's head, and he smelled the sharp, fatty smell of chicken soup. He gagged.

'What happened?'

'Nothing,' Omar said, 'nothing.'

'You on something?'

Omar shook his head.

'I'm worried about you, man,' he heard Reggie say. But Omar couldn't answer. His throat burned. As soon as he closed his eyes he felt his body undulating gently, like he was bobbing on the surface of a lake.

'You only come by when it suits you. Look at yourself. What do you expect me to do? You scare me sometimes.'

Omar thought of the poets from New York. He wanted to tell Reggie about the good-looking black Latino with the unbuttoned shirt. The aggressive poet in his dashiki. Their words, which became music atop the forceful, compelling rhythms of the conga. Remember when we saw The Supremes at Ethel's in Detroit? Remember that, Reggie? Oooh ... those tight white glittery gowns. And The Temptations at The 20 Grand? I've always said I wanted to be an entertainer. Don't you remember? But he couldn't get any of it out of his mouth. The words and images just spun around in his head. Like fireworks in his brain.

He heard Reggie talk but couldn't take any of it in. Only heard the familiar lilt of his voice, how he swallowed his words, gnawed at them, how the pitch went up at the end of every sentence. How every sentence ended in a question mark. They were really young again, maybe eleven or twelve, sitting in the field behind his house on North Street, drinking cheap bourbon. He was telling Reggie about the fight at Roxy's the night before. That little creep Eric Webb bleeding on the wooden floor, and nobody lifting a finger to help him. Webb was a shoeshine boy like Jerome, about his age. Followed Jerome to all the bars and tried to steal his customers. But that night Webb got to Roxy's first. When Jerome walked in at about eleven he saw Webb already sitting on the floor, tending to one of Jerome's regulars. A sleazy, smug look on his face. Jerome went over to him, gave him a shove. 'Get outta here,' he hissed. 'This is my turf.' He was a head shorter than Jerome, with a narrow, pointy mouse-snout. Webb looked thunderstruck, which made Jerome even madder. He punched him in the face. 'Give it to him,' he heard someone shout behind him. Webb reached for his nose. 'Go on, beat the shit out of him!' And Jerome took his wooden shoeshine box, heavy with tins and brushes, and started pounding Webb with all his might. On his shoulders, his head, his back—he didn't even see his rival anymore, only heard the goading and yelping from the black men and women standing in a circle around them. 'C'mon, thrash that little black bastard. You're stronger'n him. C'mon!' He kept at it until his arm and shoulder hurt. Webb lay motionless on the floor, his arms in front of his bloodied face. Blood on Roxy's wooden floor. Jerome picked up his kit and walked out of the club. A few men slapped him on the shoulder. 'You'll be okay. Come back here whenever you want.'

Reggie's mouth hung open. Jerome didn't tell him that later, at home, he'd puked in the toilet. It was the middle of the night, everyone was already asleep. He dragged himself up the stairs, his whole body hurt, he felt like he was the one covered with bruises, like it was him who had taken a beating. He didn't feel like a winner at all. 'Take him down! Beat him to a pulp!' Webb with his mouse-face and that pathetic look in his eyes. Webb, Webb, the name throbbed in his head. In his half-slumber he felt himself stumble and fall, but he didn't fall onto the ground, he was floating on water, it got darker and darker, and quieter. All he heard was Reggie's melodious, faraway mumbling.

He woke up and through a gap in the blue curtain he saw the sky change from dark blue to gray, then green and light blue. He was down for the count. His mind was empty. Only the sound of Reggie's regular, deep breathing. The gurgle of water. Reggie's massive body on the white carpet. A thin checked blanket over his legs. He closed his eyes and let himself be transported by the rhythm of Reggie's breathing. He heard the birds' first cautious, unconvinced chirps, as though they were frightened by the clarity of their own sound. He didn't move. He didn't want to think. Everything was okay.

'I'm leaving,' Omar said. It was Sunday morning, about eleven. Reggie had made bacon and eggs and toast.

'I'd eat breakfast first if I were you,' Reggie said. 'Man, you were delirious last night. I didn't dare leave you alone.'

'Why, what'd I say?'

'I dunno. You were cursing, crying for your mama.'

'Get outta here.'

'Just kidding.' Reggie laughed and slid him a plate of food and a glass of orange juice. He looked younger and more vulnerable than he really was. Omar wanted to tell him about the group from New York and about Yellow Springs and his decision to become a poet; that it wasn't really even a decision, but something he just knew as soon as he heard them and the music; how the images ricocheted around in his head. It felt like when he was four or five and the words pressed against the inside of his skull, screaming for attention. He wanted to tell Reggie everything, about his dream about Grandma Elizabeth and about Webb, but all he could say was: 'I'm getting out of Akron.'

'When?'

He shrugged. 'Soon. I dunno, in a couple of months.'

'How come?'

'This place is making me crazy.'

'And what about us? We're friends, right?'

'We'll always be friends.'

'Damn.' Reggie put his plate on the coffee table and got up. Omar was still lying on the sofa. Reggie's big, awkward body filled the entire basement. 'But wh-wh-why you goin'?' he mumbled.

Omar wasn't in the mood for bullshit. He tried to hoist himself up, but everything went dark and he got dizzy. He lay back down.

'I've got a headache. We'll go out tonight, have some fun, okay?'

'So where you gonna go?' Reggie asked. Omar's thoughts were in Harlem. Abiodun Oyewole had written down the Poets' address on a scrap of paper, but where had Omar put the paper? He dug in his pockets.

'Pass me that jacket.'

Reggie picked it up. 'Hell, this is heavy. What-all you got in here?'

'What do you think? Evans asked me to be a guard in Yellow Springs. But there was nothing to guard. Dead as anything.' Omar didn't know why he lied. He liked Reggie, he liked him more than anybody else, it pained him to see him standing there so gawkily, his head bent and his back hunched because of the low ceiling—but he couldn't tell him about his poems and his love for the music, his desire to translate all his thoughts and feelings into words and sounds. He was afraid he'd lose it all as soon as he said it out loud and let Reggie in on his thoughts.

'New York,' he said.

'New York?'

'Yeah.'

'What're you gonna do there?'

Omar shrugged. 'I dunno. Get famous?'

Reggie laughed. 'Get famous.'

'Maybe you shouldn't stay here either,' Omar said, trying to sound as warm and gentle as possible. He had to get out of this basement. Why the fuck couldn't Reggie take care of himself?'

'Y-y-you want me go with you?'

'That's not what I meant. Just think about it, that's all. And pass me that jacket.'

Reggie gave him the jacket, and Omar took the slip of paper with the address of the Last Poets out of one of the inside pockets. 'East Wind,' he read, '125th St., next to the Apollo.' He felt Reggie's questioning look. He felt caught out. He put the slip of paper back in the pocket. 'Friends, right?' He gave Reggie an 'us guys' look, offered him a fist.

But Reggie put his big hands in his pockets. 'Whatever you say,' he muttered.

They didn't bring up Omar's plan to leave Akron again. They worked their day shifts in the hot, stuffy Firestone factory, joked with one another, and hung around in Reggie's basement at night, or else went for drinks at the Hi-De-Ho Lounge. On Tuesdays Omar drove to Cleveland for nationalist meetings. Everything seemed back to normal. But since seeing The Last Poets, Omar was changed. His decision to become a poet was like a safe haven. Sometimes he scribbled a few words in his notebook when Chris and Billy were out and he had the bedroom to himself. He wanted to write a poem for Huey Newton, the leader of the Black Panther Party in California. He'd seen Huey on TV once, marching with his comrades, their shotguns resting loosely on their shoulders. They just marched straight into the state courthouse in Sacramento. Nobody stopped them. That was a while ago; the laws had been changed in California since then and the Panthers couldn't carry guns anymore, but it didn't matter. The Black Panthers and Huey Newton had turned the whole country upside down. The whites were shitting their pants. Huey was a street kid—just like Omar—and he knew the law books inside out; he could have been a film star with that smooth, coffee-colored skin of his. Somehow Huey reminded Omar of Miles Davis. He didn't know why; Miles was hardly streetwise. He was vain and a big talker, but his music had the same enigmatic power as a Panthers demonstration. Like everybody was electrified. If Omar could only put that into a poem ... But as soon as he started writing, it was as though the paper sucked up all his words. 'Huey was a bad muthafucka,' he read, and had no idea where to go from there. But he didn't care. It was just a matter of time. He was smoldering and churning inside; he'd never enjoyed having a secret so much. It made him immune to all the shit and ugliness around him. He suspected Reggie thought he'd abandoned his plan to quit Akron, and he was happy to leave it that way. He couldn't face that pathetic, helpless look in his friend's eyes. He had to protect himself. And besides, he wasn't responsible for Reggie's happiness, was he? What Reggie didn't know wouldn't hurt him. And then one day he'd just get on the bus. Reggie would understand. He always did. Reggie and Omar were tight.

One Monday night, a few weeks after the Yellow Springs festival, Omar and Reggie were hanging around with some old school friends at the Custard Stand on the corner of Edgewood and Euclid. David Matthews was there and Louis Johnson and another group of guys. It was already dark. They used to come here often before heading to the Hi-De-Ho or driving up to Cleveland. On

Mondays it was always extra crowded after the roller rink closed. There was a little grocery next door to the Custard Stand, run by a white couple, the Brewsters. The owners and their shop had grown old together: the older and frailer the couple got, the shabbier the grocery became. The paint was peeling from the trim and the light bulbs in the Coca-Cola sign out front fizzled one at a time. Omar and his friends bought beer and bourbon and lukewarm hot dogs at the Brewsters'. Omar was nervous that night, rocking from one leg to the other and puffing anxiously on his cigarette. He didn't know why, but he couldn't keep still. He'd slept all day following a night shift, but sleep hadn't offered him much in the way of rest: it seemed like the speed he had taken before going to work was still in his blood. And he'd picked a fight with Boyd, an older black guy, a lifer at Firestone. Boyd was a good man, but when Omar brought up the Black United Front and police brutality in Akron, Boyd just laughed at him. 'You're wasting your time with that bunch. Those students in the Front are all gonna leave soon for nice cushy jobs. You don't see that? Wake up, man.' It was as though a grenade exploded in Omar's head. As though Boyd were trying to rob him of his deepest yearnings. Boyd wasn't a stupid man. He was a member of the union and Omar respected him, which made his words hurt all the more. Still, Omar rushed at the old man and snarled that it was the guy's own business if he wanted to work himself to death in that damn factory, but no way was Omar going to be the next Papa Brown. A month earlier, Papa Brown had dropped dead of a heart attack only a few weeks after his retirement. Haines, the foreman, watched them with a smile from his glass-fronted office overlooking the work floor. Omar felt like ripping that smug smirk off his white face. He raised his fist in the air. Haines just turned away.

'So what's the plan?' Reggie asked.

'You got any ideas?' Omar snapped.

'Cool down, man.'

'Why should I cool down. Didn't you guys hear what happened last Saturday?'

'What?'

'That party on Wooster.' Omar blew into his hands to warm them up. It was early November and already getting mighty cold. He felt Reggie staring. Reggie stepped back and kicked a few stones. Omar tried to ignore him. Reggie had a sixth sense about Omar's latent anger; this was Reggie's way of warning him to cool off.

'I wasn't there,' Omar continued, 'but I heard that it got real late and that the neighbors called the cops. They took two guys down to the station and beat the shit out of them. That's what I heard.'

'From who?' someone asked.

'Doesn't matter who. It wasn't in the paper, anyway. Those guys are lucky they're alive. Hasn't this gone too far? America's exploding on all sides and Akron's fast asleep. And what are *we* doing? I haven't seen any of you at the Front's office.'

'Who was it?' Louis asked. Louis was a tall fellow with a handsome, light-brown face and fine features. Like a sculptor had spent hours working on his head. Louis reminded Omar of a prince, an Egyptian prince.

'I don't know. Students. The party was at some white chick's house. That they ended up there doesn't mean they deserve to get beaten half to death.' White puffs of condensation came out of his mouth. It was getting busier at the Custard Stand. The door to the Brewsters' grocery was open, and dim fluorescent light spilled onto the sidewalk. Omar looked around for Reggie, but he'd managed to disappear. Omar's heart started racing and he felt the blood pound in his temples. He breathed in the cold November air, felt his head tingle. Behind him he heard some other guys arguing. Someone yelled something about the Brewsters. 'Black Power,' somebody shouted. It seemed to come from a distance, had nothing to do with him. Again he looked around for Reggie's bulky figure—where in God's name was he? A guy he didn't know broke off from the group and ran over to the Brewsters' shop. 'Grab what you can!' he hollered. 'Our time has come. It's all free.' Omar heard laughing, shouting. The shriek of sirens in the distance. At least ten guys stormed the small grocery.

'Do something!' Louis said. Omar shrugged. Saw the revolving blue lights of the police cars in the distance. He had the strange sensation that it was all happening far away from him, like he was seeing the tumult from above. He watched as young men carrying six-packs of Budweiser and bottles of cognac left the store, whooping and hollering like Indians. They ran onto Edgewood Ave. Omar thought back on the Custard Stand, saw Brewster's tired old face as he'd come shuffling out of the back room when he heard the shop bell jingle. 'The usual?' And he would slide a can of beer and a pack of Lucky Strikes across the counter, as though he had set them aside for Omar. The wail of the sirens came closer. 'Run for it!' Omar heard Louis shout. Someone shoved him in the back. 'Reggie!' he yelled as he ran down Edgewood Ave. There was a sudden brilliant flood of light behind him aimed at the Custard Stand. He turned and looked back. Saw the police car lights casting their long blue beams over the Custard Stand and Edgewood Ave. The sirens howled, and he saw a few boys being led out of the grocery in handcuffs. 'Reggie!' Omar screamed, but his voice was drowned out by all the racket. He caught himself thinking that as long as he didn't watch, it wasn't really happening. He needed Reggie's eyes, Reggie's sober commentary. 'Reggie!' he shouted again and ran on, alone, as fast as he could. The sharp wintry air burned in his lungs.

Omar didn't go to the Firestone factory that night. He lay flat on his bed for a couple of hours listening to the wailing of the police and ambulance sirens. Chris and Billy came home at about one, asked what was going on, but all Omar could say was 'tussle at the Custard Stand', and he turned over, pretending to sleep. Mama, Grandma Rose, and the girls had gone to bed hours ago. At about four, when the shouting outside finally subsided, Omar drifted off to sleep, still fully dressed.

He saw his father. Sonny Huling, wearing a snug black suit, his skin glowing in the red misty light that shone on him from above. Like his skin wasn't black but silver. His afro glistened with Brylcreem and he smelled of coconut oil. He sat down on the foot of Omar's bed; he was lanky and his arms and legs moved independently from his body.

'Don't listen to them,' Sonny said.

'Who?'

'Doesn't matter who. Just trust your own intuition. I always did.'

Sonny looked young, about twenty. In his dream Omar realized they were the same age.

'I'm just as old as you.'

Sonny laughed.

'I know. I have to go now.' He got up, raised his hand lazily, and left the bedroom.

Three days after the Custard Stand incident, Omar and Reggie were at a Black United Front meeting at the office on Wooster Ave. Since all hell had broken out in the city and National Guard tanks were patrolling the streets, they met every evening to discuss strategy. During the day they hid in apartment buildings and behind walls and garages. They skirmished with the police and the National Guard on Raymond St., Bell St., and Perkins Woods Park, on Douglas St. and Euclid Ave., hurling garbage cans and rocks at the tanks. Shots were fired and arrests were made. Omar was glad to have his small .38 pistol and the .45 he had bought from Leo. He felt quick, invulnerable; nobody could harm him. He knew the National Guard was far better armed than the Front, that it was a lopsided battle, but now that the riots had begun, and more and more blacks took to the streets, life in Akron would never revert to its old stifling, snail-paced tempo.

It was ten o'clock. There was an eight o'clock curfew. They had blackened the office windows but apparently a stripe of light showed through to the street. 'Everybody outside,' they heard a policeman shout through a bull-horn. 'Come out unarmed and everyone can go home. Do as we say.'

'There's no emergency law saying we can't be here,' said David Jones, a brother from Cleveland. 'They've got no right to hassle us.'

'No right, No right,' the men and women in the cramped office chanted, and a few men stuck their fist in the air. A couple of children were playing with Matchbox cars under a large table in the corner. 'Brrmmm brrm-mm,' they intoned as they whizzed their toy cars over the bare wood floor, banging them into each other and sending them hurtling through the air, just like at home.

Omar peered outside through a crack in the blankets. There were three police cars, black and white cops taking cover behind the open doors. A floodlight was aimed at the community center where the Front had its offices. And yet it was quiet outside; he saw a few policemen chatting. The small top window was open and in the distance he could hear a barking dog. He closed his eyes. He could almost see the quiet, like a thick, black mist that sucked up all the sound and took away his breath. He nudged Reggie.

'Remember that time in Detroit when your car suddenly died?'

'What?'

'Those cops, don't you remember? That one white dude who made us get out of the car and shoved us against the hood. We'd been at Ethel's, it was in the middle of the night. He asked where we'd got that Cadillac and you were stupid enough to have left the papers home. I was so drunk, Jesus I was drunk. I saw everything in slow motion. I can't remember how we got out of there—do you?'

'Why're you bringing this up now?' Reggie furrowed his brow. He kept pushing his glasses back up his nose.

Omar shrugged. 'Want to go back to Ethel's sometime?'

'Sure.'

'Those girls there, oooh, they've got a different rhythm than here, you just feel it. You know what I'm saying? Remember Joyce? What a bombshell. Why didn't I take her with us? I'd do it differently now.'

'Shh,' Reggie whispered, putting his finger to his lips. 'D'you hear that?' Louis Johnson came over to them. 'I heard that white bastard say something about tear gas.'

Omar looked outside. A white policeman pushed the

bullhorn into his black colleague's hands. 'This is your last warning,' they heard. 'Come on out, and you can all go home.'

'They were talking about gas, man,' Reggie said, panicky. 'Is the back door open?'

''Course not,' Louis said. 'But it's locked from the inside. We can get out, no problem.'

'You sure?'

'I'll go look,' Omar said. He pushed his way through the warm bodies, most of whom were only names to him. The office had never been so full. It smelled of sour sweat, cigarettes, and a whiff of musk oil. For a moment he imagined being in the Hi Hat Café, going over to get a drink from Eunice. After all, he didn't need to be on guard here. At least not as far as the people in the office. The threat came from outside. And this external threat made him feel more secure than ever. His head was burning, and this heat soon flowed through his entire body. He went into the cement-floored hallway.

'Look out!' someone called after him, and he hit the deck automatically. He smelled something pungent, sulfury. Heard a strange hissing noise. His eyes stung. He heard shouting and screaming from the office. He clambered upright, but was dizzy and almost lost his balance. The lights seemed to have gone out; all he could see was a white mist that got steadily thicker and stickier. He could hardly breathe. The sound of crying children. He tried to make his way back to the office but the others were crowding into hall. 'Outside, quick, outside!' Was that Louis Johnson's voice? 'Reggie!' Omar shouted.

'Here,' came Reggie's faraway answer. 'They're using tear gas!' Omar couldn't see him, only shadows moving in slow motion through the dense white mist. Otherworldly. The gas muffled their shouts. Omar followed the flow, heard only a dull drone. He had to get air, get outside, to the heavy steel door at the back of the building.

A burning smell. He gagged. Looked over his shoulder. Black smoke billowed out of the small office. 'The place is on fire!' he heard Louis say, suddenly close by. Omar groped around him. 'Louis.'

'Here.' Omar felt a hand on his shoulder. The two of them shoved their way toward the back door. Louis laid into it will all his weight.

'It's stuck,' he yelled.

'Can't be!' Omar shouted back. 'Then they're holding it shut. Those motherfuckers want to burn us alive. Where's Reggie?' Just at that moment it was as if someone hit him on the head with a stick. He saw stars, colors wafted in front of his eyes, green blue purple orange. Hands to his eyes. His stomach contracted, his lungs were on fire. He couldn't breathe. His eyes shut tight. He saw The Supremes' glittery white dresses. The red neon sign outside Ethel's in Detroit. This is what it's like to die, he heard himself think, his body falling slowly backward. He saw the old school notebook he had hidden in his bottom drawer, with his underwear. *Huey was a bad muthafucka.* He saw his messy, irregular handwriting. Words crossed out with thick black strokes. Just when I'm about to become a poet, he thought. In the distance he heard glass breaking on the stones out back. 'Louis jumped out the window,' an unfamiliar voice said. He felt cold, humid air on his skin. And then everything went silent.

'Bum Rush' (1991)

The Streets are calling
The Streets are calling

There's always the Streets.

AKRON, OHIO, 1968

Recollections

You could see the hill from the parking lot behind Roxy's Cafe. A barren knoll about as high as a four- or five-story house. A strange hump in the middle of a flat, vacant field. Like it had been put there by mistake. Sometimes Jerome fantasized that he was the only one who saw the hill, that it was there for him alone, a beacon. In the winter it was snow-covered and when the moon was full and low on the horizon, the hill seemed to glow.

One night Ruby Lee took him there. It was springtime but still cold, and it had rained that day. He had three dollars and a few cents; Ruby said that would do. 'So long as you don't tell nobody.'

The silhouette of the hill jutted into the blue-green sky. Ruby Lee walked a few steps away from him. He could hear the slurping sound of her footsteps in the wet ground.

'Psst. Over here.' He started, even though it was only a whisper. Her voice was silver in the nighttime. A flicker of light. He lost track of her, saw only the black branches of the prickly shrubs that grew around the base of the hill.

'Where are you?'

There was no moonlight, so he felt his way toward the sound of her laugh.

She appeared out of nowhere, like a jack-in-the-box. 'You ever fucked before?'

"Course.'

He was eleven. He had no idea how old Ruby was. She could be eighteen or twenty-five or thirty. She was stout and heavyset. Her skin was deep brown but her face had something Chinese about it. She seemed to look at him through her eyelashes. She laughed a lot.

'Do you always come here?' he asked, startled by the sound of his own voice. Maybe he wasn't supposed to say anything. It was so quiet. So quiet and dark. He could vaguely make out the contours of Ruby's face. He heard her breathing: short, breathless gasps. Jerome looked up the hill but saw only blackness. The black of the night. No stars. Ruby didn't answer. It was as though they weren't even there; they had disappeared into the darkness, just like the hill.

'I'll bet there are foxes here,' Jerome said.

'Nah.'

'You don't think so?'

He felt Ruby fiddle with the sleeve of his jacket. Her stubby fingers wrapped around his wrist.

'I feel sorry for the girl who gets you soon,' she whispered.

'Huh?'

'I mean I'm crazy to do this for just three dollars. But I'm still gonna.'

'Hm.'

'Feel this.' She took his hand and pulled him toward her. He could see the white of her teeth. She smiled and came closer, pulled up her sweater and put his hand on her breast. He felt the warmth of her skin. Her breast was big and soft. Her skin damp. It wasn't raining, but a cold white mist rose up from the ground. He held his breath.

'You're shaking,' she said.

He shook his head. Exhaled and sucked fresh air back in. He started coughing.

'Don't be afraid,' Ruby said.

'I'm not afraid.'

She laughed again. Hiked up her skirt. Pulled down his pants. And all that time she kept his hand pressed against her breast.

'Go on, honey,' she whispered.

He stood there, frozen in the purple-green night, with the soft weight of her breast in the palm of his hand, her warmth streaming into him, making the mist feel warmish and sticky and wet, like a protective layer. His throat burned. He had a feeling of déjà vu, recognized the way Ruby moved her body, how she pulled him toward her, guided his prick into her. It was like swimming into her, she was so wide and wet. So warm. As wet as the air surrounding them. He kept his eyes wide open but was too close to see her clearly. The darkness slowly closed in on them, pressed their bodies together, skin on skin, the darkness of their skin, of the night, his hand on her breast.

'Easy,' Ruby panted in his ear. 'Not too fast.' She touched him with her voice, her breathing a hoarse and high-pitched, sultry singing. His whole body shook. He wished he could stop the tingling warmth that shot through his body. His eyes stung. He didn't know if he was crying, whether the wet warmth on his cheeks was tears or mist.

'That's good,' he heard Ruby say. 'You did good.' She did not release her grip.

He felt his muscles relax. Only now did he let go of her breast, and shrank back. He saw her red-brown nipples that floated on her breasts like saucers. Ruby saw him look and pulled her sweater back down.

'I can't give you enough love, honey,' she said. 'I hope there'll be a girl someday who can.'

He pulled up his pants. And Ruby took his hand and kissed it. Then they walked back to Howard St. in silence. On the way he turned a few times to look at the hill.

Omar closed his eyes. He smelled the metallic scent of clotted blood and a pungent mix of piss and disinfectant. Somewhere in the distance he could hear a dull tapping—he imagined someone in another cell banging a coded message on the concrete wall with a hunk of wood—and muffled voices around him, footsteps in the bare stone corridor.

The hill in the field behind Roxy's Café was, in reality, pretty insignificant. No more than a mound of sand, really, with patches of grass and heather sprouting here and there. But after that night with Ruby Lee, the hill only became more mysterious and beautiful to him. Almost like its presence was trying to convince him of something. He didn't know what, but still, it comforted him. He wondered what ever became of Ruby; he hadn't seen her in years. Maybe she'd gotten too old to be a whore. He was taken aback by his own thoughts: for him, Ruby had never been a whore, even though she'd accepted his money.

He looked up and focused on the faces around him. The cell was crowded. Some men lay sleeping on the floor, others leaned against one another on wooden benches in the middle of the room. No one spoke. It took a while for Omar's eyes to get used to the bare fluorescent light, a light that made strangers out of friends. In one corner, Louis Johnson sat on the floor, leaning against the iron bars. The right side of his face was gashed half open, dried blood stuck to his cheek. Louis dabbed at his wound with a grubby white cloth. His mouth was curled into a smile. David Matthews sat next to him, his head resting on his knees, his yellow-green shirt torn. Reggie stood in the middle of the cell, hands dug in his pockets, rocking from one foot to the other. He was lost in thought, didn't notice his friend watching him, and Omar left it that way. Omar looked at the drab, colorless walls, on which previous inmates had scratched their name or a message, *Martin, Jojo, fuck, evil, love*; red-brown stripes in the form of a hand, traces of blood and shit. The gray cement floor, piss stains in the corners, the light, that bare, harsh light. Everything in the cell seemed intended to remind Omar of death and decay. The scathing smell of blood and steel and piss and Louis's wound. And yet Omar felt relieved. He had the strange sensation that he had broken loose from his surroundings, that he wasn't really here. He watched his comrades from a distance; from their casual expressions he figured they must be feeling the same way, which is why they didn't say much, just exchanged the occasional glance. That them being here in this filthy, cramped cell was proof of their victory.

He had no idea how long he'd been unconscious. When he first came to, he'd gradually realized he was in a police van, together with the other men and women that had been driven from the Front's office. It was dark and they were crammed in tight; he could barely tell one face from the next. The van was still parked. The air inside was hot and humid and sour, dampening the sound of the agitated voices around him. He wanted to call out Reggie's name, but before the sound could leave his mouth the doors opened. Omar saw a bright stripe of light, heard laughing outside, a hissing noise. The door slammed shut and the van started moving. The air became white and smoky. 'Damn it! Gas!' someone next to him exclaimed. He heard cries and shouts, he became nauseous and his eyes stung. The van jerked and bounced. He held tight to the bench. Leaned against the metal wall and closed his eyes. Couldn't talk. He fled into his own body, floated away from the bus. And then he saw the hill behind Howard Street, its sharp contours dark against the cool, silvery moonlight, and he saw Ruby Lee smiling at him inside Roxy's, the smoke-filled air mixing with the languid, sexy sound of jazz; Ruby drew him to her with her smile and when he got close he smelled the sweet raspberryish scent of her skin, and she whispered to follow her out back, to the hill. He was the chosen one. Ruby Lee saw that he was different from the other boys and men in the bar. He felt rescued, protected. 'I can't give you enough love.' The way she spoke those words, melodious and husky. As though they meant exactly the opposite.

His recollection of that night, so many years before, was more real than the drive to the police station. Only now, in the cell, did Omar realize he had been hallucinating, that he was high from the tear gas. He smiled to himself. He looked at Reggie, who appeared to be asleep on his feet. His glasses were crooked and his head hung to one side. He looked young and vulnerable. Omar felt a warm contentment flow through his body. The memories of Ruby and the hill would forever be linked to that stuffy cell with its drab, deathly fluorescent light. And it didn't matter what else happened now: they had stood up to the cops, and the fire and the heat and the tear gas had not broken them. Nobody could pretend anymore that they didn't exist.

'Love' (1986)

I cried out, Love, what do you want from me? You've got to tell me now.
Love just smiled and answered, Must I also tell you how.

AKRON, OHIO, 1969

A Visit

'Reggie's not home,' Mammio Bellamy said.

'I know,' Omar replied.

'So what are you doin' here? It's been so long since we heard from you.'

'I've been busy. Didn't Reggie tell you?'

'Tell us what? That you got fired from the factory? That you were going to New York to become famous?'

'Yeah.'

'Tell me something, Jerome. Have you ever killed anyone?'

'No ma'am.'

'I know you could.'

'Why?'

'Your eyes.'

'What about my eyes?'

'I don't know. You've got sad, pretty eyes. But sometimes they're so cold. Sometimes you look like you don't give a hoot about anything.'

'You know that's not true.'

'Is that what you come here to tell me?'

'Maybe.'

'I hope you'll be happy in New York.'

'I'll write.'

'Uh-huh.'

'I mean it.'

'Go on now, Jerome. I'm sure you've got things to do.'

'Thanks, Mammio.'

'What for?'

JIBARO, MY PRETTY NIGGER

We don't remember the men in our family.

NEW YORK CITY, SEPTEMBER 2001

Felipe Luciano

Let me tell you a story. When I was born, in '47, Puerto Ricans were considered honorary whites. So they would put *White* on your birth certificate; it didn't matter if you were blue, you were 'white'. My maternal grandmother, Margarita Olmo, was there when I came into the world. I was lighter-skinned than most of the rest of the family. I was considered the golden child. To this day my brothers and sisters say I was given privileges that they didn't have. That might well be true.

Anyway, the doctor comes to our house in East Harlem to check me out. He goes to fill in 'white' on the birth certificate, and my grandmother, indignant, says, 'Are you blind? This kid is black.'

And so the doctor writes 'Negro' on my birth certificate. Margarita Olmo was an incredible person. She really loved me. She'd call me over to her, and I'd have to lay my head in her lap and she would run her hands through my curls—she twisted them into dreads, slowly and meticulously. That was way before dreadlocks were in vogue. She loved the shape of my head, the shape of my lips, my nose, my ears, my voice. *'Tu eres el negrito mas lindo en este mundo'*, she'd say—you are the most beautiful black child in the whole wide world. She would have me sit and just read out loud to her in English. She loved the fact that I could speak English.

'Puerto Rican Rhythms' (1968)

Taking you into El Barrio now ...

driving Latin rhythms coming out of candy store jukeboxes
trumpets, trumpets, trumpets
big brass mashed with sultry congas
sprouts palm trees in the middle of frozen streets

NEW YORK, 2002

Winter

I miss Kain.

I miss The Last Poets. I don't want to go back to that time, but I do miss the camaraderie. I miss family. The street. God, how I miss the street.

'*Hola Felipe, ¿como estas?*'

I've known CC since I was eight. We're like brothers. I bump into him this morning on Lexington Ave. on my way to work. I'm surprised CC's up and about so early. Usually he's not on the street until one, two o'clock. Before I get the chance to say anything, CC lays a hand on my shoulder and whispers: 'What's up, *amigo?* You look kinda ... '

I don't answer.

'I saw you last night on the news, man. On Times Square. About that lunatic who ran down those pedestrians. Felipe, man, the guy said he was lovesick. That that was why he did it. Jesus, Felipe. But you were good. Caring. To the point. I says to Mama, I was over at Mama's, she says hi by the way, I says, "Felipe should have been on the City Council. Too bad he didn't make it. Just a few goddamn tenths of a percent. Felipe's good with words ... Felipe ... '

I'd long stopped hearing what he said. The more he bigged me up, the more my thoughts drifted. I don't even know what I was thinking about. I was in a hurry. I'd overslept. I was going to be late for the editorial meeting. I say to CC that I've got to get moving.

'Drop by at Mama's sometime?'

'Sure,' I say.

But CC's got me figured out. He knows exactly when I'm bullshitting him. He takes my arm, looks straight at me with those brown-green eyes. And there we are, standing at the corner of 112th and Lexington. It's about eight in the morning. Traffic's racing past us. It's freezing. A heavy gray day. And we're just standing there. CC's got all the time in the world. I watch the little white puffs come out of his nose. He won't let go until I've said something. I feel the warmth of his hand through my leather jacket. Like I'm making a soft, slow landing. You know what I mean? CC knows me. I know CC. I mumble something about getting up early, that I hate it, that damn office, fuck it, something banal. But that's not what it's about. What I'm trying to say is, CC understands me on the inside.

On Fox News I can't talk about offing people, or about kicking their ass, about screwing, about fucking. At Fox you have to watch your mouth; everything can be used against you. Honesty can cost you your job.

I have friends I met through my work. Good people. Middle-class people. But they're not always *with* you. Not like that street-togetherness. I miss the loyalty of my old friends. The protection of their love.

I miss Kain.

I've always led a double life. From an early age. It's exhausting. When you're fifty-four, all you want is to be yourself. But how in God's name do you do that?

EAST HARLEM, 1967

Moon River

I wonder what would have become of me if Victor Hernandez Cruz hadn't sent me away that day. It was a hot midsummer afternoon. The streets of New York stank and steamed. There were policemen on every corner. I'd never seen so many cops in our neighborhood before. It was like an occupation during wartime. Entire apartment blocks were boarded shut and charred.

I was nineteen years old and had just been released from Coxsackie Correctional Facility in upstate New York. Coxsackie—it's really called that, named for the town where it's located, in the Catskills. And believe me, the Coxsackie jail is just as vulgar as it sounds. On the bus back to the city I kept telling myself that I was turning over a new leaf, that the future was mine and that everything was possible—but once I was back in East Harlem I felt old and worn out. Nineteen, with a whole lifetime behind me. I had no idea where to start. So I just wandered around the neighborhood, which in no way resembled the place I had longed for so bad back in Coxsackie.

When I was inside I often got myself to fall asleep by thinking of home. Pictured myself in my living room, not in some cell—my mother in the kitchen washing the dishes. Pictured how it was back when we still lived in the Johnson Projects. I was always five or six, never older than that: hearing the clatter of knives and forks on plates. Sitting at the open window and looking outside. Ralph Robles is out washing his new Ford. Robles looking tough in his brand-new Goomba T-shirt. He's got music on: Trio Los Panchos. Upstairs, Mr. Chen and his wife argue in Chinese. I don't understand a word of it. I smell the strong aroma of Bustelli coffee. And just sit there at that window. Sunlight streams in, lighting up the translucent fake pearls that dangle around the lamp. The light-blue Jesus print Mama hung above the mantle. His pale, thin face and his long blond hair. And I look at the pearls, which sparkle like cut crystal, and look at them for as long as it takes to start feeling really small compared to everything else, until I feel weightless and think: this is what it's like to go to God. Until Mama comes in and startles me with her loud voice: 'Felipe, I'm out of rice. Go on over to Gonzales, hurry now, and tell him to put it on our tab.' And suddenly I'm reminded of the book about the Eskimos that the teacher made us read. The pearls make me think of Eskimos and ice.

'Mama, what happens to Eskimos? Are they all going to hell? Or do you think God'll save them?'

'No, he won't.'

'What about the Egyptians from before Jesus was born? Won't they get saved either?'

'No.'

'But that's terrible.'

'God knows what He's doing. Get going now, go fetch that rice.'

I fly out of the house, onto the street, before Mama loses her cool.

These memories comforted me in Coxsackie. I imagined seeing pride in Mama's eyes, imagined her marveling at my ability to peel the layers off an idea, to get to the core. Imagined that she was only faking being angry. And then I thought about walking down the street, rehearsing the song and dance I'd give Gonzales to get out of having to pay for the rice so he'd put it on the tab with all the other groceries we still had on credit.

Now that I was back in East Harlem, even those memories looked like yellowed, faded photographs. I wasn't able to recall those images as clearly and sharply as in my tiny cell in Coxsackie.

Mama, by the way, had moved out of the Johnson Projects long ago. She was renting a small apartment on 125th St., not far from Iglesia La Sinagoga, where she went every evening. My brother and sister still lived at home. I'd moved back in with them.

That afternoon I left the house at around three. I told Mama I was going to Queens College to enroll for the coming semester. I'd gotten early release under the condition that I go back to school. But instead of taking the subway out to Queens I just walked aimlessly out of the neighborhood. Every muscle in my body was tense. Since getting out I was more anxious than when I was inside. I was always on my guard, like something or someone was after me. Maybe that came from the isolation in Coxsackie. For two years I volunteered to be shut up in what they called the Patio, a cellblock smack in the middle of the prison, where nobody wanted to be, but where the gangs had no influence. My cellmate was Stephen Supolski, a Polish Jew. But Stephen couldn't take it. He bugged out. So one day he put his hands on a radiator, burned half his skin off. The confinement got to him.

I was in the Patio because of Shane Coleman. I knew Shane from the Brownsville Projects in Brooklyn. We were about fourteen at the time and were friends. The day I arrived at Coxsackie I saw him standing in the courtyard with a group of guys. I was so relieved to see a familiar face that I ran over to him, yelling 'Shane! Shane!' He turned and saw me. Shane was a strapping guy, a head taller than me. You could see he worked out every day. But he gave me a cold, dull look, like he didn't recognize me.

'Get outta here,' he whispered.

'What's up?'

'You're Puerto Rican, man, you can't be here.'

'What are you talking about? It's me, Felipe.'

'Fuck off.'

'But Shane ... '

'You go hang out with your Spanish pals, okay? This here's a black crowd, you got that? Now beat it.' And he turned away.

His words made me sick for days, but I couldn't let on. I lay awake at night, drenched in sweat. Started to doubt my own memory. How easily Shane turned his back on our friendship! Like it was my fault, or I'd dreamed it up.

During the day I tried to join up with the other Latinos, but since at home all I had were black friends, they were strangers to me. Chino, their leader, hated blacks. It was 'fuckin niggers' this, 'fuckin niggers' that. Even though he was the blackest-skinned Puerto Rican I'd ever seen. His skin was like dark chocolate. He was as thin as a rail and his eyes were swimming-pool blue. Something about his eyes scared me, made me keep out of his way. When he looked at you it was as if you weren't even there, like he was making you invisible. That's why all the other guys clung to him, even though I'm sure they knew what a dumb asshole he was.

So the Patio was kind of a last resort. It gave me plenty of time to read, at least. I read everything I could get my hands on. Strange books about plants and animals and volcanoes. *Robinson Crusoe, Moby Dick, Huckleberry Finn,* you know, the classics. And the Bible, of course. Poems by Yeats. I was amazed the library had that. Yeats didn't do much for me, but as long as I had something to read, I was somewhere else. I've always loved books.

Wandering down 125th St. that afternoon toward Adam Clayton Powell Jr. Boulevard I was so tense I could hardly breathe. It was about ninety-five degrees out, and the air was humid and hazy. It was my third or fourth day back in Harlem. Honking cars, radios, shoppers chatting. Soul music, salsa. Metallic Caribbean sounds. Djembe rhythms. Police and ambulance sirens. In my head all those sounds merged into a deep drone. I leaned against a storefront, pushed my hands against my temples. The noise was too much, it was too loud and harsh. Everything was churning. Off in the distance I heard a voice: 'Hey you, get away from there. Beat it.' I didn't realize this was directed at me. Someone had mistaken me for a junkie. I stood there with my eyes shut for I don't know how long, gasping for air.

After a while I calmed down some and looked around. People were hurrying along the sidewalk. A city bus jerked into motion and puffed black smoke into the street. A Dominican guy hung out of his car window and cursed at the driver in front of him. He leaned on his horn, and a low, piercing tone trumpeted out of his car. I think that it only hit me then that I was really back. It was like I could suddenly see clearly again. I took off my jacket and started walking. South. I don't know why. I just walked, and the more I walked the calmer I got. I smelled the charcoaly scent of grilled lamb, smelled the sweet, magical oils of the street vendors. The sound of Charlie Parker wafted out of a shuttered café: I recognized his nervous, high licks. A girl in a brightly colored dress passed me. Tight ass. I saw girls of all colors, beige, brown, yellow. Black. A brief glance here and there. I felt the heaviness and the fatigue and the tension drain out of my body. It was like the neighborhood was made of colors and smells and sounds. Nothing more.

Maybe I should mention this before I go on: before being transferred to Coxsackie I spent three months in Elmira Correctional Facility, another juvenile detention center in upstate New York. And before that, I did five months in juvenile prison on 257 Atlantic Ave., Coney Island.

The following incident took place on Atlantic Ave. I was sixteen. I'd never seen a prison from the inside before. I missed my mother. My grandmother. Mostly I missed my grandmother. Her smell: flowers, roses. Her kitchen, fresh air. The warm, sweetness of her skin. Her slow, deliberate gait. The way she moved around her small apartment: the living room was packed with furniture and knickknacks but she never bumped into anything. She wore her long gray hair up, and little tufts stuck out everywhere so when I kissed her the tufts would tickle my skin. I missed her. I missed school. Miss Shapiro. All I could do was cry. The slightest reminder of home brought it on. And if there's one thing you better not do in prison, it's cry. But I cried. I cried so much that maybe I secretly hoped the tears would get me sent home.

Anyway, one night I locked myself in a slop sink. I let the water run so nobody'd hear. I sat on the cold granite floor and sobbed and wailed nonstop. When someone started banging on the door, I didn't even notice till they shouted 'Open up!'

The voice was so authoritative. I didn't recognize it.

'Open up, and make it quick.'

'Hold up a minute,' I sniffed. I wiped my face with the sleeve of my sweater. My eyes stung, but I kept on crying. I just couldn't stop. I got up, turned off the water, avoided looking in the mirror.

'Hurry up in there. I know who you are.' More pounding.

I went to the door and unlocked the bolt.

'There you are. Look at me.'

I could barely see through the tears. All that came through was the gray-white speckled granite floor.

'What you doing in there?'

'Nothing.'

'Look at me.'

I tried to look up. I saw enormous biceps in a tight black T-shirt. I'd never seen biceps like that in my life. The guy's arms were folded across his chest.

'What the fuck is wrong with you?'

'Nothing.'

'Don't lie. And look at me, goddamn it.'

I was terrified. Everything went dark. I gauged my chances of slipping past him. Scuffed my feet back and forth. Every time I tried to squeeze by, the black figure leaned the same way, quick and supple, like he was my shadow. To get past him would mean physical contact. And he'd pulverize me.

'You're fulla shit, kid,' his voice boomed. 'You look at me when I talk to you, y'little motherfucker.'

I looked up. I'd never seen the guy before. He was older than me, about eighteen.

'What're you crying about?'

I didn't answer. I forgot he'd even asked a question. Forgot who I was. I couldn't take my eyes off him. He had a handsome, well-proportioned face, unblemished except for a small scar near his right eye. His eyes were brown-green and almond shaped. He looked like an Indian, a Mohican. The harsh fluorescent light reflected off his beautifully coiffed, blue-black hair. The light was like a protective aura: he was untouchable.

'I'm gonna ask you one more time: what are you crying about?'

All I did was grunt.

'You know who you're talking to? Nobody mouths off to Diabolo. What're you crying about?'

'I got five years,' I heard myself say. My voice was small and unsure.

'Five years, huh? You're crying 'cause you got five years, muthafucka?'

I stared back at that face, at the soft, cream-colored skin. His broad eyebrows that made me think of Christmas garlands. All of a sudden he grabbed me, bringing his arm swiftly around my neck. I could hardly breathe. With his other hand he pinned my hands behind my back. I started kicking; tried to yell but his big clammy hand muffled my cries.

'Calm down now,' he whispered in my ear. 'I'm not going to hurt you.' And he let go. I panted and went into a coughing fit.

'At least your heart doesn't pump Kool-Aid. Come with me,' he said, taking my arm and dragging me to the cinderblock hallway that led to the cellblock.

'You got five years?'

I nodded.

'Rice!' Diabolo shouted. Off in the distance someone shouted back.

'What?'

'How many years you got, Rice?'

'Twenty-five to life.'

'What for?'

'Attempted manslaughter.'

'Lopez?'

'Yeah?'

'How long you in for?'

'Twelve to twenty.'

'Jones! How much longer you got?'

'Depends on how old I get,' I heard a deep voice reply. Laughter and whooping from the others.

Diabolo continued this roll call until he'd covered pretty much everyone in the block. His hand was still clamped firmly on my upper arm. I had no choice but to listen to the faraway voices, all of them with names but no faces. They sounded hollow and transparent in the huge echoey space. They all did whatever Diabolo said.

He gave me a shove and looked straight at me. 'You hear that? Thirty of us here, muthafucka. We're all in here for killing somebody. You're the only one who got five years. And *you're* crying? If I catch you blubbering again I will Bust. Your. Ass. Are we clear?'

I couldn't think anymore. I was lost. It was like dream. Unreal. But Diabolo was talking to me differently now. He was less threatening. I don't know why, but I sensed he wouldn't hurt me. And maybe he could tell that I'd forgotten my own troubles for a minute, standing there with him. I mean, I'd never seen such a good-looking guy. I wasn't in love or anything, hell no. And he knew that. It was something else. Magnetism. When I looked at him, I really *looked*. I wanted to be near him, I felt protected.

He said: 'We knew about you before you came in here. We heard about all the rabbis and priests and teachers that testified for you. We knew you wouldn't get no time, muthafucka. You're a golden boy. Everybody loves you.'

He laughed. A mocking laugh, but I wasn't afraid. He put his arm around me. 'I'm gonna teach you some things. Number one: don't trust anybody. Two: don't take cigarettes from nobody. I'll bust the muthafucka's ass who offers you smokes. I've seen it. They set you up with cigarettes, and then you owe them. You have any problems, you come to me, you hear me?'

I just stood there.

'Now beat it,' Diabolo said quietly, and let me go. He turned and walked off. A springy, light gait. No footsteps, no sound. I can't remember what I did then ... I guess I just went back to my cell. But from that day on, everything was different. In one fell swoop I was no longer a child. Under Diabolo's constant protection—even when he wasn't around, like at night, alone on the bunk in my cell—I grew, replaying his words in my head: 'You're a golden boy.' I wasn't even embarrassed. Didn't feel guilty that I had to do less time than the others. Or because my teachers had testified on my behalf. 'Everybody loves you.' Diabolo's protection justified it all. He could just as easily have beat the shit out of me. I was only sixteen.

Later, too, in Elmira and Coxsackie, I never had any troubles. Diabolo's authority reached far and wide. If he said to keep your hands off someone, you did.

It wasn't like we were friends. Not at all. Diabolo was way above me. He was a leader. He knew exactly how much distance to keep between himself and the rest to maintain his authority. His looks did the rest. But I did love him. Thanks to him, my time in prison was tolerable.

One day I was passing by his cell and saw him sweating over a sheet of paper. A little chewed-off pencil stub in his hand, mumbling to himself. He didn't know I was looking. I saw the scrawls and the scratched-out words.

When he looked up and noticed me, he whisked the paper from the table and onto the floor.

'Whaddayou want?' He was blushing.

'Nothing. Just happened to be walking by.'

'C'mere.'

I went into his cell.

'You keep your mouth shut, understand?'

I nodded.

'Could you write to my girlfriend for me?'

'Me?'

'Yeah, you. You're so damn smart, right?'

'Shouldn't you write it yourself?'

'Will you do it?' I saw the awkwardness on his face, got a glimpse of the paper with the illegible scrawls on the floor under his bed. I realized Diabolo was probably illiterate.

'Sure, I'll write your letters. But don't you think she'll notice?'

'Notice what?'

'That you didn't write them yourself?'

'I'll tell you what to say, won't I?'

'Okay, sure thing. Go on.'

'Tell her, like … You know, that I love her, romantic stuff. Say that flowery shit.'

That's when I started writing love letters for Diabolo. *My dearest darling*, that kind of thing. And later he wanted me to coach him, so he could recite those letters and the poems in them by heart. His girlfriend had been to visit. 'Oh Diabolo, say all those sweet things you told me in your letter.' 'Which ones, baby?'

'You have to look her right in the eyes,' I said.

'Oh.'

'And don't just rattle off the lines. "The sky is blue / and I love you / can we screw now?" The girl's gonna say: fuck you, nigger.'

And sometimes at night I would sing for them. Before I got sent to Atlantic I used to sing in the All-City Chorus, a huge glee club, first as a tenor, then as bass. Diabolo heard me sing once. I didn't even realize I was singing, it just came out. He said he liked it, that it reminded him of the old days. His mother was a Sinatra fan. I sung everything I could remember from the choir. Broadway numbers. *West Side Story.* 'I Whistle a Happy Tune'. 'I Believe'. 'Moon River'. Within fifteen minutes the whole cellblock was snoring. I became their radio. Just imagine: some kid singing 'Moon River' in a prison full of blacks and Puerto Ricans.

I never saw Diabolo again after that. But as I sauntered out of the neighborhood that afternoon and took in all the sounds and smells, the whole thing surreally Technicolor compared to the drabness of Coxsackie, I felt my strength return. I realized I was no longer anxious or afraid. Like Diabolo was still protecting me, even then.

I went to The Gut Theater on 104th Street. I'd heard about it from my brother. It was a theater for jazz and the occasional poetry event. It was late afternoon, much too early for any performances. I looked at the pictures in the glass display windows next to the entrance. Artists I'd never heard of. Their shiny blue suits in the soft light of the theater. The enormous string bass and the deep yellow light reflecting from its wooden sound box. I could imagine touching it. The dazzling brass instruments—I could almost hear them playing. The audience's faces, full of expectation and awe. I got sucked into the pictures. I'd been gone for three years. It was so weird. I jiggled the door and it opened at once. Inside I found myself in a small, dark space—the cloakroom, I guessed, but it was too dark to see for sure. The transition from outside was too abrupt; the bright sunlight was still shimmering on my retina. I smelled the pungent mix of cigarette smoke, alcohol, and ammonia. I went further in, arrived at another door, heard a dark murmur. I couldn't make out the words, just monotonous voices and the hum of a fan. I pushed open the door and blinked at the light that illuminated the narrow theater.

'Who's there?' someone at the back asked. The light was so intense that I couldn't make anyone out.

'The door was open ...' I stammered.

'Damn.'

'Can I come in?'

I heard the squawk of a chair scuffing against the wooden floor. Heavy footsteps approached.

'Felipe, is that you?'

I looked straight at the grinning round face of Victor Hernandez Cruz. 'Jesus, Felipe, is that you? Mustache and all. How are you, man?'

Victor was a friend of my brother's. Before I went to prison he used to stop in at our house. He was a few years older than me, but had a real adult look about him. Like he was already weighed down by responsibilities, something like that. He had a heavy build, always wore a suit. He had a pleasant, deep voice.

'What're you doing here?'

I shrugged. 'I was in the neighborhood. I ...'

'When'd you get back?'

'A few days ago. And how about you, what're you up to?'

Victor laughed. 'Take a seat. You want something to drink?' He gestured magnanimously, like he owned the place.

'Yeah, make it a cognac,' I said nonchalantly. It sounded ridiculous, but only to me. Make it a cognac. I hadn't had a drop in three years.

Victor went over to the bar and poured two glasses of cognac. Now that my eyes had gotten used to the bright light I noticed, along the side wall, a small table with a purring electric Remington on it.

'Were you typing?'

Victor mumbled something unintelligible as he returned with the two glasses. He sat down next to me on one of the red velour seats.

'Drink up. Bet you missed this in there, huh?'

'Dunno.' I took a swig, felt the cognac burn in my chest. Victor was the first acquaintance, aside from my family, I had spoken to since getting out.

'What are you writing?' I asked, just to say something. I didn't want to talk about Coxsackie. The theater was small but nicely done up. The walls were painted with brightly colored likenesses of actors and singers and dancing couples. The ceiling was ornamented with arabesques and ornate moldings. The carpeting was just as soft and red as the plush of the seats. I felt myself unwind, sink into the surroundings, shed my history.

'Just fooling around,' Victor said. 'I've got a performance tomorrow—if you feel like stopping by ... '

'You singing?'

Victor burst out laughing. 'Just picture that!'

'What then?'

'Poems, man. Did you forget?'

I hadn't forgotten that Victor wrote poems, but I was having trouble keeping my mind focused. My body was soaking up the cognac. I hadn't eaten much that day. My cheeks were flushed. The velvety, woody taste of the drink brought back memories, but the images that came with them were always just out of reach, out of sight; it was no more than a feeling.

'What are you going to do?'

I shrugged, mumbled something about Queens College. I heard myself talk; the words rolled mechanically and indifferently out of my mouth.

'So you're going to study?'

I nodded.

'Have you seen the shape the neighborhood's in?'

'The cops?'

'You don't know the half of it, Felipe. It was war, man. I don't know what all you've heard but it won't be easy for you. Take your time. I'm trying to figure things out too, in my poems I mean. I can hardly just write about love anymore, you understand? It all suddenly seems so trivial. I don't even know whether to write poems in English or Spanish. In both, maybe.'

'Read me something.' I was glad Victor was talking about himself now.

He got up and went over to the Remington. Pulled the paper out of the machine and handed it to me. I started reading but it didn't sink in. I just saw individual words. *Beats. River. White. Sands. Street.* In my mind I felt the soft, comforting warmth of the cognac. I thought of the letters I'd written for Diabolo and the other guys. The simple rhymes about roses and happiness and loneliness and yearning. 'Moon River'. It all seemed so long ago. The quiet up in Coxsackie. I didn't write letters or poems for anybody there, just helped them with their homework. If they dared ask me, that is. 'But if they see me in the Patio, I'm a goner.' 'So do your homework yourself.' But gradually they started to come. Dragging their feet. Blacks and Latinos, even whites. Even Shane Coleman lowered himself to talk to me once. His big bulging shameless green eyes. It was like I had no color or background as long as I was in the Patio. *Fuck you, nigger.* The sky is blue and I love you. 'Come sit with me, Felipe. Read to me. I want to hear your voice. No, not in Spanish. Come here.' It sounded like an order but my grandmother's voice was gentle and a little wobbly. I sank into her warm bosom, her breathing. Sometimes I'd lay my head against her chest and I'd hear her heart beating, dull and strange and deep, not a thump, more like waves. Beaches. *White. Sands.* I sat there in the red plush seat with the paper in front of my face and it was like I had a fever, the images bouncing around inside my head, all on their own. I don't know what Victor thought. I just stared silently at those few words on that sheet of white paper.

'Nice,' I said after a while.

'You didn't read it.'

'I can write too. Poems, I mean.'

'You?'

'Why not? It's easy, man. You know, just playing around with words?'

'Playing with words.'

'Yeah, can you help me?'

'Thought you said it was easy.'

'You know what I mean, Victor. I think I can do it, but I need input. You understand.'

Victor just looked at me. 'I can't help you.'

'Why not?'

'You're too impatient.'

'Me?'

'Too full of yourself.'

'What's that got to do with it?'

'Your attitude, Felipe. I can't deal with it. Didn't I just tell you I'm struggling with my own work? You need somebody else.'

'Like who?'

'There's this guy on 125th Street. A poet and playwright. Kain's his name. Gylan Kain. He's black. I've heard he's looking for young poets. He's probably better for you than I am.'

'Because he's black?'

'Just go there. Their studio's called the East Wind. Close to the Apollo Theater.'

And that's how I ended up walking back up from 104th to 125th Street. It was early evening and dusk was closing in. I found the East Wind easily enough. It was in a loft on the second floor, halfway down 125th. You had to go up a set of narrow stairs and came out into a big, empty space with a timeworn wooden floor. There were low couches, pillows on the floor. An old-fashioned dark red and yellow carpet. It looked lived-in. At the back was a small stage. A desk next to it, with a green glass lamp that shone onto the mess of papers and books. I remember it exactly. On the walls there were all kinds of posters, performance announcements. Amiri Baraka and the Spirit House Movers. James Brown in the Apollo Theater. I went in. There didn't seem to be anyone there, at first. I mean, someone had buzzed me in, but I couldn't see anyone now.

I waited, thought it might be better to come back tomorrow.

'Did we have an appointment?' The voice coming from behind me was nasal and melodious. I turned to face a lean, elegant man. He was smaller than me, and his blue-black skin glowed in the indirect yellowish light of the desk lamp. In a flash I was reminded of Diabolo, of our first meeting, the tension and its promise. The man's eyes glistened. No trace of mistrust. He seemed to think it was completely normal that a complete stranger would just walk into his loft.

'I heard you're looking for poets,' I said.

'And you're a poet,' Kain said.
'That's right.'
'Can you direct?'
'Course I can direct.'
'Okay, let's see then.'

NEW YORK CITY, SEPTEMBER 2001

Clayton Reilly

'I was working as a journalist for *The New York Times*, the Arts & Culture section. On Saturday afternoons I played basketball with David Nelson at this little outdoor court in Harlem. We lived near each other. One afternoon David says, "Hey Clayton, I didn't know you did movies too." He had read something about me in the paper.

"Yup," I said. I was on the crew for a film called *Nothing But a Man*.

"So you can handle a camera?"

"I think so."

"See, I'm performing with some poets and we want to make a film about ourselves. Could you do that?"

I laughed. The carefree way he asked.

"But that costs money, David. Lots of money."

"Money's no problem."

That's how I met The Last Poets. Gylan Kain, Abiodun Oyewole, and David, of course. Felipe joined later, but he was already hanging around the East Wind back then. I don't know where they got the money from, but anyway they managed to get their hands on a camera and sound equipment and lights. They rented this fantastic loft up on 187th St. Lots of windows. Beautiful light. We started shooting. They weren't just poets, they were performers. Totally natural. There was nothing artificial about them. They used strong imagery. And each one of them sketched, without overstatement, a portrait of his own background. Kain had grown up in the Pentecostal church. You could hear that in his poetry, you saw it in his delivery. That almost messianic tone. Of all of them, David was the most cerebral poet, the intellectual. And Abiodun, the youngest, he was so powerful and alive. So young. That was the secret of his poetry. The anger it expressed, the latent aggression you heard in his delivery, in the timbre, the rhythm, the melody. Abiodun could really sing. They brought a drummer with them too, Nilija, a low-key guy and an incredible percussionist. Never really got to know him.

I needed a lot of time to get the lighting right. As soon as I saw them perform, I knew I had to get their color right on film. It was the most powerful way to emphasize their uniqueness. Each had his own specific color. Kain's skin is a rich coffee-brown, chocolate. David's color is closer to my own: amber. And Dun was in between.

So because of this I fussed a lot with the lights and they got kind of irritated; I think they were afraid I wasn't listening to them, to what they had to say. And David kept going: "You can trust Clayton."

After a few days of filming I showed them the rushes. I said: "So you can see how you look on film." It wasn't a whole lot, maybe a half-hour in all. And when I put the lights back on it was dead quiet. They were speechless. They'd never seen themselves on film before. I could tell they were shocked. I don't think any of them had ever thought of himself as attractive. Skin color was important, it was political, but *attractive*? Attractive was not an issue. But they were good-looking men. They really were. Only nobody had ever taken the trouble to tell them so. "See how handsome you look? You're a good-looking guy."'

The 'Last Poets' Explore New Art Form

[…]

'The Last Poets' Kain grew up in the Black ghettos of the Bronx
and Queens. He started writing seriously at 16 years of age
and decided that is what he wanted to do three years later.
Soon he became frustrated with the Western form of
play-writing which was limited and bounded him in. He longed
to make something new and discovered that poetry was the
freest form of the written word to get where he wanted to go.

[…]

The whole conception of Western poetry is stagnant and
alienated from the people, Kain told muhammad speaks.
'Something happens on the stage away from the people.' On
the other hand, 'Black poetry is derived from our great poets.
People like Billy Holliday, Bessie Smith and John Coltrane.'

From: *Muhammad Speaks*
March 14, 1969

'Untogether People'

Niggers resurrected Christ
And christened him with ego
They smile less now
They dance less now
They're more cool now
Ever seen niggers get cool?
They don't get cool
They get ice

Niggers are obsessed with blindness
With the power of death in their hands

Niggers kill Malcolm
Fuck the CIA
Niggers held the guns
Niggers are very untogether people

NEW YORK CITY, FEBRUARY 2002

Felipe Luciano

Kain's eyes. I know he always wears sunglasses these days, but he has beautiful eyes. A hesitant, guarded look. No trace of anger or aggression. Kain would never be able to off somebody, never. That's why he lives in Europe now. He was no match for his brothers' violence.

We were both looking for family. Neither of us had a father. Our mothers were married to God. We grew up in the same church, different temples but the same Pentecostal community. Every evening we saw God in the quivering bodies of the women in the first and second row, whenever they felt His presence enter them. The ecstasy on their faces. The rousing music, the whooping, the sermons, the warmth. The children who stood outside the window making faces at us on the inside. It didn't matter that they were laughing at us. Not then, anyway. The sumptuous dark red carpeting that you sank into, like walking on a cloud. 'Great great God my father / sweet puddin' pie Jesus / you brought me out of the midnight hour / and planted me in a lighter day.' I understand every word Kain says, the free form of his poetry, it takes no effort.

Even now that he's on the other side of the ocean I feel his presence. We're blood brothers. We were talking on the phone recently, and he said, 'Only now I realize that The Last Poets weren't the reason I fled New York. It had to do with me, with Mother. You know what I'm talking about.'

I remember my mother getting out of bed in the middle of the night. I was twelve, and wanted to go to the school dance. I'd bought a nice suit. And suddenly my mother was standing there next to my bed. 'God told me you can't go.'

'Mother, I'm going. I'm going,' I said.

'You're not going, Felipe.'

'Am too.'

She proceeded to beat me within an inch of my life with an ironing cord. I didn't go to the dance. I couldn't, my arms were so bruised up. But not because I gave in to my mother, you understand?

The same thing happened to Kain the first time he wanted to go out with a girl. But it wasn't like him to yell and curse at his mother or to run away. They were so close. Hilda was her name.

Untitled

Red Clay Terracotta Lady of Indian Summer
I can't breathe without remembering
I love you
I know
I tried it once
Tried my best to leave you
The way that lovers try their best to do without one another
To be in the world without the one one thinks the world of
I think the world of you
Like language
Like God
Like water
Memories move in mysterious ways

HARLEM, 1968

Childhood Memories

'Just think, Felipe. Mother and I lived above the temple on 114th St. and Adam Clayton Blvd. The Greater Refuge Temple, run by Bishop Bonner and his son Nathaniel. We lived together with Sister June and her son Sonny. Sonny didn't have a father either. We shared three small rooms, with a kitchenette in between. You could hear Pastor Bonner preaching downstairs. When his voice wailed it would come right up through the floorboards. Couldn't understand it word for word, sometimes just a snippet—"He appeared unto the eleven ... evil spirits ... serpents"—when his voice really swelled. He had a beautiful voice, like a blues singer. I was about eight or nine. I lay on my bed in the dark. The door was cracked open; I could see a stripe of yellow light. Sister June at the stove wearing a greasy apron, stirring in a huge pot with a wooden spoon. Sister June cooked for Pastor Bonner and his son, and for us too. Soul food. Steam rose out of the pot. A dense white cloud that got thinner as it rose, then vanished. Sister June's forehead was wet. You could see the drops glisten in the yellow light of the bare bulb above the stove. She leaned forward, closed her eyes from the hot steam, and stirred. Deep furrows on her forehead. Like she was in a trance. Wiped her hand on her apron. The apron covered her enormous belly and broad hips. I had turned off the light so she didn't know

I was watching her. I listened to Pastor Bonner: "Deadly ... tongues ... the Lord." There was a powerful rhythm, a beat to his preaching—I always knew when a coherent word would float up to me, because they came on a four count, like clockwork: one two three four, and then I'd I pick up a single word. And sometimes he'd be lamenting, beseeching, booming, and there'd be silences in the middle of it all—he always knew just when to throw in a pause. I mean, I don't think Pastor Bonner had any idea of what he was on to. The sound of his voice mixed with the greasy white steam and the smell of chicken and soup. As if God himself was rising out of the food.

Anyway, Sister June took food seriously. She spent hours preparing it.

One evening she said to me, "Gylan, go fetch Sonny." I went outside, where Sonny usually hung around.

"Your mom says to come back."

"What is it now?" Sonny was older than me.

"I don't know." We went upstairs. I don't know where my mother was. Probably still in church, I guess; she often helped out with the service. Anyway, when it was over, Sister June brought in the food. Sonny and I sat down at the table to wait.

Bishop Bonner always sweated a lot during his sermons. If you sat up front you could see the drops sparkling on his forehead and his temples and his upper lip. Sometimes it ran down his head and I imagined I could smell the sweat. A strong, sickly smell. Masculine. It was the middle of summer, and the church wasn't air-conditioned like it is now.

So there's Sonny and me waiting there in the kitchen, and after a while we heard Sister June's footsteps on the stairs. She opened the door. Held out a sopping wet white shirt like a trophy. A big smile on her face.

"Tonight's the night," she said, in her loud, crisp voice.

"What?" Sonny was bolder than I was.

"You boys can take turns sleeping in the Bishop's shirt. I've been waiting for this moment. You have the Bishop's blessing."

"I'm not sleeping in that filthy shirt," Sonny said.

"Go wash out that mouth of yours," Sister June shot back.

I think I got to wear the shirt first. Against my bare skin, because it worked better that way, Sister June said. It felt cool to the touch. It didn't even smell bad. Fresh man-sweat mixed with sandalwood or lavender. Bishop Bonner was a vain man. I slept really deeply that night. I truly believed God was close by. That something mysterious and sacred happened to me in my sleep.'

'You can use anything you want in your poems, Felipe, anything, as long as it's real. That "in the forest" poem of yours sounds fake, you can hear that yourself, right? Have you ever been in a real forest? Well? It's nothing but flair and pathos. Air. And why're you writing about white women like that? Let's hear it, Felipe. You can't stand onstage at night and shout how white women are dragging us down, and afterward go out with Ronnie. You love Ronnie, don't you? I've seen you two. How you look at her. You love her. Invite her around sometime.'

'Here? To the East Wind?'

'Why not?'

'They'll razz you.'

'So what?'

'Did you feel the Holy Spirit in you, Felipe? Or did you ask too many questions? Didn't you believe enough?

I did. I was ten years old. For days I could feel it coming. The evening sermons always went until about nine, ten o'clock, and then the people who felt that the Holy Spirit had visited them came forward. With me it happened during the day. On Lincoln's birthday. We had the day off from school. My mother was at the hairdresser's. Maybe it wasn't a coincidence that she wasn't there. Pastor Bonner and his son Nathaniel were in the church. I can hardly explain what happened. I felt my arms and legs go all heavy, a strangely tired sensation in my back. I listened to the music. An older woman went up front and sang. Her voice was deep and warm. "His blood covered my sin. He has conquered my soul." It was like I could touch the words. I could see them. Sparkling and clear, like stars. The sunlight in the tall church window. "His blood covered my sin." The red of His blood. I heard the sound of the organ, its high tones hypnotizing and the low bass resonating in my belly. It was gospel but she sang it jazzy, free, unpredictable. Her voice was everywhere. "He has conquered my soul." I can't remember who else was in the church, as far as I was concerned it was empty. My fingertips trembled. I got dizzy. I pretty much blacked out. Fainted. I heard voices, they kept getting closer, they were heavy and slow and they were speaking a strange language. The music in the background. "My sin." The nervous humming of the organ. I fell over. I must have banged my arm on the wooden pew in front of me because later I was bruised. I lay on the floor, on that soft carpet, and my body twitched and jerked. The voices kept on whispering in my head, and I started imitating them. Unintelligible words—just sounds, really—but I understood exactly what it was all about. Like they were fighting inside of me. I rolled around on the floor. A voice tried to reassure me. I was alone, but I didn't need to be afraid: God saw me. He said

I wasn't a child anymore. I spoke with Him. I heard myself talk, spit out sounds. My voice was deep and crackly. The voice of an adult. I saw the red of blood again. So beautiful, like soft velvet. I felt so light, like I was being lifted up. I don't know how long it lasted.

I remember coming to. I was exhausted. The music had stopped. My throat felt raw and parched, my lips were swollen, and my head pounded. Nathaniel offered me a hand and pulled me up. "I know exactly how you feel," he said. I believed him. Nobody kissed or hugged. Bishop Bonner gave me a real formal handshake, and Nathaniel did the same. "Now you're a member of our congregation," the pastor said.

Dazed, I went outside. The light hurt my eyes. But I was so happy. I'd never felt so strong, so big before. Independent. I started to run. Ran as fast as I could to the hairdresser's on the corner. I wanted to tell Mama the news, see her face light up.

My mother was sitting under a dryer. The pink cape was snapped tightly around her neck. She was thumbing through one magazine or another.

"Mama!" I shouted as I burst into the salon. It had an intoxicatingly sweet, plastic smell.

She didn't hear me at first. Another woman tapped her on the shoulder. She turned toward me, and I could see she was startled. Her raised eyebrows. Deeply furrowed forehead. That rattled look.

"I had the Holy Spirit, Mama," I yelled. I couldn't care less that everyone heard. I nearly keeled over from excitement. My mother pushed up the hairdryer. It took way too long for my liking. I ran back outside. It was fine summer weather, everything looked so beautiful.

I'd almost gotten back to the church, back home, when my mother caught up with me. She'd taken off that ridiculous cape, but her hair was wild; she wasn't done yet at the hairdresser's. She yelled, "Gylan, stop." I stopped. She came over to me, gave me a hug. But it felt different. She held me too tightly. It wasn't right. I was an adult now, but that didn't seem to occur to her. She pulled my head against her bosom. Held my face tight, kissed my cheeks, my mouth. She whispered, "How wonderful for you, sweetheart," but I didn't like it. I could hardly breathe.'

'I was her little man.

On Columbus Day we moved to Long Island City, in Queens.

Mother was pregnant. She had a boyfriend, a guy from Ohio. I didn't like him, but Mother was happy. I made friends in Long Island City. My mother got married. Had my sister. Two weeks later her husband split. I was thirteen. I got up at 3 a.m. to deliver the *Daily News*. I had my own route.

Walking among those big brick apartment buildings. The heavy newspaper bag slung over my shoulder. Nobody around. Only the bluish moonlight, the sky silver, gray, green, white, blue. The sound of my footsteps. The first chirping of the birds. The streets clean and empty.

I'd be home by sunup. Would get my little sister out of bed. Change her diaper. Play with her. Mother wasn't a morning person, and she was in the dumps about that guy abandoning her. I was so proud because I paid the rent. "Hey Mama, I'm going to school now. Kettle's almost boiling. Bye."

But she wouldn't let me go to the school dance. Not with a girl. At first she said yes, but then a few days later it was "You're going with me." Soon after that we moved to the Bronx.

I could've said, "The Lord wants me to be with this sister," and she wouldn't have been able to go stop me. And
we probably wouldn't have moved. But I wasn't like that.
Not with Mother.

Instead I got depressed.'

◆

It rained. It was hot and then it rained. Thick drops came
down, sparsely at first, splatting on the dusty asphalt,
on the big leaves of the oak trees above us. Tick tick tick
tick. As though we were being offered fresh air at last, as
though we were finally going to be allowed to breathe.
Then the sky opened up and it started coming down
hard, the drops dancing on the street. Around us, people rushed indoors, into shops and snack bars, quick
quick. Priscilla's long hair was soaked through. It hung
in thick strands along her pretty face. Her pale cheeks.
The air smelled fresh, a chemical freshness of exhaust
fumes and dust and rain. It was late Saturday afternoon.
Priscilla and I had walked all the way to Mount Morris
Park because she didn't want anyone to see us together.
Priscilla was a Mexican princess. Well no, of course she
wasn't. She was plain old Puerto Rican, just like me, but
the way she looked ... No other girl in church looked like
her. She could've been eighteen, with her looks. Glossy
black hair that reached all the way to her butt. Long legs.
A narrow face, fine features. Her skin a satiny light
brown. In church I always sat so I had a good view of her.
Then I'd forget everything. She reminded me of the postcards my mother kept in the drawer of her nightstand.
The white beaches, the azure sky, the sea, the palm trees.
I wanted to go away with her. She had nothing to do with
my grandmother's Puerto Rico. On Grandmother's island

it was always overcast and bleak. Not a ray of sunshine. Priscilla was a Mexican princess and she wanted to make out with me after Bible class. Can you believe it? In Mount Morris Park, where nobody knew us.

Our clothes were drenched. She leaned against a tree. I could see her small nipples through her light-blue blouse. Two pointy little nibs. She could tell I was looking. She turned away, as though reading my thoughts. Of course I wanted to fuck her, but we weren't there yet. Making out was enough. She didn't say anything, just leaned back against the tree, resigned. She let me kiss her. Priscilla had a way of carrying herself. Is that the way to say it? Yeah, carrying herself. Almost like it wasn't her own body, like she'd somehow ended up in it by accident. You understand what I'm saying? Her good looks were a burden to her. She was always a little distant. Actually she was untouchable. But I loved her, Jesus was I in love. And the rain just kept coming down, which actually wound me up even more, but I couldn't tell her that. The tepid rain on her skin. The rain in my mouth and in her mouth. The taste of raw earth and leaves and grass. She smelled like strawberries or cherries. Sweet, anyway. I kissed her neck.

'We can't,' she whispered.

'Can't what?' I just kept on going.

'Do this.'

'Why not?'

'Y'know ... last time.'

'Shh ... ' I laid my hand gently over her mouth. I could sense she enjoyed it as much as I did. We only kissed. I didn't even put my hand under her blouse.

'It's a sin,' she sighed in my ear. She was taller than me.

'Nooo.'

For me, these words were part of the game. The more she said, the hotter I got.

'Don't,' she said.

I licked her lips, pressed my tongue into her mouth. She answered my kiss but then pushed me off her with both hands.

'What's wrong?'

'We can't do this.'

'Yes we can.'

'I'm going home.' She took a few steps away from me and straightened her blouse. 'What time is it?

I wasn't wearing a watch. 'About five, I guess. Why?'

'Walk back with me?'

'Sure thing.'

We walked all the way back to East Harlem in the rain. There was hardly anyone out, only cars and taxis. Occasionally one drove through a puddle and splashed us, getting us even wetter than we already were. We didn't talk. Priscilla held her satchel with the Bible and her notebook tight against her. It was like I was walking alongside a stranger. I felt lost. What had I done wrong? What was I supposed to say? It's not like she was my first girlfriend. Priscilla took big strides. I looked at her out of the corner of my eye. She seemed lost in thought. A vague, empty look. As though nothing had happened between us. As though she barely had any idea where she was going. Everything seemed to glide off her, just like the rain.

When we got back to our neighborhood she stopped abruptly. 'I'm going left here,' she said, and turned off toward Pleasant Ave.

I went home too. I comforted myself with the thought that Priscilla's conscience was bothering her, that she felt guilty. I clung to the memory of our necking. I didn't care that she stopped looking at me in church. That was part of our secret, my secret. That she lowered her eyes when she saw me, went off to talk with her girlfriends. For me, the memory was more genuine than the reality.

A few weeks later she came to church with a Puerto Rican boy. They didn't walk, they strode. Like they were already married. Everybody stepped aside for them. Her parents behind them, prancing and glowing with pride. I don't know his name. He was a slick bastard, a super-stud, whiter than the whitest white. I wanted to sock him in the jaw. How could I have been so blind! I wasn't good enough for her. Or for her parents, anyway.'

"'You know what color your skin is, Felipe?"

"Course I do. Why?"

"Well?"

"What?"

"Say it then."

"Black."

"Black?"

"Blue-black?"

"Take a better look."

"What do you mean?"

"I mean I know exactly what color I am. Every second of the day and night. I'm always aware of my color. Sometimes it's like I'm nothing more than my color. Like I hide behind my color. Look at me. Take a good look. You don't even know what you look like, Felipe. Do you have any idea how privileged you are? People look differently at you. And because of that, you have another self-image. You should think about that.'"

HARLEM, 1955

The Trip

It was still nighttime. I was in bed, and woke to the sound of the high-pitched squeak of a door. In the faint light from the hallway I saw my grandmother's face in the opening. I only saw her silhouette, her angular shoulders, her tousled hair, but not her face, her expression.

'Get up, Felipe, get dressed,' she whispered, so as not to wake the others. We were living in the Johnson Projects, eight of us in a small apartment. My mother, my brother and sister, and my aunt and her children. My brother was asleep on the top bunk. I heard him turn over. The bed rocked and creaked a little. He mumbled something in his sleep.

'Where are we going?'

'Shh, just get dressed.'

'Where's Mama?'

'Hurry up now.'

I slid out of bed, shivered as my feet touched the cold linoleum. Grandma stood waiting until I'd gotten dressed. She stretched out her arms and I leapt into them, my legs wound around her waist.

'You're coming with me and Abraham. You want that?' she whispered in my ear. I nuzzled my head into her neck, nodded. I hadn't the foggiest idea what she meant. I didn't know who Abraham was.

'You're hot,' she said. 'Been dreaming?'

I didn't answer. I was still half asleep. I tightened my grip on her neck.

'Mama and the others will come later. I want you to be with me. I want to show you something.'

I heard what she said, but the words didn't really sink in. She went to the kitchen with me still in her arms. My mother was sitting at the kitchen table. The warm yellow light of the ceiling lamp fell across her face. She was leaning on her elbows. I could see she was thinking. She didn't say anything when we came in.

'I'm taking him with me, Aurora,' my grandmother said.

Mama nodded absently.

'Say good-bye to your mother.' She set me on the ground, and I walked over to Mama.

'Bye Mama.' I kissed her cheek. She looked up, but she didn't really see me, she might as well have been looking right past me. 'You're coming too, right?'

She nodded. Looked up at my grandmother. 'Call when you get there?'

'It's for the best,' Grandma said. They were talking in code, but I didn't care. I liked going places with Grandma.

'It'll do you good to get away from Joseph, Aurora. A change of scene, a little sunshine ... '

I didn't get it. Joseph was my father. He hadn't lived with us since I was three. My mother had kicked him out of the house. I remember him standing at the bottom of the stairs, late at night. Their arguing had woken me up. I was on the landing. I'd pulled the covers off my bed and dragged them with me.

'You're not coming back in here,' my mother screamed from the top of the stairs.

'Papa!' That was all I could do, call out 'Papa'. He looked

up. Saw me. He didn't answer me, just stared.

'Come on, Aurora,' he pleaded with my mother, never taking his eyes off me. I was only three, but I had the feeling he was asking me something, that he was hoping I might intervene.

'Out!' my mother said, and I didn't know if she meant my father or me.

'I love you,' he said.

'Tell that to your floozy,' retorted my mother as she stormed back inside. I stayed put, holding the covers against my face. My father looked at me again, didn't say anything. He never did say much. Then he turned and left.

After that I only saw my father once in a while. Sometimes he'd come pick me up on Sunday and take me to a diner or to Central Park. Or to visit his girlfriend. I was four or five. I don't even remember her name, but they were always real nice to me. I didn't care that he had a girlfriend. I knew he still loved my mother—I'd heard him say so myself. Sometimes I'd come back with lipstick on my cheek. 'Where'd you get that from,' Mama'd ask. But I never told her; no matter how hard she beat me, I'd never rat him out. My father knew I wouldn't, and that's why he often brought me with him to her. Never my brother or sister, only me.

'Where's Papa?' I asked, looking at Grandma.

'We'll be going,' she said. Mama got up. She picked up a small suitcase and gave it to Grandma. Then she crouched down and looked me in the eye. 'You,' is all she said. She kissed me on the forehead, a thick wet kiss. I immediately wiped it off. 'What am I going to do with you,' Mama laughed. She held me tight. She smelled slightly musty and warm, like sleep. She was wearing a pink housecoat over her nightgown. The housecoat hung open and I could see her breasts, the gap between her big breasts. I thought of Papa again. It was good that Mama was away from him, Grandma had said. Where were we going? I'd never noticed that Grandma didn't like Papa.

'Promise you'll be a good boy for Grandma?' Mama asked.

I nodded. Leaving took so long. Mama just stood there. And Grandma didn't say anything either. I heard the silence echo in that tiny kitchen. Way off in the distance, outside, I heard the siren of an ambulance or a police car.

'You do that,' Mama said. 'And make sure that guy drives safely,' she told my grandmother.

'Yes, yes,' Grandma replied, irritated. She cast a sideways glance at me. Laughed. Like we were in cahoots, only I didn't know what about.

Grandma picked up the suitcase and we left. We walked down the stairs and when we got outside there was a shiny white Cadillac parked at the curb. A graying man with a beard was holding the front door open. When he saw me he opened the back door too and gestured elegantly at me. 'Is this him?' he asked my grandmother.

'That's him.'

'Ever been on a trip, Philip?' the man asked.

'No, sir.'

'Abraham. You just call me Abraham.' I got in the car. The seat was soft and the leather smelled new. The sky above our apartment building was getting lighter, as if it were a puddle of ink, dark blue ink that someone kept adding a little water to. Mama came running downstairs. She pulled her housecoat tight, holding it closed around her neck. It was winter, freezing cold. She waved to me. The door banged shut. I waved back. I saw Mama's mouth move. She was saying something but I couldn't make out what. Abraham had already started the engine. I shrugged. She moved her lips again. I'm pretty sure she said: I love you.

I must have fallen asleep right away. When I woke up we were driving through a vast, hilly forest. The sun was low on the horizon and it shone through the bare trees. The black branches looked like shadows, or thin out-stretched arms. The sunlight was soft and dusty. I couldn't believe my eyes. It was my first time outside New York City. I rubbed my eyes. Abraham was at the wheel. He drove calmly. Grandma sat up front too, watching the road.

'Where're we going, Grandma?' I asked.

'To California. You know where that is?'

'Way out there?'

Grandma turned around. 'Are you hungry? There are sandwiches in the bag, the red one next to you.'

I wasn't at all hungry. I wasn't sure what to think, to feel. I was excited about the trip, but anxious all the same.

'When's Mama coming?'

'In a couple of weeks. We're going to find a house first.'

'A house.'

'And then she'll come.'

Grandma turned to Abraham. 'Can you pull over?' He laughed. To me he was an old man. He was white, but Grandma seemed to be at ease with him. He parked the Cadillac at the side of the road. Grandma got out and climbed in back with me. Right away Abraham restarted the engine.

'Your mother needs rest,' Grandma said. She put her arm around me. 'Everything's different in California. Your family can start over again.'

'How come?'

'Sometimes you just need to start over again,' she said. She mumbled it, as though saying it more herself than to me.

'And what about you?'

'I'll stay as long as necessary. Listen, Felipe. We'll be on the road for about five days. I want you to pay careful attention to everything. This is new for me too.' She stared silently out the window.

'Grandma?'

'What is it?'

'Will Papa come too?' I knew the answer already, but I still had to ask. Grandma wouldn't get mad. She took my face in her hands.

'No. And it's better that way, for your mother.'

'But ... '

'No buts. Your mother loves him too much. She's so different from me, Felipe. Love makes her weak. She's much too sensitive. But you don't really understand, hijo.'

'I do too understand,' I sputtered.

'You *think* you do. I'll tell you a story about your mother ... ' She leaned back into the soft seat of the Cadillac. The car glided through the landscape. It was as though Abraham wasn't there, as though the car was driving itself. Now we were passing through farmland. The sunlight reflected brightly off the snow-covered ground. No people, no other cars, just the occasional truck. The drivers honked and waved to us as they passed.

'Once, when she was a child, your mother got very sick. She was eight. She had a terrible fever but the doctors couldn't find anything wrong. Day and night I sat by her bed. I was at my wits' end, Felipe, you can't imagine. There was nothing I could do, except pat her head dry, change the sheets. She got thinner and thinner. She didn't eat, eventually she couldn't even drink. She was slipping through my fingers. Just a little angel, Felipe, a transparent angel.'

'But she didn't die.'

'No. On the fourth day I was so desperate that I ran out onto the street, left her alone, ran to our doctor. We still lived in Brooklyn, near Front Street. I dragged him out of his office. He knew our family. He checked her for the umpteenth time, and said, "If this child doesn't get to see her father very soon, she'll die."' Grandma paused. I figured I should keep quiet, that she wasn't through yet.

'Mister Olmo had left a few weeks earlier.'

'Mister Olmo?'

'Your grandfather.'

'I don't know him.'

'Of course you don't,' she said. I heard the irritation in her voice, could tell I'd broken her concentration.

'Is he dead?' I asked.

'Aurora was everything to Mister Olmo. And Mister Olmo was everything to Aurora. Now do you understand when I tell you your mother can't handle love? She was like that even then. She literally loved her father almost to death. What could I do? So I sent Manolo, the neighbor's boy, to fetch him. I had to bring him back to my house, otherwise I'd lose Aurora. Aurora wasn't an accident, Felipe. I loved Mister Olmo. Maybe not as much as he loved me, but every one of my children was a wanted child, Aurora most of all. She was my healthiest, most beautiful baby. That's why you're my favorite. When you were born ... '

'And then she got better?'

'She got better. Slowly. Mister Olmo didn't leave her sickbed for a single moment. When she had recovered completely, he had a talk with her. And then he left for good.'

'Why?'

'Do you need to know *everything*?'

I shrugged my shoulders. I just didn't want her to stop.

We drove on. It was still morning. The sun was higher and wispy strands of mist hovered between the snow-covered ground and the treetops. Grandma was lost in thought. I nudged her.

'What?'

'Mister Olmo.'

'Mister Olmo. You're named after him, Felipe. Your mother gave you his name. Philip. Felipe.' She stopped, and I didn't dare ask any more questions. It was the first time Grandma had ever told me stuff like that. She wasn't a talker, certainly not about herself.

'Do you really want to know why he left?' she asked, after a while. I just keep on staring at her. 'One morning,' she said, 'very early, there was a knock at the door. It was still nighttime, we were asleep. Your grandfather wasn't home, which wasn't unusual, he was often away on business. I got up and went to the window. I saw a group of policemen, about five of them, standing at the door. I got the fright of my life. Something must have happened to Mister Olmo, I thought. I opened the door. They didn't say a thing, just stormed into my house like wild dogs and searched everywhere, the cupboards, the drawers, behind paintings, under the sofa cushions. They ransacked the place, and there was nothing I could do. I didn't ask questions. Any word could be one too many.

But inside I was cursing Mister Olmo. I ran to the children's bedroom. Your mother was sitting up, rigid, in her bed.'

'Mama?'

'That child was petrified. She was speechless. I believe she didn't talk for three whole days after that.'

Grandma paused. 'Mister Olmo took good care of us, but I didn't want to put my children in danger, you understand that? He'd hidden liquor under the floorboards without me knowing. What if the FBI had found it? What then? I was alone with the children.'

'Liquor?' I asked. I didn't get it.

'He sold bootleg liquor to clubs and bars. He was a gangster, Felipe. Maybe not a ladies' man—not that. He was faithful to me. But I couldn't live with the fear. For my children's sake. When he was gone I started taking in ironing again. And sometimes he'd send money. He was a good man. He let me bring Aunt Albertina and Uncle Manuel and Frankie over from Puerto Rico. He didn't mind at all that he was paying for someone else's children. They belonged with me, with their mother. That's how he was. Proper. Distinguished. His father came from a wealthy Spanish family on the island. That's why he was so light-skinned. His mother was like us. I don't know much about her. Only that he was an illegitimate child but was still given the name Olmo. I don't know ...' Her voice trailed off. Then there was only the hum of the engine to listen to.

Then Grandma cleared her throat and sat up straight. As if she'd suddenly realized she was in the middle of a story. 'Mister Olmo did what he had to do, Felipe. There was hardly any work for men like him. And he didn't want us to be poor.'

We stayed overnight in a small motel somewhere in Virginia or Kentucky. I shared a double bed with my grandmother; Abraham slept on a cot set up against one wall. I could hear his calm breathing. I felt Grandma's feet against mine. They were hard and leathery. She lay on her side, her back to me, her long hair in a braid. Every once in a while she snored. I was too wound up to sleep. Every time I closed my eyes I thought of Papa. It was like a dream, but I knew I was awake. I could see him dancing with his girlfriend. I was sitting on their piano bench and licking the lollipop he bought me at the candy store. I heard the music: a female singer, a high, lean trumpet. Papa's girlfriend's white dress swishing through the room. My father's laughter. He never laughed except with her. He was very tall and looked like an Indian chief. When his girlfriend spun around, Papa looked at me and winked. I sucked on my lollipop, and the sourness of it burned my tongue.

I opened my eyes and saw the lime-green motel-room wallpaper. Grandma had left on the bedside lamp. I closed my eyes again so I could see Papa. Like I was doing something dangerous. I rolled over on my side and pressed my legs against Grandma's. She shifted in her sleep, mumbled something. I wanted Papa to say something, but he just kept dancing and chatting with his girlfriend. She laughed loudly, tossing back her head. He held her even closer. The jazzy music was sultry and sad. I shouted that I had finished my lollipop, but the music drowned out by voice. My tongue stung, like I had cut it. 'Papa!' I shouted. He finally looked my way. Put his finger over his lips. An inaudible 'shh'. His face again serious and strict. An Indian chief. I could practically see the secrets that were floating around Papa's girlfriend's living room. It wasn't scary, wasn't annoying—just strange.

'Shh,' Papa repeated. He looked so dashing. I was proud. I opened my eyes, the music kept playing in my head, I nuzzled against Grandma's back. I waited until the songs were over and then fell asleep.

The next day we drove more or less nonstop. We paused once or twice at a roadside diner. I could hardly believe those sleazy joints got enough customers. It seemed to me they were out in the middle of nowhere. As far as the eye could see it was nothing but barren cornfields, hills, meadows, woods, the occasional farm. But I enjoyed the greasy, rancid smell of grilled hamburgers and onions. Abraham sometimes gave me a quarter for the jukebox. I randomly punched in a couple of numbers; I didn't have the patience to read through all the titles. A man's voice crackled out of the speakers. 'Sinatra,' Abraham said. I recognized the voice, the name. Mama liked Sinatra too. It was all so different from our neighborhood. Nobody to scold me or breathe down my neck on the playground, taunt me until I hit back. I didn't miss Mama. That was strange. The farther we got from East Harlem, the more I forgot about home. As though the trip was the first thing I'd ever experienced in my short life. And suddenly all the books I'd read about the pioneers, or about Eisenhower, came to life. This was America. I think Grandma was enjoying herself too. She looked younger. She wasn't exactly wrinkled anyway, but now it looked like the wind and the dust had smoothed out her skin entirely. At night, before she came to bed, I heard her laughing with Abraham. I still didn't have the faintest idea who he was, but I didn't care.

On the road, Grandma talked constantly.

'Aurora was the eldest of my American children,' she

said. 'I told you I had to leave Aunt Albertina and Uncle Frankie and Uncle Manuel in Puerto Rico, right?'

I nodded.

'It was much too dangerous to take them all with me on that boat. I had no money. No husband. Manuel's father was dead. We were already American citizens, so I didn't have to go through Ellis Island like those immigrants from Russia and Europe. I can still remember the boat landing. It was a huge steamer. We'd been underway for almost a week. I was so glad I was alone, the children would have been sick as dogs. I slept on a wooden floor in steerage, way down on the bottom deck, like most of the passengers. There was nothing. Nothing to keep us busy. Hardly enough to eat if you didn't have money. It was a misty November day when we sailed into the harbor. Brooklyn. But you couldn't see anything— everywhere you looked, it was white. We couldn't even see the Statue of Liberty. It was white and quiet. No sound. There was something spooky about it. I joined the throng of other Puerto Ricans as they charged off the boat. We were in America. But I didn't feel anything. I was numbed by the journey. I also can't remember the air smelling any different from in Puerto Rico, although of course it did. Everything was different. But at that moment I had no memories. My only thought was survival. They brought us to an office on shore where we had to register. But I won't bore you with that. I found a room on Front Street—it was an Italian neighborhood but Puerto Ricans could also live there. I rented a room in the basement from a family, and started to take in ironing. That's how I met Mister Olmo.'

'How did he know you were in that basement?'

'He didn't, *loco*. He brought in his shirts and trousers to be pressed. I had made a name for myself on Front

Street. Mister Olmo had nice suits. I thought he was rich. Pretty soon he was bringing me his ironing so often that I caught on he liked me.'

'Where were Aunt Albertina and Uncle Manuel and Frankie?'

'With their grandmother, naturally.'

'Did they like it there?'

'They didn't have any choice.'

'On the island?'

'Carolina, in the northeast. That's where I come from. My mother died there. If you had only known her ... '

'Is it pretty?'

'Pretty? I don't know. It was warm. Sometimes we swam in the ocean. My mother hated the Spanish. She worked for a rich Spanish family. Once, when I was very small, she hid me under a hatch in the cellar, because the Catalonians came to Carolina. I'll never forget it. So dark ... '

'There's an ocean where we're going, right?'

'An ocean, sure.'

'And palm trees?'

'Palm trees.'

'Beaches?'

'Those too.'

'Just like the postcards.'

'Which postcards?'

'The ones Mama has. Of the island.'

Grandma sniffed and turned her head the other way. Looked through the window. It was already dark out, and Abraham had switched on a small lamp, so all we could see was our distorted reflections in the glass.

'Your mother doesn't know anything about the island,' Grandma said curtly. 'She was born here.'

'Why don't we go there, then?'

'Because there's nothing there, my treasure. We're going to California. Enough about all this for now.'

The farther we drove, the warmer it got. I saw prairies and boulders. For hours we drove through the desert without seeing another car. Abraham seemed to know the way. He told us he was a preacher in a church in East Harlem and that he had to be in Los Angeles for a conference.

Los Angeles? I tasted the name in my mouth. Warm, dusty, sandy, yellow. I thought of all the westerns I'd seen on TV. It was just before sunset and beyond the boulders in the distance the sky was purple and orange and pink.

'You're going to Wilmington—that's near Los Angeles. An acquaintance of mine will help you look for a house.'

'But is it as nice as Los Angeles?' I asked, anxious. Wilmington sounded a lot less exciting.

'Nicer,' Abraham said.

Grandma rented a house for us in Aliso Village. It was the poorest area of LA but for me it was a vacation resort. Our ranch house had two bedrooms, a big living room and a yard all the way around. I had never lived in a real house before. Mama came out a few weeks later. She liked the house. I played with the neighborhood children: there were black kids, Chinese kids, Puerto Rican kids, Dominican kids, white kids. I got to be friends with Wai Ling, a Chinese girl. We played on the field at the end of our street. It was overgrown with flowers, poppies, cornflowers, sorrel, daisies; the grass smelled like honey.

I know of a wasp nest Wai Ling said come with me

I went with her
beyond the water
but we're not supposed to go there
let's go anyway
you see those palm trees
which palm trees
there are no palm trees in New York
really come on stay there slowpoke last one there's a rotten egg
I ran and I ran I saw mountains and horses and boulders and prairies and Wai Ling ran ahead of me she had short black hair she looked like a boy and I smelled the honey and the warm earth and the dust and I was on the prairie and we were going to sneak up on the bad guys
where are you
I'm coming I'm coming then we were at the water and the water was a lake and the sun shone on it and it looked all silver and I shut my eyes and didn't see Wai Ling anymore
here here
where are you
she laughed and I ran around looking for her and the air was blue with thin white stripes and all of a sudden Wai Ling rolled down the grassy bank toward the water in the mud
watch out I said the water but she just kept on rolling until she was brown from the mud and I ran over to her and grabbed her
don't do that she said it was like her eyes were shut don't do that but I wouldn't let go of her she burst out laughing again
what are you laughing at
at you silly
why

she planted a kiss on my mouth and I saw a butterfly
dart across the water I heard the butterfly hum like a
helicopter you see that a butterfly
a dragonfly
butterfly
dragonfly
dragonfly
and Wai Ling got up and ran back to our street and I ran
after her and when we got back she said see you tomorrow okay where's the wasp nest
what wasp nest tomorrow
tomorrow
and I went home and tasted the kiss on my lips it tasted
like mud and river and I licked my lips and I tasted honey
and flowers and palm trees and the prairie the prairie we
were indians

I think Mama was just as happy there as I was. She had a
boyfriend, Romero. He was an Air Force guy, a big black
man with an enormous chest and pumped-up arms. He
was a friend of my uncle's. Romero let me sit on his lap.

'Your mother is a beautiful woman.'

'Uh-huh ... '

'Is it okay with you if I take her out?'

'Sure,' I said, and I meant it. And they went out. Mama
wore a low-cut flowered dress and a necklace with imitation pearls. God was less strict out here in California.

At school I did track and field. I was the fastest sprinter
in the class.

Papa came to visit once or twice a year. He slept on the
sofa. He took me out in the car and we went to the ocean.

'You see that?' he asked, pointing out to sea. I saw a
ship with three sails.

'A three-master,' Papa said. 'How'd you like to sail on
one of those?'

The bright blue of the sky and the water and the sun stung my eyes. 'Did you come to America on a ship like Grandma?' I asked.

'Yup.'

'How old were you?'

'Older than you.'

'Were you alone?'

'Yes.'

'Did it storm?'

'No.'

'Where were your parents?'

'Smart aleck.'

'Did you miss them?'

'Yeah.'

'Your father?'

'No.'

'Why not?'

'Because.'

'Your mother?'

'I missed her.'

'So why didn't she go with you?'

'She was dead.'

'Oh.'

He shielded his eyes from the sun with his hand. He stood as stiff as a statue, stock-still. There was no wind. The heat was soft and dry. You could hear the lazy rumble of the waves in the distance. There was no one else around, just Papa and me and the ocean and the ship and the sky. I didn't move. If I did, Papa would get distracted and I didn't want him to get distracted I thought I heard him think about his mother who was dead in Puerto Rico I felt sorry for him but I didn't want pity he was my father I wanted to say something about Mama and that I was doing well at school and I was the fastest sprinter and ...

'I can't remember her face anymore, Philip,' he said.

I held my breath.

'It's so strange ... Her voice, I just don't know anymore. Sometimes just a flicker. I'm older now than she ever ... she was young ... and then it didn't look like it, but she was young ... '

He mumbled a bit. I didn't say anything.

'She wasn't afraid of anything, not even the Americans. She was a go-getter ... and her brother ... my Uncle Calmero ... was in jail for ten years. I was just a kid, I heard things. Shootouts, killings. A lot of killings. But she wasn't afraid. I ... '

'Did she get shot?'

'No. She got sick.'

'That's sad.'

'Yeah.'

It was the first time I ever heard my father talk about himself. I couldn't follow everything he said, but I was proud and sad at the same time. Everything around us was so pretty. I didn't know how to comfort him. It felt like we stood there for a long time. The ship had disappeared over the horizon, leaving the ocean smooth and empty. Papa lowered his hand.

'Let's get a move on,' he said, 'before your mother gets worried.' We drove home and my father left the next day.

One day my mother called me into her room. It was early morning. A Sunday. She was still in bed. I sat down at the foot. The shades were drawn; the sun bled through them and colored the room yellow. I smelled powder and perfume. Saw her stockings draped over the back of the chair.

'We're going home,' she said.

'How come?'

'It's too expensive here. We have to go back. Grandma has an apartment for us.'

'But I don't want to live in an apartment.'

'We leave the day after tomorrow.'

'What about Romero?'

'I can't marry him.'

'But I like him.'

'It's not right. Your father … '

'But Romero loves you.'

'You don't understand.'

'Will Papa come live with us again?'

'What on earth makes you say that?'

'But you said … '

'God wants us to go back. I can't do anything about it. I'm a married woman. Go pack your things.'

'Jibaro, My Pretty Nigger' (1968)

Jibaro, my pretty nigger.
Father of my yearning for the soil, the land, the earth of my
people.
Father of the sweet smells of fruit in my mother's womb
The earth brown of my skin, the thoughts of freedom that
butterfly through my insides.

Jibaro, my pretty nigger.
Sweating bullets of blood and bedbugs, swaying slowly to the
softly strummed strains
of a five string guitar
Remembering ancient empires of sun gods and black spirits
and things that were once so simple.

How times have changed men
How men have changed time.
'Unnatural,' screams the wind
'Unnatural.'

Jibaro, my pretty nigger-man
Fish smells and cane smells and fish smells and cane smells
And tobacco
And oppression makes even God smell foul.
As foul as the bowels of the ship that vomited you up on the
harbor of a cold metal city to die.
No sun,
no sand,
no palm trees

EAST HARLEM, 1959

The Coat

José walked about fifteen feet in front of me. His white shirt was dirty, his shoulders sagged. You could see by the way he trudged through the slushy brown snow that he was in pain. His left hand was bleeding; once in a while it dripped on the sidewalk, the red droplets spreading into the watery snow like little stars. Our little procession up Park Avenue was a sight for sore eyes. The store windows sparkling with Christmas lights, Christmas trees, silver balls. Shoppers in long, heavy winter coats who stepped aside when we passed, who turned to look at us. José with his marbled face, as though the blood had drained out of it. His torn shirtsleeve. The deep silence that hung between us, connected us. I could see the silence. A misty white blotch. Nobody stepped in that blotch, not even by accident. We exuded danger; you could see it for miles. I know for sure. My head was on fire. I still had my coat; José refused to wear it, refused to speak. He just kept walking; where to, I didn't know. I just followed. I followed him past the stores with the warm, brightly lit, sad Christmas displays. I felt strange and light after what had happened. Calm, peaceful, almost happy. I'd never felt this before. Like an epiphany, that was it, only I didn't know what that was.

José turned right onto 121st Street. He pointed to a small diner on the corner. It had loud neon lights and the owner had boarded over one of the broken windows. We went inside and sat at the back on the torn red leatherette booth seats and waited in silence until someone came over to us.

José was my cousin. José Rodriguez from Brooklyn. He picked me up that afternoon to go buy presents for our girlfriends. José looked good in his new shearling coat. It was light brown, exactly the same color as his skin. He had greased back his hair, which made it look in danger of smearing, like ink, especially when the light caught it. José didn't have curly hair like me. You'd never guess we were family. He had true Latino looks. He was older than me, and taller. He'd been shaving for a while now. I liked him. He always had money on him.

'We're going to Buddy Blake's,' José had said.

'Who's Buddy Blake?' I asked.

'Don't ask questions. He's got good stuff, cheap. You want nice duds or not?'

We walked down 112th St., my old street. When we first got back from California my grandmother had found an apartment for us in the Foster Houses on 112th between Lenox and Fifth Avenue. We had just moved again, to the Brownsville projects in Brooklyn, but my old friends still lived in the Foster projects so I still went there occasionally. Richard Battle. Billy and Carl. They're the ones I hung around with most. I used to go eat at Billy's when my mother was upset about money or my father or was just mad at me. Billy's mother Catherine always set a place for me. She cut my hair too. She'd put a plastic bowl on my head and snip around it. 'Your hair is so soft,' she would always say. I miss her. And Chicken. Chicken lived in the Foster projects too. I didn't tell Billy or Carl that I had sex with her in the basement stairwell of the building. Billy and Carl called Chicken a tramp, too loose and wild for a girl, but I liked her even though she wasn't pretty. She was just into sex, and so was I. She was really good at it. I wasn't in love and neither was she. We laughed a lot.

But Mama wanted to move again, out to Brownsville, because we could get a bigger house there. And maybe also because she wanted to go to a different church. Mama and I associated mostly with blacks, and at La Sinagoga they gossiped about it. Called her a 'nigger lover,' that kind of thing. I knew they were dissing us. And I saw how they looked at us, as though we were strangers.

Once in a while I thought about California. Especially in wintertime. Then I missed the mild weather and the palm trees and the space. But I was glad to see my father more often. At school I hardly had to study to get good grades. Mama applied for a scholarship for me to go to a private school. It was my history teacher Mr. Rabinow-itz's suggestion. And I was happy to have my friends back, even though I saw less of them now we were living in Brooklyn. But then I also made friends in Brooklyn.

There was something else. A strange incident. There was this kid we called Alligator, a fat black kid with just one tooth—sometimes we called him 'snaggletooth', too. Alligator was a bully. I felt sorry for him without being any less scared of the guy. He was nothing but rage and hate and disillusionment, you could feel it a mile off. You could see it in the way he carried himself, his pudgy bow-legged way of walking, his chin jutting out like he was proud of his ugliness. One day I'm hanging with Billy and Carl and a few other guys from the neighborhood, and over comes Alligator. He starts shoving me. 'Keep your filthy paws off me,' I say. I pretend not to be afraid but Alligator just keeps at it until I have no choice but to hit him. A little ways off are a couple of Puerto Rican guys, Vincente and Nico, who I never hung out with. So Alligator and I start fighting, Alligator is stronger than me and I do my best to keep my distance, because I'm quicker and more agile than that ugly, toothless fatso, but the strange thing is, my friends start egging Alligator on: 'Come on, take him down, kick his ass!' I even think I hear Billy and Carl encouraging him. I take a few mean punches. My jaw hurts, I duck, trying to kick Alligator in the stomach but he jumps back and laughs at me. But then I hear Vincente and Nico: '*Derecha*', to the right, they're giving me instructions in Spanish and as I listen to them I feel myself getting stronger, as though I'd been given a shot of adrenaline or something. Alligator rushes at me, grazes my shoulder, *izquierda*, I hit him on his left side, he crouches, *espalda*, I kick him on the back and he tumbles over and *derecha*, another right and he falls, his fat, limp body rolls over the sidewalk and eventually he beats a retreat.

Afterward, Carl said it wasn't a fair fight, that I only won because Vincente and Nico helped me in Spanish, that I had an unfair advantage over Alligator. 'But you guys helped *him*,' I said. 'Did not,' Carl replied. I knew he was lying but kept it to myself. We stayed friends.

'You don't look so good, honey,' said the waitress in the light-blue uniform. She stared at José but it was like she was looking straight through him, with an empty and indifferent look on her face. Her bleached-blonde hair was put up in a beehive. Her name badge said 'Rebecca'.

'Two double burgers and two chocolate milkshakes, and how about a little privacy?' I was glad to hear José talking again. Sweat dotted his forehead and upper lip.

I couldn't imagine he was hot. He walked all that way outside without a jacket. Rebecca retreated behind the counter.

'What're you looking at?' José said.

'Nothing,' I answered.

José started picking at the wound on his left hand. It was a nasty scrape. The blood had dried, and he scratched at the brownish scabs around the edge.

Rebecca came back with the burgers and milkshakes. She set them on the table and vanished noiselessly. I wasn't the least bit hungry. I looked outside. The window was half fogged up and the street looked hazy and dark, punctuated by trails of light from the passing cars. I could see the vague shadows of people bent forward and skidding along the sidewalk. José didn't touch his burger either, just sucked in a mouthful of milkshake before pushing the glass away from him. We sat like this for a little while. There was no music in the diner; the only sound came from the kitchen, the clatter of pans, the sizzle of oil on the grill, cutlery being dropped into the sink. Only when a customer came in or left did you hear street noise through the open door, the familiar rumble that seemed to come from the center of the earth. The tinkle of a Christmas tune wafting in. We sat in silence. I still felt that strange sense of calm in me. Like my feet didn't reach the ground anymore. My eyes stung, but my vision was clear and everything was extra sharp: the fluorescent ceiling lights reflecting off the stainless steel counter, the frayed tear in the red plastic upholstery in the booth, the mint-green door where someone had written LADIES in childlike letters. José was staring at me intensely and I looked right back at him. I wanted to tell him how I felt, but couldn't find the words. All we could do was look, as though we were looking inside one another, as though we both saw, in a flash, the same dangerous feelings, the same dark place that no one else could see. I had never felt our family bond as strongly as this.

'I'm going to kill him,' José said.

"Course you are,' I said.

'And, whoa, Felipe—you surprised me back there, the way you laid into that guy. That *cabrón*'ll be pissing blood for a week.' José laughed. I was relieved he could laugh again.

'But he's got your coat.'

'That's why I'm gonna kill him.'

José's face tensed into the same cold, stony expression as a few minutes before. It alarmed me. But he was my cousin and those assholes had stolen his brand-new hundred-dollar leather coat. It all happened so quickly. After we turned the corner José said he had the feeling we were being followed; we didn't see anybody, though, and kept walking. It was already getting dark. The streetlamps went on and it snowed a little. I remember thinking how pretty it all looked, the white snowflakes fluttering down like tiny feathers, silently, in the warm light. Maybe that's why I didn't see it coming. José nudged me in the ribs and I looked up and saw two stocky, dark figures standing in front of me. They weren't that big, but they held their jackets open and I saw the glimmer of steel and realized this was no good. 'Run,' José whispered, but before I knew it the smaller of the two grabbed me and put his knife against my throat. A few people were out on the street but they just looked the other way, picking up their pace. The other guy, the bigger one, took hold of José. He wore a thick woolen cap pulled down so far I could barely see his face. I heard him hiss, 'Coat off, make it quick.' Felt the cold steel against my throat. I hardly dared breathe. It was the first time I'd ever been mugged. José made no move to take off his coat. He stood there calmly with that dude holding him from behind and I saw the snowflakes settle on his beautiful leather jacket. They melted slowly and left little dark wet blotches behind.

'I'll rip your balls off,' José said.

'Gimme the coat.'

The black guy pressed his knife deeper into the leather of José's coat. José didn't budge. I couldn't have moved if I wanted to. I mean, I thought about trying to kick backward but felt the tip of the knife against my Adam's apple; with his other hand the guy twisted my arm practically out of its socket, and it hurt like a son of a bitch.

'Your coat or you'll bleed to death, stupid spic muthafucka.'

'I'll get you,' José said.

'Wha'd you say?'

'You heard me.'

An old city bus came rattling around the far corner. I heard its squeaking brakes, the rumble of its engine.

'Tell your friend to give us his coat. Now.' The guy who held me was hissing in my ear; I could feel his warm breath on my skin. His breath stank like a sewer. The bus stopped a ways farther up. My arms tingled, my blood pounded in my temples. What could I do? The bus pulled out again; groaning and panting, it heaved itself in our direction.

'You're dead meat,' the one with the cap snarled at José, and before I could do anything, he shoved José against the passing bus.

'José!' I screamed. I felt the second mugger loosen his grip. I kicked him in the shins and rammed my elbow in his stomach. The bus had already disappeared around the corner; José was lying in the street. The guy with the cap ran over and started pulling off José's coat. I jumped on him from behind. We both fell and I climbed on top of him and pushed him backward. He was on his back now and I pinned him down with my knees on his upper arms, the rest of my weight fully on his belly. His writhing body underneath mine. He spat in my face. 'You think you're stronger than me, asshole?' he asked, but I didn't bother to respond; no time for chitchat. I fumbled in his coat pockets for the knife. José's coat lay on the curb. A gentle silver clang: knife in the gutter. It happened automatically. I felt no fear; I felt nothing besides power, a power so strong that it hurt, like I was bursting out of my skin. My anger was stronger than me, red and soft, like cloth, like velvet, like blood, it tingled and gurgled and burned; I heard the racket inside me, the crackling drone, my head throbbed, and I saw nothing aside from the black silhouette that lay thrashing around under me, cursing 'Asshole, muthafucka, I'll kill you, y'ugly bastard,' but he couldn't do a thing besides swear and spit; I felt his warm, disgusting saliva glide down my cheeks and forehead but I didn't care, I yanked off his cap and bashed his face with my fists, left right left right. His face was a black blotch; he could have been anyone. I felt his skin, his flesh, the lukewarm blood that trickled out of his nose and eyes, and I smelled his blood, it smelled like steel and rain and snow and sidewalk and I just kept punching, I had to keep going he was mine so close and I thought I felt something snap in his head, his head flopped from left to right from right to left. 'Felipe,' I heard a distant voice call, but I couldn't respond, as if there was a wall of black glass between me and the rest of the world. 'Felipe, stop.' I felt the body slacken under me. The noise in my head receded, my anger was spent, my muscles relaxed. I looked up and saw that the other guy had taken off with José's coat. I gave the bleeding head beneath me one last mild swat. The guy drooled blood and mumbled a few unintelligible words.

'Come on, Felipe.' José's voice sounded close by, now. 'Leave him.' José pulled himself up and crawled onto the sidewalk.

I looked at the guy under me but couldn't make much out. I was still trapped inside that black glass wall.

'We'll get them, don't worry,' José said. 'C'mere.'

I got up. My head was spinning. I saw everything in bright Technicolor. Purple and red and dark blue and silver flashes. I held onto a lamppost and waited until I could see normally again. The black guy was slithering like a fish in the wet snow. I picked up his cap and tossed it to him. For good measure I kicked him in the groin.

'Quit it!' José commanded. He got up. 'You've gotta learn when to stop, man. Shit, the cops'll be here soon.'

I obeyed. Looked back at the guy on the ground. His face was swollen and bloody. No one could tell, now, what he normally looked like. I'd never recognize him. He tried to get up but kept falling back in the snow.

'He'll manage,' José said. 'We've gotta get out of here.' He grimaced and rubbed the spot where his white shirt was torn. Following him, I could see he was limping. I never even bothered to ask how he was. I was in a wordless euphoria. Floating a few inches above the ground. Nobody could mess with me. I had no idea I was so strong. And yet at the same time I was aware, deep down, of fear. Not for the muggers, God no, my fear was a shadow; I knew that something momentous had just happened to me, that there was no turning back. What I felt now, I wanted to feel again and again and again. In one fell swoop all my fears and pain and sorrow had suddenly become meaningful, and then dissipated—but my God, what was I supposed to do? I was scared to death. I felt my blood pulsing in my veins. I didn't want to think about it anymore. I just followed José. He hobbled and his left arm dangled limply at his side. Wet snow was still falling. The sidewalks and streets were blanketed with thick gray slush. So long as the snowflakes were airborne they were still white and pretty and made me think of angels.

'I'll introduce you to a few dudes,' José said.

'Huh?'

'If you can fight like that, you'll need backup. You can't operate on your own, you understand?'

I said 'yes' but didn't really follow him.

'Guys like us, we have to organize, otherwise we're nowhere. I always thought you were a sissy, what with those good grades and all. A goody two-shoes. But now I know better. They'll accept you, you'll see. I'll put in a good word for you. The rest is up to you. But keep your mouth shut, you got that? Or else you're a goner. The folks I'm gonna set you up with are different from those other buddies of yours.'

I nodded. Jose's words excited me, even though I could hear the menace in his voice.

'You're going to have to say goodbye to a lot of stuff.'

'Like what?'

'You can keep being a bookworm, but it's unimportant now. We need family, Felipe.'

'But you're my family.'

He laughed. As though he felt sorry for me.

'You know what I mean.'

I didn't.

'Look at yourself, you little shit. You can fight, man, I

mean really fight. And you're smart. But you'll always be that little muthafuckin' nigger from Puerto Rico. You have to know who you're sharing your strength with, is what I mean. Make sure you get something in return.'

I nodded.

'Get going now,' José said. 'I'll be in touch.'

'But you don't have a coat.'

'Don't worry about me.'

'Really?'

'Buzz off, man.' He laughed again, and I did too. I put a couple of dollars on the table for the burger and the milkshake, but José slid them back. 'I owe you,' he said. The way José acted, talked, gave me a warm feeling. I made for the door. Before leaving I turned and looked back. José was picking at his wound again. I wished I could do something for him, but the way he sat there, bent forward, his shoulders hunched, I could tell he wanted to be left alone.

'The Library' (1968)

I've kissed books before
Held them close to my brown skin
Learned why my mother got moody at the end of every month
But they never taught me how to fight
Or how to run from cops sperm bullets
"Zig zag, Butchy,
Zig zag, don't run straight fool."
Taught me to know
But not to believe
Moms believes in God
I believe in revolution
We both believe in something
Devoutly

BROOKLYN, 1960

The Frenchmen

I didn't know there was so much dust in air. A thick stripe of white sunlight streamed into our classroom, right across Miss Shapiro's desk, across her blue-green jacket and her face. She was lost in thought. The fingers of her right hand paged absently in an English dictionary but she was staring out into the classroom. Her hair looked almost transparent in the sunlight; it sat high on her head like cotton candy. Even when the wind blew old newspapers and garbage across the playground and Miss Shapiro's beige raincoat flapped behind her, even then her black hair stayed in place. As though it was glued there.

In front of me, Parnell Hargrove was writing furiously in his notebook. I could hear the scratch of his pen on the rough paper. Could hear his breathing too, which would stop occasionally, and just as I was about to nudge him, for fear that he might suffocate, he'd heave a deep sigh and continue writing. I looked back at the strip of light. Flecks of dust crept up and down it like tiny, diligent insects on invisible threads.

Miss Shapiro's pale cheeks were pink. I could smell her perfume. The warmth of the sun spread her scent throughout the classroom. Didn't all that dust bother her? She closed her eyes for a moment. As the sunlight reached her, her features, usually so sharp, seemed to fade in the misty yellowish glow. She seemed, herself, to be glowing. I opened my eyes wider, slid back my chair over the hard linoleum floor, and raised my hand.

'Yes, Philip, what is it?' I was relieved to hear her voice. It didn't matter what she said, so long as the silence was broken.

'Could you repeat the assignment again?'

'Don't you remember it?'

I shook my head.

'What did you say?'

'No, ma'am, I don't.'

She closed the dictionary and stepped out of her spotlight. She looked at her watch. 'Class dismissed. Pack up your things and leave quietly. I'll see you tomorrow. Philip, stay in your seat for now.'

The eruption of thirty-one children's voices and the squeak of metal chair legs against the floor broke the silence in the warm classroom. Parnell got up and turned to me. His cheeks were flushed, and a few tiny drops of sweat were beaded on his forehead. He sniffed up a glob of snot.

'See you at recess?' he asked.

'Nah ... ' I said.

'How come?'

'I've got stuff to do ... maybe later. I'll be around.'

'Okay,' Parnell said, picking up his bag and sauntering out of the classroom.

Miss Shapiro took her time putting her books and notebooks into her big leather bag. The sun had disappeared behind the gray wall of the schoolyard and the sky looked normal again.

'So you've forgotten the assignment,' she said, without looking up. Her voice echoed in the empty, high-ceilinged classroom. I could hear that she wasn't mad. She had a light, melodious voice, and enunciated her words meticulously, as though speaking required all her concentration. She came out from behind her desk. Through an open window I heard a bird chirp. I could ignore the background buzz of the city. Miss Shapiro unhooked the big wall map of Europe without saying a word and carefully rolled it up. I followed her every move. Saw how the stiff wool fabric of her dress hitched up when she reached for the map, saw her firm calves and ankles in the flesh-colored hose, her dark blue pumps which seemed to me too small for her feet: her instep bulged out. I had no idea how old Miss Shapiro was. Older than my mother but much younger than my grandmother. She hardly had any wrinkles. Her skin was white, really white, white like fresh paper, like the newly painted walls in the principal's office, but from up close you could see the jet-black fuzz that thinned as it fanned out from her temples over her cheeks. She was serious, and had a serious look in her eyes, almost absent, as though always deep in thought ... but when she spoke to you the spell was broken, she seemed to forget whatever had been preoccupying her and would look straight at you, intensely, with a searching expression that didn't contain even a trace of condescension.

I wasn't used to adults looking at me like that. In the eyes of my mother and grandmother I saw everything —love, annoyance, warmth, anger, fear, worry—but seldom the calm and genuine interest I read in Miss Shapiro's unreserved glance. As though I were an adult myself, that's how she looked at me, that's how she looked at all children, which is why her class was generally pretty orderly. Her classroom was an oasis in a noisy, filthy school where all the teachers were white and most of them were baffled if one of their black pupils managed to perform above average.

I looked at the classroom clock and counted the seconds as they ticked slowly by. Miss Shapiro put the chairs upside down on the desks, one by one, without paying me any notice. I started to get uncomfortable. I was supposed to meet the guys down in our basement. I had to report there every afternoon at four thirty.

José had kept his word, and introduced me to Dee and Samuel and Johnny and a few other guys. They call themselves the Frenchmen, and they controlled the neighborhood. José was in another gang, the Canarsie Chaplains, the largest black gang in Brooklyn. He said I'd be better off joining the Frenchmen because the Brownsville projects were part of their territory. And if necessary, José said, the Frenchmen and the Chaplains teamed up anyway.

I'd been assigned to Johnny, a stocky black kid of an indeterminate age with a deeply furrowed forehead and a wide, masculine, stubbly face. His expression was so distant and sad that it seemed as though he was looking inward rather than at the world. But I caught on right away that I shouldn't underestimate Johnny. José had told him about the incident with the leather coat, how I fought and saved his life. Johnny just nodded nonchalantly and gave me the once-over with those impenetrable gray-black eyes of his. 'We'll see,' he said.

It was like I was blind. I'd never noticed any of those Frenchmen before, even though they all lived in my neighborhood. Somehow I always managed to make them invisible. In fact, nobody knew the Frenchmen existed, except the Frenchmen themselves and the Canarsie Chaplains.

Every afternoon I went down the filthy cement stairs to the basement of our building. It was cool and clammy down there, even when it was warm outside. A vague smell of urine hung in the air; the homeless guy's crumpled gray blankets were tossed in a corner. The basement was divided into several areas: a large laundry room that smelled of soap powder and diapers, and on the other side of the narrow hallway a collection room for the garbage thrown down the chutes. I had to cut through that room. It stank like hell, like rotting fruit and fish and meat. I held my breath and slipped through the gap in the back wall, into a small, square, pitch-dark space. I had to knock on a wooden divider and wait for an answer. Then an improvised door would open and usually I stood face to face with Johnny. The other guys sat on an old mattress on the floor or leaned against the wall. The lair was lit by a small gas lamp; the place made me think of a war bunker or a kidnapper's hideout.

When José introduced me to Johnny, they made a point of reminding me that loyalty to the Frenchmen superseded everything else, including my school friends and my family. I should think about whether I could handle it, they said. But then they said I didn't really have much choice anymore because I already knew too much.

We got up to all kinds of no-good. If rival gangs intruded on our territory, we'd rough them up. We fought for control of the neighborhood schools. We kept the King family under control. The Kings lived in my building. They were a big, poor family. They had seven or eight kids, all boys, you could hardly tell them apart. Their skin was so dull-colored it was like it was saturated with dust, and their clothes were tatty. They were unruly but nobody wanted them in the gang. Dee said they stank.

We shoplifted and pickpocketed. But I could never just mug someone. I needed a reason. Justification gave me the right. And Johnny had me figured out right from the start. He took me aside, once, and asked if I was getting a guilty conscience.

'What do you mean?' I asked.

'You know what I mean.'

'Fuck off, man.'

'Remember: I've got my eye on you,' he said. 'I don't miss anything.'

I had no trouble keeping my new life a secret. I felt that I was finally being afforded the responsibility I deserved. I was used to being the man of the house: I organized everything, filled out forms, did the shopping, explained Bible passages my mother didn't understand. But if I made even the most cautious attempt at explaining the theory of evolution to her, she'd slap my face like I was a little kid. I knew she couldn't help it, knew that she loved me. That's why I went with her to church every evening. I didn't mind, especially because now I had my own life with the Frenchmen. It made me feel indomitable. Like I was better than those people in the church, better than my mother.

Parnell Hargrove was my best friend at school. He lived at 345 Dumont Ave. His family came from West Virginia. Parnell didn't know about the Frenchmen either. He never asked where I went after school. We were kind of like brothers; we didn't talk that much except about schoolwork and books. I imagined that my secret life made me somehow mysterious to him, that in one way or another it was clear that my life had more pizzazz than his. And this in turn made my life with Johnny and Samuel and Dee all the more attractive for myself.

'Look, Philip, come and look.' I heard Miss Shapiro's high, whispery voice behind me. I turned around.

'There.' She pointed to the playground. In the middle of the sidewalk sat a small squirrel. He held his head in the air and sniffed furiously from side to side.

'He's lost,' I said.

'Looks like it. Cute, isn't he?'

'They always find their way back.'

'You think so?'

'Course.'

She took the chair off Parnell's desk and sat down in front of me. 'So you forgot what the assignment was?'

I shrugged. It was quarter after four. If I didn't hurry up, I'd be late, and Johnny didn't tolerate lateness. He would give me the third degree. Johnny was as paranoid as anything.

'An essay about dreams,' I said quickly.

'Real dreams, not daydreams. Why are you still here?'

'Because you said I had to stay behind.'

'Is there anything you want to tell me, Philip?'

'Like what?'

'You raised your hand, remember?'

'Yeah … '

'And?'

'I thought I'd forgotten, but now I guess I remember.'

She shook her head. Gave me that pitying look. 'Go on then. I'll see you tomorrow.'

I picked up my school bag and got up. I felt disappointed but didn't know why. I headed for the door. Miss Shapiro was still sitting in Parnell's chair.

'Philip.'

I turned. 'Yes, ma'am?'

'You could go to college if you wanted to, you know that, right?'

'I think so.'

'Would you like to?'

'Sure, but ... '

'But what?'

'I have to go.'

'Too many secrets can make you sick, Philip.'

'I have to go.'

'Where?'

'You're not my mother.'

'Oh, but I *am*.' Miss Shapiro got up and walked over to me. Looked me straight in the eye. Like she was holding onto me with her big dark eyes that glistened like stars in her pale, matte face. 'I *am* your mother,' she said, smiling. 'Do you want to become a gangster? Because it seems that's the way you're headed. But I am personally going to see to it that you are the gangster with the best syntax in the world. You are going to articulate and to enunciate until you love and embrace the English language, because you will never be able to achieve your objectives in this society without a decent command of language.'

She raised her eyebrows. I was too flabbergasted to answer.

'Go on now,' she said.

But I just stood there. Her words had sucked all the strength out of me. My legs felt heavy and listless. I would never get to the basement on time.

'Go.'

'But—'

'Don't be afraid, Philip. Just go.'

I raced back to the apartment with my bag slung over my shoulder. On the way I bumped into an older lady pushing a baby buggy. I didn't even say sorry. I just kept running. It was only early March but it felt like spring already. The sun hung large and pink behind the red brick buildings. My shirt clung to my back. I skidded down the five steps to the basement and made a beeline for the garbage room. I tried to hold my breath against the stench, but my lungs burned from the running. So I leaned against the wall and let the rotten air flow in. I gagged, doubled over. I wanted to go back outside, but when I stood up I felt my guts push against my stomach. There was no holding it back. I tasted the bitter gall and threw up on the filthy gray cement. I puked until only white slime came out, white slime and thin strands of red-brown blood.

◆

I sit on the olive-green sofa in the living room at the back of Miss Shapiro's apartment in Brownsville. It's dark outside. I count five lamps in the room, five brass lamps with white lampshades on end tables next to the love-seat and the brown leather sofa and on the sideboard, and they give off a soft, white-yellow light. A haze of cigarette smoke hangs over the furniture and hovers above the lamps. It's as if the air in the room is completely inert, as if the fine particles of smoke are part of the decor, were put there precisely to muffle the voices of everyone in the room. I'm the only one sitting down. Miss Shapiro has taken off her jacket. In her thin white blouse she stands at the mantelpiece chatting with her friend Miss Lepnish. There are three other people in the room. Miss Shapiro introduced me to everyone but I can't remember all their names. There are two older men, one of them with a close-trimmed dark beard. And a lady in a lilac-colored suit, Miss Binder or Bindall, she teaches music, but not at our school. She's on her own, inspecting Miss Shapiro's bookcase, her head cocked to one side so she can read the titles and authors. I take in only a general murmur; occasionally a single word jumps out: Hollywood, outdoors, verve. The men rattle away in a language I've never heard. Miss Shapiro told me they come from Russia. Their sentences sound liquidy and gooey and questioning, the words flowing seamlessly like in a song. Once in a while one of the men looks my way, nods politely and returns to his conversation with his countryman.

It's the first time I've been to Miss Shapiro's house. 'I'll lend you some books,' she said. 'Wait for me.' She wouldn't take no for an answer, so I waited. I didn't know she had so many friends. It's practically a party, they drink sherry from long-stemmed glasses and bourbon on the rocks, but their voices are subdued, serious.

'Philip.' Miss Shapiro walks over to me. 'Those books I was talking about ... ' She nudges the woman in the lilac suit and smiles at her. 'Philip is my star pupil. I'm going to give him some extra tutoring.' She gestures to me. I get up. 'Miss Binder is a wonderful singer, she knows all the Jewish songs—won't you sing for us, Rose?' Miss Binder blushes. She looks embarrassed. I don't know what to say. 'Did you get something to drink, Philip?' Miss Shapiro asks. I know her first name is Ethel because that's what her friends call her. Ethel Shapiro. She looks a lot younger in her own house, with the thick reddish-brown pile rugs on the parquet. The top buttons of her blouse are open. Everything in this room seems to give off heat. 'There's some soda in the kitchen, help yourself.' She goes over the bookcase and pulls out two hardcover books with dusty dark-green bindings. I stay where I am. 'Did I ever tell you I used to work at a publisher?' She doesn't wait for an answer. 'I used to assist writers with their manuscripts. Writers are just like children, you know. Most of them are frightened and insecure and desperate for a pat on the back—perfectly natural, of course—but they don't dare show it, they're bad at taking criticism and overdo everything. I didn't have the patience for it. That's why I started teaching. That's why you're here.' She shoves the books into my hands. 'If you want, I can teach you something about our history. I think it might interest you.'

'Yes,' I say.

She bursts out laughing. 'Don't worry, I'm not planning to make a Jew out of you.'

'No.'

'Always remember who you are, where you come from.'

'I come from East Harlem.'

'I know, honey.'

It sounds like I've said something stupid. She puts her hand on my shoulder. 'Always be vigilant, Philip,' she says. 'You never know what might happen, never. Look at us. This is America. But we still have to be cautious. Now more than ever.'

I'm not entirely sure what she's getting at, but I have the feeling I understand. Her words remind me of José, of what he said before he introduced me to the Frenchmen. He was just as solemn about it. As though he expected me to make some kind of pledge. *You have to know who you're sharing your strength with. Make sure you get something in return.*

Miss Shapiro folds over the cuffs of her blouse and hitches the sleeves up a little. She sticks out her lower lip and blows a puff of air at her face; a few jet-black tufts of hair waft upward. She absently glances across the room, where her friends are in animated conversation. Miss Binder has joined the two Russian men. They all laugh, Miss Binder holds her hand in front of her mouth.

'Are you married?' It's out before I know it. I've noticed that Miss Shapiro doesn't wear a wedding ring but that doesn't necessarily mean anything. My mother doesn't either and she is still married to Papa.

'What?'

'Do you have any children?'

'Why do you ask?'

'I don't know … I was just thinking.'

'Thinking what?'

'Nothing.'

'Nothing?'

Raised eyebrows. A faint smile.

I wonder how long her friends will stay. What will Miss Shapiro do once they're gone? Watch TV? Read the newspaper? Check our homework?

'Have you gotten yourself something to drink yet?' she asks. Her voice sounds hurried. She glances toward the kitchen.

Suddenly I feel the weight of the heavy old books in my hands.

'May I take them?'

'You weren't planning to read them here, were you?' She gives me a playful shove. 'See you Monday.'

'Monday,' I say and look past Miss Shapiro, into the room. I raise my hand to the others, but they're too involved with each other to notice me.

The books had an earthy smell. Their dark green bindings made me think of grass and rain; the thin, finely printed pages evoked images of rice and biblical stories. I wandered home, imagining the books had changed me; I didn't even have to read them, simply pressing them against my body evoked a sensation of transformation. As though I'd passed an exam. I now had access to a strange new world. The books were my passport. If I really tried, I would understand the Russian words I'd heard in that living room, they would transport me to a city crossed by a wide river and full of tall, slender, onion-domed towers. The water in the river was as murky and deep and dangerous as the Hudson's, but the city was ancient and its people were ancient, their skin like parchment, and I didn't mind any of it, it didn't scare me, it made me think of mummies and the pyramids in Egypt and the golden desert sand and dry heat, it was like feeling electricity, as though any minute now my heart might burst out of my chest. I squared my shoulders and walked past Molly's Bar. A few old black men sat drinking on barstools out in front. 'Where's your mama?' one of them lisped. 'I can make her thighs quiver like a newborn fawn.' I pretended not to hear and kept on walking. It was already dark, chilly, but the air retained the warm scent of the spring sun.

I got home at about seven. My mother was in the kitchen. She was all ready to leave for church. She wore a beige dress and brown pumps, and had powdered her face: in the pale light I could see the minuscule flakes dotting her wispy hairs. She was fumbling in her black handbag on the kitchen table, and said nothing when I came in. I wanted to rush over and throw my arms around her neck and tell her about Miss Shapiro's fancy living room and the books with the green covers, but from the way she held her shoulders, taut and pulled back, I could tell she was impatient and in a hurry.

'I suppose you're not joining me?'

'I'd like to,' I said.

'Where were you?'

'At Miss Shapiro's.'

'Don't lie.'

'It's true.' I held up the books. 'Look.'

'So what about what I've heard?'

'What? From who?'

'Betty Brown.'

'Who's Betty Brown?'

'Don't be fresh with me. Where were you?'

'I told you. At Miss Shapiro's. And there were some other teachers there and she said she wants to give me extra lessons and she's got a whole wall of books and five lamps with copper—'

'Little Bobby's in the hospital.'

'Oh no.'

'So you do know.'

Nondescript Little Bobby. He always sat in the corner of our hideout, cowering behind Dee or one of the other boys. Johnny said he was a retard, because he never spoke. Once Johnny spat in Bobby's face, just to see how he'd react. Little Bobby didn't even cringe. The spit dribbled down his nose, over his lips. Johnny laughed, mussed Bobby's curly hair. Little Bobby just retreated into his corner.

'I was at Miss Shapiro's.'

Mama pulled out a chair and sat down. She glowered at me.

'His ribs are broken, his front teeth knocked out, and his left eyelid's ripped.'

'What happened?'

'You tell me. Betty had to scrape him off the street, like old garbage. Betty said you and he are pals, that you hang around in the basement with that Owens boy. Bobby told her the whole thing before he passed out. There was a fight … Why am I in the dark about everything? And you come home with a couple of books. What'm I supposed to do with you, Felipe? God doesn't just dole out mercy and forgiveness, if that's what you think. Not my God.'

My legs trembled. It was like being shaken awake. As if that nice apartment with the soft white light and thick carpeting was just a dream. What had gone wrong? Bobby usually got lookout duty whenever we pulled anything. Didn't he run off in time? I tried to think of Johnny and the basement, but all I saw was black. As though they'd all vamoosed without telling me. Why hadn't I told them I wouldn't be there tonight? What had I done?

'I was at Miss Shapiro's.'

Mama sighed.

I set the books in front of her on the table.

'I've been thinking,' she said, no longer staring at me, but at the flowers on the plastic tablecloth. 'We're going to go back to California.'

'What?'

'The devil's not going to get my child.'

'But I don't want to leave.'

She got up, fussed a bit with her hair, took her bag and said, 'I'm going now.'

'But—'

'But what?'

I looked at the books and at Mama. I wanted to hold her and say that Little Bobby just had bad luck. That Johnny had tested him for his own good. Johnny only wanted to protect him, but Bobby was stubborn and stupid and wanted to stick with us. He wasn't quick enough. It was a good thing he was in the hospital. We wouldn't let him back in the basement. Little Bobby would keep his mouth shut, sure he would. I wanted to tell her that I'd saved José's life and that I couldn't go to California, not now. It's not what you think, Mama. We're brothers. The guys need me. And I've never lost a fight, never. I can think better when I've fought. Then it's totally quiet and peaceful inside me. I crawl under the clean, stiff sheets you've ironed and I don't feel the bruises anymore. Only the surrounding air, soft and cool, and the freshly ironed sheets. It's a little like praying, Mama. I'm not tired. I want to read. I want to feel the thin pages of Miss Shapiro's books between my fingers. Ethel Shapiro thinks I could go to college. Her name is Ethel. Do you hear what I'm saying? I can't leave.

'I can't leave,' I said.

'Doesn't it bother you at all?'

'Mama.' I took her arm.

'No.'

'Let me go with you.'

Her face tightened. Her cheekbones scrunched up, her eyes squeezed shut.

'We're going to California,' she said. 'California.' I heard the hesitation. The way she said California. As though it had nothing to do with me. She reopened her eyes but wasn't looking at me. She seemed embarrassed. I thought of Romero and the letters with the colorful stamps with exotic flowers and birds on them that arrived in the mail every month. It had never occurred to me that Mama might have written back.

'When?' I asked.

She managed a smile, as if my question signified acquiescence and deserved a show of thanks.

'As soon as possible,' she said, and then left for church.

I went into the living room and sat down on the couch. It was so quiet in the apartment. I looked around, saw the low armchairs with the brown Naugahyde upholstery, the low, gleaming coffee table, the watery blue prints of Jesus above the mantelpiece, but everything looked strange and bare. Silence had taken control of the objects in the room. I thought back on our last days in the little bungalow in Wilmington. Our clothes and books and other small things were packed in moving boxes, but the furniture stayed behind; we had rented the house furnished. We were supposed to leave for New York in two days. I didn't feel like playing outside anymore. I lay on my bed, looked at the bare walls and listened to the outdoor sounds. The shrill children's voices, the occasional car, the hum of the cicadas at nightfall. The window was open, the blinds rolled down, so I heard everything, the squeak of the neighbor's gate, the scuff of Mrs. Bower's footsteps—she always wore sandals—after she came home from work in the city. I smelled the warm, dusty scent of grass and fresh yellow sand. I even fantasized I could smell the ocean. It was like being an invalid; everyone except me could play outside. I had to stay in bed. Every sound, every smell filled me with an agonizing sensation of loss and longing. I couldn't face having to say goodbye to my friends.

I got up and went to the front door, ran down to the basement. The garbage room was dark as usual. I felt my way through the gap in the wooden partition and knocked on the door. Johnny opened it.

'What're *you* doing here?'

He was alone. On the floor lay an unzipped overnight bag. Johnny pulled out a wide brown belt and put it on.

'Nice,' I said.

Johnny didn't answer. He rubbed the leather.

'I'm moving to California,' I panted.

'Good for you,' he said.

'That's it? "Good for you?"'

'What am I supposed to say?'

'Fuck, man. I took the oath. I'll be back. What happened to Bobby?'

'Nothin'. Just a fight. He tripped over his own feet. Maybe he'll learn something.'

'Shit.'

'Yeah, and where were you?'

'I had to go to my teacher's. What was I supposed to say, that I had to go fighting with the Frenchmen?'

'Since when you got trouble with lying?'

'Me?'

Johnny laughed. He dug a T-shirt out of the bag, sniffed it, and shoved it back in. 'I'll bet you're gonna go surfing, that's what all the pretty blond boys do in California, right?' His voice was thick with condescension, but his eyes sparkled, like he really did want to know.

'I'll be back, Johnny, I promise. I belong here, with you guys.'

'Sure,' he said mockingly.

'I mean it.'

'When you going?'

'I don't know. Soon.'

'Don't forget to write.'

'Really?'

'No, 'course not,' he said. He turned down the lantern. The faint light shone on his tough skin, on the wrinkles in his forehead that were so deep they looked like cuts. I realized I knew nothing about Johnny. How he lived, who his family was. As far as I knew, he lived in the basement. He was always the first one there. I could hardly imagine that he had parents. He looked like he'd already had a long life.

'I'm sorry about Bobby,' I said.

'He'll survive.'

'That's not what I mean.'

'Oh.'

'I'll miss you.'

'Yeah,' Johnny said.

That Monday Miss Shapiro treated me no differently than usual when I got to class. I decided to hold off telling her about our move for the time being. It was a way of postponing it for myself too. And I was afraid she wouldn't ask me around again if she knew I was leaving.

But as the week wore on Miss Shapiro seemed to have totally forgotten I'd met her friends and knew what her living room looked like in the fine, soft light from the five brass table lamps.

During class I made a point of trying to catch her eye, in the hope that she would smile at me, just as a gesture of friendship, of familiarity, but when she finally saw I was looking at her, her face was so calm and empty that I immediately lowered my eyes. And whenever I thought of the nonchalant way I had seen her blow that tuft of hair out of her face, her hands resting casually her hips, looking at me, I got a knot in my stomach.

By Thursday I couldn't contain myself any longer. Class was almost over and Miss Shapiro was reading to us from Shakespeare's *The Merchant of Venice*. None of it was sinking in. Of course I should have waited until after class, then casually mentioned the books she'd lent me—in retrospect I think that's what she was waiting for—but I was blinded by my impending departure for California and the fear of losing Miss Shapiro for good.

I raised my hand and asked to be excused to go to the bathroom.

'All right, then, quickly,' she said and returned to her book.

I walked to the front of the classroom and hesitated at her desk. I smelled the refined scent of her perfume. She was standing behind her desk—she never read out loud sitting down. I looked back at my classmates, but their faces were nothing more than gray blotches. All I saw were the blemished yellowed walls that seemed to get higher and higher. I held my breath. This, I thought, was my last chance. My heart pounded in my throat, my mouth was dry. The books Miss Shapiro had lent me, lying on my nightstand, flashed before my eyes. I thought of Isaac and Rosh Hashanah. Mahalia Jackson, who sang Psalm 23 to the music of Duke Ellington. 'He leads me beside still waters, he refreshes my soul.' Papa, grimacing as he listened, like he was in pain. 'Still waters.' Why couldn't he convince Mama to let us stay? I heard Miss Shapiro's voice—not the words, only the melodious, luminous sounds that danced around her like fireflies. I threw my hands around her waist and pressed my nose into her neck. Her neck was warm.

'I want you to say you love me,' I whispered.

'Philip, this is *improper*,' she said. Her body felt limp and soft even though she was standing up straight.

'I need you to say you love me,' I said.

'I'm going to send you to the principal's office, Philip. Stop this at once.'

I heard the roars of laughter and the hubbub from the class. I couldn't care less. I closed my eyes. My classmates had vanished.

'First you have to say you love me.'

'If I say it, will you go back to your seat and behave yourself?'

'Of course.'

She grabbed my hand and freed herself from my embrace. 'I love you,' she whispered so quietly and quickly that no one could hear it except me.

BOYLE HEIGHTS, LOS ANGELES, 1961

Paradise

I see dogs, horses, crickets, mules; salamanders scurrying up the white stucco walls of our house; the sun, every day; the air at daybreak: cobalt-blue, sea-blue, whitish-blue, purple-blue, pink, turquoise, yellow, orange, purple, green. Wide vistas, oil wells, the smell of petroleum mixed with a warm sweetness that wafts over from the neighbor's yard. Yellow flowers, white, red, purple oleander. Fine yellow sand, red-orange sand, dark brown oily sand the deeper you dig. Sand in the air. The wind in the clean sheets hanging out to dry. Grass. Garishly green grass. Akiri Arota's hair. Hair so straight and black like I've never seen. Purple, when the sun hits it. Her hesitant, cautious laugh. Her finger on my nose, my lips. Her fat Japanese grandmother in a wicker rocking chair on the veranda of their house. My friends are Latinos. I am black. I hear Spanish all day long. I get a scholarship. I'm elected student body vice-president at the second biggest high school in LA. The gangs. Never once arrested. Captain Morgan Spiced Rum. Getting drunk with Fredo and his brother. Coming home. A note from Mama. Elegant, curlicue letters. 'I'm out with Romero. There's food in the icebox.' Romero promises to take me for a spin in a sport plane.

'When?'

'Soon.'

'When?'

I'm greedy. I'm in a hurry to absorb all those sun-drenched images, to store them away. I know that sooner or later Mama will hear Papa's call in the balmy California wind. I see her guardedly sizing up Romero. The first overcast, rainy day. Mama sleeps in; the door to her bedroom is closed, the blinds drawn. The telephone rings at the strangest times. 'Come here, Felipe. Papa misses us. He needs me.'

When I think back on that year and a half in California I see only disjointed images. There is no narrative. It's like I am made up of loose images. Snippets, fragments, colors, a smell, a sound. I know I have to be quick, as quick and supple and wily as a panther. Only haste can save me.

'When are we going back to New York, Mama?'

'Soon. As soon as possible.'

'Hey Now' (1968)

Chaplains ...

Hey now

Where are you?
Brothers I need you
Fort Green, Mau Maus, Canarsies

Hey now

Hey Blood, hey Signatary
Hey Chico, hey Chain

Hey now

Where are you men?
They are fucking me up

Hey now

Ain't even given me a fair one
The pretty boys have taken over the city

Hey now ...

BROOKLYN, NEW YORK, 1962

1 The Harbor

The California warmth stayed in my body for the first few days back in Brooklyn. I was constantly flushed. We were staying with Aunt Calada and her children. On the third day my mother, my brother and I went to check out our new apartment near the harbor on the East River. The water stank of fish and rotting leaves. Everywhere gray and dark-green steel. I heard a ship's horn and the drawn-out squeal of the cranes. But I couldn't see the harbor. Our back window looked out onto the brick wall of some warehouse. The wall was so close that you could see the moss eating its way into the bricks. The front window faced another huge yellow apartment building, just like ours, with countless tiny windows like pin-holes in the brick façade. And behind all those square black holes were minuscule apartments where dwarves lived.

I slid open the window, stuck out my head, and looked up. The sky was blue. A seagull glided between buildings. The wind tugged at my hair. I felt the chill on my skin. Imagined that I could hear the damp air sizzle against my overheated forehead.

'Close that window!' my mother shouted.

I let the window slam shut. The glass jiggled in the sash.

'Was that really necessary?'

All I could see was brick. Brick in front, Brick at the back.

I can't remember how I ended up on the floor. My entire body was trembling and jerking. I couldn't talk. I slid across the worn parquet floor like a mad dog, gasping dust and mucus and air. And I was so hot. The sun was inside me. Red and gold and burning. The sun was so big and overwhelming and it pulverized all my dreams and desires into ashes. An anxiety attack.

'Look!' I heard my brother saying, 'he's got the Holy Spirit.'

And my mother: 'That's not the Holy Spirit. Do you think it just possesses you all at once? Is that what you think? Oh Felipe, Felipe, *mi hijo!*'

2 The Rain

My brother got beat up by some dude in Brownsville.

Sunday was revenge day. My cousin José and seven other guys from the Canarsie Chaplains, plus Johnny and me from the Frenchmen. By that time José had moved up to leader of the Chaplains.

It was raining, but there were gaps in the cloud cover where the sun shone through. A thin layer of glass was draped over the city that glistened in the wintery white.

I especially remember the sounds from that afternoon. It was like they reverberated off the glass, making them clearer and crisper than otherwise. The slam of a garbage can lid. The slurping of my rubber soles on the wet asphalt. A car drove through a puddle, and it was like thousands of pebbles pelted the bus stop.

And beyond all those sounds, it was quiet. The city seemed to be sleeping. Or else everyone had left.

I didn't know the kid with the knife. Afterward, José told me he wasn't even a member of the Chaplains, just somebody's friend who wanted to come along. That's why everyone ran. No one felt responsible for him. Cody was his name.

In a corner of a dead-end alley, where the buildings were too tall to let in the lazy winter sun and the rain was just rain and the asphalt was soaked, lay the guy who I had pointed out as that afternoon's enemy. The asshole who'd broken both of my brother's shoulder blades. Blood trickled out from under his body, mixing with the rainwater and meandering in a thin stream into a puddle. The guy's eyes were open, but he wasn't looking anywhere in particular. His arms were limp alongside his body, his hands open, and thick raindrops splashed disinterestedly onto his upturned palms.

Cody stood in the alley with the bloodied knife in his hand. His chest heaved wildly. I could hear his breath scraping his lungs. There was froth on the corners of his mouth. Paralyzed, he stared at the limp body of the boy he had just stabbed.

'It's okay,' I whispered. 'We'll get rid of the knife.'

'Yeah,' he grumbled.

'Not here.'

'Okay.'

'Give it to me.'

He handed it to me. Wiped his hands on his corduroy pants.

'Run,' I said.

'Run,' his voice echoed.

A few blocks away, I put the knife under a garbage can, after I heard the sirens wailing in the distance. The glass had melted away. No more rain. But before we could go any further, we were intercepted by a police car. A big black policeman got out and pointed his gun at us.

'End of the road, fellas.'

3 Interrogation

The DA came in.

'Where were you last night?'

'In Carnegie Hall.'

'Where?'

'Carnegie Hall.'

'I can't understand you. Speak up.'

'Carnegie Hall.'

'Carnegie Hall? And what were you doing in Carnegie Hall?'

'Listening to Gregorian chants.'

'Gregorian what?'

'Chants.'

'Oh, so you're one of them, ya sick fuck. One of those intellectual killers.'

'I don't know who killed that kid.'

'Tell the Sarge what you told me. Where were you last night?'

'Carnegie Hall.'

'Where?'

'Carnegie Hall.'

'*What?*'

'Carnegie Hall.'

'You buy that, Sarge?'

NEW YORK, OCTOBER 2000

My dear Felipe,

You asked me why I thought of you running for City Council next September. During our brief telephone conversation you said you were worried that your past might catch up with you, could become a campaign liability. Well, my dear friend, I don't believe you have any reason to be afraid. Afraid of who, anyway? A mean-spirited journalist who takes pleasure in dragging your name through the mud? A dirt-hungry political opponent? Come on. You're afraid of that? You've been through worse ordeals, Felipe. You've never hidden your past, never. Not from employers, not from journalists. And, more importantly: you've done your time, you've paid your debt to society. Later, too, as a poet, political activist. Why so timid all of a sudden?

I've been thinking, Felipe. I tasted a different kind of fear in your words. Tell me if I'm wrong, but are you afraid of losing? I know how proud and ambitious you are. And at the same time I know shame sometimes gets in your way. Ashamed of your success, your flair, the ease with which you win people over. They're two sides of the same coin, Felipe.

(And don't tell me it's not true! A guilty conscience is part of our generation's baggage. I'm well aware of the inner struggle that goes with success, material or otherwise—as though you're being rewarded for something that's not totally aboveboard. I too know the suspicious glances from comrades. I remember you talking about 'nigger money'; that you were worth more than what Channel 5 offered you for an hour-and-a-half program. You were right, Felipe! It was shit. You're better than that. But it also gave you an excuse not to have to work for Channel 5. You took that job as a pro bono lawyer in the Bronx for not even half as much. And I respect you for making that decision, really I do. I recognize your struggle. I know how you feel about Kain and David and Abiodun and even Umar. I feel your pain. Speaking of 'nigger money', black poets in America still have to grovel in the dirt to earn a living wage!)

The important thing is that you run, and that you let your voice be heard as a representative and advocate of the people of East Harlem, your neighborhood, your home. Win or lose, the point is that by being a candidate you're making a statement. You don't risk anything if you run only to win, when losing isn't an option.

Maybe back in the '60s we were ill-prepared for losing. Forgive me, Felipe, but my thoughts invariably return to those days.

I was working for *The New York Times* back then, and at the same time was active with neighborhood political papers in Harlem. I remember going to a meeting in this gorgeous house on Striver's Row. An acquaintance of mine had invited me. I thought he'd asked me as a journalist, but once things got underway in that mansion I caught on that it was something else altogether. It was a meeting of revolutionary black nationalists. Not the Panthers. The discussion revolved around the drugs inundating our neighborhoods and undermining the revolution. It was '68 or '69. Everybody agreed that we had to send a message to the dealers and junkies. There was a plan—a serious plan—to go out in three armed groups and mow down the addicts and dealers from passing cars on Eighth Ave. and 126th. Between 3:30 and 4:30 in the afternoon. By the time the cops got wind of it, traffic would prevent them from getting there.

I recall being intrigued by their plans. I was a calm young man, dreamy and idealistic. But for one reason or another I considered that talk of machine-gunning junkies and dealers perfectly reasonable.

The plan was never carried out. The group, as it turns out, had been infiltrated by the FBI. Their counter-intelligence program was in full swing. Often it was the undercover FBI or CIA agents who agitated for violence the loudest. Later on, a few guys from that meeting were murdered.

I also remember, incidentally, how a good friend and I—he's now a prominent architect—spent weeks fantasizing about blowing up the Empire State Building. How we could do it without causing too many casualties. We didn't care if we got caught. That's how much we loathed the authorities and everything they stood for. We felt we were outside the system—and to be honest, Felipe, I still feel that way. Deep down I'd still like to kick those motherfuckers' asses.

I'm not sure why I'm telling you all this. I think what I'm trying to say is: our hate made us vulnerable. We were so naive. Whenever you talked over a political plan with more than two people, chances were one of them was a snitch. We isolated ourselves. The violence we faced was so much bigger and stronger and smarter than we were. It reduced us to one small voice crying out in a godforsaken wilderness.

And that's why I respect your courage to run for office, Felipe. To take advantage of the meager resources at our disposal. I'm rooting for you. When I talked about shame just now I did it mainly to reassure you. Because I think deep down, you're afraid you're not good enough to win this election.

Believe me, Felipe, if I say you are, then you are. You're ready.

Your friend forever,
Clayton

NEW YORK, OCTOBER 1970

The Fall

I am in a building in East Harlem. An abandoned old factory at the edge of Manhattan, near Thomas Jefferson Park, on the water. I don't know where Pablo is. We came here to accompany the girls. They want to cross over to Wards Island. They promised to pay us for protection. Nobody goes through East Harlem without protection. Nobody. But now Pablo has suddenly disappeared. Only Lula's here. Was that her name? She's standing at the open window. Lula. Cold winter air on her deep-brown skin. She smiles. Chubby cheeks. She's a big woman.

She says something but I only see her lips move. No sound. A few seconds later the words reach me: they sound fat and hollow and elongated.

'What you standin' there like that for?'

I see the brown walls. The red and green electricity wires dangling out of plastic tubes. The peeling paint. Damp spots on the high ceiling. The blotches begin to change their form; they become enormous jellyfish and amoebas. I see an octopus. I smell the hard, steely odor of the river water. It's so cold.

'Can you close the window?' I ask.

She replies with a toothy smile. Slides the window further open.

'I'm not taking any chances with you,' she says, and again her words reach me with a delay. My facial muscles hurt. I slowly stiffen. The blood quivers in my veins. I shouldn't have smoked that joint. Jesus. Lula. The walls keep getting higher, like they're liquid, pushing the ceiling upward.

'Lula.'

'Are you scared?'

She doesn't move. Just grins.

'Close the window. Please.'

'The leader of the Young Lords is scared.'

The leader of the Young Lords is scared. Scared. Scared. The words ricochet in my head. I don't know what they mean. I only see the leaden sky above the water. It's dusk. I wonder what time it is. The window is wide open. The piercing wind whips into the empty concrete space. No light. I've lost all sensation in my body. I raise my hand but feel nothing. I look at my hand, my body, an empty shell. I'm standing at the window. The water is brown and deep and viscous as oil. I want to get out of here.

'Come on then,' Lula says.

I shake my head no. I'm at the window already, aren't I? I want to go downstairs. All I want to do is go downstairs. How many stairs did we climb to get up here? Why did we have to come here? For the money? Didn't they want to go to Wards Island? What business do they have on Wards Island? Where's Pablo?

'Pablo.'

'He's gone, honey.'

'Pablo!'

'We're alone.'

The screech of seagulls. Fat, satiated gulls swoop low over the water. The pedestrian bridge in the distance. Tiny black figures moving across the steel construction.

'Is it true what I heard?' Lula asks. 'That you guys are gonna take over the church? You've got guns, I hope?

Otherwise it'll backfire, just like the first time.'

Guns.

I'm petrified from the cold. I can't talk. What the hell did they put in that joint? I want to leave but can't move. The gray cement walls begin to vibrate, they're closing in on me, I can't breathe. Maybe I'm dead already. Is this the end?

'Lu ... Lu ... Lu ... ' I stammer.

'Calm down.' Her voice is firm, resolute.

I close my eyes. Drop to my knees. The smell of piss and old dust. I'm suffocating. I have to get outside, to the window. My fingernails crack on the hard concrete. I'm almost there. I feel the breeze on my skin. Almost. A hand on my back. Where are you, Lula? A hand pushes me to the floor. Lula? I open my eyes, see only gray. Gray concrete, gray skies, gray water.

'Lie there,' I hear some faraway voice tell me. The warmth of the hand on my back. I hear only a deep, soft rustle coming from within my body. Black. Black with brilliant, sparkling gold dots in the distance. Are they stars?

When I came to, I saw Lula sitting in a corner. She had tucked her knees up to her chin; her eyes were closed. The window was open a crack. It was dark outside. Evening, or maybe even night. I had no idea how long I'd been unconscious. Or had I just been sleeping? A bare lightbulb dangled from the ceiling, spreading a faint orangish light. I tried to heave myself up. All my muscles hurt. I was cold. My head pounded.

Apparently Lula heard me move. She opened her eyes and smiled at me. At once I thought of Iris. I had left home at around nine that morning, and had promised to call.

'You feeling better now?' Lula asked.

She pushed herself up and came over to me. I vaguely remembered Lula saying something about guns and the church. She crouched next to me and ran her hand over my cheek. I shivered. I could hardly believe this was the girl who had shoved the window all the way open when I asked her to shut it. I didn't know what exactly had happened, but my body remembered my fear. I was stressed, sapped.

'You must've taken some bad stuff. You were flipped out.' Lula cocked her head to one side.

'Where's Pablo? And your friend?'

'You wanted to come here, don't you remember? You wanted to be alone with me. That's what you said.'

'But the money ... '

'Shh. Pablo's got it. It'll be all right.'

'Who are you?'

'You know who I am. You're supposed to protect me.' She laughed. 'Now look who needs protecting.'

'I've gotta get going.' I was panicking. I was hungry. I had to let Mickey and the others know where I was. We kept in contact, always. That was the deal. I could be dead, for all they knew. Could have gotten into a nasty situation. You couldn't put anything past the police.

'Here. Come lie down on my coat. You can't go anywhere in your state.' Lula bent over to help me up. Her small breasts grazed my bare arm. I did what she said. I was too weak to resist. When I got up the room started spinning, and I saw all kinds of colors. Red, green, purple, yellow, blue. I leaned on Lula.

'C'mere,' she whispered. She had spread her long fake-fur coat on the cold floor. 'You just lie down. I'll be right back.' Unresisting, I lay down on the coat, closed my eyes and felt sleep wash over me. I heard the tick of Lula's heels on the concrete as she walked off. I opened my eyes, saw the strange orange light.

'Don't go,' I called.

She turned toward me. 'Can't I even go to the bathroom? You really are something, y'know that?'

Off she went. I heard the tired creak of a door opening and then the soft click as it shut again.

'Lula!' I shouted. 'Lula.' I heard my voice reverberate off the walls. Hollow echoes. I muttered to myself. Tried to pull myself up, but my body was too heavy and limp. Those colors again. Glistening blue and orange and silver.

I don't know how long I lay there. I was paralyzed. I desperately tried to remember how I got into the factory in the first place. When I last saw Pablo. But it was like trying to climb out of a deep, narrow hole, and constantly falling back in. I couldn't even picture his face. His name echoed softly in my head. Pablo. Pablo. I must have fallen asleep.

'You still lying there?' I opened my eyes. Lula was crouched next to me. Only now did I get a good look at her face. Her skin was silky and flawless; you could hardly make out any pores or wrinkles. She had a high forehead and a fine, hooked nose. Must have some Indian blood in her. She couldn't have been older than eighteen, nineteen.

'I have to go,' I said.

'Easy does it. We've got time. Let's talk a little.'

I pulled myself upright. I shivered, but was no longer sick.

'Pablo and Janet will be here soon,' she said matter-of-factly, sounding almost motherly. She nudged my shoulder, motioned for me to lift up my butt so she could pull the coat out from under me.

'Don't want it getting dirty,' she said with a smile. I

smiled back. It all sounded so everyday and familiar. 'Don't want it getting dirty.' Why would Lula lie? If Pablo was on his way, then that was okay, because it meant Mickey also knew where I was, and Mickey will surely have called Iris to say I'd be home late and that I could wait for him. The best thing would be for me to wait.

'You know what I thought the first time I saw you?'

'Hm?'

'That you looked like Che Guevara. With that beret.'

'What beret?'

'You wore it that time, don't you remember? At the East Wind. You spoke.'

'Did I see you then?'

'Only you don't have a beard. But the way you talked about the Garbage Offensive. You remember? Burning the trash in the middle of the street because the city hardly did any pick-up in the Barrio. You got everybody riled. Che Guevara—I thought of him then. Che Guevara in Harlem. Funny, huh?'

I didn't answer. I remembered that meeting. There were about fifty people crammed in the loft. My throat hurt from the cigarette smoke, and from having to raise my voice. And later, a few young people joined the Lords. It was a Saturday afternoon, more than a year ago. Hot as hell. Late summer. The long shadows on the sidewalk on my way home. I remember those shadows. Like I was being followed. But I did not remember Lula's face.

'Don't you write poems too?'

'How do you know that?'

'I know your friend Kain.'

'Kain? How ...?'

'He's an actor now, right? In the Village. Too bad. I thought you guys were good together.'

'But ... '

'What?'

'Who are you?'

'I'm Lula.' She got up and walked slowly away from me. She was wearing a tight maroon turtleneck sweater and black pants. She had wide hips; her buttocks were round and stuck way out, like they were too big for her body and didn't totally belong.

'How do you know Pablo's coming?'

'He said so.'

'When?'

'Before we headed out here. You were already too far gone. I had to stay with you. What else was I supposed to do, Felipe? You said you liked my company.'

'I'm going,' I said, and got up. Too quickly. Dizzy again. I nearly fell over.

'You can't.'

'Why not?'

'Pablo.'

'Pablo'll find his way.'

'You don't just leave your comrades in the lurch, do you?' Lula leaned against the wall.

'I know lots of Puerto Ricans,' she mused. 'Me and Janet love East Harlem. You all have better clubs than we do, y'know? I love salsa. Janet even more than me, but her mother doesn't want her going with Latinos. Says you're too hot-tempered. Her mother's a racist if you ask me. Don't you think?'

She sounded like a schoolgirl. I looked around the room for my leather coat. I was wearing just a T-shirt. Lula saw me look.

'Your coat's downstairs. Pablo'll get it for you.'

'How'd it get there?'

'You took it off. I don't know why, you were acting crazy. You cold? Put my coat on. I've got a sweater anyway. C'mere.'

I went over to her. Who knows why. Maybe I was afraid to go downstairs. I was tired and hungry and still shaky from the trip. I don't know. She held her coat open. I could simply step into it, wrap myself up in the warmth and her scent and her arms. But instead I took the coat from her and grabbed her wrists. They were thick and strong. She resisted, but I pressed up against her, reached for her ass and her back. She was cornered. I don't know what possessed me. I wanted to climb into her. I wanted her to hold me. Comfort me.

'Please, baby,' I panted in her ear.

'Felipe,' she said, trying to push me away.

'Isn't this what you want?' I said.

'Here? Like this?'

I started kissing her neck. My hand crept under her sweater, under her bra. Her breast was small and round and firm. She was so warm. I pressed my erection against her pelvis. Tried to undo the clasp of her bra without loosening my grip so that she could wriggle loose.

'Lula,' I whispered. 'Who gave you such a weird name?'

'My father.'

'What kind of guy is your father?'

'He's my father, that's all. What do you want to know?'

I had no idea. I didn't want to know anything. Maybe she sensed my hesitation. Maybe she thought she'd be better off going along with it. I don't know. But I felt her relax. She cautiously ran her hand over my face. The coat fell onto the cement floor, and with the toe of her shoe she spread it out.

'Go on.'

'What?'

'On the coat.'

I let go. Took a step back. I watched Lula undress in front of me. The wide black pants slid over her hips; she wriggled out of her sweater. She lay down on the coat. I sank to my knees. Pulled down her panties. Unzipped my trousers. It was neither beautiful nor romantic—it was the only thing I could do at that moment. Lula extended her arms like a child and I lay on top of her, inhaled her sweetly satisfying warmth. She looked at me with big, questioning eyes in which all I detected was a brief, burning desire, soft and warm and comforting. I slid into her. She closed her eyes as I slowly fucked her. I didn't hear Pablo come in.

NEW YORK, MAY 2002

Mickey Melendez

'Felipe was the first Young Lord I recruited in New York. It was one night at the Blue Guerrilla, a club on 125th St. He performed there with H. Rap Brown. Poems and politics. He was already a Last Poet. We knew each other from Queens College. So afterwards I go over to him. "Listen, Felipe," I say, "I want to start an organization, like the Black Panthers but for Puerto Ricans. I've got contacts in Chicago. We should talk." Felipe looks taken aback. "But I'm black," he says. I laugh. "Yeah, sure enough, but you're also Puerto Rican, a black Puerto Rican." I guess that got him thinking. Felipe grew up in a black community. In The Last Poets he was the Latino. I saw him perform "Jibaro, My Pretty Nigger". "Father of my yearning for the soil, the land, the earth of my people"— but he hardly had any contact with the Puerto Rican community.

I was born in East Harlem but pretty soon my family moved to the Bronx. My father comes from Puerto Rico. He worked on board a merchant ship. Was almost never home. My mother is Cuban, raised in Tampa, Florida. I went to Puerto Rico only once as a kid. When my mother got her tubes tied. You could only get it done on the island, it was an experiment with birth control. I was four. Airsick on the way there and airsick on the way back. That's what I remember most. The nausea, the vomiting. We were in a storm. It was the only time I saw my Puerto Rican grandmother; she died shortly after that. Puerto Rico meant nothing to me. I used to spend summers with family in Ybor City, Tampa—not on the island. There was one strange aspect about being there. I was about ten, it was '60 or '61. We always had fun outings, but on Thursday we never went anywhere. Not swimming, not to the movies. "How come we're not going out?" I asked my aunt once. "I'm bored." She told me that Thursday was the day that black people could go to the Cascade pool, to the Ritz Theater, and the carnival. Then on Friday there was an hour-long line for the swimming pool. You had to wait, because they first drained it and then refilled it with fresh water for us. I didn't get it at all. I got very dark in the summer. Why could I swim every day except Thursday? Back in New York I played basketball with black and white boys. Only later, when I watched the civil rights marches and riots on TV, did I understand the situation in Florida. I saw the police and the dogs, the demonstrators being dragged over the streets, whites shouting and cursing and spitting at the blacks.

Queens College was the whitest university in New York. I enrolled to avoid having to go to Vietnam. A year later they changed the law and students got drafted anyway. When we met, Felipe was much more politically oriented than me. He organized antiwar assemblies. He was charismatic, likeable: you wanted to be around him. Felipe can roll out of bed in the morning and stand in front of a television camera like there's nothing to it. He was like that back then too. He commanded respect. He had just been released from prison. We became friends instantly, he and Pablo Guzman and me. The three of us would slip into the university library at night, after closing time. We had memorized all kinds of names and dates—especially Pablo, he knew more than we two. 1868, the "Lares Uprising", the first Puerto Rican revolt; 1937, the nationalist march and the Ponce massacre; 1950, the assassination attempt on President Truman. We looked it all up on the library's microfiches. We were self-taught. We read about Dr. Ramón Betances, a doctor who bought and freed slaves in Cabo Rojo. About Don Pedro Albizu Campos, "El Maestro", a mulatto who went to the US and returned to the island ten years later with eight or nine degrees, including a law degree from Harvard. Don Pedro was for Puerto Ricans what Malcolm X was for blacks. It blew our minds. You see? They've been trying to hide this stuff from us all these years.

There's a saying among Puerto Ricans: *Cásate con un blanco para mejorar la raza*—Marry a white to better the race. As though our race wasn't good enough. As a child I only knew we were different because we spoke Spanish at home. My parents were Americans, period. Once I started school, it was like: "You can't speak Spanish here".

At first the Young Lords was a Puerto Rican gang in Chicago. Cha-Cha Jiménez was their leader. Cha-Cha had met Fred Hampton, the chairman of the Illinois chapter of the Black Panther Party, in jail. Fred had a gang history, and later he was murdered by the police. He had a huge influence on Cha-Cha. He taught him that gang rivalry was senseless. That they had to concentrate on real issues: health services, education, that kind of thing. So Cha-Cha turned his gang into a political organization. One day Pablo and Felipe and I are sitting around together and we read in the paper that the Black Panther Party was being integrated into the Rainbow Coalition. It was a sort of declaration. The Panthers had merged with the Young Lords and the American Indian Movement and the Young Patriots, an anti-racist group of poor whites. Their goal was to focus on the masses, get active in the neighborhoods, mobilize everyone, not just students. We read their revolutionary pamphlet in our study group, the Sociedad de Don Pedro Albizu Campos. That same day we jumped into my VW and drove to Chicago to talk to Cha-Cha. It was July 26, 1968. We wanted Cha-Cha's blessing. We wanted to be the Young Lords, the Young Lords in Spanish Harlem. That's how it started.

Felipe became chairman. Pablo was minister of information and I set up the urban guerilla wing. Juan Gonzáles was there too, as minister of education. And David Pérez from Chicago. In August were the first Garbage Offensives. Burning a huge pile of garbage on Third Ave., blocking all six lanes of traffic. We had asked residents about their gripes, expecting to hear housing, health care. But no: garbage. Garbage! "And what about the dictatorship of the proletariat?" *Garbage.* The city didn't dare to act. They were scared after the previous year's riots. But the garbage trucks did come do their rounds more often than before. It stank less.

In December we took over the Spanish Methodist Church on 111th and Lexington. The church was only open one day a week. We wanted to set up a free health clinic and a childcare center. But the pastor was a Cuban refugee. And there's us with our beards and berets. He sees Fidel and Che. About has a heart attack. So there's a service the following Sunday. We go. One by one the congregation takes communion. Felipe gets up. Starts talking about the church, that the church should be there for the people. He only gets a few sentences out, and suddenly there are cops coming out of the woodwork. They jump him. The pastor had brought them in. It was a hell of a brawl. Fourteen arrests, Felipe in the hospital with thirteen stitches and a broken arm.

Two weeks later we went to the church with crowbars and chains and locks and broke the doors down. Eleven days after that we had a free health clinic and offered free breakfast for the poor. Until we were thrown out and a hundred and three people were arrested.

We were a paramilitary organization. At first we only had oriental weapons. Stainless-steel ninja throwing stars. Nunchuks—two wooden sticks connected by a cord—excellent for neutralizing your adversary. We learned self-defense. We occupied Lincoln Hospital on 141st St. & Southern Blvd. With the approval of the doctors and nurses. We set up a drug rehab clinic—at that time, one out of four people in the Bronx was hooked on heroine. We got lots of media coverage, negotiated with the city council. There was so much support. You'd hardly dream of it these days.

Felipe was married to Iris Morales, also a Young Lord. One night he goes out somewhere with Pablo, to give a talk, I think. He doesn't want protection, which was strange because we never went anywhere without it: the police murdered political activists and the Mafia was after our asses. Later it turns out he screwed that girl, Lula. While he was married to Iris. It caused a ruckus in the organization: shouldn't our leaders set an example? Or can we just go fooling around as we liked? Okay, maybe Lula was a cop, or was working with them, there was enough evidence to that effect, but that doesn't change the fact that Felipe cheated on Iris. We stripped him of his leadership; he could have rehabilitated himself but just couldn't hack it. Later he publicly said ugly things about the organization when we occupied the church for the second time.

Julio Rosan, a young Puerto Rican inmate at Rikers Island, had died in custody. Suicide, according to the police. Murder, we said. We organized a funeral in East Harlem. Julio's coffin was crammed full of weapons. Once inside the church, we took out the guns. We held a three-day wake for Julio, our rifles slung over our shoulders. Got our picture on the front page of the *Daily News*. We demanded an inquiry into prison conditions. And got the church back.

Felipe said publicly that we didn't know how to use the weapons, what kind of bullets they needed. I was sore at him for that. Even if it was true, you don't go saying it in public. Those men and women in the church were prepared to go all the way.

I didn't see Felipe for a long time after that.'

NEW YORK, 2002

Exit

Felipe remembered walking home with Pablo. Lula had left on her own. She didn't want him to bring her home.

'Don't say anything to Iris, okay? I'll tell her myself.'

'Uh-huh.'

'And don't go to the Party.'

'But they think we're dead.'

'I don't care. I just need to think. You understand? I don't really get what just happened back there.'

'What are we supposed to say?'

'Nothing, that's what.'

'Nothing?'

'I can trust you, right, Pablo?'

'Sure.'

'She was strange, Pablo. I don't know. You remember that joint I smoked?'

'What joint?'

'Jesus, Pablo.'

'What's with you?'

'Nothing. Lula. She asked me things. About the church. I don't know what I said. Drives me crazy to think about it. What if she's an undercover cop?'

'You fucked a cop? Come on, Felipe. That girlfriend of hers was as naive as all get-out. We've got their money, that's what counts. Go home. Sleep off that joint. See you tomorrow.'

'T'morrow,' he answered in a monotone.

Pablo stuck up his hand. Avoided eye contact and turned. Felipe watched him amble off. The back of his jeans jacket. It was past midnight. No wind, hardly any traffic. Mist hung low over the glistening asphalt and sidewalks. It must have rained.

Even after all those years he thinks he senses a guilty look in Pablo's eyes whenever they happen to meet.

The next day Pablo went to the Central Committee. 'You guys know what the chairman did?' Three months later he bumped into Pablo and Lula at a party. Hand in hand.

Pablo pretended not to see him and turned his back. From across the room, Lula looked straight at him as she talked to Pablo, with the same calm, disillusioned expression as when they made love. As though she touched him with that look, infected him—but with what, he didn't know.

He went to the kitchen. Pulled a knife out of the drawer. It was a reflex; no thought went into it. His thoughts evaporated into a grayish haze, into a dull throbbing in his body. He charged into the living room. No one seemed to notice him; the party noise continued. A few couples were draped listlessly on each other, rocking gently to the sultry music. The small, dark room was thick with smoke. Where were they? Then he heard Pablo's voice. He was sitting in one of the low leather armchairs. Lula sat on the ground next to him, her head on his lap. Pablo was talking to a few young comrades. He couldn't make out the words, but from his misty, watery eyes and animated air it was clear he was talking revolution. The church. He seemed so earnest. Like his expression was a few sizes too big, didn't fit with his patchy beard and innocently boyish face, his unconditional faith in the Party and the future. Even if it meant blackmail. The Party needed money, didn't it? And Janet and Lula had protection. 'You guys know what the chairman did?' He saw Pablo's hand glide over Lula's face, over her short hair. Lula shifted, closed her eyes, pressed her face deeper into his lap. Pablo had no ideas of his own, just did what was expected of him. Felipe felt the knife burn in the palm of his right hand. But no one saw him. He was a spectator. A stranger. The way Iris looked at him when he told her about the bad trip and about Lula, his fear, his desperate urge to jump out the window of that bare, brown factory. 'I don't know what came over me, Iris. I was afraid. Forgive me. Please.' As though Iris looked right through him. Her screams, tears: 'Go away.'

The knife slipped out of his hand and fell noiselessly onto the soft beige rug. He pressed his way between the warm bodies to the front door, inhaled the tepid, damp September air and walked down the street.

'What It Is'

Giving honor to the deeper register of our persons
To the sun inside our bellies
And to the fountain above our heads
Filled and overflowing
With the wellspring of fresh ideas
Just to consider about our words

[...]

To the poetry and to the genius of Amiri Baraka
To a Love Supreme Mister John Coltrane
To James
To the book of James
To James Baldwin
To James Joyce
To James Brown
To James

NEW YORK, FEBRUARY 2002

June Lum

'Sometimes it's like Kain has become invisible. His poetry isn't published here. Amiri Baraka thinks he should come back. The circle's complete. His children wish he were closer. Just as Langston Hughes and Baraka were examples to him, he could be an example to young poets today. But for Kain, going back in time is too painful. He feels safe over in Holland. And I'd prefer him feeling safe there than going crazy over here. He wouldn't have survived it. So much is unresolved. I don't know what all happened back then, Kain kept most of it to himself, he wanted to protect me and the children. And then sometimes he'd drink too much and say things … I've seen Kain and Abiodun scream and argue during rehearsals. About poems, about a word. That was shortly after The Last Poets appeared on *Soul*, a black television show. That was their breakthrough. And after *Soul* was when things started to unravel. Abiodun went off with Umar and Jalal. And when Felipe and David and Kain brought out the album *Right On!* the others went to court, demanding the rights to the name "The Last Poets". That's when it got really unbearable.

I met Kain and Felipe at a girlfriend's party in Brooklyn. It was in the fall of '68, I remember it still being warm out. I was taken with them. Kain told me that he knew Amiri Baraka and that we could go over to his house in Newark.

"Really?" I said. I was a fan of Baraka's. Kain recited a few of his poems. I loved it. I've always been attracted to intelligent men. Kain was a real philosopher. He read Nietzsche, Kierkegaard, Camus. I was twenty-one. Still really young. I had a son from an earlier relationship. We got married pretty soon after we first met.

My father came from China. He was a sailor on a Norwegian cargo ship. One of his brothers lived in Baltimore; my father jumped ship there. They went looking for him, so he fled to New York and settled near Chinatown. My mother was his contact person in case he got caught and needed a lawyer. Her sister was seeing one of his cousins, which is how my parents met. In those days you had miscegenation laws, which actually were meant to block black-white mixed marriages. But all mixed marriages were taboo. My mother was black, a very open woman, from South Carolina. So I grew up with gospel music; with her, everything revolved around the family, hospitality, and food, food, food. I think I would have been a very different person if my mother had been Chinese. I'd have learned the language, the culture. You are what your mother is, in the end. My father knew that to survive in America, you had to assimilate. So we went to the Episcopal church, we spoke English. But personally he was very Chinese, a closed-up man. I only learned about martial arts through Kain, although my father was a master fighter. He was a Maoist. His parents were killed during the Japanese occupation, and he considered Mao the Chinese people's liberator and the one who beat the famine. But he had no empathy for the black civil rights movement. The idea that the FBI would appear on his daughter's doorstep, oh no. Go to prison for your ideals? No, no, no. My mother thought of Kain as an African hippie. She saw herself as 'colored', not black.

We moved into the East Wind. I worked as a secretary at a music company. I was independent, but Kain looked down on me having a job. "What do you mean, you have to go work for a boss?" He felt that if I loved him, I should stand by him. So I quit my job. We hardly had any money. Lived off donations from visitors to the loft. Every night there was something going on. Poetry on Friday, theater on Saturday, political workshops—Felipe did those—conga lessons, family day on Sundays. Kain was the director, and I saw to it that everything ran smoothly, East Wind as well as our family. Actually we lived like Gypsies, moving from apartment to apartment, dragging the kids with us. Whenever we couldn't pay the rent we'd just move. We lived everywhere. In the Bronx, Brooklyn, Harlem. But my heart always belonged to the East Village, where I grew up. The Lower East Side, Chinatown. Delancey St., Avenue A and B. I felt most at home there.

Kain and the other poets talked about a fine black world for their black women. I really thought: my God, these are strong men and we'll make beautiful black babies and we'll help each other and have good black schools ... But most of the women of my generation are single mothers. We had to work hard, but we still studied, had a career, children ... while the men ... I don't understand why so many of our men are so destructive. The '70s and '80s were tough. All those drugs. It took resilience to stay true to your art and yourself. Certainly in those days. The political reaction was so fierce. And still ... if you see how little has changed in the past thirty years, with the prisons still full of black men ... It's become an industry. And the poverty here in New York ... Felipe, now *he* was successful. Because of his charisma. He worked on TV. If it hadn't been for 9/11 he'd be in the city council for sure. Felipe always helped me, and my daughter too.

Kain's mother was wonderful to me and the children. She never tried to foist her religion on us. Even when Kain and I split up, she was supportive. I think she was trying to compensate for what went wrong between Kain and her. And she knew I couldn't count on him for support. I remember once when the kids were at Kain's for the weekend. "Where are their shoes?" I asked when he brought them back. He shrugged. Looked surprised. "Oh … yeah," he said. He just didn't see that kind of thing.'

THE BRONX, 1970

Tell Me, Brother

'Who did this?' I asked.

We were in Kain's apartment. He sat at the end of the sofa. I stood in the doorway and looked at his face, which was as big as a watermelon. His left eye was swollen shut and dried blood stuck to his chin. He smiled. Winced and brought his hands to his face. It was like he had little pillows of wetness on his purple skin.

'It's okay,' Kain said.

'It's not okay. Who did this?'

'This isn't why I asked you to come, Felipe.'

'Then why?'

'Have a seat.'

I went into the small living room and closed the door behind me. Looked around to see if June was there. She'd tell me what happened. Kain and I fell in love with her at the same time, but she picked Kain.

'She's gone to get the kids,' he said, as though he read my mind. 'She doesn't know anything.'

'My God.'

Kain groaned as he got up from the sofa.

'What can I get you? Stay there.'

'Water.'

I went to the narrow kitchen and got a glass from the cupboard. Turned on the faucet and held the glass under it. I let the ice-cold water run over my hand until my fingers tingled.

'When did this happen?' I asked when I returned to the living room. I gave him the glass; he took it but did not drink.

'Day before yesterday.'

'And I only hear about it now?'

'It's for you own good, Felipe.'

'Fuck off, Kain.'

'I'm sorry.'

'*You're* sorry? Tell me who did this and I'll make sure they get fucked up good. Even if I have to do it myself. Tell me it wasn't the police.'

Kain laughed. A growling, cynical laugh.

'I shouldn't have gone,' he stammered. 'It's my own fault ... I ... '

'What?'

'Nothing. I'm so sorry, Felipe. It's too late ... Too late. Leave them.'

'Them?'

'I'm glad you're with the Lords. You do good work, y'know ... for your own people. That's better ... we ... the Poets ... '

'What are you talking about?'

'Don't give up.'

'Who's talking about giving up? What happened?'

Kain closed his eyes. His arms went limp, a few fat drops of water splashed onto the bare linoleum. He slipped into a daze of pain and fatigue. I wanted to go over and shake him. I couldn't stand seeing him like that, sitting there locked up in his own violent secret. It was almost like looking at a stranger.

'Why'd you ask me to come? Why? I love you. You can't do this to me, Kain.'

His good eye opened. Slowly. He reminded me of a walrus, or a hippo, or a huge, sluggish, prehistoric animal that has all the time in the world and conceals a wealth of wisdom under his thick, rubbery skin. I caught his eye. For a moment I thought I saw pity in his right eye, pity for me, which made me feel even more fraught than I already was.

'I love you too, Felipe,' he said weakly. 'I can't say anything. I'm sorry.'

And then Kain fell fast asleep. I could hear it from his heavy, regular breathing. I took the thick woolen blanket from the sofa and draped it over him, and carefully removed the water glass from his hand, brought it back to the kitchen. I didn't really know what to do. I was ashamed of my anger. I appreciated that it was for my own good that Kain kept what had happened to himself. But why'd he call me here then? 'Don't give up.' It gave me a vague, nasty feeling. I remembered when I was very young and heard my parents talking in the next room. I heard exactly what they were saying but it was like they were speaking a foreign language. Even the most everyday words like *sock* or *street* or *butter* or *flour* suddenly sounded mysterious and exotic, as though they meant something totally different to what I had previously thought.

I waited a little while for June and the children, but when after an hour they still hadn't arrived, I crept out of the apartment.

NEW YORK, NEW YORK

'Sacred to the Pain'

Temporary pleasure becomes permanent emotions
That separate ...
Leaving me in so many many places

HARLEM, 1970

Niggers Are Scared of Revolution

'You going out tonight?' Cookie asked. She lay on the narrow double bed in the corner of the small room, her head leaning lazily on her arms.

Omar stood at the mirror putting on a fresh shirt.

'You going out?' she repeated.

He saw her in the mirror. Her round face, her small, sturdy body hidden under the thin sheet. She smiled. Cookie's eternal smile, even when she was tired or angry. Sometimes this irritated him. Like she was laughing at him. He took a bottle of Arabic sandalwood oil from the dressing table, sprinkled a few drops into the palm of his hand, and rubbed the oil onto his face. The bitter-sweet scent wafted through the room.

'C'mere?' Cookie said.

Omar turned around, banged into the only chair in the room. 'Damn,' he hissed.

'What's going on, Omar?'

'Nothing.'

'Do you have a gig?'

'No.'

'What, then?'

Omar sagged into the uncomfortable, high-backed chair. 'It's so cramped here.'

'I thought you liked it that way. It's big enough, isn't it? You want me to go with you? We haven't eaten yet. We could go to Sylvia's.'

'I'm not going out.'

'But I thought ... '

'I have to think.'

'About what?'

'I'm not hungry. You go ahead.' He fished around in the pocket of the leather jacket draped over the chair, found the butt of a crumpled joint, smoothed it out, and lit it. He took a long drag, held the smoke in his lungs as long as he could and exhaled a blue-gray cloud into the room.

Cookie coughed demonstratively. She didn't like it when he smoked. Marijuana was strictly forbidden in the Alamac Hotel. If they were caught they'd be kicked out. And Omar changed when he smoked pot. Like the blue haze was a kind of shield. But she kept her worries to herself.

'Go on now,' Omar said.

'I'm not going anywhere. There's still a sandwich in the icebox. I'm tired.' She rolled over, the sheet slid from her hip. She was wearing only a T-shirt and panties. She closed her eyes.

Omar looked at her bronze thighs. Soft as satin. The thought crossed his mind that he could snuggle up to her. Even from a distance he could feel her warmth, taste her scent. She smelled of powder and perfume and how he imagined a baby smelled. Sweet, like honey. She would wrap her legs around him and let him melt into her body. Whisper loving words in his ear. Cookie took care of him. He could forget everything. He was safe with her. But he stayed seated, taking hard drags on the joint, pinching it between his thumb and index finger. He felt the hot glow on his fingertips.

Their silence buzzed in Omar's head. He heard the gentle hum of the fan. The water that flowed invisibly through the pipes in the wall, like a gurgling brook. Muffled voices in the hall. He tossed the remains of the joint into the sink. Breathed deeply. His nerve endings felt warmed up. He relaxed. Looked at the old-fashioned brass lamp on the nightstand, the green glass lampshade that cast a misty light and made the room look smaller than it was. The dusty venetian blinds. Was it already dark outside? He didn't hear the city. Only the occasional yelp of a distant siren. From this dim, stuffy room he had shared with Cookie for the past couple of months, New York sometimes felt like a fantasy. Like he'd never arrived. And when he had to go out for an appointment, to a rehearsal with the poets at the East Wind, or a gig, or just to take his pants to the dry cleaners across the street, it was like he faced a monumental hurdle. As though once he left the security of the cramped room and the familiarity of Cookie's love and her body, he wouldn't be able to return.

Her recalled the morning he arrived at Port Authority. It seemed like eons ago, a previous life, but it had been hardly a year. It was before noon, but 42nd St. was as dark as nighttime. The glitter of neon lights that screamed and beckoned in a whole spectrum of colors made him think he was on Broadway. He walked past the clubs whose glass-enclosed poster cases burst with beautiful blonde women in bikinis or just skimpy panties that let their black pubic hair show through. Bouncers in faux-fancy suits guarded the entrance to the peepshows. The overwhelming thud and rattle of traffic. He almost didn't dare look up at the glistening towers, the gray and red brick buildings with their countless windows that made him think of eyes. It was February and freezing, but the lights and the stores and the cars gave off so much warmth that he unzipped his jacket and took off his wool cap. It was as though New York had no sky, just a glass roof.

He might have walked for hours. He stopped at every marquee, every seedy movie house. He didn't talk to anyone; there was no one to talk to. People dashed past him like hunted animals. He couldn't make out faces, not at first. In their haste they were impossible to tell apart. His pace slowed so that he could soak up the onslaught of impressions without tripping or losing his way. His mind was blank; he just walked. The wind cut into his face. The air smelled different than in Akron: it was thinner, deoxygenated. The longer he walked, the better he felt. He forgot he had no money on him; he had used his last quarter to buy a Mars bar at a Greyhound station on the way. He forgot he had nowhere to sleep. All he had was the crumpled scrap of paper with the address of The Last Poets that Abiodun Oyewole had written down all those months ago. He forgot everything, including himself. Even his hunger pangs evaporated in all the hubbub.

'Hey, you.'

Omar started. It seemed impossible that a human voice could break free of the monotonous background rumble and call out to him. Omar turned and looked. A stout black man in a green army coat was leaning against a lamppost. His dreads were tucked into a colorful knitted cap. 'Psst, how about a little wager?'

'Whaddya got?' He tried to sound as nonchalant as possible.

'Try your luck, man, what have you got to lose? You're new here, aren't you?' He held out a red handkerchief.

'What's the deal?'

'Just a little game.'

'What kind of game?'

'You'll see.' The man looked nervously to both sides. 'For a dollar you can guess how much money's in this handkerchief. Guess right and it's yours.' Omar was pretty surprised: this Rasta brother obviously thought every backwoods nigger was a sucker who'd let himself be robbed blind. Well, he had nothing to steal, but this dude with the weird hat didn't know that. The guy thought he was so slick.

'Hold it,' the man said.

Omar took the handkerchief. The Jamaican bent over to pull something out of his sock.

Omar ran so fast he couldn't even feel his legs. Behind him he heard, 'Grab that sonofabitch! Stop him!' But he was too fast. Without bumping into a single pedestrian, he tore down 42nd St., crossed a wide, busy avenue, zig-zagged between taxis and cars, back onto the sidewalk, heard sirens and car horns but didn't look back, just kept on running, another street the same as the last, like he was flying over the traffic, wasn't even out of breath. He ran until he reached a small park, crouched behind some bushes and opened the handkerchief. There was a hundred-dollar bill in it. Omar waited a moment. He could hear the Jamaican's deep, coarse voice across the park. 'He's gotta be here. I saw him. He robbed me.' Omar peered out from behind the bare branches, made himself as small as possible. Good thing he was wearing dark clothes. The Rasta guy had brought a policeman with him, but the white officer just shrugged. 'You've lost him, pal,' he said indifferently. 'No!' the Jamaican screamed, now turning his anger against the policeman. Omar rolled himself up even smaller, like when he was eleven and hid under the bridge from his father: 'It's *my* money! I earned it myself!' Papa's quick, agitated footsteps. His muffled voice. 'Where are you, Jerome? I'll find you, you little beggar.' The pounding of his heart. He wasn't afraid. He just had to give his father the slip. The only thing that worried him was that someone might see Papa teetering down the street and hear his helpless cries.

Omar watched as the Jamaican and the police officer left the park. He got up, dusted himself off, and emerged from behind the bushes. He took the exit at the opposite end of the park and ducked into the nearest subway station. Jumped over the stainless steel turnstile—he couldn't buy a token with a hundred-dollar bill, could he—and felt the earth quake and tremble under his feet. The heat hit him in the face. With a squeal the train rumbled into the station. The number 2 train. 'Does this go to Harlem?' he asked a black girl of about twelve. She had a bright pink ribbon in her hair and an open, childlike face. She nodded as she took a few steps away from him. What did she see? He didn't have time to think about it, the doors opened and disgorged passengers onto him. He wriggled into the subway car, flopped onto a seat next to an older black lady with a large shopping bag. He couldn't see what was in it. He closed his eyes as the train jerked into motion. The car was crowded but no one spoke; he heard only the subway's heavy metallic grumble. It was warm. Omar leaned back, bobbed along gently with the monotonous vibration of the train. He felt a satisfying calmness wash over him. Took in the stale, stuffy air. Savored every moment of it.

'Why don't you come lie down for a bit?' Cookie asked. She lay motionless with her back to him. 'What's wrong?'

'Nothing.'

'Really?'

He got off at 125th St. and allowed himself to be carried by the crowd, the passengers hurrying to alight and apparently knowing exactly where they were going. No trace of hesitation on their faces. And not a single white one among them. He climbed the cement stairs, held the steel handrail tight. His body shuddered hitting the cold air on street level, but also, he figured, because he was exhausted. He wasn't sure which way to go, but still felt certain he would eventually find The Last Poets' loft. Between Madison and Fifth, Abiodun had said. Near the Apollo Theater. Apollo Theater. Apollo Theater. Being close to the place where James Brown had caused such a furor spurred him on. He emerged onto a wide sidewalk alongside an even wider avenue. Suddenly there was air and space again, no skyscrapers pressing down on him. Only simple brick and concrete apartment blocks and stores, no higher than four or five stories. A pale sun shone through the wispy clouds. He squinted at the light that reflected off the concrete sidewalk. Like it had snowed. He stopped. Leaned against a fence. He shoved his hands into his pockets, blew a white cloud into the freezing air. Pedestrians passed him left and right, but it was a while before he really took in his new surroundings. The slowly passing cars, as if they had all the time in the world. The brightly lit supermarket across the street next door to a boarded-up church. The street was something of a marketplace: sidewalk vendors had spread out their wares, radios, cassettes, shoelaces, gold-colored chains, charcoal portraits of Malcolm and Dr. King and Eldridge Cleaver and Angela Davis. Panther pamphlets. He had never seen so many black people in one place before. He saw women with vibrant head scarves, whining kids tugging at their arm; men in suede jackets, men in white robes, in army fatigues—

some of them wearing sunglasses even though it was the middle of winter—and girls with cropped hair and huge earrings. He searched in vain to find something recognizable in their faces. Nobody seemed to notice him. He felt invisible. He listened to the gentle rhythm of the voices, the traffic in the background. The music coming from the improvised sound system of one of the street vendors: lazy jazz, a saxophone or a trumpet. Everything was new and strange, but at the same time the sounds and the music were like echoes, memories. As if Howard St. was just around the corner, Roxy's a bar on 125th St. Eunice tending the bar at the Hi-Hat, her disarming laugh. Charlie Brown, downing one whisky after the other, groping the ass of one of his women. He thought back on that time he and a few other shoeshine boys beat the crap out of a white guy. He was about ten. The guy was on the prowl for a black hooker. They lured him into an alley behind Howard St. and lit into him with their shoeshine kits. And him yelling all the while, 'Keep going, keep going.' It made Omar sick to his stomach. He didn't even steal the guy's money. He thought of Ahmed Evans and Reggie and the cell at the Akron police station, the red-brown scabs on Louis's head. The images were no more than passing flashes, like he was sitting on a merry-go-round.

He ambled on, his hands deep in his pockets. The hundred-dollar bill crackled in his fingers. The bold and indifferent and timid and warm and proud and violent expressions on all the strange new faces nestled into his consciousness, getting reflected back as the looks and characteristics of friends, family, acquaintances in Akron. Slowly, he was finally swooping down upon the place he had so often dreamed of back home, that he'd seen on TV. And as he walked, a deep and powerful feeling grew in him, the realization that no one knew where he was, that no one here knew him, that he was alone, as alone as a person could possibly be. He recalled the time one winter when he stood on the Spring St. bridge wearing only jeans and a sweater. He was eight or nine. It was cold. He just stood there in the freezing rain. Let the ice batter his cheeks, the wind blow through the thin cotton of his sweater. He stood there until he no longer felt the cold, until his cheeks were on fire and his fingers and toes burned and tingled and ached. It was a pain he welcomed and which strengthened him. He felt the hot tears stream down his face. He didn't care. No one saw him. The freezing cold was like a blanket. An invisible hand protected him. He closed his eyes and felt the wind lift him up and carry him away.

And he never again felt the cold when he roamed from bar to bar at night, lugging his box of brushes and rags and shoe polish. Never again.

Now, as he wandered down the wide, white street in Harlem, occasionally bumping into an unfamiliar shoulder or arm and walking on without apologizing, having someone grumble 'watch where you're going', now that he felt the warmth of all those anonymous people on the go, tasted their exotic odor and breath on his chapped lips, the promise of it all, he was overcome by the same liberating and dangerous sensation as on that bridge. As though he had already lived up to his dreams. He could do whatever he felt like, and more. Go as far as he wanted. Nothing and nobody could hold him back. He wasn't afraid of anything. There was nothing to be afraid of.

He walked on without feeling the concrete under his feet.

The sudden awareness of his own freedom was so absolute and so much bigger than himself that Omar almost forgot where he was. He couldn't remember how he got to the East Wind loft. He only knew that Abiodun was there, and Nilija, the drummer, and that Dun told him Kain and Felipe Luciano and David Nelson had quit the group and that he and Nilija rehearsed there a few times a week. It only half sunk in. Dun had taken him to an apartment on Riverside Drive where he lived with his girlfriend, gave him fried chicken and rice and beans. He lent Omar twenty dollars and fixed him up with a room at the Alamac Hotel on 71st and Broadway.

In the days that followed, Omar felt anxious, agitated. He slept badly, never more than an hour or two at a time, and only left his room to buy a sandwich or beer or some candy.

One evening Dun invited him to a performance at Columbia University. He could recite a few of his poems if he wanted, and the audience would decide whether he could become a Last Poet. He had his old notebook with him, the one he had started writing in back when he shared a room with Chris and Billy, the notebook that smelled like home, like dampness and sand and coal and Mama and greasy fried fish. He went up on stage and started chanting: 'Huey was a bad muthafucka ... Malcolm was a royal muthafucka ... ' The audience laughed and whooped. He just kept going. Let his voice ride the waves of his aggressive words. The sound of his own voice excited him, which made it go even more high-pitched and lyrical. It wasn't a real poem. Nilija improvised like they had been playing together for years. And when Dun asked the audience whether this brother from Ohio could call himself a Last Poet they unanimously yelled, 'Yeah!'

That's how it went. But it was only a few months later, on a warm spring day in Mount Morris Park when Abiodun asked him what he had learned since arriving in Harlem, and Omar spontaneously said 'Niggers are scared of revolution', only then did he truly realize that he was a poet.

'Write it down,' Dun said. 'Go home and work it out. It's good, man, it's a poem.'

He had no trouble finding the words. He wrote in pencil; his hand could hardly keep pace with his thoughts. Breathless. *Niggers are scared of revolution / But niggers shouldn't be scared of revolution / Because revolution is nothing but change / And all niggers do is change. Niggers come in from work and change into pimping clothes / And hit the streets to make some quick change. Niggers change their hair from black to red to blond / And hope like hell their looks will change. Niggers kill other niggers / Just because one didn't receive the correct change ... change ... change ... change ...* He paused for a moment. His neck and back were sore from sitting hunched over on his bed. It was like writing down memories but seeing only colors. A flickering red neon sign on Euclid Ave. A glimpse of Charlie Brown's white Pontiac. The soft gray-green dawn light beyond the hill behind Roxy's. The white of the lilies in the neighbor's yard on Chestnut Street. Gray images on the TV in the back room. *Niggers are lovers / Niggers love to see Clark Gable make love to Marilyn Monroe / Niggers love to see Tarzan fuck all the natives.* Every sentence was a color behind which lay a story, a story only he knew. But if you listened carefully, Omar was convinced, you could hear the story. He felt himself pressing his energy into the words. *Niggers talk about the mind / Talk about: My mind is stronger than yours / 'I got that bitch's mind uptight!'* As if he were lecturing himself, hearing Ahmed Evans preaching in

Cleveland. 'You're nothin' but a big stupid muthafuckin' nigger. You could be doing things for your own people.' Now his words and phrases banished his pain and disillusionment. Left a total absence of fear. *But I'm a lover too … / I love niggers … / Because niggers are me / And I should only love that which is me …*

'Omar?'

He heard Cookie's sleep-rasped voice but did not answer. His poem was still resounding in his head. The music came automatically when he read it to Dun and Nilija the next day. The tight rhythms. As if the words dictated how Nilija should play. He knew that wasn't entirely true, but he was euphoric anyway. Almost as euphoric as on that first day in Harlem. Only it no longer bowled him over—just the opposite, in fact. His words gave meaning to all those loose memories and images stored up in his body. Calmed him down.

'Omar?'

He wished Cookie would just keep quiet. He needed to be alone. But he couldn't bring himself to get up and go outside.

'Is it true what I heard?'

'Is what true?'

'About the bickering over at the East Wind. Everybody's talking about it.'

'What do you mean, everybody?'

'I'm not making this up.'

'Who says you are?'

She sat facing him and pulled her knees up. 'What does Abiodun think?'

'Dun's in North Carolina.'

'He is?'

'I told you.'

'Did not.'

'Look, let's just not talk about it.'

'So who's fixing the gigs now?'

'I don't want to talk about it!'

'What about that record? When's it coming out? It is coming out?' Cookie leaned forward and opened the door to the small icebox near the foot of the bed. She felt around for the leftover tuna fish sandwich, peeled off the plastic wrap, and took a bite. She made a face and tossed the sandwich at the wastebasket under the sink, and she missed.

Omar pretended not to notice.

Cookie got out of bed and stretched. 'C'mon, let's go out.' She squatted, laid her hands on his lap. 'I don't want you to be like this, Omar.' She cocked her head. He could see the sleep in her eyes, the thin lines on her forehead, the enlarged pores around her nose. She worked too hard. She ran the Harlem Teams for Self-Help. Dun had introduced them. Cookie was a serious woman. She was saving up so she could study. She said she didn't have time for boyfriends. But Omar persisted, waited for her after work, until she gave in and went out with him.

Cookie let her shoulders droop and rested her head on his lap. 'What am I gonna do with you?'

He felt the warmth of her breath through his cotton trousers. He dug his hand through her thick black hair.

'Do you love me?' she asked.

'Why d'you ask that?'

She pulled away from him, got up, and walked over to the sink. She took off her T-shirt and splashed water on her face and neck. He looked at her back. The taut skin, the vertebrae underneath. He enjoyed running his fingers over the bones while they made love, silently counting them. Cookie would giggle like a girl. And then he would continue, letting his fingers travel slowly downward, pressing them between her buttocks. He'd feel her body tense, her breathing falter, as he gently pressed against her narrow hole. 'Don't,' she would sigh and he would reassure her, kiss her neck, and continue pushing his fingers slowly into her; she would giggle again and moan, and he wanted to tell her not to be nervous, that he'd be careful and make her hole wet first. He wanted to whisper that he loved her, but didn't, afraid it would break the spell.

'Sometimes I think I should leave,' she said.

'What d'you mean?'

She pulled on her jeans and took a clean t-shirt out of the suitcase that lay on the floor under the sink.

Omar followed her every move, but he had a hard time concentrating; his thoughts kept going off on their own.

'Where were you last night?'

'I told you. I had a gig.'

'Um-hm.' She brushed her hair. Examined herself in the mirror.

Omar heard the crinkle of her thick hair. He loved those familiar little sounds. His gaze traveled over the cracked red-brown linoleum and the blotchy yellowed walls, to the narrow hotel bed, whose mattress was too squishy and lumpy and reminded him of all its previous users. Even the air smelled temporary, despite Cookie's incense, the oils from the flasks, the sleep and the sex. That was why he liked this room so much. The stuffy warmth, the monotonous hum of the ceiling fan. That was why he kept coming back.

'I called my mother last night,' Cookie said. She sat down on the foot of the bed and rested the hairbrush in her lap.

'What'd she say?'

'The usual: her rheumatism's acting up and she's worried about my brother. Hasn't heard from him in months. He said he was going to California to look for work and then the radar went blank. What am I supposed to do?'

'He's just lying on the beach with some babe.'

'You know that's not true, Omar.'

'Well, what am I supposed to say?'

'I dunno.'

'You shouldn't worry so much. C'mere.'

She got up and shuffled apathetically over to him. He pulled her onto his lap. She laughed, but behind that cramped smile he could see her anxiety.

'Let's make a baby then. A little Omar. How about it?' He put his hand on her belly.

'And then?'

'And then we'll have a child together.'

'You're talking shit. Where were you last night?'

'Are you gonna keep interrogating me? I don't want to talk about it.'

'You don't want to talk about it. Just like those arguments with the Poets.' She jerked away from him, stood up. 'What do you want from me, Omar? What do you want from me?'

'Nothin'.'

'Nothin'?'

'I just want us to be happy here,' he said, and he meant it. It was so simple, why couldn't she see that? Why did he have to prove he loved her? He always came back to her, didn't he? Last night he'd tiptoed in. He didn't want to wake her. She lay on her back, her arms spread, taking up the whole bed. He looked at her beautiful slumbering face for a while. He washed and climbed in bed next to her. She turned in her sleep, face to the wall. He wrapped his arm around her waist, pressed his cheek against her warm back. He heard her heartbeat, and fell asleep almost at once. He didn't give that chick in the park another thought. A college student, he'd already forgotten her name. She had gone with him after the gig. They wandered down Lenox Ave., bought a bottle of bourbon in a deli, and went into the park. It was unseasonably warm for January. Almost spring. The air was warmish and humid. She rattled on about his poems and the Panthers and the occupation of the area behind 125th St., where the city wanted to tear down the apartment houses and playgrounds so they could build an office building. He let her words glide off him. She had taken off her beige Afghan leather coat and draped it over her shoulders. He could tell she was sexy. She had long, tight legs; the bright-red scarf over her afro accentuated her fine, innocent features. They got drunk in the park and then she took off her clothes. She wasn't ashamed of anything. He sat on a wooden bench and she climbed on top of him. Whispered in his ear that he had to recite a poem while they fucked, that it wound her up. He just kept quiet. Took a swig of bourbon. And still she rode him like her life depended on it.

Even now, now that Cookie stood facing him, glaring fiercely, desperately at him, even now he had trouble feeling the least bit guilty about fooling around. He looked at her well-toned body. He loved her, what else did she want from him, for God's sake? And as painful as it was to see her standing there like that, he was at a loss for words. He had never promised her anything.

'You want us to be happy,' she said.

'We *are* happy, Cookie.'

She laughed and plopped down on the bed. 'Look at me.'

'I'm looking at you.'

'No, really look at me.'

He smiled, felt himself blush.

'You know what it is with you, Omar?' she said. 'I can tell you love me, and you know I love you, but it's not enough. The things you do make me sad. Don't you understand? I'm not saying you don't give me anything, but I can't hold on to your love ... I don't know how to say it. I only feel safe with you when we make love. Only then, Omar. God ... Sometimes it's like afterward you take your love away with you, like I don't deserve it. Do you get what I'm saying?'

Cookie's stream of words came across as some kind of foreign language. Omar's mind wandered as she searched, hesitantly and with furrowed forehead, for the right expression. He thought of the meeting he had tonight with Gylan Kain at the East Wind. Ever since Dun had left for North Carolina to devote himself to the Yoruba religion, he and Alafia were in charge of the recordings. Kain didn't want Dun, Alafia, Nilija, and him calling themselves The Last Poets. Kain acted like the name belonged to him. But shit, he was the one who split. Alafia Pudim had only been a recent addition to the group, but he was a fantastic poet, a street cat from Brooklyn with a tongue sharper than a razor blade. And what he could do with rhyme! Omar wasn't sure if he liked him or not. He had a big mouth and tried to lord it over Omar because he was older. But Alafia had also shown him Brooklyn, introduced him to shady club managers and bigwigs from the 'hood. They had a lot in common. Spoke the same language. Now they called themselves 'The People's Poets'—but who'd ever heard of The People's Poets? They were short of gigs.

'Did you hear what I said?' Cookie asked.

'I heard you,' he said, under control.

'And?'

'And what?'

'What am I supposed to do?'

'Nothing.'

'Nothing? Come on, Omar.'

'What do you want me to say?'

'It's not about what you should *say*.'

He saw the tears well up in her eyes but still did not reply. It was always like Cookie was a step ahead of him. As though she wanted to grab something from him. His thoughts. He felt the words get stuck in his throat. Suddenly he was back in Grandma Rose's cramped living room. They were all there: Billy and Chris and Sandra and Suzy and Georgie and Mama and Grandma. He heard Sandra's raucous laugh. 'You want to be a poet? You won't be nothin'.' He laughed along with them. Sandra didn't know yet that he'd hocked her record player to buy a bus ticket. He loved Sandra. He knew she'd forgive him. She understood him. Goddamn it, Cookie, why are you doing this to me? I want things to stay just like they are. Us, you and me, here in this shabby little room. I want us to breathe the same rancid air. Always. The window closed. The blinds drawn. The table lamp on. The warm yellow light on your skin. Your skin is golden here. Your calm, steady breathing. Come on, Cookie, please. We'll go out tomorrow. I promise. His head was spinning, his limbs felt heavy. He was thirsty. He looked at his watch: quarter after seven.

'I'm going out soon,' he said.

'You're going out.'

'I'll wake you when I get back, okay?'

She shook her head absently, as though she didn't hear him. She bit her bottom lip. 'I only want to help you, Omar,' she said meekly.

'I know, doll.' He tried to conceal his impatience. He

was supposed to be at East Wind at eight.

'It hurts. What you do.'

'Have you seen my wallet?' He got up. Rubbed his stomach. Went to the icebox, removed a half-full bottle of orange juice, and took a swig.

Cookie threw her hairbrush on the floor. It slid across the hard, bare linoleum, banged against the baseboard. Omar bent over and picked it up.

'Here,' he said, handing it back to her. He ran his hand over her cheek. She let him. He got his coat out of the closet and put it on.

'Where're you going?'

'East Wind. Kain's coming around.'

'To do what?'

'Talk.'

'Talk?'

Omar tried to ignore the sarcasm in her voice, but his irritation grew. Was she still not satisfied? What did she mean? He thought of Kain. That asshole thought he was the only real Last Poet. He'd seen him perform a few times. He admired Kain; Kain had been an inspiration for him, and he was willing to tell him so. Tell him how 'Untogether People' had stuck in his head for days. The poem had excited and provoked him—the urgent, driving rhythm of the words had throbbed through his body. But no way was he going to let some arrogant black muthafucka who'd rather die than work with a white producer rob him of his future. As though they'd sold their souls to the devil by signing up with Alan Douglas. It was purely business. And damn it, Douglas had made Jimi big. Jimi Hendrix! Who the hell did Kain think he was, with that two-bit off-Broadway shtick of his with Felipe and David? He'd taken a wrong turn, only didn't know it yet.

'Your wallet's in the shower,' Cookie said. 'I hope it's still dry.'

'Shit.' He opened the door to the shower stall and saw his wallet lying on the tile floor, next to a crumpled hotel towel. He picked it up and stuffed it into his back pocket.

'Watch some TV,' he said, just to say something. He had to get going. He broke into a sweat; the cramped, stuffy room was starting to get on his nerves. He could barely move. 'See ya later,' he said hastily as he opened the door and inhaled the musty corridor air.

'Be careful!' Cookie called. 'You know how Alafia is.' The sincere concern in her voice made him more uptight and pissed off than he already was. He hurried to the elevator, saw it was in use, and headed for the stairwell, charging down all eight flights. He ran so fast that he hardly felt the stone steps under his feet. He thought only of falling.

PARIS, SEPTEMBER 2002

Alan Douglas

'My wife saw them on TV. She was in the bedroom, sitting on the edge of the bed, and her mouth fell open. I walked in.

"What's up?" I asked.

"Check this out. It's wild. I can't believe they're saying this stuff. Just listen."

I saw four black men performing in a courtyard somewhere in Harlem. *Niggers shoot dope into their arm / Niggers shoot guns and rifles on New Year's Eve / A new year that is coming in / The white police will do more shooting at them / Where are niggers when the revolution needs some shots!? Yeah, you know. Niggers are somewhere shootin' the shit.*

The next day I called the TV station and asked for their phone number. At that time I had my own label, Douglas Records. I had worked with Charles Mingus, with Duke Ellington, Max Roach, Eric Dolphy. I was a fan more than anything. So I called the East Wind. Got Jalal on the line. He was still Alafia Pudim back then, before he converted to Islam. He knew I was white. Right away lot of hateful bullshit. But I was used to it. I knew the game. Jalal said, "If you want to see us, be at 137th and Lenox in an hour." So I drove straight to Harlem. I had a silver Jaguar. So I show up at this basketball court. The Poets were surrounded by a group of about fifteen black men, who moved aside when I approached. Jalal was the spokesman. He had the biggest mouth. Lots of bitchin' and bellyachin'. They recited their poems.

"You guys want to cut a record?" I asked.

"Now?" Jalal replied.

"Now." They piled into my car and we drove to a studio owned by a friend of mine, somewhere on West 60th. We recorded that album in a single afternoon. I hardly had to do anything except explain how to use the microphone. That if they rapped they had to keep their mouth up close to it, and for quieter sections pull back a bit ... They'd never been inside a studio before. Their call-and-response technique was an art in itself. The background singing too. The sound was so full. And Nilija's beats ...

I knew about the infighting. Didn't get involved. I can vaguely remember something about a lawsuit. Kain and Felipe and David Nelson wanted to cut an album at the same time, and they couldn't agree on who could use the name "The Last Poets." I didn't care one way or the other. Wasn't my problem. I had a product to sell. I saw to it that they got themselves a manager, an impresario. They earned a lot of money on that album, it sold half a million copies. They toured all over the country. Dun was in jail by then, I never really understood why. It was a real pity. For the second album I had to add a lot more studio sounds, echoes and such, and had to bring in other musicians. It missed the richness of *This Is Madness*. Without Abiodun their passion seemed to fade.

Jalal, though—I could have made him famous. He was more polished than Omar and Dun. Had his sights set higher too. He was a real rapper. Wrote brilliant "jail toasts" like "Hustler's Convention," a classic. *I was snortin' skag while other kids played tag and my elders went to church to pray ... I was a down stud's dream, a hustler supreme, there wasn't no game that I couldn't play. If I caught a dude cheatin', I would give him a beatin' and I might even blow him away.* It's a long, rhyming epic story about a hustler, Sport, who gets out of jail and goes with his pal Spoon to a convention of big-time hustlers to gamble and party and drink with the girls. They fight, guns get drawn, and Spoon ends up half-dead in Sing Sing and repents. Music by Kool and the Gang in the background.

He came by once while I was making recordings with Jimi. Buddy Miles was there too. Jalal started rapping. Jimi heard him and got his guitar, and it became the number "Doriella du Fontaine". That's how easy it was. But Jalal's problem was, he mistrusted everybody. He was torn between his ambition and the loyalty and responsibility he felt for his own people. We got along all right. He used to drop by my place, brought his wife—he had a pretty, young wife—but I was always aware of his antipathy just under the surface.'

'Malcolm'

Where is the pain? I love you brother. Self-hatred wrapped
up in a twisted, demented but well-controlled smile. Where
is the pain?
I love you brother.

HARLEM, 1970

The Hammer

'Muthafucka's late,' Alafia Pudim said.

Omar was still out of breath. He sought Alafia's narrow eyes through his wild afro, through the reflection in his glasses. His colorful dashiki hung on his lanky body. He looked boyish, almost breakable, in the bare light. His appearance did not tally with his nervous, guarded expression.

'Where's Nilija?' Omar asked.

'What's he got to do with it?'

'I thought maybe ... '

'Kain's late, damn it,' Alafia repeated, more to himself than to Omar.

'You got anything to smoke?' Omar asked.

'Not now, man. Are you crazy?' Alafia sat down on the small stage at the rear of the loft. 'I don't want any surprises. Have some coffee.'

'I don't drink coffee,' Omar replied.

'Beer, then.'

'Beer.'

'Quit your bitchin', Omar. Where's Kain?'

'He'll be here,' Omar reassured him, 'just try and relax.' An aura of electricity surrounded Alafia. A thick yellow haze, as though he himself was luminous. In a way it calmed Omar down. He was glad to be out of the hotel. He had taken the subway and got out one stop early on purpose. He needed to run. If he ran fast and far enough, his thoughts would dissipate all on their own. He only heard the rhythm of his footsteps; loose words bounced around in his head like fragments of an unwritten poem. *Voice. Rustling. Wind.* He felt his shirt stick to his back. He went to the kitchenette and opened the refrigerator. No beer, only a few bottles of water. He flicked the door shut and wiped the sweat from his forehead with his sleeve.

'Where'd you disappear to last night?' Alafia asked.

Omar laughed, wetted his lips.

'Never mind.'

'Jealous?'

Alafia ignored the comment. 'It was a good show,' he mused. 'Kain should've seen us. I can just picture that arrogant face of his. By the way, I wrote some new stuff yesterday. I was thinking ... I'd like to use more jazz, y'know, a sax, maybe a soprano or an alto ... I dunno, but when I hear Miles ... '

'Use the music in your words.'

'Don't I already?'

'Everybody loves Nilija. Be glad we've got him.'

'Um-hm.'

Omar opened the fridge again and took out of a bottle of water, drank half of it. He felt warm and lethargic. He sank into a chair. 'Do you ever pray?'

'Huh?'

'I was just thinking ... I've been reading Malcolm. Jesus, man ... '

'How far have you got?'

'He's in jail and his brother keeps visiting him. His whole family's with the Nation of Islam ... and ... '

'Fuck the Nation.'

'I don't mean that. I was only thinking ... I never pray.

But the way he describes it ... you know what I mean. It gives him peace, strength.'

'Peace? You?'

Omar felt trapped now. He didn't even know why he'd brought it up. Maybe it came from the running; he could still feel the cool January air on his face. On Lenox Ave. he had passed the flicker of neon-lighted bars. Two high-strung young guys in army coats were leaning against a shop window, behind them shiny new TVs and ugly, oversized refrigerators. 'Psst, hey man, you in a hurry?' He smelled the sweet, intoxicating scent of marijuana. He just ran on. 'Jerk,' he heard behind him. 'Faggot.' He felt the tension drain from his body, saw Cookie's serene face. *I just want to help you.* He ran even faster, as long as necessary for thoughts of Cookie to be safely stashed away. So she couldn't get at him. The lights from the store windows and the bars, the traffic, the chill, the dark, the steam escaping from the cracks and crannies in the pavement, the hot voices of the hustlers and the whores—they all melted together at a distance. Like he had to smash through an invisible glass wall, run, run, run.

'So you gonna become a Muslim?' Alafia asked.

'Maybe.'

'I know some folks in Brooklyn. They've got their own temple.'

'Drop it.'

'Where the fuck is he?'

'We could go to his place.'

'No.'

Omar took a closer look at Alafia. He saw the fatigue in his shoulders, his crumpled forehead, the tense, empty look he hid behind those intellectual glasses of his. His dusty skin.

'Ever seen *The Thief of Bagdad?*' Alafia asked.

Omar shook his head.

'The main character is from India, I think. Handsome guy with smooth, jet-black hair. I don't know how old I was when I saw it … it was showing in a small neighborhood movie theater. There was a magic lamp in it, and beautiful music. The women all fall for him, except for the one he wants, she plays hard to get. She had those blackened eyes. I loved it. Later I fantasized about … y'know, flying carpets, that kind of thing. Reenacted the whole film in my head. D'you know the *Thousand and One Nights?* I always wanted to get out, even as a child. I think I even believed that all I had to do was wait, and one day I'd wake up somewhere else.'

'Anywhere except Brooklyn, you mean?'

'Sure enough.'

Omar didn't question him further. He wasn't used to hearing Alafia talk like this. Alafia was always on his guard. To be honest, he could hardly imagine him as a child. But he knew just what he was talking about. That was the thing with Alafia. Sometimes he felt like his big brother, with a common past, but he couldn't ask him anything personal. As soon as you did, he'd brush it off, make him feel like a fool, like a stranger.

'You know, what Kain did to me … ' Alafia muttered. 'He wouldn't even listen to me the first time I came to the East Wind for that poetry workshop of his. I did "The Signifying Monkey" and right away Kain starts putting me down. "Poetry doesn't have to rhyme," he says, the asshole. As though "The Signifying Monkey" ain't poetry. Just because it's got swear words in it … because it's a legend, folklore … damn … you should have seen his face. Like I was some street thug or something. Kain, the high priest of poetry. He talks about niggers and shit, but he doesn't know shit about niggers. Kain's a pussy. That look of his. He hates himself, if you ask me. He could hardly bring himself to look at me … because I'm lighter than him.'

Omar listened to Alafia's cynical words. They sounded funky, slick, and scary all at once. His anger made him glow.

'I could rhyme and rap before I could read or write. But Kain doesn't know that. He doesn't get it. He was still in diapers at his mama's.'

Alafia guffawed, closed his eyes. Omar laughed along with him. He tried not to hear the bitterness in Alafia's laughter.

'My mother gave me money for the pictures,' Alafia continued. 'She wanted me to have fun. She knew there was nothing for me to do at home. If it hadn't been for her … My ol' man never said a thing, he just sat there in his chair and stared into space with those watery, absent eyes of his. I never knew what he was looking at. He'd been in Europe during the war. Who knows what-all he saw over there. He never talked about it. Not even to Mama. I was scared of him when I was small.'

'You, scared?'

'Why not? Everybody's scared sometimes. Scared is good. It helps you concentrate.'

Omar just smiled, let his mind wander. Alafia's insistent monologue echoed throughout the loft, he heard the hard, strident sounds but the words meant nothing to him.

'You know what my mother did?' Alafia said, paying no attention to Omar. 'She used to put on Mahalia Jackson, really loud, and sing along. She couldn't stand quiet in the house. That's what she said. She was a pretty good singer.'

Alafia looked at his hands. It was like he'd forgotten where he was. He had long, slender fingers. With the one hand he picked at the cuticles of the other. He hummed some or other tune. 'She was so happy when I got discharged from the army. Shit, man. If I'd stayed any longer I'd surely have got my sorry black ass blown to smithereens in Vietnam. Can you see me mowing down a bunch of Vietnamese? Shit.'

Omar couldn't really imagine why Alafia was telling him all this. Maybe he was searching for something himself.

Alafia cleared his throat. Looked straight at him. 'Kain hides behind his erudition. But I can tell he's scared. He thinks he's superior just 'cause he happened to read more books than me.'

Omar scuffed back and forth in his chair. The mix of nostalgia and anger in Alafia's words—what a downer. And the last thing he wanted right now was a downer. He got up, took a few steps into the big empty space.

'Where you going?'

Alafia's facial muscles tensed under his light brown skin. As though he wanted to erase all expressivity from his face. Become invisible.

'This is taking too long,' Omar said.

'You're impatient, that's all. Sit down, man.'

He dug his hands into his pants pockets. 'I'm gonna go get something to smoke.'

'Now?'

'Why not? I'll be right back.' Before Alafia could answer, Omar was out of the loft, down the stairs, and onto the street. He took a deep whiff of the brisk evening air. Felt his head spin. He crossed the street and went into a coffee shop. The bright fluorescent light hurt his eyes. The space was only large enough for a bar and two

Formica tables with red-and-white tablecloths. Airline company posters on the wall: a deserted white-sand beach with palm trees, an amber-colored couple posing in front of a golden sunset. He sat at the bar and ordered a Miller from a gangly kid who sat thumbing absently through a magazine. It was Monday evening and Omar was the only customer. Through the front window he kept an eye on the East Wind entrance.

He slowly drank away the lukewarm beer. Shook off Alafia's stifling stories, pretending they had nothing to do with him. Pretending he wasn't waiting for Kain anymore. The kid behind the bar put music on. Ben E. King's melancholy voice filled the bar. It made him wistful. ' ... and the land is dark ... ' He saw Cookie. He tried to suppress the image, sipped his beer. But Cookie smiled at him as only she could. As if she wanted to say something about him. It only made him more curious. He remembered the first night he took her back to his hotel room. He had bought a rose for her from a street vendor. She said she couldn't stay long, that she had to meet her sister. It felt like a triumph. He liked her a lot. Cookie had style. She knew he was a Last Poet but didn't seem the least bit impressed by it. She laughed when she saw the small room, his few clothes hanging neatly in the closet. The made-up bed. His bottles of oil on the shelf next to the sink.

'I can tell you're not from around here,' she said. 'You're cute.'

'Cute?'

'C'mere, baby.' Off came her blouse. He saw her large breasts in the white silk bra. It touched him: that expensive, glossy white fabric against her black skin. The gentle rocking of her heavy breasts.

'I know what you need. Get undressed.'

He did what she said. The roles were reversed once they were behind closed doors. She lay down on the bed and spread her arms. He climbed on top of her.

'Not like that,' she said quasi-reproachfully. She pushed him off her and rolled on top. 'I'll tell you something,' she whispered in his ear, 'I'm gonna see to it that that hungry, dull skin of yours is going to shine tomorrow, and the next day, and the next.'

He smelled her strong, sweet scent. She pinned his arms to the mattress, kissed and licked his neck, tickled the hairs on his ears with her tongue. He shivered.

'Tomorrow morning we're going to have bacon and eggs and grits and oatmeal for breakfast,' she said. 'You've got to put on some weight. What have you lived off all this time? Really, what's with you? You've got the money to feed yourself, don't you?' She looked concerned, caressed his hair. He nuzzled her breasts, felt the hot tears burn behind his eyelids. He was speechless.

'You don't fool me, Omar honey,' she said. 'Just trust me, though, otherwise it won't work.'

Even now, after all these months, he could still effortlessly recall the feelings from that first night. It was like drifting around in an unfamiliar space, where his memories evaporated and everything went dark and warm and moist. He had kept his eyes closed the entire time. Cookie's arms and legs were everywhere. He sweetish scent, her tongue, her wetness. Like she'd spun a web around him, a warm, sticky web that trapped her words like tiny insects.

The next morning he woke to the warmth of the sun on his face. He heard Cookie shuffle through the room. The rustle of her blouse. Water splashing on the cold white sink. He pretended to sleep. Through his eyelashes he saw her scribble something on a piece of paper. She leaned toward the mirror, wet her finger with her tongue and smoothed out her eyebrows. She tiptoed out of the room. He wanted to call after her: 'Where're you going? What about that bacon and eggs?' but he stayed put. She was gone. He felt paralyzed, his tongue stuck to the roof of his mouth. His body still belonged to the night. He squeezed his eyes shut against the bright light, and the red and yellow specks dancing on his eyelids lulled him back to sleep. He only woke again that afternoon. Cookie had left a note: 'Now I know I can stay. Sorry about breakfast. I have to go to work. Tonight?'

The self-assurance of her words, the confidence that radiated from her scribbly, irregular handwriting, pushed him back into the flush of the night. He was no longer in control of his body. It frightened him. He got up and shut the blinds; calmed by the dimmed light he sat down on the chair, and waited ... what for, he didn't know—for thoughts to relate to, maybe; memories, something to help him find himself again—but his head remained empty. Empty except for Cookie's words. Sorry about breakfast. Tonight? I know I can stay. Tonight? Tonight?

She came back. With a valise of clothes. He didn't tell her about being so shaken up. He wouldn't even know how to begin to explain it. They went out to eat at an Indian restaurant on Amsterdam Ave. Chicken curry.

A few nights later he was on his way to the East Wind and had just scored some marijuana from a nervous Jamaican when a girl spoke to him. It was dark and he couldn't see her face. She stood in a doorway. 'Wanna get spoiled?' she said in a shaky voice. He caught a glimpse of the girl in the headlights of passing cars. She was diminutive, frail. Her jeans clung to her scrawny legs.

'Ten bucks,' she whispered. 'Okay,' he answered without thinking, and went into the doorway. 'The money first,' she said. He dug loose dollar bills out of his pocket and handed them over. She squatted and started tugging at his zipper, groped for his dick. The doorway stank of gasoline and garbage and mildew. He felt himself get hard. He looked down at the girl; this was clearly not her first blow job. A stinging warmth shot through his body. He got a shock when she glanced up at him and he got a glimpse of her hollow, indifferent expression. Her thin, jaundiced face. When she had finished she shoved him away, spat on the ground. 'You like that?' she asked flatly. He zipped up his fly and hurried off. He wasn't far from the East Wind now, but quickened his pace anyway in an attempt to erase the memory of the girl. She was like a ghost who had been waiting for him there, evaporating into the darkness as soon as he left.

He stopped outside the door to the loft. Pressed his hands to his face. The stench of the doorway had stuck to him. The smell of his own sperm—it always smelled new to him—made him shiver; it was as though he were harboring a secret, a pathetic and ugly secret that thrust him back into his solitude, into the intoxicating solitary freedom he remembered from his first few days of drifting around New York. He was relieved by the anonymity of his encounter with that girl. He could pretend he'd imagined it. Only in his imagination could it be transformed into something beautiful and meaningful. Suddenly he missed Cookie terribly. He caught himself fearing she wouldn't be waiting for him when he got back.

Omar set his empty beer glass on the bar, tossed a crumpled dollar bill next to it, and nodded at the kid, who was still engrossed in his magazine. He crossed 125th St., weaving between the cars that drove languidly past, slapped the hood of an olive-green Chevrolet that nearly knocked him over. The reflection of the streetlamps on the windshield blocked out the driver's face. 'Asshole,' he hissed. As he climbed the steps to the East Wind he heard Kain's nasal drone echo through the stairwell— just the sound itself, he couldn't make out the words. He hurried up, threw open the door.

Alafia looked skittishly in his direction. He was still at the back of the loft, where Omar had left him. Gylan Kain was leaning against one of the side walls, his right hand tucked into his unzipped black leather jacket, staring fixedly at Alafia.

'He's got a hammer,' Alafia said.

Kain's face twisted into an uncomfortable smile. 'Hi, Omar. Didn't expect to see you here too.' Kain's voice was light and pleasant, like he was actually glad to see Omar. He shifted nervously from one foot to the other. 'Should've known,' he added.

'What's going on?' Omar asked, realizing how impotent his words must sound.

'Shut up, fool,' Alafia said.

'Leave him.' Kain said.

Omar looked at the two poets. They were both frozen, like they were waiting for him to act. Alafia looked even skinnier than he already was. His eyes were glued to Gylan Kain, who raised his strong, compact shoulders and shut his eyes, laughing quietly to himself. Omar knew Alafia heard the contempt in Kain's private mirth. He saw the bitter tautness of his mouth. He heard him think: you arrogant nigger. Because you're blacker than me. Intellectual motherfucker. Because I can rhyme and you can't. You don't know anything about me or my poetry. You're nothin' but scared, scared, scared.

He looked over at Kain. The pale fluorescent light isolated him, sucking the blue-black shine off his skin and leaving him desiccated. Omar almost felt sorry for him, the way he stood there with that bewildered look on his face. But he hated him too. Kain might be stronger than Alafia, but he was crumbling under Alafia's frozen, impassionate gaze. And that laugh, Kain's pitiful, supercilious laugh.

Kain opened his eyes. 'I can't do it,' he sighed, letting his right arm drop. The hammer slid out of his hand and fell to the floor with a thud.

'Can't what?' Alafia asked.

'I don't know,' Kain said.

'What were you gonna do?' Omar asked. He was relieved to see a little movement in the two men.

Kain sagged to the floor and leaned back.

'Grab the hammer,' Alafia whispered.

Omar didn't budge. He could see that Kain had lost all interest in it.

'You can't just take the name like that,' Kain was saying, 'you have no idea how much it means to me. You have no right.'

'No right?' Omar said. 'What are you talking about?'

'Didn't I tell you?' Alafia interjected. 'He thinks he's God.'

Kain laughed again. That same laugh. Infuriating, disgusting.

'When Baraka said we needed poets, poets who could swing like The Temptations ... where were you guys? Out hustling, that's where.'

'Why'd you bring that hammer?' Alafia asked, his voice earnest and measured.

Kain looked up, looked straight into Alafia's contorted face. 'I just thought ... I forgot that words ... I mean ... a poem's not a weapon, it's more than that. You can get into somebody's head with a poem, into their blood. That's what The Last Poets did, what we did … do … goddam … '

'What do you think we're doing?' Omar said. Kain's solemn tone annoyed him. The whole conversation was ridiculous. What was Kain's beef now? He'd wanted out, according to Dun. He looked like a whining little kid demanding to have his way. He couldn't stand to see Kain humiliating himself like this.

'Fuck off, man,' he said.

'No,' Alafia hissed.

'Why not?'

'If we don't fix this here and now, this bastard's gonna keep stalking us.' He spoke as though Kain wasn't there.

'It was my dream … ' Kain mused. 'Why'd you have to sign up with the first rich white guy who crossed your path? Douglas tried to butter me up too, with some fat ol' contract. Do you think I fell for it? We've got to do this ourselves. What're you guys in it for? Fame? Don't make me laugh.'

'Shut up,' Omar said. Kain's words zoomed around his pounding head as though they were his own thoughts. Did he come to New York for this chickenshit? Kain was just out to drive a wedge between Alafia and him.

'Why do you guys keep hassling me then …? Calling me at home. You think your threats scare me? What'll be left of you? Come on, tell me.'

'Who's the one who came waltzing in here with a hammer?' Alafia said.

Omar didn't hear any more of it. Kain's words stuck to him. He was defenseless. Did Kain think he was the only one with dreams of his own? Is that what he was trying to say? Shit. Shit.

Kain's shoulders drooped. He pushed himself up off the floor.

Like a panther, Alafia shot forward and grabbed the hammer.

'You think you can just walk outta here? Is that what you think?' Alafia whispered.

Kain raised his hands. 'Wait … wait … we'll discuss this another time.'

'No way "another time". You've put me down.'

'I've what?' Kain said, surprised.

'Grab him, Omar,' Alafia said.

Omar ran over and took hold of Kain. He pulled his arms behind his back. Kain didn't resist. He was as limp as a rag doll, which made Omar even madder. Did the dude have no self-respect at all? Grab him, grab him … it echoed in his head … beat the shit out of him, go on … let's see who's boss. Beat the shit out of that little black creep. He felt the charged, overheated voices of the men and women in Roxy's Café breathing down his neck. 'Beat the daylights out of him.' He pulled Kain's arms tighter. Kain's muted groan was an invitation. Alafia ran at them, raised the hammer in the air, and brought it down on Kain's right shoulder. Kain didn't even cringe. Swallowed back the pain. Omar saw only red and black, like he was looking into a huge fire. He didn't see Alafia hit Kain again with the hammer. The fire blinded him. He felt only the dull reaction of Kain's limp body against his own. As though he were the one taking a beating. He didn't retain any other coherent thoughts from that evening, but his body remembered the numbness that flowed through his veins like lukewarm blood.

DAVID AND DAVID AND DAVID

'The Last Poets'

We are a new breed of men
Black warriors
The last poets of the world
We will create this world in honor of our fathers
Whose unwept tears even now well up inside us
Tears welling inside us waiting to gush out
Tears gushing out turning into spearpoints
Each spear tear
The spirit of a great fallen warrior
We are the last poets of the world
And our spirit breath rhythm words
Will temper and harden those tears
Hot tears
Harden in the fires of our souls
Tempered in the flames of our suffering

CLEVELAND, OHIO, SEPTEMBER 2001

Meditations

It happened to him every once in a while. He'd lose track of time. An hour, a morning, an evening would pass and he couldn't remember what he'd done, what he'd thought about. He woke up without having slept. Inside he was completely empty, no colors, not even white or gray, only the uneasy feeling that the solution lay hidden somewhere in one of the dark recesses of his consciousness. Solution—he couldn't come up with any other word for the insight he so longed for at such moments. Or maybe 'revelation', but that sounded so weighty and religious. The nagging feeling that pursued him was too personal and too close by for that.

Take this afternoon. He was sitting alone on the polished wood floor of the large communal living room, going through music he might use for a performance in Detroit next week. David, his eldest son, had sent him a few new numbers from New York. David knew the best musicians. He had his own agency downtown.

The wind whooshed through the willows out in the yard. The rocking chair on the veranda swayed slowly back and forth, like a ghost was sitting in it, peacefully enjoying the warm September rain, awaiting the arrival of fall. Thick drops stuck to the windows. Upstairs Tray was practicing a new sermon. His fierce, lively voice trickled through the cracks between the floor planks.

Tray was preaching himself into a trance. There was no one else home. The little ones were at school, the mothers at work. The Prince and his wife had gone to a conference of fellow believers in Israel.

He listened to the music, and found himself surprised at what David had sent him. Especially because he had sounded so hesitant over the phone.

'You know I'm busy.'

"Course, son, but I'll bet you can help me out.'

'How many poems did you say: two?'

'I've recorded them all. I'll send you the cassette. See what you can do with them.'

'Yeah, easy does it. I'll see if I've got time. Anything else?'

'How're you doing?'

'Can you call me back later? I'm in a meeting.'

'Sure, David. I love you.'

'Yeah.'

'I'll call you.'

And then they hung up. A few weeks later the CD arrived in the mail. Without a note or even a scribble on the envelope. All David had done was write the names of the musicians on the inside. He recognized the neat handwriting. The small, angular letters, nowhere a loop or a swirl or a sloppy smear. Almost like they'd been typeset. They told him nothing about his eldest son's emotions or motivation, or maybe they were only a product of that same reticence, the caution he had heard on the telephone and which, in an instant, no more than an instant, had sounded to him like fear.

But the music! 'Black Bodies on the Line' sounded almost like a soul number. His words melted together with background singer LaMena Smith belting out those passionate rhythms. And that harmonica—the lean, high notes compensating for the weightiness of the poem. Of course he'd have to re-record the text over the music in a real studio, but what David had done with it already ... The electric guitar under 'My Ole Man' sounded almost like a sax: searching, velvety, sexy. He heard the crackle of an LP. A Hammond organ. Languid drums. It was like being in a nightclub. He chuckled at the thought of hearing his own voice, and not Barry White's. But it was good, jazzy, plenty of atmosphere. His spare text thrived in this music. Fortunately David hadn't been heavy-handed on the bass line, none of the throbbing rhythms that were so in these days.

The song lasted about two minutes. He recalled walking to the kitchen to make himself some lunch. A vegetarian hot dog, some broccoli and rice. He brought his plate to the living room and sat down on the sofa. And then his mind went blank. From that moment on, time stopped, although the wall clock in the hallway ticked away, tick-tock tick-tock tick-tock, and hours later he was suddenly in his bedroom, in the low chair at the window, staring outside without seeing anything.

◆

'Nina Simone's in the audience. Nina Simone's in the audience.' He saw her from the wings, the diva, the woman with the broad, stoic face that could suddenly open up, and then it was like the sun was shining even though it was nighttime. The fox stole around her neck. Had Woodie King convinced her to come? The Cubiculo Theater was packed. Despite the NO SMOKING signs a blue haze hung in the auditorium. The rustle subsided when the lights went out, and he and Kain and Felipe walked onstage. He nudged Kain and nodded in Nina's direction, but Kain didn't see anything; he was turned inward, closed off, concentrating too hard to notice. But he never let Nina out of his sight, not even—especially—when it was his turn to recite his poems. As though she'd come just for him. The Juilliard-trained pianist, the singer with the dark, musty voice. 'Are you ready? Are you ready to do what is necessary? Are you ready to kill if necessary? Are you ready to smash evil things? Burn buildings? Are you ready to give yourself? Your love, your soul, your heart? Are you ready?' He didn't sing, but the words danced on the muffled, uniform rhythm of the drum. They were bare, ugly, threatening words, but she understood that they were music to him. That all his poems began with music, with beauty. 'Are you ready to turn yourself inside out through and through and change yourself?' He felt the invisible thread that connected Nina and him. And for a brief moment, ever so briefly, he felt as though he were levitating, floating above his own words, and he heard the gentle, lazy melody Nina played on the piano. The melody absorbed the words, transformed them into pure sound, into colors he had never seen. That evening was the first time he didn't feel the shortcomings of language, the powerlessness, the impotence of words, just words, no matter how suggestive and significant, no matter how much he trusted them. It was so long ago—my God, more than thirty years. Nina was an old woman now. Back then she included 'Are You Ready?' in her repertoire and was shadowed by the feds. Now she was living somewhere in the south of France. Did she remember that evening? Would she remember him? How he had kissed and caressed her toes, one by one, in her hotel room? Nina, whose rough, stumpy feet betrayed her vulnerability. She only laughed. She had chosen him. Would she remember?

Sometimes it was as though he'd slipped out of history—yeah, that was it, like he'd just quietly faded away. He was only a name: David Nelson, founder of the legendary Last Poets from Harlem. Period. He was the nice one, the intellectual, the poet who didn't fight, while the others spat nails at one another. Maybe it was because he never felt as much anger as the others: not that real, all-consuming, serpentine, malicious anger that gave them strength and was the driving force behind their poems, but which at the same time made them forget, forget, forget.

His anger was more resigned, gentler, more questioning, and maybe that's why it sometimes seemed like that whole period when the group became famous, broke up, made history, had taken place without him. As though he were invisible, a spectator at most. Even that time Umar and Jalal had waited for him on 125th St. 'Hey David, asshole, the name is just as much ours, man. Ours.'

'Sure it is,' he'd said, softly, and he meant it too, 'sure it is.' Too softly, since they didn't even hear him. Umar hit him a few times, not hard, and that was it. No harm done. They just sauntered off. As if nothing had happened.

All the articles and features about The Last Poets credited a poem by the South African poet Willie Kgositsile as the source of the name. *'This wind you hear is the birth of memory. When the moment hatches in time's womb there will be no art talk; the only poem you will hear will be the spearpoint pivoted in the punctured marrow of the villain ... '* It had been repeated and written so many times that it had become a fact. A few years earlier, Umar had registered the name and officially claimed the rights to it.

But the term 'last poets' never appeared in Kgositsile's poem. When David first read it, God had whispered to him: 'We are the last poets of the world / and our spirit breath rhythm words ... '

That thought gave him hope. God was more reliable than history. God wouldn't forget him.

◆

He tried to recall David's music, but all he could hear was a soft, blank hum. Tray had stopped preaching. Even the slow ticking of the clock dissolved into the silence.

◆

'Do you know your name?' the doctor asked. He was a young white man whose sandy hair was slicked back in a long outmoded cut.

'Nobody fools with me,' he said.

'What's your name?'

'David Nelson.'

'Do you know why you're here?'

'Do you?' He didn't feel like kowtowing to this doctor, whose name he didn't even know.

'Why don't you answer?'

'What's *your* name?'

'We're not talking about me.' The man leaned over to page through the thin dossier on the table in front of him.

He looked at the tall window. The grayish plastic film stuck to the glass filtered the sunlight into a watery and dull and meaningless white. The walls were white. The doctor's coat was white. No nametag. The space devoid of any identity.

'Poet, did you say?'

'Did I say that?'

'You don't remember?' The doctor pushed his glasses higher up the bridge of his nose, the thick black frame hiding his eyebrows. He sniffed. Furrowed his forehead.

'Poet, um-hm,' he mused.

'Yeah.'

He wished the doctor would keep his mouth shut. He remembered the scene in the deli. How he had spread out his mat on the red linoleum floor in front of the counter and sat down to meditate. Was he a poet? He remembered how, after a few yoga exercises, he would glide into a world of pure poetry where words were superfluous. They were like glass, transparent, fluid, and clear as gin, they came to him without any intellectual effort whatsoever, like air that he breathed, cool water he drank, that cleansed him, emptied and protected him against the violence all around him.

'What year is it?'

'1970,' he answered without hesitation and without looking at his interrogator. He wanted to hold onto his thoughts. Not so he could explain his puzzling presence in Bellevue Hospital to the doctor, who, it seemed, had already written the answers to his questions in red pen. It didn't matter what he said. He just wanted to get back to the sunny afternoon in the deli, so he'd know where to pick up his life once he got out of the loony bin. How long had he been in here? A day, three days, five, a week? He felt as if he'd slept the entire time. All he could remember was the last meal. The anxious glances of the other men in the dining room, the colorless food that stuck to the roof of his mouth—was it oatmeal? Then it must still be morning.

'What are you thinking about?' the doctor asked.

'You interested?'

'Wouldn't have asked if I weren't.'

This was what he remembered: it was war, the deli was full of uniformed soldiers. He was lying on the street under a car parked out in front, his legs trapped, he couldn't move. He stared up at the azure sky, saw bright yellow buttercups, watched downy white fluff drift by. The air was thick and warm and wrapped around him like a coat. He heard shouting, shots. He saw the bullet heading straight at him, a shiny gold bullet, and just before it reached him, a few inches from his head, it floated in mid-air, proud, glorious, big, glowing in the clear sunlight. Wasn't that enough proof? It wasn't the first time God had come to his rescue, and he knew it wouldn't be the last. He had no idea how he got there, only that he woke up in a metal bed in a white room under a tightly tucked sheet. No blanket, though; he was shivering. A nurse had helped him get dressed, and led him to the dining room.

'Are you afraid?' the doctor asked.

'Afraid?' The warm sound of his voice in the empty office. The quiet irony of it. Saw how his silence disconcerted the young doctor. The doctor's long pink fingers sifted aimlessly through the paperwork, but he clearly wasn't reading a word.

'Afraid? What should I be afraid of?'

The doctor laughed, shook his head. Closed the dossier and cleared his throat. 'I've seen you on TV.'

'Oh.'

'Are you going to perform again?' He was taking a different tack. Trying to sound as though he was in the know. As though he could be trusted.

As David listened to the dry silence absorb the man's sparse and senseless words, it dawned on him that in the deli that afternoon he had never been so close to the ultimate goal of his crusade. A personal crusade that had begun shortly after he left the group, despite ongoing contracts for TV shows, offers from producers and theater directors, after he had refused to set foot in a white courtroom to defend his right to the name 'The Last Poets', because of which the record that he and Kain and Felipe had cut now lay rotting in some lousy warehouse.

Amiri Baraka put it perfectly: 'We live in a reality that requires us to destroy our old spirit and find a new one.' David knew damn well what Baraka meant by this. From the very beginning, the Poets had the same mission as their mentor's. 'We are a new breed of men. A new breed.'

In a certain sense, Baraka had freed him from the nagging feeling of being a con man, a liar. Every time he did 'Are You Ready?' with the Poets, and without batting an eye yelled 'Are you ready to kill if necessary? Are you ready? Are you ready?' When he accepted the applause, answering the affirmative 'yeahs' and 'oohhs' with an elegant bow, a fist in the air, a grin. When he walked off stage, to the dressing room with those bright round light bulbs around the mirrors, wiped the sweat from his forehead with a clammy towel, saw himself in the mirror. Are you ready? Was he ready to put a bullet in a traitor's head? Bump off policemen? Was he really ready? Ready for war? For revolution? He broke out in a massive sweat. Admitting doubt was almost too much for him.

For days he'd been holed up in a tiny, airless apartment in SoHo an old friend had lent him. Left the apartment only to replenish his supply of weed and milk and bread. The rest of the time he smoked pot, meditated, practiced the yoga exercises he had learned at a workshop at NYU. There was no phone. He spoke to no one, only to himself. And slowly, ever so slowly, the memories of the life he had lived until then started to fade.

Like ink drawings left in the light for too long, or like faded and yellowed photographs, the images of Kain and Felipe and Abiodun, of his friends and teachers at college, of Brenda, his parents, his siblings, of Josephine and the two boys, his boys, his boys, gradually became faint and vague and surreal. He could scarcely believe he had been married, had children, was a father, a father, a father. He immersed himself ever deeper and longer in the calm flush of meditation and marijuana until he felt no more pain.

'I think we'll have to let you go.' The doctor interrupted his thoughts. 'Your father's here. Your brother too.'

The doctor was going too fast. His father? In New York? Had he driven all the way here from Detroit? Didn't he have to work?

'We found a phone number among your things. They came right away.'

'Uh-huh.'

'Does that alarm you?'

'Why should it alarm me?'

'You look so ... how shall I put it ... Tell me what you feel.'

'Nothing.'

'Really?'

'Where is he?'

'Out in the hall.'

David got up and went to the door. He was so light-headed that for a brief moment everything spun.

'You don't have to see him if you don't want to,' the doctor said.

'Where is he?'

'Relax. You're still weak. Take your time.'

'Where?'

♦

The rain had stopped. The thick clouds were torn now, and fresh orange-yellow light shone on the birch tree in the yard, made the bark go silver. The wispy leaves quivered in the breeze. One of the kids had left a red plastic bucket on the picnic table, and it had filled with rainwater. A blackbird landed on the surface, lifted its wings and ducked its noble head underwater, it fluttered and squawked, droplets spattered in the air, sucked up the sunlight. Pearls, he thought, pearls.

On the way from New York to Detroit he had stared continually at his father's rough, cracked hands on the steering wheel. The nails white and spotty from disinfectant, from too much washing, scrubbing away the traces of meat and clotted blood with a small steel brush. Once, when he was small, his father had taken him to Hartgrove's Packinghouse, where he worked as a deboner in the abattoir. He was the foreman and could easily smuggle his son inside. 'Don't touch anything,' he whispered as he pointed to a stool in the cluttered, glass-enclosed office and headed off; David saw his father give a younger colleague a friendly clap on the shoulder, watched him laugh and talk and give orders with a superior kind of charm and self-assurance. With a keen, controlled eye he checked the dripping carcasses which hung like limp coats on big, shiny hooks. Ignored the sweet stench, the puddles of syrupy dark-red blood. He was the boss. Traveled all over the country with a suitcase full of sharpened knives to teach apprentices the trade.

Don't touch anything.

No questions. No reproach. Only the quiet drone of

the engine. His brother's regular snoring on the backseat. The countless dark miles of asphalt that disappeared under the car.

'Can I turn on the radio?'

His father nodded.

He twisted the beige knob and soft night-music filled
the space. From the sound of the jazz station, they were
nearing Detroit. He had not asked to return; his fate was
in his father's hands. He smelled the deep, sweet smell of
his skin. Felt the warmth his huge body gave off. He was
glad the music drowned out the indistinct hum of his
father's thoughts. He closed his eyes. Heard the smooth-
ness of Coltrane's soprano sax. The music was like a shallow river that weaved its way through a rolling green
landscape. The water was cold and clear, he could see the
smooth stones on the bed, the small fish that were carried along with the current, the fragile yellow tones that
danced upon the water's surface, he saw the rays of the
sun; it was as though Coltrane created them, made them
audible, tangible, his breath in the notes, warm, whispering breath, no gaps. He briefly imagined he heard
Trane's voice through the music: a deep, sonorous drone
about God and the sun and words and memory. Trane
was always close by.

When he'd first moved to New York and was looking
for an apartment for Josephine, young David, and himself, someone had given him a saxophone. Just like that.
It was an older man who managed a few cheap apartments on 120th St.; they had struck up a conversation at
a barber shop on Lenox. David told him he'd come to
New York to study, had a basketball scholarship at NYU,
but was really a poet. When they parted, the old guy blew
the dust off the case and put it in David's hands. 'You can
have it,' he sighed, 'it only gives me grief.' Only a few

days later, when he unpacked the instrument and put it to his mouth, blew, squeezed, pushed, until a ragged, shrill squawk came out, did David realize what the old man meant.

He opened his eyes. Saw patches of mist hovering above the vacant fields on either side of the highway. Every now and then a few houses, a cluster of trees whose silhouettes rose like ghosts against the early-morning light. He heard Coltrane's voice. His meandering search in the upper register of the sax.

'See that?'

'Hmm?' His father's voice sounded tired and raspy. He followed David's eyes.

'There, that mist.'

'What, son?' His father switched off the radio, but the music carried on. David pointed outside. He opened his eyes wider in his attempt to better make out the tall, thin shapes in the mist. Were they men, women? He saw their open but mute mouths; heard short, menacing bass notes, restrained drumbeats, as though the drums were holding back the rhythm rather than propelling it—not too fast yet, wait—ah, there was the sax again, he looked at the translucent figures in the field and heard their shrill voices in the song of the sax, their slow, heavy footsteps, the muffled cries. A truck passed them on the right, honking. The huge wheels thudded over the road surface. Sucked the air out from under their car, so that it was almost like they were being lifted up, blown away. When truck had overtaken them the mist had lifted; the ghosts were gone. Trane kept on playing, though. David leaned back in his seat. That comforting, sultry music swirled around his head, grazed his cheeks, caressed him: relax, everything's all right, you're almost home.

'What, son?'

'Never mind.'

Without Coltrane he'd never have become a Last Poet. One night, long ago—he had just sent for his wife and son from Detroit—he met the sax player Archie Shepp at the Lenox Lounge. Being a Monday evening, there were no performances, so Shepp sat at the bar, absently sipping a bourbon. David recognized him from his picture on album covers. It was a few months after Coltrane died, and nothing seemed more appropriate than to offer his condolences to Shepp on the passing of his mentor.

'Shit, man,' was his reaction.

'I'm sorry,' David said, 'I only thought ... '

'No, no ... Let me offer you a drink.'

Not a word about Trane the whole evening. They both did their utmost to avoid saying his name. As though they were both painfully aware that their words and thoughts circled like vultures over Trane and his legacy. And what they wanted most for him was peace.

'I've got a sax but can't get a note out of it,' David said. 'Sounds like an old geezer with asthma.'

'I could give you a few pointers.'

'Really?'

'Why not?'

A few days later Shepp showed him how to attach the mouthpiece, how to warm the instrument up, wet the reed, lick it, suck and carefully blow, whisper into the mouthpiece. He showed him the fingerings, demonstrated scales and intervals.

'And now all you have to do is listen, listen, listen. You understand?'

David took out Coltrane's albums and locked himself in the bedroom where the stereo was. He listened to the music almost nonstop, most of the time with his eyes closed so as to get closer to the music, to the jagged melody lines, as though Trane was playing two saxophones at once. At a certain point he did not even hear the music; all that remained was the feeling behind the notes, and for the first time in his life it was like all the images and memories he had collected up until then, and which floated around in his consciousness like loose puzzle pieces, finally fell into place.

When was thirteen he played basketball with Emmett Till, his elderly neighbor's grandson. They lived in Pinewood, not far from downtown. Emmett was his own age, and lived far away, in a town somewhere in Mississippi, but spent summers with his grandfather. He liked Emmett, who spoke so differently than he did, like his tongue was thicker, his words greasy and juicy. Emmett in turn liked Detroit. The blacks here were different than the ones back home, he said.

'Like how?' he asked.

'Just are,' Emmett said, shrugging his shoulders. 'Y'know. Different.' And they went back to shooting hoops, dunking like their lives depended on it. David seemed to feel his muscles grow, in bed at night, the irritating itch under his skin. He was already bigger than Mama.

At the end of August, Emmett went back south. Two days and two nights in the bus. They hugged and promised to pick up their basketball training next year. 'Why don't you just stay here?' David asked.

'With Gramps?'

'Why not?'

Emmett looked at the ground, kicked away a few stones. 'It snows here in the winter, right?'

'Yeah.'

'I dunno ... I'll be seeing you.'

A few months later, one dark late afternoon, the back door opened and David heard his father's familiar, calm footsteps on the wood floor in the hallway. He tossed a newspaper on the table, shaking his head, his hand clamped tightly over his mouth. Mama grabbed the paper, stared at a photo on the front page, and started rocking back and forth on her chair, muttering in a contorted voice: 'That poor, poor man. He shouldn't be put through this. That poor man.' David stood behind her chair. The photo was unclear, he could make out a dead body on an improvised bier, but it wasn't just a regular dead body—the face was hardly a face anymore, it was like a mask, the eyes were dark holes, the nose strangely narrow, like a bird's beak, the skull was cracked open, he saw blood and tissue that made him think of Hartgrove's Packinghouse, the watery chill that seeped through his thickest clothes, the white tiles spattered with blood, the smell of death, death smelled sweet and icy and pungent.

'Who is it?' he asked. The letters under the photo were reduced to black stripes.

'Oh my God,' Mama groaned, pulling him close. She pressed her face into his neck, kissed him, jabbered snippets of prayers. 'Oh God Almighty, be merciful to that poor old man, his mother, oh God, oh God.' He felt the warmth of her tears on his neck, tried to wrest loose from her grip. He looked over at his father.

'Emmett.' His father did not say the name of his friend as much as exhale it. David forgot what happened after that, what he did, felt. In the weeks that followed he gradually got wind of what had happened. How Emmett had whistled at a pretty white woman, how white men grabbed him, locked him up in a wooden shed, beat him with bricks and then shot him through the head. What happened to Emmett after that, he hardly dared think about. He saw the river, smooth and still. The blindingly white sunlight above, the yellow-green leafage of the weeping willows that dangled over the water. It could get real hot in Mississippi, Emmett had told him, 'real hot, in the summer it's like your skin's made of salt, like your body fluids, your blood, your tears, have evaporated, your knees and elbows are like cardboard.' He laughed, proud of the fact that David had no idea of the heat and the swamps and the haunted forests. They had dragged Emmett to the riverbank. Weighed down his limp body with stones. The two strongest men picked Emmett up by his ankles and wrists, and like with a playful child, swung him back and forth a few times before flinging him into the water. He sank at once. David could see the ripples on the surface, concentric circles of wavelets with the occasional bubble. The ripples dissipated in the wind, like vanishing snippets of sound. The water was again still and opaque. Emmett lay on the rocky bottom, silvery fish swam through his legs, over his chest and his broken face.

'Can we go out to Pinewood?' David asked.

'To your sister's?'

'I want to see the house again. D'you think she'll mind? Maybe I can stay awhile.'

'Stay ... ' His father's gaze seemed glued to the highway, as though the endless miles consumed his thoughts and words. Nothing to say, nothing to ask. Only the secretive language of his aging body. The sweetness of his skin mixed with the weakly sour smell of perspiration. His worn-out hands on the steering wheel. David felt a wave of panic and retreated into the music; it was easy for him to evoke Trane's lucid tones.

He drew the curtains. His body hurt and his joints were stiff, but the music emanating from the second-hand stereo made him feel safe, and he hungered for more. Coltrane expressed his own grief. The black hole that Emmett's death had left in him, the silence in the house after his mother had wiped away her last tears and begged God one more time for compassion, 'Merciful God, stand by me, stand by me, just help me raise my six children, help me.' His father said nothing. Stood in the corner of the kitchen, invisible. Even Emmett's death didn't give him the right to comfort Mama. He just stood there like a wooden cigar-store Indian. It didn't occur to David that his father was hurting too, that it must have been painful that something as awful as Emmett's murder would be enough reason to show up —unannounced and unexpected, on a regular weekday—at his former house. David's parents had recently separated.

The next summer, Emmett's shadow followed him everywhere. It was 1955. He studied at Cass Technical High School in midtown Detroit; the school was called the 'brain factory' because most of the students, black and white, would win scholarships and go on to study at universities all over the country. David liked school, and he lived with Big Ma, his proud black grandmother who shuffled through the house in fluffy slippers, made him scrambled eggs and sausage, sweet toast and black tea for breakfast. She lived within walking distance of the school. He reveled in his prowess on the basketball court: the cheerleaders on the sideline responded to his dunk shots with a roar of support and a swirl of pom-poms, like pink and yellow birds that might take flight at any moment. He was one of the tallest boys in his class. He noticed the blonde girls sneaking looks at him in the cafeteria. They sat separately, near the window. 'Hey David,' they would coo when he walked past, but he didn't look. Emmett was shadowing him. No one else could see him, luckily; poor Emmett, he had to look out for him, comfort him, now that he'd lost his voice and his fine young body. David went over to his own table in the corner of the cafeteria, crossed the invisible line that divided the white and the black students. At Cass Tech there was officially no such thing as racial segregation; even talking about it was to deny everything the school stood for, the silent dreams his father harbored for him, and that his mother had no trouble expressing out loud.

'I was the only black child in my class.'

'I know, Mama.'

'I was Miss Brody's pet. She always gave me odd jobs to do.'

'How come?'

'I liked it. I could even deliver papers to the principal's office! Did I ever tell you about my Shirley Temple project? You know who Shirley Temple is, don't you? That adorable little girl with the blonde curls that bounced on her head and her round cheeks that went all pink whenever she danced. Miss Brody asked me to read my essay to the class. I told all about Shirley and her curls, but didn't say her name until the very end. I kept up the tension. Miss Brody thought that was brilliant, holding off like that. I think I looked a little bit like Shirley, I was just as small and chubby. Everybody liked me. And I was very good at spelling. You've got my knack for language, David.'

Since his death, Emmett seemed to look over his shoulder every second of every day. Only when David played basketball and lost himself in the game and sweated like crazy, only then did he feel the weight of his dead friend slowly glide off his shoulders. Only then was he completely free. But after he had showered and dressed, as he ambled down the long, shiny-floored halls to the schoolyard or the cafeteria, he felt his tread become heavier and wearier with every step. He passed a group of white boys, the same ones who had just cheered him on out on the court, and for whom he was now, in jeans and T-shirt, invisible. They just kept on chatting with one another.

Emmett taught him that the tolerance at Cass Tech was no more than a ceasefire, and had never been anything but that. Hope and yearning did strange things to your outlook: look at your father, the 'boss'. Did he have a single white man under him? Look, David, look how tired and washed-out your old man is, every year he's more hunched than before, he's doing double shifts and do you know why? Because he's scared, scared of squandering his hard-earned authority. Just look: his colleagues at the slaughterhouse joke with him, 'respect' him—but do you still not see it? Their hidden contempt? Their embarrassment? If you look closely, David, you'll see they're ashamed of your father.

Shut up, Emmett.

Just look. Look at me.

But Emmett had vanished. Whenever David really needed him, Emmett hid in the bathroom or in a student locker. Some friend.

Ten years later, while David sat listening to Trane in that small apartment on 120th St., to the short, self-assured phrases, the pauses—just as steeped in feeling and as fragile as the notes themselves—and to the phrases that followed, gradually becoming longer and more unpredictable and daring and thin, almost transparent as they approached the end of the number ... when David heard the music that seemed to melt together with his memories, only then did he feel a sense of peace. Finally, he had found his refuge. The images followed the same intuitive and logical pattern as Trane's notes, a form that captured his pent-up emotions and desires. In the weeks and months after that, he did nothing except play the sax. He only had to grasp the feeling, and the notes came all by themselves. He played with them, lustily, aggressively, lovingly. He had read somewhere that Trane often worked with short poems he wrote himself, composing music to the rhythms and sound of his own words. Just like Emmett Till all those years ago, Trane figured in David's daily life—though he was never as smotheringly present as Emmett. Trane offered him a way out. He was David's example regarding poetry, musical structure, complex rhythms that could carry and propel words.

They arrived at his sister's house early that morning. His father parked the car in front, leaned over him and pushed open the passenger door. His brother, on the backseat, rubbed the sleep out of his eyes.

'Aren't you going in?'

'Nope.'

'But Beleda doesn't know ... '

'She's your sister. You're on your own now.'

'But ... '

'Your bag's in the trunk. Go on. Move it.' He practically pushed him out of the car, didn't look him in the eye.

David got his bag and walked around back. The curtains were still shut. Behind him he heard the thud of the car door. He looked over at the car. His father hadn't started the engine yet. He was just sitting rigidly with his hands on the steering wheel, staring straight ahead. Even from this distance David could sense his disappointment. He wanted to turn back, but just then he heard the heavy rumble of the engine. Without looking back, his father drove off and turned the corner. The sky above the road and houses and trees was striped and pink. Windless. It would be a nice day. David went up and opened the screen door and tapped on the kitchen door. 'Beleda, are you awake? It's me, David. Beleda ... open up.'

How long had he lived up in that attic? Three years? Four? The ceiling was too low for him; he was always having to duck. Beleda gave him a mattress and bedding, she dug out some red-and-white checkered cloths from a cupboard and improvised curtains with thumbtacks. A single bare bulb lit the space, which like any attic was a repository for old junk: a child's toy car with one wheel missing, a wooden scooter, an old-fashioned iron, a chest where their mother used to keep the off-season clothes, but which now held only a set of faded blue velvet curtains.

He used the curtains as rugs. Beleda had offered him the guest room, the big room at the front that he used to share with his brothers Larry and Philip, but David felt safest in the attic. It had nothing to do with nostalgia. All his curiosity and longing for the house he grew up in vanished the minute he stepped over the threshold and got a greasy whiff of fried eggs and hash browns and onions. He could scarcely conceal his nausea, gagged behind his hand. Beleda didn't seem surprised to see him. She shuffled across the kitchen in her lilac quilted housecoat, took an additional plate from the cupboard, and set it on the table. 'Say hello to Uncle David,' she told her two eldest girls, who were sitting timidly on the wooden bench against the wall.

'Hello Uncle David.'

'Hello girls,' he answered. He looked at his sister. Glanced upward. 'Is it okay if I ... ' He didn't have to finish his question. Beleda nodded. 'Whatever.' Her surly hospitality reminded him of his mother. Made him feel at home. Had his father warned her he was coming? But when?

It was getting dark outside. He switched on a lamp. Smiled at the gaunt face in the window. Friendly, wide-open and deep-set eyes. Thin braids that glistened with silvery threads. Chapped, cracked lips. David leaned forward and put his hand on the cool glass, pressed his left cheek against the face of the old man. He felt the window vibrate, the glass reverberated with the busy sounds downstairs, excited children's voices, chairs scuffing on parquet, curtains being drawn. It was like he'd plugged himself in and only had to concentrate to be able to decipher and translate the familiar, mundane hubbub into words and sentences.

'You got any washing, David?' Beleda asked. Her head jutted into the attic just above floor level; she stood on the folding ladder.

'Nope.'

'It stinks up here. The kids are talking about it.'

'Oh.'

'That's all? "Oh?"'

'I'm fine up here, Beleda. Don't you worry.'

'Do I look worried?'

'Relax.'

'I am not relaxed.'

'I could teach you some yoga exercises.'

'David, look at yourself.'

'Vanity.'

'That's not what I mean. What happened to you down in New York? What did they do to you?'

'Nothing.'

'You want me to call Josephine?'

'Josephine?'

'Your kids' mother.'

'No, Beleda, no.'

'You're thinking only of yourself.'

'I wish that were true.'

'Damn it, David, think of the boys.'

In all those years in the attic, not a single line of poetry. As though he wanted to shield his poetry from the crudeness of language.

'Why don't you answer her?' Emmett asked. It was night-time. Emmett only visited at night, when everyone else was asleep; it was almost like the house itself slept, you could imagine you heard its quiet breathing.

'I asked you something.'

'I don't know,' David answered.

'Can I tell you something?'

'Take a seat.'

Emmett took a pillow and kneeled down on it. He was wearing a gaudy silver shirt, untucked. His face looked as it did in life.

'You been out?' David asked.

Emmett laughed. 'They won't let me in anywhere, man. I think I look old enough, but they don't fall for it.'

David chuckled.

'I was at the river.'

'When?'

'I go there a lot, at night. Then all you hear are the owls. And the water. The water calms me down. D'you think there are wolves in the woods? Coyotes? Maybe it was just some stray dogs I heard howling. I dunno.'

'What'd you want to tell me?'

'D'you remember that guy, the one who held my feet? Not the dude who stuffed my pants full of stones, the other one ... the redhead.'

'Nah.'

'He had broad, rounded shoulders, don't you remember? Was wearing only a white shirt. He thought I couldn't see anything, but the whole night I was staring straight at his face. The sweat trickled along his sideburns. He looked ridiculous. So anyway, that kid—how old d'you suppose he was, eighteen, nineteen?—he's got a dog, I saw him walking it a while ago ... what was it? Not a sheepdog, but something like that. Anyway, I—'

'At the river?'

'Yeah, and it wasn't the first time I'd seen him there, either. And always at night. It's nice there, David. Especially with a full moon. When the water twinkles and the sky's purple. He threw a stick in the water for the dog. Dog jumped in after it, just like that, dropped it in the grass at the kid's feet.'

'And?'

'He threw the stick again, and then again and again. The dog couldn't get enough.'

'At night?'

'Didn't I say so?'

'What was he doing there at night?'

'Ain't nobody there.'

'Except you.'

'I hid. Y'know, David, I felt kind of sorry for him. It's

pitiful, seeing him with that dog, wagging its tail and panting and begging the kid to throw the stick in the water, over and over again. You can tell the guy's tired of it, but he keeps on throwing it ... '

'He feels guilty,' David said.

'You know what the worst part is about being dead? I've never really loved a girl—or a woman. You understand? That messing around, it wasn't love, it was only wishful thinking. I don't know what it feels like to really be in love, David, and yet I still miss it. D'you get that?'

'I don't miss it.'

'Because you aren't alive. And you're not dead either. You're somewhere in between.' Emmett stood up, shook his legs. Ran his fingers through his short hair.

'You going?'

'Yeah.'

'Coming back?'

Emmett shook his head. Smiled wistfully. 'Do you know I seriously considered staying in Detroit? I mean back then, with my grandfather. I saw you and your friends hanging around on the street corner doing those doo-wop numbers and telling each other stories in rhyme. I wanted to be able to do that too, rattle off whole strings of words without making any mistakes. Dumb, huh? Anyway, my mother would never have let me stay up North. I didn't even mention it.'

Emmett walked over to the ladder. He had to duck so as not to bump his head.

'Don't wait too long, David,' he said.

'For what?'

But Emmett had already vanished through the dark hole in the floor.

'Today Is a Killer' (1968)

I often sit and stare at the sea
And dream dreams and hope hopes
And wish wishes and lately I listen to the wind sing

I listen to the wind sing as it dances a beautiful dance
for me

But these moments never seem to last
Never last
Cause after the hopes and dreams and wishes

[...]

comes the stark reality of today

washing away our memory

DETROIT, FEBRUARY 2002

Essie Mae Nelson

'We lived in an apartment complex on Vernor Highway. My mother was the manager. The neighbors were Polish but in our building there were only colored people. My mother used to write poetry. I still know one by heart: *"Are you an active member / the kind that would be missed / or are you just content your name is on the list / Do you attend the meetings / mingle with the flock / or do you stay at home / criticizing ... "* She had another long poem, I think it was about the railways, but it got burned, most of it was burned ... I've lost part of my memory. I had a stroke without even knowing it. Had a terrible headache, so I took a bunch of painkillers, and only called somebody on Wednesday evening ...

Nobody believes I'm eighty years old.

David and his older brother Bill Nelson rented a room from us on Vernor. They came from the south. Oklahoma. David brought the rent. I had hair down to my behind. One look at me and he fell right in love. I was seventeen and had plans to be a teacher. I was a good student. In the summer I used to look after the little ones in the building, played games with them and such.

I didn't know much about love. I was just a teenager.

I'm not the worrying kind, you know, because I believe in God. When I was fifteen the Lord spoke to me. I came home from school and asked: "Where's Grandma?" and they said: "Grandma's dead," just like that, Grandma's dead, nothing else, so I locked myself in the bathroom and I screamed and hollered and cried: "God, I hate you for letting my grandmother die, I hate you," and then the Holy Spirit spoke to me, loud and clear: "You don't hate me, you love me ... " I was scared ... I heard the voice but couldn't see anyone. I was fifteen, but on that day I placed my life in God's hands.'

'Portrait of Dad' (1989)

My ole man,
sleeping in his easy chair.
Sometime grumbling 'n complaining
but always keeping on
trying to make a way.
Smilin' from deep inside
some dark secret places ...

DETROIT, NOVEMBER 2001

The Party

It was still dark outside when David Nelson III tried in vain to spot his father among all the unfamiliar faces in the arrivals hall. He swore to himself, sat down, and paged through the last issue of *The Source*, read a blurb about one of Tupac Shakur's posthumously released CDs. He wondered who was raking in the bucks from the murdered hip-hop legend's old recordings. Afeni Shakur, Tupac's mother, the former Black Panther activist? Didn't his father know her? Where was he, damn it? He slapped the magazine shut and got up. Paced back and forth with his overnight bag tucked under his arm. Listened to the unintelligible canned voices from the PA system and thought of his return flight to New York, tonight at 6:40.

I'm an adult now. He chuckled at the thought. As though he wasn't ten years ago. Ten years ago he stood here waiting, just like this. Grandpa Nelson had died. He hardly knew his grandfather, but his father still talked him into flying to Detroit for the service.

'You were named after him.'

'Yeah. So what.'

'The man worked himself to death. Hartgrove's sucked all the life out of him.'

'I thought you couldn't stand him.'

'I want you to come, David.'

It was the way he said it. Almost like begging. He felt a strange sort of pity for his father. His grandfather's death had nothing to do with it.

'I have to lead the service. I'm the eldest son. I don't know what to say.'

'Can't help you there.'

'I know. But will you be there?'

He stood at the back of the church for the entire service. He hadn't seen his father in years, knew he was a preacher out in Denver, that he had remarried (Pat, the loud woman in the loud clothes, next to Kenya, their daughter and his half-sister), but he couldn't bring himself to walk up front. He couldn't even remember what kind of eulogy his father gave. He just stood there and looked at the tall, lean figure alongside the white casket on the altar, at his thin, elegant hands, which every so often went up in the air; David heard the measured and well-chosen but meaningless words, his father's deep voice, the echo of that voice against the high gray walls of the church, how the voice inflected upward, became thinner, at the end of each sentence so that each sentence became a question, the reassuring rhythm that followed, like he was speaking to him alone. It was the sound of that voice that made David Nelson III forget where he was, forget his annoyance and aversion, just for a brief moment. He no longer heard the voice itself, but memories of it, and did not know what he should feel.

So he felt nothing. Right after the meal Grandma Essie and her church friends had served in the basement of the building, he took a taxi to the airport and flew back to New York.

He sat back down. Glanced at his watch. Five endless minutes had gone by. He had to cut his father some slack—maybe he was stuck in traffic. He took out the invitation from his nephew, checking that he at least had the address of his grandmother's party. Grandma Essie was eighty, his father sixty, and he would turn forty in a couple of months. Nice round numbers. Not that he was superstitious, but since receiving the invitation for Grandma Essie's birthday party a few months ago, he had thought of his father more often. Indirectly, at least. He thought about himself, about his work, his ambitions, his dreams, as though evaluating his life up until now. At the strangest moments, snippets of long-forgotten memories flashed before his eyes, and his father was a permanent background fixture in all of them, as if he couldn't do anything without his father watching over his shoulder. He never spoke, but he was there, like a ghost, and gradually it began to dawn on David III that maybe it had never been otherwise, that his father, despite his absence, had whispered all kinds of advice and guidance in his ear. That was the confusing part. There had been periods when he didn't see his father for four or five years, when he didn't call or write— not even Josephine knew what he was up to, where he lived, with whom; for all they knew, he could have been dead. He was gone for so long that David hardly missed him. His father was the shoebox full of clippings his mother kept in her closet.

Junior High School. 1973 or '74.

'Isn't your father ...?'

'How'd you know?'

He took out the shoebox and read the clippings one by one. Like putting together a jigsaw puzzle, he pieced together the story of The Last Poets, adding to it his vague memories of their rehearsals. He was five or six; his father took him and his little brother Duane to Uncle Joe's store. Uncle Joe sold African art and jewelry and clothing. They could choose whatever they wanted, a silver bracelet or a brightly colored dashiki. Spiffed up in their new things, their father took them to a big empty space with a wooden floor on 125th St. They sat on pillows. His brother was tired and lay his head in David's lap. David himself was too excited with his new duds to notice his father's friends. Only later, in junior high, did he play the record and recall how his father's voice bled into Kain's in 'Today Is a Killer'. It was February, Black History Month, and anyone could perform if they wanted to. He and Duane and a few friends did The Last Poets. He was Felipe. 'No, not my father. I want to sing. Felipe's a good singer. And he's young and sexy.'

He took the clippings with him to college. Not only as mementos of his father. Looking back on it, those clippings had been a kind of insurance policy, a birth certificate, a passport. He remembered the time he saw a poster for The Last Poets on campus. It was 1982, the beginning of the hip-hop era. Grandmaster Flash had just become world-famous with 'The Message'. The DJ Afrika Bambaataa made waves with 'Planet Rock'. All the clubs had DJs and MCs who rapped to throbbing beats and samples from older recordings. David knew everybody in the scene, and everybody knew David, who occasionally appeared as MC for his father, David Sr., Last Poet and godfather of militant rap. He and his friends went to see The Last Poets in the campus auditorium. For David they were just names: Jalal Nuriddin, Suliaman El-Hadi, and the drummer Nilija—he had never met them before. But they were The Last Poets and he was proud that they were performing on his campus. He was so excited about going up to the stage with his friends, introducing them to Jalal, that he rocked nervously from one leg to the other, hardly taking in the poems or the music. Jalal had been in the group almost from the very beginning. He'd surely remember his father.

But Jalal didn't give him the time of day. 'Yeah, I know your old man,' he mumbled in a dull, disinterested voice, and then turned to give an autograph to a girl.

Worse than his own disappointment was his friends' silence. As though the snub cast doubt on his background, as though he were some fraud, a show-off. No one said so, of course, but that evening he took out the box of faded clippings read them all and when he calmed down and felt his friends' imagined jibes and wisecracks fade, he bundled the material up and crossed the hallway to the room opposite his. The door was ajar; he went in, spread the articles out on the linoleum floor and said to the guys, 'Here. Read it for yourselves. The tall one with the beard? That's David Nelson, my father.'

He unzipped his bag and stuffed the magazine in. The arrivals hall had started filling up, the hubbub echoing off the glass. Maybe he should have his father paged. He could have gotten lost; it's such a big, busy place. Good thing he was getting a lift: he would never be able to find his way around Detroit, with its maze of highways, the abandoned yellow factories that stood there like war casualties complete with bullet holes and ragged plastic sheeting flapping in the broken windows. The deserted avenues downtown where no one dared go. He only knew the city from taxi rides. It gave him the creeps, but he never told his father that.

His father always showed up unexpectedly. Like one Friday afternoon. He was nine.

'Packed your bag?'

He shook his head.

'We're going camping.'

They drove out of the city in his father's silver Buick. The headlights of oncoming cars shone through his half-shut eyes. He pretended to be asleep. They drove for hours; at the end there was hardly any traffic. The road got narrower and snaked upwards. Down below he saw a thin black line.

'The river,' his father said. And later: 'We're here.'

They got out. He felt the mud suck at his sandals. He followed his father down the dark path, stayed close behind him. A strange, lonesome sound came out of the woods, a sound he'd never heard before. 'Are there bears here?' he asked. 'Sure are,' his father laughed. They pitched their tent on an open patch of ground, rolled open the mats and sleeping bags and gathered dry branches for the campfire. Then David Sr. brought out a bag of marsh-mallows and pronged one on a thin green twig to roast.

'Are there really bears here?' David asked.

'You afraid?'

'No,' he lied.

'We'll go back tomorrow. I want you to see the night. It's never night in New York. D'you hear that? It's nature breathing. City life isn't real life, it only seems like it because it's so busy there all the time, because every-thing's moving. But it's not so, son. The real world is somewhere else, behind things. What we see with our eyes is not real life, it's a kind of play. I want to you dis-cover that. Come on, let's hit the sack.'

David looked at the smoldering orange branches on the ground. All he could think of was sleep; when you slept, time went faster, and soon it was daytime again.

He still didn't entirely understand what his father

meant. But last summer, when he listened to that cassette tape of his father reciting his poetry, it brought that camping weekend in the woods back to him, and his father's words, strange and ominous, as though something precious had been taken from him.

The cassette had lain on his desk all week. Every time it caught his eye he got that same feeling in the pit of his stomach. He wasn't sure if it was irritation or guilt—maybe both. But why should he feel guilty? One Thursday evening, after a full day of meetings, David put the tape into the player and listened.

The first poem was 'Black Woman': *I wanna make a beautiful world for you black woman / a world of beauty for beautiful you / a world where black women can bathe / naked and unashamed in gentle streams / a world where poetry is you black woman / bathe in gentle rhythmic ways / I will create create create / until I create that world for you.*

His father's words sounded so genuine, so sincere and absolute, that David was almost embarrassed. Not a trace of doubt. It was like his father had banned all ugliness and routineness from his thoughts while he wrote, as though he put all his hope into his lyrics, thus making them reality.

There was some older work at the end of the tape. 'The Last Poets' and 'Today Is a Killer' and 'Are You Ready?' Poetry that even now carried the hot breath of revolution; after all these years you could still hear the urgency, the fear, the bitter desires. David knew the words by heart. They were a part of his past, even though he always had a hard time taking it all literally. But now, his father's uninhibited delivery made him sad. He knew right away he would find music for them, for all the poems, first thing tomorrow morning he would call a few studio musicians to talk it over. He felt uneasy, harried, no time to lose. His father had never been afforded the respect he deserved. He would recast these poems together with the music, he imagined smoky jazz and earthy beats; the dreamlike visions had to sound ordinary, up front, real. He would use sexy rhythms. The older, militant poems would get a sober treatment, maybe only an African drum underneath, just like back then, maybe that would keep them from sounding plucked out of the past, like some retro parody.

That night in his office, David stared at the worn patches on the black carpet, saw how the pallid fluorescent light reflected off the framed platinum albums on the wall, he heard the wailing sirens and honking taxis outside and realized he had set himself an impossible task. He wanted his music to protect his father from being let down by his own prophetic words. He knew it was too late, but it didn't matter. For the first time in his life he felt that he really had something to tell him.

He picked up his bag and followed the signs to the taxi stand. It was a little past eight. Far too early to go to the party. He realized he had no address with him, Grandma Essie's or one of his aunts or uncles. He barely knew their names. His father was driving in from Cleveland and didn't have a cell phone. He slowed his pace, walked over to a small self-service counter and got himself a coffee. It was down to being stuck there, or deciding to take the next plane back to New York. Overcome by a vague, empty feeling, he wondered what the hell he was doing here. What did he expect? Reconciliation? Everything suddenly hunky-dory? He had resolved to really listen to his father, and not jump to the defensive as usual. He sat down and drank the lukewarm coffee.

How old was he then—six, seven? He and Duane were

asleep in their bunk beds in their apartment on 120th St. He on top and Duane on the bottom. It was still dark when he woke, his father shaking his shoulder. 'Psst.' He put a finger over his lips, patted his knee. David climbed out of bed and onto his father's lap.

'Listen, David,' he whispered. 'Daddy's going away for a while.'

'Where?'

'I just have to go. I've got business to take care of.'

'What kind of business?'

'Go back to sleep. I love you.'

'I love you too.'

He climbed back into bed, his eyes sore with sleepiness. He heard his father tiptoe out of the room, into the hallway, and out the front door. Real softly so he didn't wake Mama and Duane. David lay on his back. The first light of day shone through the thin green curtains. He couldn't get back to sleep. He didn't understand why Daddy had to leave, but the earnestness in his voice suggested he wouldn't be back anytime soon. But he was proud that his father woke only him, not the others, as though letting him in on some future plan—only he didn't know what.

Even his mother couldn't understand his sudden disappearance. All she told him was that his father could be a loving and responsible and caring family man the one minute, and gone the next.

He felt a clammy hand on the back his neck. He started, splashing coffee on his new sneakers.

'Damn,' he said, wheeling around to see his father's tawny, smiling face.

'Sorry, David ... my car ... an old sedan ... borrowed it from the Prince ... been sitting at the side of the road for an hour ... sorry.'

David wiped the coffee from his sneakers, but it left yellowish stains on the white leather. 'Never mind,' he mumbled. Damn that Prince and his jalopy. The Lord might have chosen him to save mankind, but a decent car wasn't part of the package.

'Is that all you've got?' his father asked, nodding at the valise.

'I'm going back tonight,' David replied.

'So soon?'

'Let's go, okay?'

'I want to go around to Uncle Bill's first.'

'Who's that?'

'Your grandfather's brother. I heard he didn't want to go to the party. He's blind and unsteady. The guy's ninety. He lives on Santa Rosa Drive, it shouldn't be any trouble to swing by there.'

'Guess not.'

'I'm happy to see you, David.'

David nodded. Wanted to say he was glad to see his father too, but he decided to save it for a better moment.

'When We Are Weak' (1998)

We are sounds spit into a sea of silence
Black characters inscribed on the pages
of history. We are the swollen river
of the night seeking to empty
ourselves into the purple orange
sunrise

DETROIT, NOVEMBER 2001

Uncle Bill Nelson

I'm not going anywhere. So it's Essie's eightieth birthday today. I'm not going. Was that David's boy who called?

'I raised your father,' I told him.

'I know, Uncle Bill, 'cept I've never heard the whole story.'

His voice sounded just like my brother's, God rest his soul.

'I'm blind,' that's what I told him. 'The only place I go is the bank, with my niece. I bought her a new Ford for twenty-four thousand dollars so she can do my shopping for me every week and take me to the bank.'

But he wasn't listening.

At home I see everything. I might be blind, but I see everything I need to see. Every day is the same. My life's made up of memories, that's why dates are so important, they're all in my head and I go through them every day. Practice. Dates give me something to hold on to. Yesterday I tripped over an empty box my niece had left in the dining room. Didn't break anything. I got back up. I saw the lamp hanging above the table, the yellow light reflecting off the shiny tabletop. Saw my wife sitting there. We were married for fifty-four years.

'I don't want to go.'

But David's boy insisted.

'I'll come pick you up.'

'I raised your father.'

'It'll do you good to get out.'

I said, 'When I was thirteen, my mother came back in a dream. She was young and beautiful. Her hair jutted out in all directions. She was worried. "I want you to look out for your little brother," she said. The next day my sister Odessa showed up at the door with Jake, that's what we called your father. David, I should say. David Jordan Hubert Truman Nelson. Odessa lived in New York but she had traveled to Coweta, Oklahoma to Uncle Nathaniel's to check up on us. But Uncle Nathaniel was dead. Jake was living with Clemmie, our stepmother in Sapulpa, Oklahoma and I was in Kansas City, working as a gas station attendant. That was 1926. Jake was ten. I raised him.'

I heard how cold and empty my words sounded. They had nothing to do with what all's in my head. What you say is always so much less than what's really there. The grooves in the dark wood of the freight train that brought me to Tulsa, or to Denver or California and back to Oklahoma. The damp that rises off the bales of hay in the fields. The mountain peaks that disappear into the morning clouds. The bright orange-yellow flowers on the banks alongside the railway. How the wind yanked at their fragile, silky blossoms as the train rushed past. I dangled my legs out of the freight car and smelled the hot, dusty air, saw the yellowed grass in the distance. I was eleven. I stole a hunk of bread from a shop, ran for my life back to the station. I stared at the greasy black locomotive like it was the most beautiful thing I'd ever seen, and when the train slowly ground into motion I hopped on. Nobody saw me; I hid among the sacks of wheat or grain and bales of cotton.

'Uncle Bill?'

'What do you want from me?' I didn't mean to be gruff. But what in God's name was that boy thinking, just calling me up and insisting I go to some party? I'm blind. All that racket, the strange voices, it'll only befuddle me. I don't want to see any new faces. All the faces I want to see are in this here house, this kitchen.

'I'll drop by anyway,' he said. I could hear the hesitation in his voice. My brother's voice. His son's a poet or something.

I don't know how long ago he called. An hour? Two? Time is irrelevant. Even death has become irrelevant. I call it the blessing of blindness. No new memories. My life has done an about-face; I can only go back.

205 North Hickory Street, Sapulpa, Oklahoma. That was our house. Just a ways up from the railroad tracks. The phone rang. Our number was 1182. It was just getting light outside; indoors, everything was grayish. Papa lay in bed. He said: 'Send them over.' It was 1920. Usually he never had them send anybody over. White people never crossed the tracks without his permission. He was the chief of police. Had three pistols, a .38, a .40, and a .45. He'd shot two men dead, I saw it with my own eyes. That kind of thing sticks with you forever ... like the telephone ringing at dawn.

The laborers with their huge hands, loading the bales of cotton. There were no other houses in the neighborhood, just the Frisco Railway building, where they built new trains.

205 North Hickory Street. 1918. I ran like mad through the fields. My shoes wet from the dew. 'Go get Dr. McCoy. Quick.' Dr. McCoy was a black lady doctor. The only one I ever saw in my whole life. She'd delivered every one of us, all six of my mother's children. I was born on July 20,

1913. Papa had six more children with another woman, Clemmie. I have a half-brother, Clemmie's eldest child, he's a year and four months older than me. Mama must've known. I still believe she was murdered. They said she died after eating spoiled cabbage, but can you die from that? Papa married Clemmie the day after the funeral.

Everybody was jealous of Papa. He had twelve children and we lived better than any of the colored people in the whole county.

So anyway, I was five, Jake was two. He was too young to remember. Too young for anything. Clemmie didn't want any pictures of Mama in the living room. There was a yellowed photo with curled-up corners, the thick paper felt like cardboard and the edges crumbled in your fingers.

Everything's in my head, everything, but wordless, a deep, dark pool of sludgy, steaming mud in the middle of the woods. And sometimes, all by itself, on its surface the sight of the St. James Theater appears, with its worn velvet seats, the smell of burned sugar, silver flickering on the screen. Hoot Gibson and Jack Hawks. Their mouths moved but no sound came out. Stylish letters told the story.

1922.

'Will the Nelson boys please report to the ticket window?' And then: 'Your father's been wounded.'

We left the movie house. Walked straight into Ed Glass's hearses on North Johannes Street. Tom Brown walked alongside. 'I didn't kill your father. I swear it on my brother's grave.'

It's like the images in my head start taking control. They don't want to be told, only seen. When I put them in the right order and make a story out of them, they seem to lose their punch. But what if Jake's kid starts asking questions? What then? He's a poet, I think, or a priest. He's gonna want a story.

1922.

My father is Richard Nelson. He was a US marshal. The fastest gun in the West. Shot nine men dead. His father brought him from Waco, Texas to Sapulpa even before Oklahoma became a state. Sapulpa's in Creek County, named after the Creek Indians. Legas Brown was an Indian. Selling whisky to Indians was prohibited, but Legas Brown was drunk. He was with his brother Tom in a car, their women on the backseat.

Papa was on his way from Sapulpa to Beggs, Oklahoma to fetch a robber. He had a deputy with him to do the driving. A 1919 Model A Ford Touring without windows, just some celluloid on the side to keep out the dust. And they had another passenger in back. None of the roads were paved, they were just narrow dirt paths.

Halfway there they can't go any further. A car's blocking the way. Legas and Tom Brown. Legas is drunk, refuses to move over. Papa walks over to Tom. 'What're you and Legas doing here?' They argue. But Papa doesn't know Legas has a gun. The deputy yells: 'Watch out! Behind you!' Papa turns and Legas shoots him right in the mouth, the bullet goes straight through his neck, and before he hits the ground my father shoots Legas in his left eye. Legas stumbles over to the car and shoots the deputy. Then the man on the backseat jumps out and empties his rifle into Legas.

That's how Tom Brown told it, anyway. And again he swore he didn't kill Papa. He had to testify against his own brother in court. Tom Brown had oil on his land. He sold the land and gave Clemmie five thousand dollars. But she only got to enjoy it for two weeks, because then a black fellow stole it all from her.

1922.

I was nine. Jake six. Clemmie sent us to Louise, Mississippi, to my great-grandmother, Mama's grandma. We had a chaperone. Clemmie gave him a hundred dollars and brought us to the station. We weren't but a few miles out of town and I pulled the handbrake. 'I ain't going to Mississippi,' I said. I'd been to Louise once with my mother. I thought we were going to see my grandma, Granny Hill in Beggs, Oklahoma. Mama laughed. 'This is your great-grandmother,' she said. I got a taste of the Mississippi whites. They blocked the road so we couldn't get in. They just stood there in the middle of the road. Didn't matter that it was boiling hot, we just had to sit there in the car until they got tired of taunting us and ambled off.

So we walked back across the tracks to Clemmie's. 205 North Hickory.

In Sapulpa the whites didn't dare cross the tracks without my father's permission. He was the fastest gun in the West.

I couldn't call Clemmie 'Mama'. What did Jake call her? I can't even remember Jake talking. He was my little shadow.

Fortunately, on the train from Sapulpa to Coweta, Oklahoma he fell asleep.

'Uncle Nathaniel, how come we're not eating steak?' He asked that.

'You want steak, go fetch a rifle,' Uncle Nathaniel said. ''Nuf steak walking around out there.'

Jake looked at me. 'Let's go,' I said. We went out to the barn. The hunting rifle was too big and heavy for Jake— he put it to his shoulder and tumbled backwards. I told him to hide in the tall grass. Hide and watch. I shot two rabbits and a hare. Uncle Nathaniel said: 'Still ain't no steak.'

There were raccoons in the woods.

Skinning a cow. The blood in tin buckets. Pulley and winch to hoist the carcasses in the smoking shed.

It was okay to leave Jake behind there. There was enough meat in Coweta, Oklahoma. And Uncle Nathaniel was my father's brother.

I spent two years tramping through Oklahoma, Colorado, Arizona and California. Sometimes I thought I heard footsteps behind me. It was cold. Wispy clouds passing in front of the moon. I'd stop and look back. Nobody. Silence. Only the owls. I'd walk further, and the footsteps followed. Footsteps on the wet ground. I always thought it might be an Indian. Indians can make themselves invisible, sneaking barefoot through the woods. But there was never anyone, never.

I'm bushed. I'm doing my best, but the images are too quick for me. As though my thoughts are chasing them off, as though life is slipping through my fingers.

The doorbell. Is that the doorbell? If it's Jake's boy, he'll walk around back and knock on the kitchen door. What'm I supposed to tell him?

'I raised your father.'

When my mother came back in my dream, Uncle Nathaniel was already dead. That was news to me. I was living in Kansas City, on Troost Ave. I was a gas station attendant. I was nineteen. I was really thirteen but my ID said I was nineteen. I stole my older brother William's ID after he'd gotten crushed to death playing football. Now I was William.

'You got to look after Jake,' Odessa said. She stayed one night on Troost Ave. and then went back to New York.

Jake didn't go to school. I told him what to do. He shined shoes, helped me out at the gas station. We earned seventy-seven cents a day.

Seventy-seven cents.

A dollar.

A dollar fifty.

Eventually Odessa moved from New York to Detroit. She wrote to us. She said: 'Ford pays five dollars a day. Blacks are coming here from all over the country. They'll hire you both in a jiffy.'

Three days was all I could stand. You had to wear this heat-resistant suit, but it was like I was on fire. Jake did some hustling in the city. I found work for us at Hackett's Butchers. Slaughtering cows. At first we did fifty a day, and at the end, two hundred and fifty. We lived in a boarding house for coloreds. I told Jake he had to pay the rent to Mrs. Boyd. Essie was her youngest daughter.

I don't want to go to Essie's party.

I don't know if she ever loved Jake. Jake was only doing his best. Sometimes I still feel like he's close by. I can hear him breathe. He went with me when I marched past the Ford factory with a megaphone to organize the workers. But he didn't say anything, he was just there, like when we were back in Coweta, Oklahoma and he hid in the tall grass and watched me shoot rabbits and hares. He was always hiding. Sometimes I forgot he was there. Jimmy Hoffa and the Teamsters sent one of their guys; he walked up to us, a rolled-up newspaper under his arm with a steel bar hidden in it. I knew their methods. 'Fuck off, ya black scum.' Even that slick Italian didn't pay Jake any notice. Only me. But I was too fast.

Too fast.

I'm tired.

God, I'm tired.

IF WE ONLY KNEW

'25 Years'

I couldn't write for just myself
I had to write to give a Damn
Entertaining not Complaining
About the changes we go through
Is a sucker M.C.'s message
Cause we've got work to do

CENTRAL PRISON, RALEIGH, NORTH CAROLINA, 1970

When the Revolution Comes

Never knew dark could be so dark. So utterly devoid of every trace of light. Not a single tint of gray or blue, purple, no shadow, only black, black, deep and impenetrable. I'm surprised I can breathe through the blackness, that there's oxygen in this space whose dimensions I can only guess by running my fingers along the walls. I feel rough stone, moisture, coolness; three feet, six feet, a sharp corner and the same distance back until I feel the steel of the door, behind which I'll bet it's just as dark and silent, because the only sounds I hear in here are the sounds of my own body, the swish of my blood in my veins. I imagine I'm sitting in a box that's inside another box, and another ...

I know that this is as far as my eyes will adjust to the dark. I've been here for too many hours now. If I bring my hands close to my face, I see only the white edges of my fingernails, as though they're floating in the air, separate from my fingers, as though I've drunk some magic potion that made me invisible even to myself.

And yet I'm not panicking. Just the opposite. In a strange way, the quiet is calming. Like I'm taking a break from myself, from life. The world has been turned inside out and I'm sitting right in the middle, in its deepest and warmest core. And on the other side of these walls are mirrors, huge silver surfaces that reflect all the hubbub and excitement and noise.

It reminds me of when I was kid and lay in bed early in the morning, after Daddy Joe woke me up at 5:30 to feed the rabbits and chickens and dogs. I knew I still had another ten minutes or so while Daddy shaved. And in those precious ten minutes I did nothing but lie on my back under the warm, soft covers with my eyes wide open. I didn't think of anything in particular; the thoughts just came to me. I saw the fringe of the orange tablecloth on the kitchen table, the apron strings tied behind Aunt Beanie's back. She was making gumbo, and all the while talking a mile a minute to me about the neighbor's son who went to a special school in the Bronx because it was better for him and for his mother. She stirred the gumbo without taking her eyes off it, and I thought: Why doesn't she open a window? It stinks in here. I saw Peaches' red-and-green checked skirt. She was skipping rope with her girlfriends on the corner of 142nd and Lenox. Every time she jumped, her dress floated up, and I caught a glimpse of the white edges of her panties contrasting against her deep brown skin. I was sitting on the stoop in front of Aunt Baby's house in Harlem. It was Sunday and sometimes we would drive there from Jamaica to visit Daddy Joe's sister. 'What you lookin' at,' Peaches sneered. I quickly averted my eyes, stared at the sidewalk. She ignored me, just kept on double Dutching. She had hair all the way down to her waist. She was cute and tough and not scared of anything and I'll bet she didn't have to get up at the crack of dawn to feed chickens or weed the garden like I did. In Harlem there were no gardens or chicken runs or rabbit hutches. In Harlem there were shop windows and street vendors and bars and restaurants and lights and men with fedoras and cashmere coats and women with painted nails and pretty dresses.

I saw all this in the ten minutes I stole from Daddy Joe. Until I heard him shout a second time: 'Charles, get downstairs. Now!' I knew I didn't have a second to lose—jumped out of bed, threw on my clothes, and ran down the stairs.

Here my voice means nothing; I don't have the illusion that anyone hears me when I yell, and if they did hear me they would probably just laugh and shrug. They feel emboldened by the power they believe they have over me.

It was my big mouth that got me here, and now no one can hear anything I say. We're even, in other words.

I never realized how dependent I was on my voice. How I trusted the strength of my own sound, my rhythm, timbre, the way I use pauses, the emotions I put behind my words. I believed that a story is only a story when it's told out loud, a poem is only a poem when it's recited, sung, when the sound of the voice flavors the words, colors them, gives them warmth, meaning, breath, a soul. I'd have understood that even without my African background and Yoruba religion. Until now I'd done everything with my voice. Everything. I can still hear Aunt Beanie saying: 'Don't yell! Use your diaphragm! Throw your voice! Don't yell!' I'm in the basement rehearsing for Easter, when I'll be allowed to do the Lord's Prayer; she wanted to hear me up in the kitchen without me yelling. 'Use your diaphragm!' And when the Everly Brothers came on the radio, she'd let me sing along. 'Whenever I want you, all I have to do is dream, dream, dream, dream ... ' Then she'd go and get the neighbors. You didn't hear the Everly Brothers, you only heard me. But only when Daddy Joe was at work.

I know what they think: the silence will humble him. He'll beg for forgiveness. Well, the begging part they can forget, and I'm not sure about the humbling either. I'll have to make sense of being stuck in this unyielding darkness. Otherwise it'll have been a waste of time. Dead time. I've already lost my name. Here I'm 'Charles Davis 202464 Out-of-State'. Abiodun Oyewole only exists as long as I feel he exists. I have to do something. I don't believe in coincidence. If I had a pen and paper and light, I'd write. And then I'd put the words in my head and on the paper into sound. But I have nothing. Only memories.

As though she's afraid to hurt them, Marlena slices the watermelons carefully and meticulously into wedges. She's made quite a bit of headway by the time I've unloaded the last melons from my car. She leans over the improvised table, takes the long-blade kitchen knife with both hands and attacks the next melon. Sweat beads on her forehead and upper lip. She straightens herself, holds the knife in one hand and pushes her afro back with the other, sticks out her bottom lip, and puffs air into her face. She stands there like that for a moment, her eye absently passing over the hundreds of red half-moon slices lying on the wooden table waiting to be slurped up by the thirsty neighborhood residents and other sympathizers. It's still early morning, June 30, 1969. A year ago, just a year and a few months, but it's still like I'm looking at a stranger when I see myself standing next to the open door of my beige 1965 Impala, a shiny dark-green watermelon under each arm. I remember feeling pretty ridiculous carting around those melons—a pretty menial job for a revolutionary, for a man—but in here it's hard to call the sensation to mind. I've got to try harder. Freeze the image, and examine it for as long as it takes until every detail reveals its significance. The juicy red flesh of the melons in the hot June sun. The countless flat black seeds. Marlena's petite fingers grasping the handle of the knife.

'You want me to go to the market?'

'In the Bronx, you know where. Get as many watermelons as you can, okay?' Marlena handed me a crumpled twenty-dollar bill. We were building tables out of trestles and old doors. Just after dawn I had driven out to the lot on the corner of 125th and Seventh Ave. with a few women from the Harlem Committee for Self-Defense. We used a bolt cutter to snip holes in the chain-link fence. Just one more day until Rockefeller's bulldozers would come raze the vacant apartment buildings and shops, the old elementary school and the playground. They were planning to build a high-rise office building on the property. The last thing that neighborhood needed was a high-rise office building.

'Why me?'

'Because you have a car.'

'So do you,' I snapped, and saw Marlena subtly bring back her shoulders, tilt her head, and knit her brow, her face becoming a question mark.

'So?'

There was an element of involuntary, matter-of-fact superiority in her voice, in the calmness with which she asked the question. I had no answer for it, nor had I ever seen this kind of assertiveness in any other black woman. My anger ebbed before it got the chance to burn in my chest.

Marlena Franklin was my girlfriend. She was a Panther and was active in the neighborhood. We'd been living together in an apartment on Riverside Drive for a few months. Marlena had a certain natural elegance about her. Whenever she walked in a room, you saw people look at her, not because she was so beautiful or eye-catching, but because of her insouciant aura; she seized her surroundings without it ever occurring to her whether she had the right to. It had more to do with naiveté than with arrogance. During the occupation, too, it was more like Marlena was puttering around in her own little kitchen rather than a ramshackle building site that could be surrounded by police cars at any moment. She was finely built and had the kind of face that drew all your attention to her eyes. Eyes that displayed knowledge and intelligence, yet, at times, a flash of suppressed panic.

Marlena was the daughter of Cicely Tyson, the actress who lived with Miles Davis. This was common knowledge at the Committee for Self-Defense, but no one made a point of it, least of all Marlena. It was almost taboo: as far as the Marxist-Leninists were concerned, Tyson and Davis were bourgeois artists who craved white acceptance. But I saw the curiosity when comrades were in Marlena's presence, a kind of awkward neediness, as though they hoped that some of the glamour of Marlena's mother and stepfather might rub off on them. And because they were ashamed of these feelings, their curiosity twisted into contempt.

I have to be honest here. If I'm not, I can just as well shut my eyes right now and let the dank darkness swallow me up. I dug Marlena. I loved Marlena more than I've loved any other woman. More than Olubiji, my wife and the mother of my only son. It was Marlena who said I should marry Biji, who at that time still went by the name Carolyn.

'Well Dun, if Pharaoh is really your son, you might as well get married to her, because I'm not having any children.'

I was crushed. 'What's that all about?'

'What?'

'About not wanting children. You're a woman.'

She cocked her head and looked pityingly at me. It caught me off guard. Her expression was dull and inward-looking, quasi-bored and indifferent. She was drifting away from me and the worst of it was that I wasn't the cause of her mood. She wasn't angry at me because of Carolyn, who I'd only been to bed with once, and that was before I even knew Marlena.

'What do you really want?' she said.

'Carolyn's not down at all, Marlena. She has no idea about the revolution. Have you had a good look at her? She buys her clothes at Saks Fifth Avenue. Sneakers and jeans, no afro. She's never set foot in a jazz club. She's this bourgie upper-middle-class person living in fucking Queens with her mother.'

'Something the matter with that?' she snapped, as though I had insulted her rather than Carolyn. And maybe I was self-consciously trying to do just that. I was so hyped and confused about suddenly finding out I had a son that I hardly recognized my anger over Marlena's indifference. Anyway, I was ignoring her pain. I knew she adored her mother, protected her. Cicely was so wrapped up in her career that she'd shipped Marlena off to a Catholic boarding school as a kid. She told me about her loneliness and about the priest who, night after night, snuck into her room and whispered 'shhh' and laid one hand over her mouth while pulling down her panties with the other. I knew all that, but at that moment I was thinking only of myself. Scared to death of losing Marlena, the only woman at that point in my life I'd have asked to marry me.

'Well?' she repeated. 'What's wrong with living with your mother in Queens?'

'I dunno, Marlena. I don't love her.'

'Come on, Dun. You have a son. You say you want to be a revolutionary. Who for? How can you really mean something to the movement if you're too chicken to set an example for your own son? Huh?'

'Are you calling me chicken? Did you say that?' It was the word 'chicken' that blinded me and turned my panic into anger.

'Can't I say that?'

'I should never have been so honest with you.'

'Excuse me?'

'Carolyn has nothing to do with this. I know what you're thinking: the poet's afraid. He's just a poet, a charlatan, a coward who preaches revolution but is too scared to stick his neck out. Who gets a kick out of fame. Isn't that what you mean? Just say so. What are words, after all? You know better than anyone what it's like when an artist gets all the attention, don't you? Just look at your mother and Miles. Do you remember our first night, Marlena? Do you? I thought my words were safe with you. I thought you understood me. Marlena, a true Panther, my girl.'

She stood staring at me impassively while I spewed all that at her. The louder and harsher my words, the more absent and frail she seemed, as though part of her had left the room long ago—or maybe she was just trying to protect herself.

'What are you talking about, Dun?'

'Leave me alone.'

'Come on, Dun. You don't have to prove yourself to anyone. Have you ever heard me badmouth The Last Poets?'

'It's not that,' I muttered as I went to the bedroom to grab some clothes and shove them in a bag. 'I'm fed up with The Last Poets. They're turning into celebrities, acting like rock stars.' I looked up and saw Marlena standing in the doorway.

'I'll be seeing you,' I said, bag in hand, as I stormed out of the apartment.

I have to think of a way of not getting ahead of myself. My mind works differently in this cell. You have no grip in the dark. There's too much space, too much time and freedom to think whatever you want. And who's to say what's true? What's the correct order? The silence seems to want to rob me of my own narrative, push me outside it. The characters can do what they want, say what they want. Where am I? I have to concentrate, concentrate. This is a test, I know it, the silence is testing me. I'm here. I close my fists and feel my fingernails cut into the palms of my hands. I'm here. There must be a truth. I have to stay calm and look and listen carefully, keep on breathing. I close my eyes, in the distance I hear a faint breeze-like hissing, I know it's my own breathing but I hear the wind cautiously playing with the thick leafage of the birch trees in Daddy Joe's backyard, I see the misty white sky, the clouds.

'Charles, go fetch your mother. Hurry up, go on.' Even before I see him, I feel his deep bass voice reverberate in my stomach. I rush inside. Aunt Beanie is on her hands and knees on the kitchen floor, she's looking for something in a cabinet, I hear a bottle fall over, a muted sigh.

'Daddy Joe wants you to come.'

She looks up, blows a tuft of hair out of her sweaty face. 'Do you have any idea where I left those rubber gloves, son?'

'What gloves?'

'Never mind. Just help me up. It's already bad enough

you see me like this. What did you say?'

'Daddy Joe wants you to go outside.'

'Is he home already? Good heavens, what time is it?'

The radio is on. I hear lazy dance-band music. It reminds me of Hollywood movies. The sun shines through the open window and makes the kitchen orange. I bend over and offer Aunt Beanie a hand.

'What were you looking for?' I ask once she's righted herself. She pants; it was an effort to stand up. I'm taller than she is. I see the glittery silver threads in her hair. Her face is swollen from the heat. It's the first time that I really notice that Aunt Beanie is old. She wipes her hands on her apron.

'I thought we might still have time for a glass of lemonade in the backyard,' she says, a forced smile on her face. She winks at me. 'Homework finished?'

I nod.

'Practice your singing?'

I nod again.

'Go on then.' She pushes me toward the door.

'But—'

'No buts. Go on now.'

I don't see Daddy Joe. I stay in the kitchen. I smell the floor wax and lye. I lay my hand on the thin cotton tablecloth, feel the warmth of the sun on my face. I squint just enough so that everything's hazy. The yard. The tall cornstalks, the golden wheat, the tomato plants, the peppers and the gnarly beech tree trunks. I see the dust that rises off the dry ground and hangs like mist above the crops. It's August. Our house is in Jamaica, Queens, but I imagine we're in Savannah, Georgia. That's where Daddy Joe comes from. He never told me, but I heard it from Aunt Beanie. Daddy Joe is a man of few words. He doesn't like wasting time with idle talk when there's work to be done. I see the garden he's made out of three parking spaces. As though beyond it there's nothing but fields and hills and woods and meandering creeks. No city, no houses, no traffic, no movement. I hear the dogs barking, the rustling of the rabbits in their hutch. The whole neighborhood's jealous of our land, of the sumptuous gardens surrounding our house. It's strange to see myself back in a garden. I'd give my eyeteeth right now to stick my nose in a pile of freshly dug potatoes and smell the dirt, moist and clammy and full of promise. But it also feels disloyal to Daddy Joe. Like I don't have the right to return, even in my mind, without his permission. Like I never had enough respect for his dreams. I couldn't imagine Daddy Joe having dreams. I was scared to death of him. I don't think I ever told anyone that, not even Aunt Beanie. How could I? It would be too painful for her, because she couldn't protect me from him. She tried, though, with love, with little gifts, with our secrets and our private jokes.

'What you all laughin' about? What's funny?'

'Nothing, Daddy.'

I'd been weeding in the garden. Spent hours cutting away all the clover and dandelions and carpetweed, chopping at them with a hoe and a rake. I thought I'd done pretty good job, but when Daddy Joe came home he grabbed me by the scruff of the neck, dragged me into the yard and shoved me onto the ground. 'If you don't pull out the weeds root and all, you ain't doing nothing. They'll choke the rest of the plants. What's the matter with you? You afraid to get dirty? Go on, get on your knees and pull them up by the roots! That's right. Don't come back in till you're done.'

Now that I think about it, it was perfectly innocent,

but at the time I was scared stiff. I felt the coldness of his anger. A coldness that bordered on cruelty. Subconsciously I knew that for him, there was no sacrifice too great in order to achieve something in life. So my life was subject to his regime. Every moment I lost to rest or idleness could and would be punished. As though I ceased to exist as a person when I was around him—I was his tool.

I remember one story Daddy Joe told. Once, when he was young, he was working the land for a white foreman. Plowing. Halfway through his shift, his mule went lame and he went to the foremen to ask for another animal. There were two more mules out in the field. 'Do it yourself,' the foreman said. So Daddy Joe put the leather straps around his waist and dragged that plow up and down the field and come evening the whole thing had been plowed.

He told this anecdote without a trace of emotion, as though he were reading a report. As a kid it didn't make any sense to me. To be honest, I didn't like it when Daddy Joe talked normally. I was so used to his bitter silence and his harsh orders, both of which frightened me and made me wary; still, one way or another I got used to it and knew how to behave. So when he suddenly spoke in a normal tone of voice, I was far more anxious. Was almost ashamed of him.

I'm on the backseat with Aunt Beanie. Daddy Joe and Aunt Baby are in front. I don't know where we're going. We drive down Lenox Ave. and right around 125th there's tumult. Dozens of men and women and children are standing on the corner. Standing a little higher than the rest, maybe on a soapbox or a stepstool, one man is giving a speech. I don't have a good view of him, can't hear him either, because the car windows are shut. 'He won't live to see old age,' Aunt Baby sighs, with a pitying shake of the head.

Daddy Joe stares peevishly ahead. We wait at the stoplight. 'He's only stirring things up,' he whispers to Aunt Baby. 'No good'll come of it.'

I'm curious, and crane my neck to see him better, but with all the people thronging around him, all I can catch a glimpse of is his reddish hair. Funny, I've never seen a black man with red hair before.

'Who's that?' I ask, looking over at Aunt Beanie.

She pretends not to hear me, looks the other way. I'm sitting behind Daddy Joe, and I see his neck muscles twitch. The starched white collar of his dress shirt cuts into his blue-black skin. The silence pounds in my ears and I wonder what I said wrong.

'Aren't you going to tell him?' Aunt Baby exclaims. With a jerk she turns to me. 'That's Malcolm X, son. His biggest mistake is telling the truth. Not everybody appreciates that.' She shoots her husband a fiery glance. He just keeps looking straight ahead. 'They'll kill him, for sure,' she says.

'Who will?' I ask naively, but no one responds, not even Aunt Baby. The light turns green and we drive on, leaving the crowd behind. I look out the rear window, trying to catch another glimpse of Malcolm X. But all I see is the strange orange aura that surrounds his trimmed orange hair.

Thinking back on it now, I almost feel sorry for Daddy Joe. I'm glad he didn't have to see all this. He'd have felt like a failed parent. I can see that now. So clearly it hurts. Daddy Joe, staring straight ahead, big workman's hands firmly on the steering wheel. Why do I only realize now that he just couldn't bring himself to afford Malcolm even a bit of respect? He had to pretend he didn't exist, because everything about that proud, tall Afro-American, with his snappy, melodious speech and his orations about the slave mentality that imprisoned us ran contrary to his own existence, contrary to the luxuriant garden he had created with his own two hands and where he felt invulnerable. No matter how much he and Malcolm resembled one another, in their black Sunday suit and heavy-framed glasses and rigid, determined attitude.

Daddy Joe's determination brought him everything he needed in order to prove his worth: a big house, two cars, a bank account, property, animals, a family. Do I belong on that list? I'm not sure. Maybe Daddy Joe was always secretly afraid I wouldn't accept him as my father. He projected his own shortcomings onto me. But didn't I choose to go to New York with him and Aunt Beanie? That's how it was, right? Please tell me it was. I was four. I remember standing at the top of the stairs in our house in Cincinnati, Ohio. Mama was downstairs on the couch. It was evening. The clear plastic lampshade cover sparkled like tinfoil. Being the only lamp in the living room, it made Mama and Aunt Beanie look like they were floating in midair, like there was no floor, no rug, no windows or doors or cupboards or chairs, only the old sofa she was sitting on and the pink lampshade with the plastic cover, whose light shone on their serious faces. I sat down on the top step and laid my hands flat on the soft brown carpeting. This gave me the illusion that I could hear them better, even though I hardly understood what they were talking about.

'He's just as much yours as he is mine, sister,' Mama was saying. 'I don't know what I'd done without you.'

'I'd lay down my life for Charles, you know that,' Aunt Beanie replied. 'It'll be all right, May, God willing, it will be all right.'

'And Joe?'

'Don't you worry about Joe.'

'Does he want a son?'

'Oh May, May ... ' Aunt Beanie shook her head and put her arm around Mama's back.

She whispered something in her ear, I couldn't hear what. Mama's shoulders twitched a bit and she rubbed her eyes. Aunt Beanie held her tight and together they rocked back and forth.

'Come join us when you've got stronger, May,' Aunt Beanie said. 'We'll help you find a house in New York.'

'A boy needs a father,' Mama said.

'It's all right, May, it's all right. Nobody blames you for anything. What you need is confidence. You're still young.'

'Quit, Beanie.' She wriggled loose from her older sister's embrace.

'I'm right, May. God knows, I'm right.'

I was still sitting on the top step. I looked down at Mama, who got smaller with every word. It made me think of an angel in one of the pictures on the wall of our Sunday school. Mama looked so trim and tidy and transparent. She was quiet as a mouse, as though the darkness in the room squeezed her so she couldn't move. I only remember tiptoeing back to my room. I got my holster with the two toy six-guns, the cowboy hat and matching vest, and charged down the stairs.

'I'm going to New York with Auntie,' I announced. I did not look at Mama.

'And you're bringing your guns with you, I suppose?' Aunt Beanie said.

"Course,' I answered, dead serious.

'Well then we'll never have to be afraid of anything again, will we, Charles? Look, May, Charles is going to protect us in the big city.'

'New York, New York' (1968)

New York is brogan boot shape state
of Madison Ave negro button-downs
hungry lost nigger souls screaming
screaming downtown for death
semi-black obscured blackness
plastic trees and phony grass
New York is a state of mind that doesn't mind
fucking up a brother

HARLEM, FEBRUARY 2002

Telephone Call

All I said was, 'A week from Saturday. Louisville, Kentucky. The festival. We fly out the night before.'

'From New York?' Umar asked.

'Where else?'

'Louisville ... '

'Kentucky.'

'Uh-huh.'

'Three thousand dollars.'

'Each?'

'Fuck off, Umar. For the three of us. Since when do The Last Poets get three grand each? It's a forty-five-minute set. What's wrong?'

'I could rent a car and drive to Louisville ... from Flint ... If I first have to take a bus to New York ... fourteen hours ... I'll be a wreck.'

'You always take the bus, man. If you get here Friday it'll be enough time.'

'But ... never mind.'

'What, Umar?'

'You know I live in Flint.'

'So?'

'Couldn't you get me a ticket from here to Louisville?'

'Too complicated.'

'For who?'

'I gotta go, Umar. You okay?'

'Uh-huh.'
'Next Friday, all right?'
'Friday ... '
'I'll call you.'

'Brothers Working' (1994)

I want to work with you brother
take that pain that you carry inside your heart
that pain that hangs from your lips
that pain you show in your eyes
that pain that says
nobody to love
nobody to trust
and loneliness has become an incurable disease
I want to help you brother

RALEIGH, NORTH CAROLINA, 1970

Run Nigger

It was one in the afternoon. It had rained that morning and my boots were heavy with moisture. I pulled the hunting hat down over my eyes and looked at Alex. He was a strange sight in the dark-blue jacket he'd borrowed from a friend on campus.

'You okay?' I asked.

'You bet,' he replied.

The Watkins Brothers' filling station was out on E. Hwy. 64. They also had a general store: car parts, hardware, bread, bottles of pop, guns, knives, candy, coffee.

'It's not far now,' I said, looking straight ahead. The wide, gray road we were walking down just dissolved into the downy clouds that hung low over the city. There was hardly any traffic. No wind. A few crows watched us from their perches high up on the power lines. I heard the squish of our footsteps.

'What'd you tell Biji?'

'Nothing.'

We kept on walking until we saw the red, white, and blue pennants of the gas station. Alex stopped. 'Got everything?' he asked.

'You're asking me?' Did I see a trace of doubt in Alex's eyes? Doubt was the last thing we needed here on a deserted stretch of asphalt outside Raleigh, on the way to the Watkins Brothers, respectable shopkeepers and members of the local Ku Klux Klan. I felt like an actor in a movie; much different than it felt when I asked Alex a few days ago to assist me in a robbery.

We stood there for a minute, peering at the tiny gas station off in the distance.

Alexander Young, my best friend at Shaw University. He was a member of the Yoruba society but was disgruntled because of his Marxist-Leninist convictions. Still, we had complete respect for each other; he was one brother I could trust one hundred percent. But now I didn't know what to say. We'd gone through the plan dozens of times. All we had to do was walk into the shop, take out our guns, and demand the money from the safe—and once we had it, make our way to the getaway car. It was an airtight plan. But Alex kept looking at me, wanting me to say something.

'This time tomorrow, the brothers'll be free,' I said, 'and all this never happened, okay? We raised their bail from collections, got it?'

'Jesus, Dun, I'm not one of your students.'

'Meaning?'

'I don't know. What if it doesn't succeed?'

'It *will* succeed.'

'And then?'

'Then what?'

'It never happened.'

'Correct.'

'But ... '

'But what?'

'Nothing,' Alex said. He looked away. 'Let's go.'

The Pepsi truck wasn't there when we went inside. The white guy behind the counter, cigarette dangling from his lips, wasn't much older than us. The fluorescent light made him look pale and sickly, so he kind of melted into the rest of the cement-colored interior. He didn't look up from his newspaper. Alex hung back, next to a rack of tires. I walked up to the counter, took out my .45, and cleared my throat. I said: 'You know what this is.' I hadn't rehearsed that line. It was like I was hearing my own voice for the first time; it came from outside of me. I was startled by the dryness of the words, by the man's total lack of response. The lethargic ordinariness of the silence that followed. I had gone through the scene umpteen times in my head, but now that I actually stood here with a cocked gun in my hand I felt kind of disappointed. As though I'd secretly hoped there would be an audience, witnesses who could tell me it all really did happen. In a flash I imagined we could still say 'sorry' to the man, 'just a little misunderstanding' and walk back out of the store, 'Bye, thanks'.

Silence.

The sluggish hum of the soft-drink cooler.

The vague smell of rot and disinfectant.

The vibration of the light fixtures.

'Well?' I said.

Without a word the man punched a button on the cash register, and the drawer flew open with a loud jingle.

'Uh-uh, no. The safe,' I said. 'Take me to the safe.' Alex was backing me up now. Out of the corner of my eye I could see he was nervously looking around to see if anyone was coming.

'Move,' he hissed.

The man didn't budge; his bored expression was frozen on his pale face. He was completely blasé, like he was watching a play. I tried to suppress my panic, and waved the gun around. He took his cigarette out of his mouth, tossed it onto the floor and blew out a puff of smoke. He turned toward a door behind the counter; I shoved him into the storage room where the safe had to be.

'Get the money, asshole,' I snarled.

'A truck's just pulled up!' Alex yelled.

'Shut up.'

'Stupid niggers,' the man muttered to himself. 'Can't even hold up a gas station.' He shook his head pityingly.

'The money,' I repeated. The gun wasn't shaking, but now my insides sure were. I felt like a two-bit gangster, a pimp; there was no time for political discussions, no time to inform this racist shithead of his own violent past, no time to explain our motives to him or to the people of Raleigh, who would soon be hearing about two crazy niggers in their twenties who had held up a gas station.

These thoughts continued to play in my head, along with the worry that I'd overlooked something while planning this venture. Seems I'd assumed that, in this situation too, I could simply count on my voice, even if I didn't use it. People would know just from looking at me that I was a gifted and convincing political orator, a revolutionary, a cultural activist—even this sap of a gas station attendant would have seen it.

They weren't even real thoughts. More like a cold, sickening realization that slowly sunk into every fiber of my body.

With the money in a rolled-up paper bag under my jacket I ran out of the store. Alex followed a few yards behind me. I couldn't see anything but Alex kept yelling, 'the truck, the truck'. I heard the rhythm of his words but their meaning escaped me. Alex caught up with me and grabbed my arm.

'Dun, the Pepsi truck. We're finished, man.'

'Just keep walking,' I panted. Now I did see the large delivery truck with the prominent logo parked in the entrance lane, right near the gas pump. Two white guys got out and started walking over to the store.

Alex was still holding onto me. He squeezed my upper arm. Gave me a desperate look. He opened his mouth but no sound came out.

'Get to the car, man, just act like everything's cool,' I said under my breath. Nodded 'no problem' to the truck drivers. I tried to pull loose from his grip, shake his panic off me, but with every second I felt the fear nestle even deeper in my consciousness and drive out what little was left of my anger. Not thirty seconds later I heard shouts from the store. The glass door opened and the Pepsi guys started running toward their truck.

'They've got rifles for sure,' Alex whispered. 'All these Southern crackers have guns.'

'The woods,' I said, having forgotten all about the getaway car. In half a minute we had been transformed from robbers into fugitives, on the run from a pair of armed truck drivers, the Watkins' Klan brothers, and every law enforcement agency in the state of North Carolina. Even at that moment, the bitter irony of the whole situation didn't escape me. But I saw no other option than to dive into the woods. We heard shots behind us. I grabbled for my .45 and shot wildly, emptying the magazine in one go. Then the thought flashed through my head: I might have just killed someone. I heard twigs break under my boots. Felt the mire of mud and water and dead leaves sucking at my feet. I remember the bag of money slipping out from under my jacket and how I quickly dug a hole with my bare hands, threw the bag in it and covered it up with moss and branches. Then I ran deeper into the woods.

'Can we use your bathroom, ma'am?'

I heard myself say this. The innocence of a simple request. The comfort of the everyday. Going to the bathroom. Unzipping your pants. Peeing. Washing your hands. Drinking some water. As though events can just erase themselves.

'Can we please use your bathroom?'

'It's out back,' the elderly black woman mumbled, pointing to a bleak outhouse behind the white-shingled dwelling.

'My friend here and I were out hunting. It's cold ... we were wondering if ... '

'Bathroom's out back,' she repeated.

'Okay, thanks.'

'You can come inside.'

'Thank you.'

'But take those boots off,' she said, 'I don't want you dirtyin' my rugs.'

Alex dragged himself up the steps to the veranda and I headed for the outhouse.

'Didn't y'all shoot anything?' she asked, nodding at my empty hands.

'A few pheasants,' I said. I didn't know the first thing about hunting. 'We'll pick them up later.'

She slapped her forehead and laughed out loud. 'If the foxes don't get to 'em first.'

I opened the door to the rickety outhouse. The smell of stale piss hit me; I held my breath and let the door swing closed. I waited before returning to the house, didn't want the old lady to think I thought her outhouse too filthy to use. I stood there in that little shed, listening to the shuffling on the veranda, to their unintelligible voices, to the squeak of the screen door and, a few seconds later, to the faint thud of the main door falling shut. They were inside. I was so relieved that I closed my eyes, granting myself a moment of oblivion. I heard the excited chatter of the birds. The autumn air felt warm and soft on my cheeks. I licked my upper lip. Tasted the salt of my sweat and laughed to myself. I opened my eyes without seeing anything in particular.

'Mister?' The little voice came from down below. I looked down into the glowing face of a little boy of about six. He gave me a serious look and tugged at my sleeve. 'Are you one of the bandits they're looking for?'

'Wha—?'

'Grandma!' he shouted, ran away from me, up to the veranda, into the house. Just then I heard the sirens.

'When the Revolution Comes' (1968)

When the revolution comes
when the revolution comes
black cultural centers will be forts
supplying the revolutionaries with food and arms
white death will fall off the walls
of museums and churches
breaking the lie that enslaved our mothers
when the revolution comes
Jesus Christ is gonna be standing
on the corner of Malcolm X Blvd. and 125th St.
trying to catch the first gypsy cab out of Harlem
when the revolution comes

[...]

but until then
you know and I know and we know
niggers will party and bullshit
and party and bullshit and party and bullshit and party
and some might even die
before the revolution comes.

CENTRAL PRISON, RALEIGH, NORTH CAROLINA, 1970

Last Rites

I remember Marlena saying to me in bed one night, 'You're holding your breath.'

'Am not.'

'Are too.'

I sighed and rolled over to her. 'Now I'm not.'

'I'm serious, Dun. Even when you're asleep your muscles are tense. You're bracing yourself for something.'

'C'mere.'

'Why do you love me?'

'Is that important?'

'For me it is.'

'I just do, that's all.'

'"Just do"?'

'Yeah.'

'You've stopped writing poetry.'

'I don't need it.'

'Why not?'

'I've got you, don't I?' I said, laughing. I didn't take the conversation seriously. I saw it as a game. I was reading Frantz Fanon's *The Wretched of the Earth* and didn't feel like talking.

'Could you write me a poem?'

'What?'

'A love poem.'

'You're kidding.'

She grabbed the book out of my hands and pushed me on my back.

'Well?'

'Love poems are for bourgies.'

'No one has to know.'

'I can't.'

'You don't want to.'

'Cut it out, Marlena.'

She tossed the book aside and sat up. 'You think you're in love with me but you're only in love with my ideals. The danger. Am I right? Why'd you want to be in charge of the occupation, huh? You and your big mouth. All you did was come have a look, and already the cops are looking for you.'

I couldn't believe what I was hearing.

'I'm just trying to warn you, that's all,' Marlena said. The concern in her voice confused me—I'd assumed she was picking a fight.

'And just what are you warning me about?' I asked.

'I don't know. I can understand that your poetry wasn't enough, and that you were fed up with The Last Poets' bickering. You were right to take the step. You're not afraid. But don't just assume everybody's going to stick up for you. People really aren't going to like you better just because you're right. Life's not that simple. We're alone, Dun. You and me both.'

I went to press my hand to her cheek, to reassure her, but she recoiled as though there was electricity in my fingers. She cocked her head, looked at me questioningly, sizing me up.

'Why can't I have a poem?' she asked. 'Just a few lines … for later.'

'Later?'

'Yeah.'

'And then?'

'And then they'll be my lines.'

'You're crazy.'

'No I'm not.'

That was the end of our discussion. Marlena turned, went to the bathroom and locked the door behind her.

A heavy droplet splatters on the cement floor. I hear it. Plop. The droplets fall to the floor in a torturously slow rhythm, sometimes one every fifteen minutes or half hour, I reckon. I try to imagine how my warm breath rises to the cold ceiling, condenses, clings to other condensation, until a drop is formed, and the drop becomes heavy enough that it can no longer resist gravity. Plop.

Just a few lines ...

You're crazy.

For later.

You're crazy.

I believed I'd freed myself from Daddy Joe's tyranny, simply because I was no longer afraid. He was dead. And I was free. And meanwhile Biji and Pharaoh and I were living his dream in North Carolina, with the Yoruba society on campus: we had our own plot of land to live from, our own world where I determined my own history and the history of my people. I was proud. Just as proud has Daddy Joe must have been when he came home one afternoon with a pig. He fattened it up for a few days and then slaughtered it behind the house. He wanted me to watch him, help him, but the sweet scent of blood that gushed out of the animal's throat made me gag. The smell of fatty barbecued pig wafted for miles. Aunt Beanie sold the meat and sandwiches to folks from all over the neighborhood, and we ate pork for weeks on end.

I believed so strongly in my own strength that I even convinced myself I could be happy with Biji. If I could just transform her into the woman I thought she should be. The lessons started back in New York. I took her to all the jazz clubs I knew in Harlem and the Village. I forced her to listen to hour after hour of Trane and Parker and Monk, until I noticed her making minuscule rhythmic movements with her head or her foot. I introduced her to Marlena and the others. She traded her fancy dresses for jeans and T-shirts, changed her hairdo. I didn't even have to ask. But one afternoon I showed up at our spot on 125th St. and saw her standing there in the soup kitchen, stirring a huge pot of chili. She didn't see me, and I watched as she joked with the other comrades, standing there like she'd been a black nationalist all her life. I was furious. What was she thinking? She was my fiancée, the mother of my child.

In North Carolina she was safer. And those African fabrics looked so beautiful on her, the bright green and red and yellow against her silky skin. She sewed dresses and dashikis without messing up the complex symmetrical patterns. I had a wife, a son, a house, a religion, and a community. I didn't even have to keep my other woman a secret from Biji. I explained everything to her about polygamy in Yoruba culture. And she got along with Paulette, attractive, sexy Paulette Jackson, who I gave a new name—Bolanile—before she officially became my second wife.

I know my relationship with Biji is over. Maybe she's relieved I'm here. She sent me a picture of her and Pharaoh a few weeks after I got arrested. She'd had it taken especially for me, she wrote. I ran my fingers over the glossy, cool paper, stared at their small, precious faces, at my own bookcase in the background. I didn't just look at the photograph, I studied it, analyzed it; even without a magnifying glass no details escaped me, and the longer I looked, the more clearly I saw that Biji had stuck a message in it for me. Maybe not deliberately, but it was a message nonetheless. Her legs were hidden under the table, but from the black sash around her waist, from the way the fabric hugged her hips, I could see that she was wearing pants and not an African dress. She smiled at the camera but had forgotten to remove the ashtray from the table. A half-smoked cigarette balanced on its edge, the filter facing Biji, and I realized she had been smoking, that she'd embraced the freedom of being her old self again.

It's over. When I get my ass out of here, I need to make a fresh start. Maybe I needed this isolation to realize it. This darkness that makes me think of silk; cool, damp silk that glides along my skin. Sometimes it feels like my whole life has been a journey to here. At least that's how it feels now. Because there's nothing else, not yet.

They hope, of course, that my strength will drain from me, that the solitary confinement and the darkness and my own memories will drive me crazy. But what they don't know is that Daddy Joe trained me just for this. Stealing time when I had the least right to it, being the boss over my own thoughts, knowing when I could let them run free and when to rein them in. And there was always Aunt Beanie, singing my name with her sugary voice: 'Charles, Charles, my boy.' Even if she didn't say anything, it was good. I always saw my own reflection in her caring face.

They don't know anything.

Nothing at all.

I still remember the first time I found myself in a cramped cinderblock cell and did a head count. Including myself there were fifteen of us. And just twelve beds. Still, I didn't give it a moment's thought. Jumped up on one of the top bunks and curled up on the hard mattress with the few possessions I'd managed to smuggle in: a baby picture of Pharaoh, a pencil stub. Every faggot who dared to give me the eye got chased off. I didn't have to do anything except open my mouth and use the right tone of voice. I'd learned it from Daddy Joe, the menace behind each word, no room for doubt. I thought of George Jackson and Huey Newton and Bobby Seale, and all the other revolutionaries who had gone before me, and I was almost drunk with pride that I was now following in their footsteps. I was convinced this was just the beginning. Baptism by fire. If I managed to show my revolutionary colors in here, transform my hopes and dreams into action and deeds, into improving the lives of the inmates, broadening their horizons, then what could possibly happen to me? I'd already shed my fear. Daddy Joe had taken all my fears with him to his grave, including my fear of death. I was so charged that I convinced myself it was a good a thing we'd been caught. The police never found that bag of money and the brothers got out on bail, just like we planned. And Marlena had made a collection for my own bail. Marlena. She hadn't forgotten me. The comrades in the Hamilton Terrace building had collected 485 dollars—just a fraction of the 50,000 dollars I needed, but that didn't matter. Even in Harlem everybody knew about me being arrested. I would never, never be a victim.

Every evening I started my spiel about Malcolm, about Marcus Garvey. Tried to ram some historical awareness into those assholes, put some insight into their isolated outlook and their imprisonment, which they seemed to regard as a tragic twist of fate directed personally at them. And they listened. Boy, did they listen ... I saw their dull eyes light up when I heard my voice echo off the cinderblock walls. My voice was an invisible ribbon of sounds that resonated and snaked through the over-crowded cell. At lights out, exhausted and high from my own rhetoric, I sunk into a restless half-slumber and a blissful sense of calmness and fulfillment washed over me. My blood tingled in my hands and feet. I kept myself warm, never suffered from the clamminess. I slept like a log. My God, when I think back on those first few weeks ... I had put my trust in the power of the spoken word, and saw that trust confirmed in the respect I got from the other inmates.

'Cigarette, Davis?'

'I don't smoke.'

'Tell us about Harlem again.'

'Yeah, soon.'

'Okay, New York. Whatever you say.'

Prison life came so easy to me that it felt like I'd never known anything else. It was my home. I felt so at home in that disgusting, dank cell that I refused to face up to my own impotence. I understand it now, now that I've got the time. Back then I was so full of myself, so angry, that I hardly took the trouble to listen to the other inmates' stories. Maybe I was so shocked by the butt-fucking because I didn't see their helpless exhaustion. Because I didn't understand that hope was a privilege, and that indifference can be your only protection. All my rousing words did was to keep me from facing the fact that I was actually in prison. I orated myself into the future, without the faintest idea what that future had in store for me.

I was blind. I mean, I'd seen them eyeing each other before—Marion Rayford and Victor Mangum—but didn't give it much notice. It simply didn't occur to me that someone would dare have sex with another inmate right under my nose. I'd preached against it often enough. Marion and Victor were both in for some picayune robberies. One night—it was already after lights out and the familiar cacophony of wheezy, husky sleeping noises took over the cell—Victor let his blanket hang down from his top bunk. Their bunk bed was in the corner, next to mine, and in the shadows I saw how Victor and Marion turned their beds into a sort of private tent. I turned over and tried to sleep, but their whispering kept me awake. I assumed they had gotten their hands on some stuff, some speed or coke or hash. I didn't want to be a spoilsport so I let them be, even though their chatting irritated me.

It was the first time since I went to prison that I couldn't get to sleep. The more I tossed and turned, the further I drifted from the warmth and comfort that sleep usually offered me. There was something about the sound of their voices that forced me to keep listening. I don't know exactly what it was. Maybe I was simply struck by the intimacy of their conversation. I couldn't pick up any distinct words, but the muffled laughs, the whispered words and the softness of their voices evoked a sad sort of nostalgia I hadn't felt before and did not want to feel. I tried to suppress my growing nausea by breathing deeply. I broke out in a sweat. I bolted upright and slid as noiselessly as possible from my bunk.

'Psst, Marion,' I whispered.

'What?'

'I'm trying to get some shut-eye over here, damn it,' I said, casually pulling aside the blanket. Marion was on all fours with pants around his ankles. I could just see Victor slip his cock back in his trousers and zip up his fly. He drew the back of his hand over his forehead and puffed out a little imaginary cloud of relief at not having been caught.

'Jesus, Marion!' I shouted, pushing Victor off the bed and dragging Marion off the mattress and onto the floor. Marion disgusted me the most. I heard shuffling and mumbling behind me. Marion lay on his back, his limp dick between his legs. I kicked him in the ribs.

'Get up, you bastard. Filthy faggot.'

But Marion just lay there, so I lifted him up and socked him in the face. Blood spurted out of his mouth but I kept on punching until my cellmates pulled me off him, and Marion could finally pull up his pants.

A few days later I was transferred to a different cellblock, where I shared a cell with Bobby Sole, Kincaid Wilson, and James De Keyser. Bobby, a light-colored brother, was an errand boy (and was also apparently getting fucked by one of the guards), so was allowed to leave the cell during the day. Sometimes he brought me a *New York Times*, which was a treat. Kincaid was a middleweight boxing champion, a dumb-ass brother doing time for rape. He was stupid enough to get turned on by some sleazy white girl on his way to work. Slipped into her bedroom one night and her uncle walked in on them; she cried 'rape' and that was that. James was the oldest. He was forty. He'd got locked up in the hole once and got into such a panic that he'd cut his little toe off with the top of the tin can. In the infirmary they had to cut off two more toes so he wouldn't die of gangrene.

And still I didn't catch on that I couldn't just go shooting off my mouth. It was Saturday and they brought us to the small chapel in the north wing of the prison. The white preacher was already waiting for us. Behind him were four little blonde girls with guitars. Two of them wore hair bands around their long curls. They couldn't have been older than sixteen or seventeen. Their eyes glowed with childlike hope. I think they thought themselves pretty hip and heroic. Wasn't there anybody who could protect them from themselves? The girls started playing and singing as we shuffled into the chapel in our dingy duds. *Come to the church ...* We were just glad to be out of our cell. The preacher was a middle-aged guy with ruddy cheeks and stubby fingers. I always look at a person's hands. Hands can tell you more about somebody than any other part of his body, more than their eyes or mouth. His hands were fleshy and soft. He started his sermon while the last prisoners were still fighting over the pews at the back of the chapel. 'God is all-merciful. To you too. He will forgive you. Even the greatest sinners can find forgiveness with Him.' I watched that redneck in his shiny suit while he rambled on about our sins. He raised his arms in the air and I reckon he felt like a big shot up on that little altar, bleating his message to a whole room full of black prisoners. One of the inmates got up and walked to the front. It was Peter Rabbit. He was in for rape. He went up there and fell to his knees and started chanting along. Had he lost his mind? The preacher laid his hand on Peter's shoulder and closed his eyes, mumbled along with him. I glanced over at Bobby and Kincaid and James, trying to catch their eye, but they seemed wrapped up in themselves, staring at the floor or their hands. Like they were hypnotized. I stepped over the pew and went up to Peter, grabbed him by the arm, and threw him against the wall.

'God will forgive you too, sinner!' the preacher exclaimed, pointing his index finger in my direction as though he was putting a curse on me. Looked straight at me. I started shouting and cursing, like a bomb had gone off in my head. 'God could never have made you his messenger. Look at you. That cheap suit, your cheap voice. Fuck you. God doesn't even see you. Nobody here needs you. Who's the sinner, anyway? We're not sheep, we're proud black men. You don't know anything about our sins … ' I kept on in this vein; meanwhile the girls had stopped playing. That awful twanging of theirs stopped and the preacher waved them off the altar. When I finally quit ranting you could hear a pin drop. Like everybody was holding their breath. I took the silence as a sign of agreement: I had put their thoughts into words. I was their leader. It never occurred to me that it might be self-preservation or even disapproval that kept them quiet. Even when the guards dragged me out of the chapel I felt nothing but euphoria and pride.

The next morning, Rogers, the prison director, came to my cell.

'Davis, get your stuff.'

And all I could think of was that Biji had finally got my bail together and that I was going home, to Pharaoh and Shaw University. Rogers never came to the cellblock personally for anything else.

'You're going to the hole, Davis,' he said. 'Then you'll be your own audience.'

'For the Millions' (1995)

It's time

[...]

to leave this American Nightmare

Alone

HARLEM, SEPTEMBER 2001

Don 'Babatunde' Eaton

'I taught drums at the Harlem School of the Arts; it was sometime in the mid-'80s. One Saturday morning, Abiodun came into the classroom with his son in tow. I recognized him immediately from the old record jackets. "You're Abiodun Oyewole, right? From The Last Poets?" His wife Ayisha was there too. Obadele, the little boy, was about six and Dun wanted him to learn to play the djembe. He worked in education and was a musician in his free time. Jazz, he had his own ensemble. We got talking. He was very respectful. Asked if I wanted to play with him.

I was ten or eleven when my older brother Jeffrey came home with The Last Poets' first album. 'Course, I didn't play drums yet. We played that album over and over, until we knew the words by heart. We ate it up. How they used the word "nigger" ... Until our mother forbade us to listen to it anymore.

We lived in the Colonial Houses on 159th. In 1970 it wasn't a bad neighborhood; most people had regular jobs. My grandma on my mother's side lived nearby, on 149th and Eighth Ave., together with her sister, Aunt Emma. Aunt Emma always gave us candy and chewing gum. My grandmother was a seamstress; she made all these way-out costumes. I remember sleeping over at her place as a kid, and hearing the early-morning click-clack of horses' hooves outside. The jingle of a bell—that was the knife-grinder. The street vendors singing. My grandmother took care of the whole family, cooked for everybody. I was crazy about her pies. She came from the South, where it made a difference whether you were light-skinned or dark-skinned. Grandma was really light and had problems with real blacks. It was an issue in my father's family too. My father didn't live with us but we saw him regularly. I think my father even disowned his own brother because he was too dark. But that's always been a mystery ...

We watched the neighborhood deteriorate. You saw more and more heroin addicts on the street; they just wandered around jerking their head. Landlords stopped maintaining the buildings. There was a lot more robbery. My grandmother was robbed a few times and I suspect my cousin was behind it. Her apartment was a miniature palace—spotlessly clean and tidy, and suddenly everything was all topsy-turvy ... My mother kept us indoors. Our only escape was the church social center. We'd go there after school, hang around and meet up with girls. Otherwise we kept pretty much to ourselves. Sure, I knew about the Black Panthers. Rap Brown set the whole East coast on fire. Everybody wore khaki in those days, the boys in military garb. We wanted to be militant. Listened to Sly and the Family Stone, the Ohio Players. And The Last Poets. "When the Revolution Comes". "The Revolution will not Be Televised" made Gil Scott-Heron popular. It was a topic of conversation, but I was just a kid then so it only took on a political significance later on.

I remember sitting in the bus one day, riding past Central Park. All of a sudden I heard drums, the melodic tones of a conga. The sound got me all excited; I wanted to climb inside it. My uncle had a conga but he couldn't play it. Those days everybody had a conga, because of the bebop and the Afro-Cuban sound that used to be popular. I nagged my mother for one until she broke down and bought me a small Mexican drum. I borrowed fifteen dollars from her and signed up for lessons at the Harlem Dance Theater, where they offered a special class from drummers. It never occurred to me to make it my profession. I loved biology and wanted to go into biochemistry.

Around the time Dun came to the school with Obadele, I bumped into an old friend, another drummer who I used to play in a group with. He told me he worked with Jalal and Suliaman and asked if I felt like going to Canada with them for a few gigs. I didn't know Suliaman, but Jalal, sure. For me, The Last Poets are still Abiodun, Jalal, Umar, and Nilija. Naturally I said yes. I opened the first gig with a drum prayer. I was already initiated into the Yoruba faith: drumming is an essential element in our religion, a way to make contact with our forefathers and the spirits, the Orishas. I regard that prayer as a ritual. But I could see right away that Jalal was irritated. "Play somethin' else, man," he said. Jalal and Suliaman were both fanatic Muslims, and they considered me a heathen. I was surprised by their intolerance, because in The Last Poets, Dun and Nilija were both Yoruba—Nilija was even a priest.

Umar suddenly showed up at the second gig in Montreal. Jalal, Suliaman and he had just done "Niggers Are Scared of Revolution" for a film by John Singleton, *Poetic Justice*, with Tupac Shakur and Janet Jackson. Man, Umar's voice ... that was my real memory of The Last Poets. But Umar wasn't easy to get along with. Suspicious and withdrawn. And a heavy user. Right away he and Jalal got to arguing. He took me aside: "It's time to start earning some money," he said. "That political stuff is cool but we need bucks." This is fifteen years ago already. I said: "I can't work with you like this, Umar, the crack's doing something to your personality. You're negative and you've got a short fuse."

Later, when Umar and Dun were on speaking terms again and were looking for a drummer, they both independently thought of me. That's how it went. It's crazy to think that as a kid I listened to The Last Poets and fantasized that I was the drummer ... '

CENTRAL PRISON, RALEIGH, NORTH CAROLINA, 1970

Two Lives

'What do you think of this?' I asked.

'Let's hear it,' Jonathan Bird replied. It was evening and we were in our cell. Bird was twice my age, an easygoing, circumspect man who kept to himself. Outside, he'd been a teacher and greengrocer. I couldn't imagine him beating a man to death. He had an intellectual's hands: long, slender fingers, trimmed and clean nails. Bird made sure he always looked presentable. We were both working on a novel, and took turns reading passages to each other for advice and criticism. Bird raised his eyebrows and looked expectantly over the top of his reading glasses.

'Well?' he said with a deep, reassuring voice.

'Okay then.' I thumbed through the loose sheets of paper, all full, on my lap. 'This is when Jesse lets his mind wander ... '

'Is he already in Harlem?'

'Yeah, has been for a while. They can't prosecute him in New York for what happened in North Carolina. He's living with a comrade on Riverside Drive. Immerses himself up in the movement. He thinks his life will only have meaning if he throws himself body and soul into the struggle. He's convinced we have to tackle the institutions keeping us subjugated, with violence if necessary. Feels we have the right to defend ourselves against white dominance ... '

'I know Jesse.'

'Yeah, but Ade—that's the comrade he shares the apartment with—is a cultural activist. He also believes in the revolution but Ade's totally down-to-earth, he studies the history of slavery, knows all about his roots, grows his own vegetables, wears African robes and learns—'

'Go on and read.'

'But this is important.'

'Then it should be in the story.'

'I want to read you a different bit. Just listen, okay ... Ade's lecturing Jesse, trying to convince him that our strength lies in retaking our own culture, that this is the way to liberate ourselves. At a certain point he tells Jesse he's acting like a nigger.'

'Hmm.'

'Of course that pisses Jesse off. He counters that Ade is naive and gullible. That the system will eventually destroy him and his African brothers and sisters anyway. What do you do when a redneck manhandles your woman and turns his gun on you? You got a bulletproof dashiki? Well? You gonna knock him out with your afro? And so on and so forth, you know Jesse. But Ade doesn't fight back. He stays calm, keeps his mouth shut.'

'Jesse can't stand that.'

'Sure can't. Jesse knows he's right, but what's he supposed to do with Ade's smug silence? It's getting on his nerves. He locks himself in his room. It's summer. The windows are open and Jesse listens to the street noise: traffic, children playing, their shouting and laughing wafts all the way up to the fifth floor. It's late afternoon and the sun reflects brightly off the Hudson, as though the water's got a silver coating. It makes him squint but he keeps looking. Just then, Jesse is overcome by a vague emptiness. He's so happy to be in Harlem, to be finally surrounded by like-minded folks, comrades, and yet he feels a weird kind of homesickness.'

'Beauty,' Bird mumbled. He sat on the edge of his bed and rested his head in his hands.

'Huh?'

'Beauty—it makes him wistful.'

'Why?'

'You ought to know.'

I stared at the deep lines in Bird's forehead, tried to follow his thoughts. He laughed and shook his head in mock pity.

'Anyway,' I continued. 'Jesse lies down on his bed and thinks. I hope I can read my own handwriting ...' I raised the sheet. 'Here: *Happiness is me being successful in my endeavors, giving order to my life, floating in the natural sounds that give birth to a Coltrane song. Playing that song on a sax or just watching it grow in the eyes and body of a child, being the love that I have, completely and never giving anything away for free, for freedom exists for everyone; to do, what and how and when and where. They want to end because this dude said so, because you have no choice. Now happiness is a million things and it's one thing. It's every element on earth that nourishes the nature of our lives ...'*

I stopped. My cheeks were flushed with enthusiasm.

'Is that Jesse?' Bird asked.

'Yeah.'

'Romantic.'

'Too much?'

'Oh, no, Davis, no. I was only wondering ...'

'What?'

'What happens next?'

'I don't know yet.'

'It's almost poetry, you should leave it. I'm curious

what Jesse's going to do. He doesn't give up.'

'He's figuring out what's really important.'

'Oh.'

'Doesn't that come through in the text?'

'Maybe. Anyway, he's confused about what's happening to him. Maybe he's the one who's defenseless against the big bad world, and not Ade.'

'I never said Ade was defenseless. He's a cultural activist. He knows where he's at.'

'Relax. What I meant was ... ' Bird shifted and squeezed his eyes shut, ' ... that at a certain point in the story Jesse has to connect his love and his sensitivity to the struggle and his own anger. That's a tall order, but it's essential. Now it's as though he's leading two lives. Am I right?'

'Maybe.'

'He's not happy. He's overwhelmed by his feelings. He's not in control.'

I stared at my compact handwriting. Paper here was at a premium, so I crammed as much as I could onto each sheet. Bird saw my face; maybe he thought I was disappointed.

He said: 'Keep writing, Davis. Jesse's still young. You know where he's going. Have patience with him.'

'Patience?'

'Yeah.'

Bird and I were cellmates for a couple of months. During the day he worked in the library; I had a job as an aide in the infirmary. Every morning at seven I tended the eight patients assigned to me, and then I shoved a table under the enormous TV that was always on, and started writing. Bird did the same in the library. His novel was about a family of black hustlers in New York. Bird was a natural. His dialogue was true to life and his characterizations were downright breathtaking. I knew I could learn a lot from him. Because we exchanged manuscripts, we got to be friendly, but still I was careful about what I told him. When I landed in the hole I decided then and there to get out of there as soon as possible. I was serving twelve-to-twenty for robbery and would be eligible for parole in two years, with good behavior. So I was going to keep my mouth shut and my opinions to myself, entrusting my thoughts and feelings only to paper. I didn't see it as cowardice or acquiescence: the incident in the chapel taught me not to expect too much from my fellow inmates. I was on my own. Writing kept me going. I never realized I'd take so much comfort from it. Without it I think I'd have gone crazy with my doubts about the revolution, the notion of a revolutionary army of black men. By writing I kept in touch with myself without going overboard, and on top of it created a world where I could escape the grim monotony of prison life. Bird understood that. In a way, it was easier to get to know each other through our writing than through just talking.

I didn't miss my voice. To be honest, I enjoyed the peace my new routine gave me. Keeping quiet and working hard gave me a new kind of freedom. I didn't bother anybody, not even the racist white guards. I was polite to them the way you're polite to a stranger you happen to meet in an elevator. Soon my new anonymity gave me all kinds of perks. Officially I didn't have mail privileges, but Perry, one of the guards, would slip letters from Biji under my pillow. Perry was a cracker from the North Carolina swamps. To him, I was probably just some nigger from New York. We talked only when absolutely necessary.

This was my day-to-day routine, and I tried not to look too far ahead. One afternoon I was walking past the washrooms when I heard an inmate singing a familiar tune. It took a few seconds before it hit me what it was, and in those few seconds I was nailed to the ground. Like my body caught on quicker than my mind did. The guy walked off, but his singsong murmur echoed throughout the bare cement washroom. 'When the revolution comes ... when the revolution comes ... ' He was singing my poem! 'Some of us will catch it on TV ... ' I hadn't given those recordings in Alan Douglas's studio any more thought, it had been more than a year earlier. Why hadn't Biji written me about it? I couldn't get to my cell fast enough.

Bird wasn't back yet and I lay down on my bed to think. That album must have been released. It was like my past was catching up with me, just when I'd decided to keep my head down and make a fresh start. The Last Poets and I were worlds apart. A few months ago Biji had written to me about the arguments between Kain, David, and Felipe and Umar and Jalal, over who had the rights to the name. Nilija, she wrote, kept her informed of things by phone; Nilija was the only Last Poet who took the trouble to ask about me. Good, quiet Nilija. I only skimmed the letter and then threw it away. Even the news that Jalal had beaten Kain with a hammer hardly made any impression on me. The Last Poets were history. I didn't want anything more to do with them. I had my hands full with myself. As far as I was concerned, their petty bickering only confirmed my own disillusionment with the revolution.

I decided not to mention it to Bird. He didn't know anything about Abiodun Oyewole anyhow. But the next few weeks I felt like I was being chased by my own shadow. At the most unexpected moments I'd hear snippets of poems echoing through the cement hallways. '*Oh beautiful black hands / reach out and snatch the death out / of the youth of our nation ...*' The words were disconnected from the person reciting them, they echoed through the mess hall, the latrines, the cellblocks and even the infirmary. '*Have you seen two little boys sitting in Sylvia's / stuffing chicken and cornbread / down their tasteless mouths ...*' Whenever I walked anywhere I had the strange sensation that the bare walls turned into mirrors, but as soon as I tried to catch a glimpse of myself I saw only a vague apparition. The words were mine, but at the same time they had nothing to do with me. Even the memory of that morning in Sylvia's—Omar had just arrived in Harlem and I wanted to show him the neighborhood, let him taste it, at Sylvia's—when a pair of little ragged boys about ten years old, junkie kids, sat a couple of tables away, stuffing their faces with chicken and potato salad and cornbread, like dogs, and when they were finished they got up and bolted out the door without paying ... I knew at once I had a poem, sittin' in Sylvia's, sittin' in Sylvia's, Sylvia's; even that memory seemed not to belong to me anymore, although the images were crystal clear, almost like I could touch them.

I heard inmates talk about the record and about The Last Poets from New York, cool dudes who weren't afraid of nothin', who said it like it was. *Niggers don't realize while they're doing all this fucking they're getting fucked around. But when they do realize it's too late, so all niggers do is just get fucked ... up!* Laughter. Applause. They effortlessly imitated Omar's fast, fiery delivery. Nobody lowered their voice when I was there or happened to walk by. I was part of the audience. A passerby. I could just as well have been invisible.

One night Bird says, 'You ever heard of those poets from Harlem? Everybody's talking about them. "Niggers Are Scared of Revolution", Jesus man, their shit is explosive. You know them?' He said it nonchalantly, while he was rearranging his bookshelf. He blew dust from the covers and ran his hand lovingly over the books before putting them back. I didn't know what to say. I didn't want to lie, not to Bird. And maybe it was my pride playing up too. I can't deny I was proud to hear inmates recite my poems. But because I kept it to myself, I had sensed I was drifting even further from my own past. I started to notice that it was getting in the way of my writing. I felt an invisible wall went up between me and my characters, found it more and more difficult to put myself in my their shoes. I'd forgotten something crucial but didn't know what.

'Bird?'

'Yeah?' He turned to face me. Wiped his hands on his pants and sat down on his bed. I didn't answer.

'What is it?'

'Bird, those Last Poets ... that's, uh, me ... I ... I'm Abiodun ... Abiodun Oyewole.'

He took off his glasses, shook his head wearily. 'Really, man ... you've been here too long. I know it's rough going with that book of yours ... But you're tripping. That's not so strange. Maybe you should take a break.'

It never occurred to me that Bird wouldn't believe me. His concern and the warmth in his voice made me feel even worse, more detached. It was almost like I was speaking a foreign language, and no matter how loud I spoke, how clearly I enunciated, he would never understand.

'Listen, Bird, really, that's me, that poet.'

'What's his name?' he asked. I could tell he was doing his best to sound patient so as not to upset me.

'Abiodun. Abiodun Oyewole.'

'You're Davis. Charles Davis.'

'Here, yeah. Here, my real name doesn't count ... you know that. Bird, you've got to believe me, man.' I felt like a kid.

'Everybody flips out here sooner or later, Davis. You're no different.'

'Ask your wife.'

'My wife?'

'Yeah. Write and ask her to bring the record with her next Sunday, the Last Poets' record. There's a picture on the jacket. Then you'll see for yourself.'

Bird covered his eyes with his big hand. He crossed his legs and leaned forward. I knew he thought I was crazy. I felt his disappointment, his loneliness. There was nothing more I could say.

Bird sighed, whispered, 'Okay then, Davis, I'll write to my wife. If you'll just promise me you'll keep cool.'

I don't know anymore how I got through that week. Bird and I avoided talking about our novels. I buried myself in my job at the infirmary and tried to work on my book. Bird was friendly but I could sense he was distancing himself. Couldn't really blame him. Why should he believe me?

The following Sunday was visiting day. I had asked Biji not to come. She'd written me about the album and said that Nilija arranged my royalties check but she needed my permission to hire a lawyer so she could cash it. I thought that was a strange request, seeing as we were still officially married; I saw no reason why she couldn't just cash the check. I didn't trust her. I suspected she had a boyfriend. Her letters became more infrequent, and when she did write, her tone was distant, businesslike. Only her news about Pharaoh was detailed: he had a new nursery-school teacher and was already learning to write. There was a drawing with the last letter. 'For Daddy,' it said, in thin, shaky letters. The rest was bright blue scrawls, the top edge in deep, dark blue with yellow dots, and in the middle floated a stretched-out figure with hands and feet like pitchforks. I taped it next to my bed. My throat clenched every time I looked at it, a mix of joy and anger. I knew he was well-cared-for. But I missed my son. And the longer we were separated, the more unreal the feeling became. I held tight to my memories of Pharaoh at the moment I went to prison: a toddler of eighteen months, still pretty much a baby, with the scent of talc and diapers, his pudgy arms clamped around my neck. When Biji occasionally brought him with her and I saw how much he'd grown and how much his vocabulary had improved, how he spoke in a sort of secret code with his mother, a language that betrayed daily contact—mealtimes, story-reading, bathing, bedtime—and when I saw this, the ground gave way under my feet, as though despite my elation at seeing my son, I'd lost something for good.

So I stayed in my cell that Sunday afternoon. At about four I heard Bird's heavy, deliberate footsteps. He didn't say anything; I knew what visitation did to you and wanted to give him his space. And Bird loved his wife.

He lay down on his bed and stared at the dark-gray concrete ceiling.

'Why, Davis?' His voice was muffled and thin. He looked over at me. 'I thought you trusted me.'

'What's up, Bird?'

'I saw the picture. Lydia brought the LP today. Man, you've changed. The white dashiki looked good on you. And that uppity face o' yours!' He laughed. 'Why didn't you tell me?'

'I couldn't.

'How come?'

'Does me being Abiodun Oyewole do anybody here any good? Does it?'

'You're famous, man.'

'I want to get out of here, Bird. In two years I'm up for parole. What's the point in touting myself as a revolutionary poet?'

'Because it's your responsibility.'

I grunted, irritated, although I knew full well what Bird meant. He'd put his finger on my sore spot. These last few years I had done nothing *but* take responsibility for my ideals, and look where it got me.

'Don't you see what your poetry does to the guys? What it brings out in them? My God, you *touch* them, Davis—the biggest criminals in here go around singing about niggers and the revolution and they understand exactly what it's all about. I can't believe you were able to keep it under your hat the whole time.'

All I could say was 'Shit.' I felt like I had let Bird down, and that was the last thing I wanted.

'Are you guys still in contact?'

'Who?'

'The Poets! If I were you ... '

'You don't know the half of it, Bird. It's a real mess. It's like ... How can I put it ... those poems of ours ... I dunno.'

'What do you mean, a mess?' He was losing patience. 'What're you talking about?'

I withdrew. Thought of Kain. Of his worried face, his sad, glistening eyes, Kain, my mentor, my tormentor, his arms raised in the air like a voodoo priest as if begging the gods for understanding, for support. He looked at me and whispered: 'You'll see, Dun. The minute we've cut that album, the minute we turn our poems over to the white vultures in the record industry, then they've got us. Don't you get what they're after? They want to declaw us, make entertainers out of us. Make us fight like dogs over a bone.'

'Oh yeah,' I said, and I meant it, even though Kain's preachy tone annoyed me, the earnest, melancholy look in his eyes, like he knew more than me, like he was some kind of clairvoyant and was rubbing my nose in it. I knew he was the better poet. But I could sing and he couldn't. He didn't have the right to boss me around, do like he was my father. I was glad when he finally got his ass out of East Wind. And when Alafia showed up all excited a few months later with a contract from Douglas, I said: 'Sure, let's make an album.' The poems were recorded in a single afternoon. Alafia beaming like he was Miles Davis in the flesh. Omar was in top form too. But I never had the feeling that I was doing something significant, there in that fancy studio, with Douglas sitting there at the controls in his hip bourgie duds. My own impatience did the rest—made sure I gave it everything I had. And shortly thereafter I put on a decent suit and sunglasses and went to North Carolina, on the run from the cops because of the 125th St. occupation. I was—

'What kind of mess, Davis?'

'They nearly killed each other over that record, Bird. You call that "revolutionary struggle"?'

'Who did?'

'Doesn't matter who ... the Poets ... I don't give a damn about getting famous.'

'Oh no?' Bird looked at me sharply through his thick glasses. 'And where were you when they were killing each other?'

'I told you. I was a militant. I thought ... '

'I thought you were smarter than that, Davis. You think poets are somehow above regular people, don't you? Because you had the guts to look at yourselves. "Niggers act so cool and slick, causing white people to ask, What makes them niggers act like that?" Oooh. Be grateful for that album, man. Those poems'll be fine if you leave them to their own devices, even if you guys mess it up for yourselves. Can you blame a poor black man for wanting success, recognition? Well? Wake up, Davis. You're no better than the rest of us here, in case you think you are. We're all prisoners. These here walls tell us more about ourselves than we want to believe. And if a poem can raise these dudes above the drab garbage that is their lives, even for a while, then you should be glad. That's hope. Your poems are blues, man, nothing else: blues.' He shook his head. Bird was not only talking to me but to himself. I heard every word he said, drank it all up, because I trusted Bird and his insight, his intentions—but did I *understand* it? Only vaguely.

'What should I do, Bird?'

'I can't tell you that. Do what you think is right.'

'I promised Pharaoh I'd be home in two years. I asked him to wait for me, and he said he would. I've got to keep my head down.'

'It's okay, Davis, you don't have to convince me. For the time being those poems of yours don't need you. But don't be surprised if one day you wake up and miss them. You're a strange one, man.' He got up and went over to the toilet in the corner of the cell. He unzipped his trousers and a few moments later I heard his water splash on the filthy porcelain.

'Pelourinho' (1993)

How long
can this go on?

I know I must be strong
to live through this journey

to live through this journey

HARLEM, FEBRUARY 2002

The Last Poets

'I'm going, Dad.' I heard Obadele's soft, deep voice from the kitchen. It was a Thursday evening. I was sitting at my desk in my workroom. Even here I could smell the musky scent of his new aftershave.

'I'm going.'

'I heard you.'

'What are you doing?' Oba said as he sauntered into my room.

'Nothing. Just taking care of some business.' I had just hung up the phone. The grumpy exchange with Umar was still echoing in my head. *You know I live in Flint … Couldn't you get me a ticket from here?*

'I won't be late,' Oba said.

I turned toward my youngest son. He was wearing a tight new black T-shirt, and his freshly shaved head glistened in the dark-yellow light of the hallway lamp. He looked good, self-assured but without a trace of arrogance, relaxed. Obadele always managed to amaze me. I couldn't remember ever worrying about him. He had a kind of invulnerability, like there was a natural shield between him and the surrounding racket. He was the only one of my children who was planned: Ayisha and I had been doing it every night for months, but only on our wedding night, now some twenty-six years ago, did she get pregnant. As though God personally had a hand in it. Eight days after he was born the Yoruba priest came to our apartment for the naming ceremony. Obadele, we called him: 'the king arrives'. And it followed that everything in Oba's life proceeded along the lines of his conception and birth. He planned his future down to the smallest detail, and now he was in his second year as a lawyer at a respected firm in downtown Manhattan. I was forever grateful to Ayisha for letting Oba live with me after the divorce.

'Why're you sitting in the dark?' he asked.

'Hmm, what?'

'You said you were taking care of business. You're sitting in the dark. Want me to turn off the monitor?'

'Yeah, thanks,' I said.

'Is Umar staying with us?'

'Nah.'

'But don't you guys have performances next week?'

'In Kentucky and then in Oakland. I think I'll be gone about a week.'

'Okay,' Oba said.

'"Okay"?' I laughed. Have you got plans or something? Need some space?'

Oba did not respond. He was staring at his reflection in the glass of a framed portrait of me from *Rolling Stone* from a few years back. It was a color photo, profile, and I thought it flattered me, so I cut it out and framed it. It was for an article about me and the rapper Ice Cube. We had to talk about each other's work, and Cube told about being inspired by The Last Poets. It was a good article. And the picture was effective: it was full-page and after that issue people recognized me on the street. The kids at school asked for my autograph.

Oba leaned forward and rubbed his index finger over his eyebrows. He saw only his own reflection.

'You going or not?' I asked.

Oba ignored my question, just kept gazing unashamedly in the glass, lost in thought.

'Umar's making himself scarce these days,' he said casually.

'Do you miss him?'

'No. I just thought ... You guys have so many gigs and ...'

'And what? Umar stays at Coney Island with his daughter.'

'The one who was in the second tower on 9/11?'

'Yeah, her.'

'How's she doing?'

'All right, I think. She got out okay.' My thoughts were not really on this conversation. But Oba kept dawdling.

'Guess I'll be going.'

'Okay, do that,' I said.

'Dad?'

'Yes?'

'Turn on the light.' Oba picked up his bag and left the apartment.

I stared out the window for a while. I love the view. Our apartment is on a hill on Morningside Drive and from my office window I have a view over all of Harlem. I looked at the countless sparkling lights in the distance. The buildings and streets seemed to undulate in the strong February wind, like a huge living organism. Occasionally the wind sent snippets of street sounds up to my window—the howl of a siren, an idling truck, ragged echoes of voices. But inside the apartment it was dead quiet. Sometimes I'd sit here at sunset and watch the brick buildings slowly turn yellow and pink and purple and blue and black. It calmed me. If I looked for long enough it was like I had broken loose from all the hubbub underneath, from the tension in my body and my mind, and floated above the city. I lived in Harlem but at the same time I was miles from here. The view was one of the main reasons I've never moved, all these years. Rent control did the rest. I had seen a slew of Columbia students and teachers come and go, but I stayed. Oba was born here. In a flash I realized I'd also probably grow old here.

I called Umar back on his cell phone.

'Hello?' He sounded like I'd woken him up.

'It's Dun. I was wondering ... Those tickets ... It's too late to change them. We have to fly out of New York.'

'You said that already.'

'When can you be here?'

'On time.' He was enjoying this, the bastard. He laughed.

'Everything okay?'

'With you?'

'Sure. I'm always okay. What are you up to?'

'Nothing.' I heard the blare of the television in the background.

'We've got lots of work coming our way, Umar ... I got a call today from a lady in New Orleans, from the university ... it's raining invitations.'

'Ah ... '

'It's sick, man. Remember what my brother said after the attacks? He thought of my poem: "When the revolution comes ... blood will run through the streets of Harlem ... " History itself is our PR agent right now, Umar. It's creepy. Cynical. Like they're only just waking up, and see the mess and violence and hate America let loose on the world, and here it's—'

'I know, Dun, I know … when was New Orleans again?'

'Next month sometime.'

'I've got some solo gigs in March … and my CD's coming out …'

'Oh, yeah.'

'We'll talk about it next week.'

'Okay.'

And then he hung up.

We were both nineteen, but I was older. I've always kept that feeling that I was the oldest. Officially I still lived at home but most nights I slept at Marlena's apartment on Riverside Drive. I'll never forget how it felt to drive into Harlem. From our house on Hillside Ave. in Jamaica, Queens I would drive down Grand Central Parkway, over the Triborough Bridge, and then onto 125th. It was a moment of triumph every single time. I felt like life was finally beginning, as though my lungs opened up and fresh air streamed in. I think Umar—Omar, he was still called back then—must have felt something similar when he first charged up the stairs to the East Wind. He was sweaty, the drops beaded up on his forehead, ran down his temples, even though it was freezing outside. He took off his jacket. He looked pretty slick in his black turtleneck, but his hungry look and that jabbering about some Times Square chase scene betrayed his Midwest roots. I recognized him right away from that Poets gig in Yellow Springs, where he was supposedly the head of security. That was nearly a year ago. I had given him our address in case he wanted to take a poetry workshop—I did that a lot with fans—but I never expected that bigmouth hick would actually come to New York to become a poet. But there he stood, nervous as anything, rocking from one foot to the other on those skinny legs, looking at me expectantly, eagerly. He launched in with: 'I want to join your group,' totally unembarrassed, like I'd personally invited him, or owed him something. Nilija kept his mouth shut but I could read his mind: nobody just 'becomes' a Last Poet, we're not some political party you can join. I was thinking the same thing but there was something in Omar's eyes that touched me, that said we couldn't just toss the guy back out on the street. I don't know exactly what it was. He kept looking at me with those big hazel eyes. I could see he was streetwise; I sensed his mistrust and cynicism, as though he might explode if I so much as laid a finger on him, but at the same time he had the innocent, vulnerable look of a child. I almost felt sorry for him. He had a hard time hiding his hankering, his hunger for everything what life had to offer.

That same evening I brought him with me to Marlena's. She had made fried fish and rice and vegetables and beans, and Omar stuffed himself and then fell asleep on the sofa. The next day I smuggled him into the Alamac Hotel on 71st and Broadway. Officially the Alamac was student housing, but I knew the concierge, Pietro, and made a deal with him so that Omar had a roof over his head.

I have never been able to shake the feeling that Omar was a kid brother I had to look out for.

Of course at that time I didn't know what kind of poet he was. To be honest, I was ashamed of him when we had that gig at Columbia and he started spouting that 'muthafucka' poem. 'Eldridge Cleaver is a thick muthafucka ... Malcolm was a royal muthafucka ... ' Man, it was more like a carnival attraction than a poetry reading. I never let him do that poem again.

I remember going to Smalls Paradise with him one

night, a jazz club on 135th Street. It's closed down now. Omar had already written 'Niggers Are Scared of Revolution' and we performed a lot with Jalal and Nilija. It was a warm fall evening. Smalls was chock-full. A thick cloud of cigarette smoke hung low and motionless above the tables. The light was red and muted. Lazy bass notes made the floor vibrate; the high-pitched trumpet was so thin and piercing that it was almost painful to listen to, like it tickled your nerve endings. The singer's hair glistened with Brylcreem. He had a mouthful of gold teeth and rocked shamelessly back and forth with his fat belly. 'Give it to me baby. Give it to me one more time.' The bassist played with his eyes closed and smiled like he was privy to a delicious secret. I knew this kind of club like the back of my hand. The light and the smoke made the air feel like velvet. The music was always second-rate but sexy and edgy enough for you to order a second glass, maybe even hang around longer. We ordered cognac. Omar tossed his back in one swig. His eyes darted every which way. It was his first time at Smalls and I saw what the club did to him. He was transformed. From one moment to the next, he was miles away, as though he had melted into the smoky warmth of the air and the music. I sat at the bar and watched Omar shuffle along the tables. I can't recall any other moment when I was so aware of our differences, the distance between us. Omar chatted to a girl, he whispered something in her ear and she smiled, allowed him to put his hand on her arm, threw back her head as she laughed. He moved his hips in time to the music, snapped his fingers and gestured to the barman for a refill. 'What can I buy you, honey?' I felt the warm flush of the cognac. Looked at Omar in the middle of the club, at the fluid movements of his body, saw how he attracted the desirous looks of women and men alike, maybe he wasn't even aware of it. But I never felt like such an outsider before. A spectator. It was Omar's doing: the nonchalance and ease with which he maneuvered in the warm, funky world of Smalls Paradise turned me into a stranger.

I had a hard time shaking that feeling. Later, too. The realization that I had to be on my guard when Omar was around. I hated that feeling, because Omar was in no way out to exclude me. He was just being himself. He conquered Harlem like a whirlwind; he claimed the neighborhood as his own with a fervor that approached insanity. He had no time to lose—like every new day was a personal victory over death. And even though I recognized his impetuosity and his drive and his desire to lose himself in his newfound freedom, I always had the feeling that I was a few steps behind.

That's how it seems now. Back then I thought it was the other way around. When Omar came to New York to become a Last Poet, I was already preparing to leave the group. I was the one who felt like a traitor whenever I went on stage to do 'When the Revolution Comes': a faux-revolutionary who didn't dare take real risks, who stayed out of harm's way, avoided pain. If, after a performance, I got talking to a mother trying to feed her eight kids on food stamps, I was ashamed of our success and felt nothing but contempt for my poetry. And at the same time I was proud of the awareness, and that Marlena had introduced me to the Harlem Committee for Self-Defense. I was ready for action. I was the strong, cool-headed intellectual, more politically savvy than Omar. Looking after him was easy, and it helped counter the alienating feeling I got when I was around him. I would never have called it jealousy back then, never. But when he performed 'Niggers Are Scared of Revolution' and went into a trance, when he spat out the words in that high, transparent voice, embraced them, sang them, called them out, it was like his body became a saxophone or a trumpet and he was just telling what he knew, what he had seen and experienced, his words bubbled up from a seething mud pot deep within him and came out as poetry—*You hear niggers say things are changing, things are changing. Yeah, things are changing / Niggers change into 'Black' nigger things, black nigger things that go through all kinds of changes. The change in the day that makes them rant and rave Black Power! Black Power! And the change that comes over them at night, as they sigh and moan: ooooh white thighs, ooooh, white thighs. Niggers always goin' through bullshit change ...* —and when I looked at him and saw how unashamedly he was as one with his poem, how his thoughts and his feelings, his ideas and his experiences, were so tight, I felt a kind of discomfort I couldn't put my finger on. Embarrassment, almost. I think I subconsciously knew I was no match for his recklessness. Not as a poet, nor as a person. He was free in a way I never could be. Yeah, I was jealous, but Omar's poem was stronger than me. Bird was right: our poems were stronger than ourselves. When I saw Omar sweating onstage, or a street corner, wriggling his legs like he's gonna take off into the air after his words, and I sang *niggers niggers niggers niggers* in the background to keep up the poem's driving cadence, then I loved him. I loved us.

It was about eleven o'clock. I got up and went to the kitchen, poured myself a glass of cognac. Why was Umar suddenly grumbling about that plane ticket? I thought he liked long bus rides. He always said the bus calmed him down, that it was a good place to think. It hadn't even occurred to me to book him a ticket from Flint or

Detroit. Besides, I never really knew where Umar hung out. For all I knew he was in Columbus or New Orleans or here in New York. Umar was a nomad. Damn it, he should be grateful I was organizing these gigs for us. Without me he wouldn't have two nickels to rub together. 'I'm tired, Dun.' Shit. Or was it about that new CD of his? Did he think he didn't need me anymore? That he could get a solo career off the ground? He always found some die-hard fan to take him under his wing. Even though he was thirty years older and forty pounds heavier, he still managed to send out the signal that he needed rescuing, that they should give him what he deserved as living legend, the godfather of hip-hop. Fuck that. And now that Carl guy in Columbus. I figure he paid for those CD recordings out of his own pocket.

I sat back down at my desk. Took a sip and tried to unwind, to shake off the negative thoughts. I looked out the window. The wind had died down; the buzz of the city was far away. It was like looking out over a deep valley. Thousands of fireflies hovered above the darkened brick wilderness. I watched the city settle into an uneasy sleep.

A few weeks back we were sitting in the lobby bar at our hotel in Washington, DC after a gig. It was a good thing Baba was there too. Baba, with his imposing figure, radiated tranquility. I'd never seen him angry. He always kept a certain distance from his surroundings without being aloof. Exactly what you want in a Yoruba priest.

Anyway, we were sitting at the bar, chatting about the show and blowing off steam. The performance was a success, even though I could sense Umar's tension. I had the feeling he was evading me during the show; he avoided eye contact entirely. The audience didn't notice.

Since 9/11, every performance was an event, a statement. A few days after the attacks I wrote 'Reign of Terror', a poetic pamphlet about America's cruel history and the lies about democracy and freedom. Well, that gave the show an edge. Even our oldest poems took on a new urgency and relevance. When Umar did 'This Is Madness' or I did 'When the Revolution Comes' the audience went wild. They were mostly in their twenties. It was exciting and depressing at the same time. Sometimes I had a strange déjà vu. I recognized the electricity in the auditorium, the same kind of energy and excitement I had felt thirty years ago, only now it was darker, less hopeful than back then.

I don't know if Umar felt the same way. He was pretty bottled up, just drank mineral water and muttered unintelligibly to himself. Baba and I sipped cognac and chatted about the Harlem Dance Theater's new show that Baba was touring with. I was relaxed. When Umar suddenly got up, I thought it was to go to his room, but he stood next to his barstool and rubbed his eyes.

'I'm tired,' was all he said.

'It's late,' I said.

'That's not what I mean,' Umar said. He looked straight at me.

'What, then?' I asked. Baba leaned back, his mouth curled into a half-smile.

'I couldn't get out of that dressing room ... Did you see that kid? A college student. His mouth hung open the whole time, you could see his fillings. He knew more about The Last Poets than I do, he even tried to correct me. "No, you wrote 'This Is Madness' in 1970, not in '69.' Like he was there. He probably hadn't even been born yet. I like the attention and all ... but sometimes ... sometimes ... '

'What, Umar?'

'I dunno.'

'You want me to order you something?'

'No.' He sat back down. He mumbled a bit, fidgeted with his hands. Like he was having a conversation with himself.

'I feel like I've got to move on … I mean … maybe it's time that The Last Poets … don't get me wrong, Dun, The Last Poets have given me everything I wanted, but sometimes I see myself, us, standing there … I don't know if I want to spend my whole life being pursued by my past. I'm still young. You know what I'm saying?'

I shook my head, but I knew exactly how Umar felt, and wanted nothing more than for him to take the elevator up to his room and sleep off his melancholy and dangerous thoughts. He was right. Sometimes I had that nagging feeling too, that The Last Poets were determining my identity more than I wanted. I was a teacher, singer, political speaker, poet. The poetry workshops I gave for those schoolkids from the ghetto were a hundred times more gratifying than a Last Poets gig. But strangely enough, I was still first and foremost a Last Poet, also for myself. As though without that title I didn't really exist. And there might be some truth in that. The poems we had made history with were so full of promise, excitement, hope, and the form we chose—poetry to the rhythm of drums—was as ancient as it was revolutionary. Back then, at least. People listened to us because we were the first. Poets were prophets. What Umar wanted to say was that we were prisoners of our own history. And I wanted to personally see to it that he swallowed those words. Sometimes I hated Umar because of The Last Poets, and I think he also could hate me for the same reason.

'Go get some sleep, Umar,' I said.

He grunted.

I felt his pent-up anger.

'Maybe we should all go upstairs,' Baba said with his quiet, kindly voice.

'Why?' Umar asked. He was wide awake, his eyes ablaze.

'Because we're tired,' Baba said.

Umar pretended not to hear. 'I don't want to spend the rest of my life being the high priest of our people, our race. Fuck the Race Question. I'm an artist. I've got responsibilities ... '

'You're talking shit, man,' I said. 'You've got the freedom to say whatever you want, about anything you want. So quit acting like that. You're doing exactly what you want, right? You've got new work and a solo CD.' I heard the unintentional reproach in my voice.

'All you are is scared,' Umar said.

'And you aren't?'

'What have I got to be scared about?'

Baba put his arm around Umar's shoulders. I saw him slacken.

'Everybody's scared of something, Umar,' I said.

He turned away and nodded absently. Took Baba's big hand. 'I'm going up,' he said.

I was about to hit the sack when I heard Obadele come in. The house was still dark. Oba must have thought I'd have long since gone to bed; he tiptoed to his room. I realized how familiar the sounds of our house were. The dry squeak of the middle floor plank in the hallway. The double click of Oba's door as it shut. The whoosh of the water in the pipes when someone opened a faucet. The gentle gurgling of the radiator pipes. I drained my glass and got up. On my way I pressed against the front door and checked to see if it was locked. It was a reflex, one that I had adopted when the children were still small and I had to constantly make sure the doors and windows were closed properly. Even now that it was no longer necessary, I still did it. I chuckled to myself. Ran my hand over the rough wood of the door. I heard sounds from Obadele's room; he had music on, sexy, languid R&B that fit with this time of night, and probably with his mood too. Oba never said much about his escapades in clubs or with girls. I figured it wouldn't be much longer before he earned enough money to rent his own apartment. He was a man now, with his own life. I noticed how differently he treated me these past few years, more adult, critical, distant and at the same time more caring, responsible. I was proud of the way he'd grown, but it also hurt like hell to be confronted with the merciless march of time, with mortality. Why did he bring up Umar? Had he overheard our conversation? Was he worried? How long ago was it since Umar last showed up on our doorstep? Damn, more than ten years ago. Oba was about fourteen. It was an evening like this one. We were watching the NBA playoffs on TV and suddenly the doorbell rang. Like an excited dog, Oba leapt up and ran to the door.

'Dad, there's somebody here for you.'

'Who?'

'I dunno.' He came back into the living room and plopped down on the couch.

'Who is it?' I asked again.

'A man. I think there's something wrong with him.'

'How'd he get up here?'

'How should I know? He asked for you.'

I reluctantly shuffled to the front door.

'Omar?' I whispered. Couldn't get any more than that

out of my mouth. He leaned against the doorpost, panting. Apparently he had taken the stairs. I recognized him right away by his eyes. His clothes hung sloppily on his skinny frame. It was like he'd shrunk. He'd let his beard grow; bits of gray blinked in the pale hall light. 'Omar?' I repeated.

'How you doing, man?' he mumbled. He started to cough, almost choked. 'Shoulda taken the elevator.'

'Where'd you come from?'

'Connecticut ... My sister ... '

'But ... ' The words got caught in my throat.

'We've got to revive The Last Poets man we have something to say I heard myself last night on the radio A Tribe Called Quest one of those hip-hop bands my own fucking voice I have to claim the rights come on Dun we've got work to do the only thing these chumps can rap about these days is bitches and whores and niggers and pussy no message at all ... '

'Whoa!' I said. 'Damn, Omar. I thought you were dead. Twenty years we don't hear a word from you. Everybody thinks you're dead. I've got my own life. What were you thinking?'

He laughed. I was angry that he embarrassed me, put me on the spot like that. And at the same time I felt for him, cutting such a shoddy figure in that cheap suit.

'Can I come in?' he asked.

'No.'

'Dad?' Oba called from the living room.

'I'm coming, son,' I said.

Umar pulled a crumpled scrap of paper from his back pocket. Started reading. *Highly intelligent in a very low way / We speak of existing but have nothing to say / We touch religion and make it seem like hell / But then we touch unholy dreams and wish them well / Faith is replaced by apathy and grief / Indifference is made acceptable and then a belief / Our left eyes glitter while our right are blind / We submit to this madness and hope it is kind / Distraught women ...*

And so on and so forth. The poem was new to me, but he could recite just like in the old days. Omar never could sing, but oh how he made the words dance, float, fly on his too-thin breath, as if trying to keep up with them—I could tell the high notes hurt. I don't remember exactly what I felt right then, but I had to protect myself against his words. Where the hell had he been hanging out all this time? What had happened? And now I'm supposed to let him in? At last I had a normal life with my children, my women, my music, my job as educational adviser for the city. The Last Poets? Two years ago Gregory Reed, this lawyer from Detroit, tried to get us back together again. Kain and David and Felipe and me. Omar was dead. Jalal AWOL. It was as if time had stood still: the same rivalry and mistrust, Felipe grousing about money, David with his head in the clouds and Kain, Kain jumping on the first airplane back to Holland after the show. We were no more than a shadow of our former selves. The disillusionment hit me hard. And now Omar shows up on my doorstep. He doesn't even acknowledge me, just launches into his poem: ... *to look at the sea and understand its motion / To understand tenderness and give it devotion / To understand courtesy and to make it a pact / to understand what love is and make it a fact / Because we all must struggle. We all must try / Because somewhere in the future we all must die ...*

I listened. Omar's words forced my own thoughts to the background. They dissolved in the transparent sound of his voice, the rhythm, and I couldn't deny that it gave me a tingling, excited feeling. Like I'd missed something all that time. A kind of greedy curiosity. I didn't know what to do with him but I realized I couldn't very well chuck Omar back out onto the street. His poem was finished. He panted and looked at me impassively. It was clear he did not expect anything from me.

'That was beautiful, Omar,' I said.

He only nodded, stuffed the scrap of paper back into his pocket and zipped up his jacket.

'Have you got more new material?' I asked.

'Oh, sure ... sure ... you?'

'You want to come in?'

'If I may.'

'Come on in.' I didn't want him acting so polite and humble. It made me feel like shit. As if what I said didn't matter: my turning him away wouldn't really hurt him. I pushed the door open and gestured for him to go in. 'You can have the sofa,' I said.

'Thanks, Dun.'

'Maybe ... maybe we should to give it a try,' I said, but Omar didn't seem to hear. He took off his jacket and went into the living room, where Oba was still watching the playoffs. He sat down next to him on the futon and asked him about the game. Without taking his eyes off the screen, Oba answered him in his special self-assured, calm way. It was quite a sight to see the two of them sitting there. As though it was perfectly normal that after all these years, Omar would walk back into my life.

BE BOP OR BE DEAD

HARLEM, 1983

Riverbank State Park

The sun was dim that childish morning

'Lemme show you something,' Umar says. They climb over the stone wall adjacent to the highway and walk down the soggy bank, among the trees and leaves, the shit and the garbage and the dirty needles. It's still early, not busy, a ways further up they see the shadow of a couple who are at it.

The roar of traffic dies down. Jane takes his hand. He feels her warmth. 'Come with me.' The sparkle of the lights across the water. New Jersey. The murky Hudson. The rocky, wooded cliffs in the distance.

'You see that?' he asks.

'See what?'

'The narrow passage between the hills. Where the ships leave the city. From here the Hudson's at its best.'

'Did you bring the stuff?' Jane asks.

'What do you think?'

'Let's go then.'

They lean against a tree. Burn the crack on a piece of aluminum foil. 'Quick, quick, you first.' Jane sucks in the smoke through a plastic pipe. Then Umar.

'Come here,' she sighs, pulling him close. Her blouse is open. He sees her ribs, her small body, the light of the city reflecting off her bronze skin. Her eyes wide open.

'Come in me, Umar.' Her eyes. It's like he can look straight through her. Her love, her pleasure, her fear. He feels her moist, warm desire. Pulls her even closer.

'Faster,' she pants. 'I'm gonna give you a blow job.'

He shuts his eyes. The lights of the highway traffic linger; they had just spent hours watching it. Hand in hand. 'I'll take care of you, baby.'

'Let's go to my mother's house.'

'In a bit.'

Her sighs so near, her sweat, her heartbeat. As though she's inside him. He thrusts deeper into her. Her entire body is on fire. He wants to touch her where no one else has ever been, but her fragile bones are like a harness he cannot break through.

'You're hurting me, Umar.'

'Almost,' he whispers, kisses her wet cheeks. Closes his eyes. He feels the strength drain out of him. He drowns in her girlish body. She is Queenie Mae. In a flash he sees Queenie. All his love begins with Queenie Mae.

'Let's get out of here,' Jane whispers.

'Where to?'

'My mother's out.'

'All night?'

'All night.'

CONEY ISLAND, SEPTEMBER 2001

Queenie Mae

'We had already been separated for a while when Umar disappeared. I told Amina: "Daddy's not coming back, he's got his own things to see to." No one knew where he was at. Not even Malika, I don't think. He was married to her at the time. I think Umar didn't want me to see him in that state. I only heard everything later, of course, but that's what I think. Umar and I can talk, really talk, I mean. Even now.

I come from Walterboro, South Carolina. My father was a long-distance truck driver and my mother was a teaching assistant in a kindergarten. I had three sisters and two brothers. We were a close family. South Carolina is so different from New York. No high-rises, just real houses. People greet one another on the street. And families are different too. My parents wanted us to work hard and further our studies. They were always there for us. My sisters and I were Brownies and Girl Scouts. Every Sunday we went to church. My grandfather was a minister. Southern blacks are much more tight-knit. My parents taught us that it's your obligation to give something back to the community.

I came to New York when I was in high school. An aunt of mine lived in Brooklyn. She owned a building in Bed-Stuy and I moved in with her. At first I tiptoed through the apartment, I thought it was so strange to be walking above other people's heads. I thought I was bothering them. I finished high school in New York. My father was disappointed that I didn't go to college, but I wanted to work, broaden my horizons. There was a lot of opportunity in New York, plenty of jobs, for black people too. I got a job at American Express as secretary to the director. Later they sent me to do a computer course. I've always been a career woman.

One day I fell asleep on the subway on my way home from work. I woke up a stop too far, at Fulton Street. So I got out to catch the next train back. I remember my aunt always warning how dangerous Fulton was. I took the stairs up to street level—you had to cross the road to get to the other platform—and while waiting at the crosswalk I saw all these men in jogging suits slouched against cars, women whose arms were swollen from shooting up, wounds oozing pus. I couldn't believe my eyes. It was so sad. And all that poverty. I was stunned. After I crossed the street I bumped into a friend of my aunt's. "What are you doing here?" he asked. He took me to a restaurant, offered me something to eat. My mother used to make lemon meringue pie, so I ordered a piece of that. He told me about Youth in Action, where he and his wife were active. They were looking for somebody who was good with computers. So I went to an interview and was hired on the spot. Youth in Action was one of the first government-subsidized poverty prevention programs; they organized sports and recreation for underprivileged black youths, so that they didn't have to hang around on the street. That's where my political awareness was formed. I met all sorts of people. Shirley Chisholm, the first black US congresswoman, was on the board. I learned a lot from her. I also went to meetings of the Southern Christian Leadership Conference, which had been founded by Martin Luther King. He came from the South, just like me. And I helped out with a Youth in Action radio program. One afternoon Omar was going to be interviewed—The Last Poets were very popular among young people. That's where we met. Matter of fact, it was really crazy, because Omar just came out and said: "You're gonna be my wife." We just laughed and talked and laughed and talked. And then we got married.'

◆

Run ... Run ... the ocean is going to sail without us

Me eat rice? You must be kidding. I was a Midwestern kid, I ate mashed potatoes. Omar, go on and make me some mashed potatoes. Queenie Mae was no joke. She could make rice twelve different ways. And fish. Queenie had three children from a previous marriage. Four months after we were married we moved to Walterboro. I had money from our second album. People talk about going to Africa, but when you're in the South Carolina hills you think you're in Africa. The tall trees, the weeping willows, the wide-open space. The light on a summer day. The women there have high cheekbones, their skin is darker, really dark. And their asses ... oooh. We went around to Queenie's friends, a couple. The guy's big, a truck driver. His wife a head shorter. She says something that pisses him off. You know how that goes. He starts hitting her. She just stands there and takes it, looks him straight in the eye. Proud. And suddenly she attacks the guy, starts biting and kicking him.
Queenie Mae was no joke.

No joke.

She was lying on her back in bed, staring at the ceiling. He saw the curve of her belly.

They had made love. It was Sunday morning.

'How does it feel?'

'What?'

'The baby.'

She laughed. Kept staring at the ceiling.

He ran his fingers over her belly, put his ear to it.

'There's nothing to hear yet, silly.' She pushed him off her.

'Why not?'

'It's only two months along.'

'So when do you hear something? Or feel it kick. Babies kick, right?'

'I'll let you know.'

It was pitch-black out. No stars, no moon. He went inside. Queenie had left a light on for him. She'd been asleep for hours. He switched on the television, tuned in to a basketball game. LA Lakers vs. Chicago Bulls. He turned off the sound, went to the kitchen and got a beer from the fridge. He chugged it down and got another. Back in the living room he listened to the hum, stared at the flickering images. The room looked just like when he left this morning, before Queenie and the children were up. Toy box in the corner, the dolls in a tidy row. Sunflowers on the dining table. No dust, no washing, no newspapers on the floor. The leather sofa and armchairs bulky and overbearing, as though they were the boss here, not him.

A few hours earlier they had performed in a smoky little theater in Philadelphia. The music was still in his head. The fluid rhythms of Nilija's drums. The sound of his own high voice. He only had to shut his eyes to see the words glisten like gold and silver. *Trying to get out to sea. The laughter of idiots bleeding in my ears. Trying to get out to sea. The laughter of idiots bleeding in my ears.* He was working on a new poem about drums. About their sound, their melody you heard once Nilija got into the groove and sped up, faster, faster, mysterious rarefied music that wafted high above the congas. He had composed a few lines but wasn't able to finish it. All the way back from the gig the words danced around in his head like an endless loop, until all he heard were sounds.

He shook his head. Took a high-backed dining room chair and set it in front of the TV, propping his feet on the coffee table. The soft carpeting muted Queenie's footsteps. Suddenly she was standing in the middle of the room in her long yellow nightgown. The light shone through the thin cotton, outlining her broad hips and her heavy breasts that rested on her enormous belly.

'I didn't hear you come in.'

'Couldn't you sleep?'

She shrugged. 'It's like I'm awake all the time, even when I'm asleep. It's exhausting me. I don't really dream. It's like I'm permanently on my guard, lying there waiting until something happens, only I don't know what. I didn't have this with the others. Slept like a rock right up till the end. You don't suppose it means something, do you?'

'C'mere.'

'I'm worried, Omar.'

'Let me feel your belly.'

She came closer. He hiked up her nightgown. Her skin was so tight and smooth that it glowed. Her navel stuck out a bit. He held his hand against the side of her belly, the place where he'd once felt the baby move. A soft, dull movement, as though the baby reacted to his touch and swam in his direction. The first time he felt it, he was startled, pulled back his hand. His hand felt too big for what was inside her. Too big and too strong. He waited a moment, closed his eyes.

'The baby's sleeping.'

She laughed, and ran her fingers through his wiry curls.

'Omar, we can't go on like this. I mean it.' She pressed his head against her belly. 'Once the baby's here I'm going back to work.'

'Why?'

'Why do you think?'

'I can take care of you, don't worry.'

'We're nearly broke. You want us to get evicted?'

'We're not gonna get evicted. I said I'd take care of you, didn't I? I've got gigs till the end of the year. I don't want you working.'

'Why not? I've always worked. I like working. I'm not the stay-at-home type.'

'Who's going to take care of the children?'

'Who do you think?' She laughed, looked straight at him without a trace of reproach or anger. 'How'd your gig go?'

'I don't want you working.'

'Come on to bed.'

'You understand me?'

Queenie shuffled off to the hall.

'I want to provide for my family, God damn it, is that so wrong?' He heard the bedroom door click shut.

'Fuck you, bitch,' he thought.

When worldly affairs and your touch make me want to run
and hide in winter storms and temptation and lust in silk
sheets of denial and rejection and begging and pleading
for your eyes to meet mine for some
soft apology over impromptu lunches and long walks into
empty arms and promising careers of pretending to be
happy by the fire and pain holding up very well considering
the fact that I find myself alone in the thought of some
ridiculous smile and half-empty glass and bar stools and
wondering why I can't humble myself to unconditional love
and poems and prayers asking you to please remember that
I am only human.

He was no match for Queenie. Naturally calm and self-assured, she won every argument. She hardly ever yelled at the children, ran the household with ease. She let him work on his poetry at night. She looked beautiful, even right after Amina was born. He saw how she looked at the baby, her soft, protective, loving gaze, the same look she gave him. The look that made his head spin. The more she loved him, the more helpless he felt.

Queenie made friends with his sister Sandra and his mother right off the bat. They could talk for hours on end, and when they weren't physically together, they would call. The phone bill got higher every month. It was like the women in his family all spoke the same language, a language he did not understand.

She reminded him of his younger siblings. Of the harsh winters when the snowdrifts piled high against the front door and they had to all push together to get it open, and then they ran out and had snowball fights. He would mix the snow with fruit-flavored syrup and pack it into small balls. The little ones always demanded snow cones in the winter.

Queenie knew how to deal with his family. She also knew she wouldn't survive without them, especially not in New York.

'Let's go to Walterboro.'

'You go with the children.'

'But you haven't seen my parents in so long.'

'I've got gigs.'

'Come on, Omar.'

'Don't nag, okay?'

He'd stayed up all night, watching her as she slept. She lay on her side, her hair covering her face. He listened to her breathing; sometimes it was like she forgot to breathe and then sighed deeply and curled up her knees. He had to force himself not to wake her. He wanted to know what she dreamed about, what went on in her head. He lay next to her, fully clothed, on his back. He felt her warm breath in his face, listened to the dull silence. Queenie had so often asked him to come to bed with her, but he always stayed up alone, when poetic inspiration might strike. But the silence seemed to erode his thoughts. It made him sick to his stomach. It felt like he was regressing rather than moving forward. He didn't mention it to Queenie—how could he tell her he was roaming around lost in the space she had given him, the space he had demanded. 'I'm a poet, an artist, I don't want a job.' Queenie turned in her sleep, made soft noises with her tongue. Through the thin white curtains he saw the beginnings of the morning light.

And I hear my mother's voice rustling in the wind reminding me of the many times he tried to rape her of her Blackness.

But she with the strength of a panther, the swiftness of a
cheetah and the cunning of a lioness would not be caged
up with the other lies that kept me from being totally free.
And when she came home at night I could smell the musty
closeness of his body and see his translucent fingerprints
on her tired weary physical structure depressed from
warding off his beastly attacks. But she would smile the
smile of a thousand Black Orchids at me not realizing all
the while that the anger of a hundred lions was residing in
my soul.

Queenie said: 'I don't want our children to go through
what you did.'

So easy to love other women. So cheap. After every performance some black princess would turn up, profess
her love for him. All he had to do was hint that she just
might be the one who really understood him. The only
thing he asked in return was pleasure, not love, but
warm, damp, fleeting pleasure, the dirty smell of sex,
hot talk, panting, groaning, the subtle, sickly taste of
swollen lips and female wetness and the moment where
everything went black and his heart seemed to burst out
of his chest, that painful fraction of a second when he
felt alone and totally free.

Queenie said: 'I know you're fooling around.'
    'Who, me?'
    'Don't lie to me.'
    'What do you want me to do?'
    'I want you to pack your things and leave.'
    'But I love you and no one else.'
    'I know, Omar, I know.'
    'Queenie?'

'You have to go.'
'What about the children?'
'That's why you have to go. Get that into your head.'

GOLDSBORO, NORTH CAROLINA, FEBRUARY 2002

Anne Hurrey, widow of Raymond Hurrey, a.k.a. Nilija Obabi

'I was born in this house. When my father died of a heart attack, Nilija and the children and I moved back to North Carolina to look after my mother. We wanted to find our own place but Nilija's health was already slipping. Once, I cooked for him and he took his plate and just dropped it on the kitchen floor. I didn't think anything of it at that time, just cleaned up the mess and gave him a new helping. But a few weeks later he started dragging one leg. His arms hurt. At the hospital they thought he had MS, but the medicine they gave him didn't help. A month later a specialist at the Greenville Medical Center did a brain scan. Turned out he had a tumor in his head as big as a half-dollar. They could operate, the doctor said, but that would mean he'd spend the rest of his life as a vegetable. They gave him three to six months to live. At the end he couldn't talk anymore or move his limbs. One of the last things he said to me was, "Don't let anybody say you were a bad mother or wife." He thanked me. Said I'd given him things he'd never expected to get out of life— love, a family. That was really touching. I said: "It would have meant so much to me if you'd said this earlier."

"I couldn't," he said. "But I've never done anything to jeopardize our family." Nilija wasn't the emotive, communicative type. But I'm thankful for that last talk we had. Three weeks later he was dead.

I met Ray in New York in 1961. I was spending the summer at my aunt's in Flatbush, in Brooklyn. Most Saturday evenings my cousins and I went dancing at the Palladium Ballroom on 53rd and Broadway. Latin music was popular among Afro-Americans. The mambo. I had noticed Ray a couple of times before, and the night before I was to go back to Goldsboro, he asked me to dance. We talked a little. He asked where I came from. "Down South."

"Me too," he said. "I used to live with my grandmother in Mobile, Alabama." I gave him my phone number—he wrote it on the back of the silver foil paper from a pack of Marlboros.

I was studying to be a physiotherapist, but my parents couldn't pay the tuition anymore, so I went back to New York to find work. I got a secretarial job at an institute for international studies. One of the girls at the office offered me a room in her apartment on 100th street and Central Park West. Raymond lived up in Harlem, on 148th between Seventh and Eighth. One evening I wanted to surprise him, so I took the bus there and rang his doorbell.

"How'd you get here?" he asked.

"With the bus."

"Are you crazy? Didn't you see all that riffraff hanging around?"

"Sure."

"They're junkies. If they think you've got any money, they'll rob you blind. Promise me you'll never take the bus on your own again."

I was in love. Ray fascinated me. He told me things about African culture I'd never heard before. About our people's history from before the time we were brought to America. Sundiata and the great kingdoms of Mali. At school, black history only started with slavery—

Africa was the "dark continent". I wasn't aware of the depth of the problems between blacks and whites. I'd gone to an all-black school, but was used to white people because my father did business with them. He had a supermarket. And my mother was an Avon consultant with lots of white customers.

Ray and I went to museums and street festivals. He already played drums. In those days everybody was active in something—theater or music or poetry. I've always danced. Modern dance. Later, because of Nilija, I turned to African dance. I don't know how he learned to play the drums; he was a natural, could pick up the most complicated rhythms just like that. He used to jam with friends in Central Park.

It was an exciting time. A kind of black renaissance. You could be walking through Harlem and just happen to hear Malcolm X speak. All kinds of interesting people lived in my building. Babatunde Olatunji, the famous drummer, with his family. Duke Ellington had an apartment there. These were people you bumped into in the elevator. One of my neighbors was seeing David Baldwin, the brother of James Baldwin, who also used to drop by. He was working on *The Fire Next Time*, which later became a bestseller.

Everybody liked Ray. They thought that was interesting, being a drummer. But he kept pretty much to himself. I think he felt he didn't belong. His mother was not a warm person. When Ray was a baby, she left him with her mother in Mobile and moved to New York to look for work. Ray thought his grandmother was his mother. She had another grandchild living with her, a boy called Junior, so he and Ray grew up like brothers. Mobile's about three hours' drive from New Orleans, and it's got a lot of the same atmosphere and style, a jazz history and all. There were a lot of mulattos living there—Ray's grandmother was one, she was very light-skinned. That woman lived to be a hundred and one! I don't know what I'd done without her after Ray died. I was left with two children. Our son Ayinde was just six.

So anyway, when he was five Ray's mother sent for him, brought him up to New York. She had remarried and her husband had a son, Ronald. Ray told me that his mother favored Ronald. That he, Ray, always had to help with housework, and Ronald didn't. "Just like Cinderella," I teased him. He was able to laugh about it. He left home at sixteen and went to live with one of his aunts. They were good to him. When I met him he was nineteen and was living on his own.

One day—we were already married and Colette was a baby—Ray came home and said he met a couple of guys whose poems he liked. "Maybe I'll go jam with them," he said. And that was the beginning of The Last Poets. Ray had a job at the printing works. He had a decent boss who always gave him time off for performances and tours, no problem. Sometimes the Poets came to our place in Brooklyn on Saturdays to rehearse. I really had to laugh. "You're the only group I know where the audience pays to be cussed at," I told them. They must have thought I was an odd duck. Dun was with Marlena Franklin then, and Kain was with June. Kain was so in love with her. I can't remember who David and Felipe were with. Nilija was the peacemaker. Later, too, with Omar and Jalal. The others had bigger egos because they were the ones writing the poetry, but as the drummer Nilija didn't have any competition within the group. He always did his own thing anyway. Sometimes he'd call me from his hotel room after a gig. "Where are the others?" I'd ask.

"You know where. Out on the town."

Nilija admired them for their texts and performance style, but it bothered him that as soon as the spotlights were off they would do exactly what they railed against in their poems. Argue. Fight. Cheat on their women. Omar was married to Queenie, and it caused her no end of heartache. Dun and Jalal were womanizers too. Nilija and Dun always stayed close. I think Dun admired Nilija for managing to keep his family together. A few weeks ago I happened to see Dun on TV, in some talk show. I was shocked, it was almost painful to see how much he's aged. It's been twenty years since I last saw him. But then, we all get older, don't we.'

'25 Years' (1993)

There is no easy thing in being the strength for the weakness
and fear of words lost in the dreams and nights of Harlem our
inspiration to leave and come back to in times of madness and
coke and jail.

[...]

We are the friends to the tears that have nowhere to go.
We are our fathers in that moment of night that speaks
only to the softness of compassion. We are the doubt and
hesitation on corners in bars and in love with our people and
being so much a part of their pain and laughter we sacrifice
ourselves to the neon lights and being close to one another
in the morning will come only when we learn to control the
darkness of ourselves ...

HARLEM, 1983

Morning

The first thing Umar saw when he woke up was a harsh
black-and-white sparkle that hurt his eyes. He brushed
away the rumpled covers and rolled out of bed. He
coughed, struggled to breathe, as though his lungs were
filled with dust. He crawled toward the crackle and sput-
ter that made him think of storm and sand. He was
dehydrated, his throat burned and his lips were cracked.
Umar sank onto the dirty red carpet and closed his eyes.
It was like being washed ashore. He listened to the crashing waves, saw the white froth and the blue-green water.
He smiled in his half-sleep. The sky was clear blue, the
clearest blue he'd ever seen, a beautiful infinite nothing.
He felt the cool water lap at his feet. Heard the faraway
sound of a trumpet. He turned on his side, listened as
the warm, velvety music approached, the music was like
a down quilt that warmed and caressed his bruised
limbs. As he opened his eyes he counted the slow, empty
seconds, as though he were outside time, until he could
register where he was. The TV was on, but just snow and
white noise. He reached out and tugged the plug out of
the socket. Jane's small, naked body was rolled up on the
queen-size mattress, the sheets draped around her like
a huge, loose bandage. She snored like a baby. The way
she lay there, oblivious and cocooned by her childlike
dreams, she was a stranger to him. Umar remembered

them making love and smoking crack until collapsing into sleep at dawn, but he couldn't recall any real feelings. Her body was so far away. Even the memory of her sultry, melodious voice as she whispered pleasantries to him and begged him to do the same—this too seemed an illusion, a distant, wistful memory. He hoisted himself up and pulled a T-shirt out from under the TV. The shirt smelled like sweat and puke. He gagged, staggered to the bathroom, and opened a faucet. Running water. The sound of running water. Thousands of needles pricking his brain. He listened to the splashing for as long as it took to suppress the nausea and clear his head. He looked in the mirror but avoided the bewildered face that stared back at him. The face of a child. Ashamed, he turned away. The dry silence in the house oppressed him.

He had spoken to Amina yesterday afternoon. Had slid a couple of quarters into a pay phone on Times Square and dialed Queenie's number on Coney Island, resolved to hang up if Queenie answered. It was Saturday so their eldest daughter would probably be home.

'Dad?'

'How you doing, honey?'

'Where are you?'

'Traveling.'

'Doesn't sound like it.'

'What does it sound like then?'

'I don't know. Farther away. What are you doing?'

'Working, doll. I'll come for you soon.'

'Are you all right?'

'I'm always all right, you know that.'

'Are you alone? Mom misses you.'

'No she doesn't, honey. You only want her to. I've gotta go.'

'Can I call you back?'

'Sure.'

'Where?' But her voice was drowned out by the shriek of a passing ambulance. He hung up and started walking, already sorry he'd phoned. It was painful to hear her voice, her thin, girlish voice utter such encouraging words—how old was she by now? Thirteen, fourteen? He'd lost track. He had no chance to ask about *her*, how *she* was doing. Or did he call just to hear her concern, her love—her unconditional, undeserved love? Maybe calling was a sort of self-inflicted punishment, but he only realized this afterward, when it was too late, and the guilt grabbed him by the throat and made him run.

He ran alongside the freeway all the way to New Jersey, the traffic roared past him, egged him on, he lost all feeling in his feet and legs, the cold burned his ears, his temples throbbed but he kept running until he saw the chemical factory with the gray wet roof shining like steel in the sunlight; the gleaming white metal blinded him and the sun seemed to lift him up, he was surrounded by light and felt weightless. He had no idea how long he stood there on the bridge across the Hudson. When the clouds drifted in front of the sun, the factory returned to its familiar brown-gray tint and melted into the rest of the industrial zone, into the traffic, the noise, the menacing blue mist rising off the river's surface; he ran on, leaving the white light behind him, and for a brief moment it felt like he was outrunning the tumult, outrunning his own pent-up emotions and the throbbing in his head, and he imagined himself calling Amina back and saying, 'I'm sorry, honey. How's school?'

But the traffic caught up with him. Truck drivers gestured angrily from high in their cabs, they honked, their oversized wheels spattered him with water from the puddles on the shoulder. He kept on running, ignoring his sopping and muddy clothes. He ran like a machine. He was his body: muscles, warmth, blood, mucus, bones, fat, liver, heart, lungs, spleen, kidneys. A magnet was tugging at him, he no longer needed to think or feel. And when he reached the familiar alley behind the bus station and his lungs sucked in the exhaust fumes and the steely air of the trains, he approached a couple of crackheads and pulled his knife. They were so far gone they didn't even realize he was stealing their stuff. He smoked some there, then he went into the station to find a pay phone.

'Jane?'

'Is that you?'

'Riverbank State Park? In an hour?'

'I love you, baby.'

'How do you know that?'

'What? I can hardly hear you. Where are you? Got the dope?'

'Yeah. How do you know you love me? How do you know?'

'I've gotta hang up now. See you at the park.'

It was already getting dark.

Back in the bedroom, Jane groaned and turned onto her back. She rubbed her eyes and pulled herself up.

'I feel sick,' she said.

'I'm going soon,' Umar said.

She rolled out of bed and shuffled to the bathroom. She had to grab hold of the doorframe to keep from falling over.

He picked up his pants and jacket and finished getting dressed. Ran a hand through his hair and fished his cap out of the pile of dirty clothes and underwear and bedsheets. He had to get out of here before Jane's mother came home. Did not feel up to her judgmental looks right now. From the bathroom came the sound of vomiting, the toilet flushing, a scream.

'Umar, come quick!'

What he really wanted was to run out of the apartment, but he went to the bathroom, stood in the doorway, and saw Jane's horrified face, her tousled afro. 'What is it?'

'I'm pissing blood, Umar.'

'It's just your period.'

'No! My God, I'm pissing blood.

The sour smell in the bathroom made him want to gag. He took a step back.

'Don't leave.' Jane started to cry.

'You smoked too much. You've got to take it easy.'

'Easy for you to say, asshole. I could lose the baby.'

'What baby? What's that bullshit?' He felt sorry for her but didn't have the energy to pay her any attention. He was exhausted, wanted nothing more than to sleep for days, weeks on end.

'I'm pregnant, Umar. Three months.' She lifted her T-shirt and showed him her scrawny body.

'You're not pregnant. I'm outta here.' He pulled his cap forward, the brim shading his eyes.

'It's yours. You're the only one I've fucked. What did you think? That nothing would happen?' She was screaming through her tears, but her voice was thin and shaky.

Umar squatted, covered his eyes with his hands. The bitch. Now this. A fucking baby. His baby. The last of his energy drained out of him. He sat down on the floor and listened to Jane's whimpering. He had nothing to say. He could never say what he felt. Fate was always a step ahead of him. Even in his weakest moments, fate didn't give him any peace, it laughed in his face and bombarded him with responsibilities, squeezed his throat and took his breath away, robbed him of the freedom to actually love someone. His eyes itched, he wept for the baby, for his uncontrollable love, which he thought he'd left behind in the apartment on Clinton Ave. where Malika and his three children lived, with Queenie and Amina on Coney Island, with Juwariya and Khadija—Khadija, his only daughter he hadn't seen being born. Forgive me, baby. Forgive me. Forgive me. He shook his head.

Jane muttered something, got up, adjusted her pants, and flushed the toilet.

'You've got to see a doctor. You're sick.'

'I just want to sleep,' Jane said, climbing into bed and pulling the covers over herself.

'Tell it to your mother.' He righted himself and zipped up his jacket.

'Yeah, sure. I'm tired.'

'Then go to sleep.'

'Uh-huh.'

'I'll call you.'

But Jane didn't answer. From her heavy breathing he could hear she was asleep. He tiptoed out of the apartment.

'Illusion of Self ' (1993)

The sun was dim that childish morning when sleep awakened
me to the cries of your distant touch. There were no crowded
rooms for our love to cross no smoke-filled fantasies to
insure our happiness. Ours had become a comedy of errors.
A tragedy from the dark side of the moon.

[...]

But still we tried

WATERBURY, CONNECTICUT, AUTUMN 1986

Rain

It was just after midnight when the bus pulled into the small Greyhound station. Everything was dark, the ticket office closed, no cafeteria. He had the slip of paper with the address of the Catholic shelter in his back pocket, but when he stepped off the bus and took it out, fat raindrops dripped off the awning onto the paper, slowly transforming the black-inked block letters LeRoy had written down back in Danbury into a dark-purple blotch. There was no one he could ask for directions. Maybe he should call the rehab clinic and ask for Lee, but he had neither their number nor change for the phone. He missed LeRoy. He even missed the chill of their dormitory, the pale yellow walls of the rec room, the hallway lights that never seemed to go out. There was a sort of comfort in that ugliness, and in the shifty, scared eyes of the newcomers, their open pores, dark rings around their eyes, bad teeth and worse breath, and the cigarette smoke that hung permanently, heavy and greasy, above the Formica tables. Knowing you were protected against your own illusions gave you a sense of security.

'Aren't you ...?' LeRoy asked him after a few days.

By now it was a familiar question. He nodded.

'The *poet*,' LeRoy said proudly. He extended his hand. 'LeRoy Alexander. Lee to my friends.'

'Hey Lee.'

'Who was that on the phone just now?'

'None of your goddamn business.'

'Family, am I right?'

'Shut up.'

'A woman?'

'My daughter. I have no idea how she found me. That child must have ESP. She follows me like my own shadow.'

He was glad Lee did not comment.

'You still work?'

'Work?' Umar asked, irritated.

'Write poetry. You mind if I ask?'

Lee was a decent guy despite his down-at-the-heel appearance, his jagged nails, and bad teeth.

He shrugged. He didn't feel like mentioning the crack house performances, although he was proud of reaching the occasional junkie. Sometimes a crackhead would show him a few lines and ask his opinion. Sure, there were poems bumping around his head, but he wasn't going to tell just anybody. He could hardly grasp them himself. His words were always quicker than he was, they offered him a glimpse of a life that was ongoing but out of reach. Discussing them was out of the question. The visions would evaporate into thin air.

This is what passed through his mind as he watched the bus disappear in the distance. Lee had warned him. 'You're not ready, man, you can't do it yet.' But every fiber in his haggard body quivered and all he could think of was air, cold fresh air on his cheeks and his forehead, the white autumn mist that hung low and mysterious above the fields and hills, the scent of rain and half-rotted leaves—he had to get out, get moving, move, run, listen to the reassuring hum of the Greyhound bus engine. Waterbury. Night.

The road reflected a dull, wet black. Umar stepped out from under the awning, closed his eyes, and threw back his head, heard the wind tug at the bare branches. The raindrops caressed his warm cheeks; he licked them from his upper lip and tasted their sweetness, their warmth. He took off his cap so the rain could dance through his wiry hair, he heard the droplets, a voice whispering to him, North St., the gurgling of the creek behind their house mixed with the sultry tones of the trumpet that wafted up from their basement. 'Sonny! Dinner!' his mother called, but his father played on. Jerome sat on the big smooth rocks alongside the creek, imagined it was a waterfall crashing against the boulders, leaving behind a layer of glistening droplets on the grass and the moss and his clothes and skin. The murmur of the creek reassured him that it was okay he couldn't talk, everything was clear and simple and Papa knew it, he connected with him through his trumpet, told him about the bears and the deer and the foxholes in the woods, the music was so thin and fragile, all his love crammed into those wispy tones, the husky melodies. 'Sonny,' his mother called again. 'Jerome, Chris, dinner's ready.' But he did not move.

He did not move. He felt the water seep through his thin jacket. A shudder shot through his body, reminded him of crack's bite. The generic, anonymous sex in Riverbank State Park. How can I ever explain that I needed that ugly pleasure, that I did it entirely for myself, my guilty conscience was just an excuse, no more than that. I experienced my happiest moments with those needy, emaciated women who would do anything for a line of coke or a few crumbs of crack. They stank like garbage and depravity and asphalt, just like me. Come on Daddy, fuck me from behind, fuck me fuck me until I see stars and have quit feeling. Come on. A few yards away, cars shot like lightning bolts down the freeway. Headlights like stiff nipples in the air, like strobe lights in a bizarre underground disco. I remember the massive thighs of the Howard St. whores, the flickering neon lights and the red-green-red-green dancing on their skin. Carla putting out in the parking lot behind Roxy's for a few dollars. The cracker's pants around his ankles, thrusting Carla harder and harder against the wall, her ass chafing against the bricks, biting her lip not to cry out in pain. I so wanted to rescue her. I couldn't risk letting her get killed—she was guarding my secret. 'Nobody has to know, Geronimo. Nobody.' I knew how her pussy smelled. That raw, salty taste in my mouth. Without her I was totally alone. How can I tell you all that? I had to go back. With every woman I've loved, no matter how twisted or perverse, I've tried to get closer to the secret. As though I could hide myself in the erose folds and wrinkles of womanhood. But what I was looking for was past her body, past love, past memories.

D'you hear the music? Listen ... off in the distance. D'you hear it?

He had waited so long, and only now, now he hardly dared hope for it, snippets of a poem trickled in together with the droplets of rain. *Hard laughter disguising softer fears / Love becomes entangled while deception cheers / Love that moment you can't understand / It's when love is asking for a helping hand / Intelligence is vital, love takes reason / Passion without wisdom is romantic treason / Love is the rain that greens the leaves / It's the part of death that never grieves*
...

He only had to listen closely and remember the words, because he had nothing to write with, no paper. And when the poem was complete and he was sure the words were safely stored in his consciousness, he started walking, calmly, Waterbury wasn't so big, the shelter must be downtown somewhere, there would be a sign, maybe a lighted one, or a cross on the roof ...

NEW YORK CITY, FEBRUARY 2002

Khadijah Hassan-Da Silva

'At college I had a friend, Jamal, from Ghana. One day I went into his room and saw a Last Poets poster on the wall—signed and everything. "That's my father," I said. I knew about the Last Poets, but didn't realize they were famous. Jamal got all excited. "Is that your *father*? Do you know what that means?" "Not really," I replied.

Once in a while, when I was a kid, he would pick me up and take me to my stepmother's—Khalil and Sabreeyah's mother. He would pace back and forth in a karate outfit reciting all kinds of strange texts. I didn't understand what he was doing; I just thought he was weird. These were apparently stage plays he was writing. In fact, mostly I remember how undependable he was. For instance: one time he called, said "come to Junior's"—that's a restaurant downtown—"and bring your brother and sister." It was snowing. We waited for an hour, but he never showed up. I didn't have only my own disappointment to deal with, but had to explain it to Khalil and Sabreeyah too. No phone call, no apology, nothing.

I saw him perform twice, most recently at a Def Poetry Jam in Brooklyn. He's a brilliant poet, his music is great, people listen to him. But for me he's two separate people: I watch him perform, think: wow he's smart, and at the same time he's a big question mark. Inside I'm going: What kind of father are you? I have to separate my feelings for him, otherwise it's total confusion.

My mother thinks I should cut him some slack. She's very spiritual and religious. A Muslim. She works as a therapist. She says, "He's sick. You can't expect him to act like someone who's healthy." I've read about him, about his childhood and his father and all that, that he was abused. But I think people can make choices in how much they let their past influence them. I've decided never, ever to let myself be a victim, even though the adults in my life have let me down. I'm going to make it. My goal is to become dean of an African-American Studies department of a university. Right now I'm setting up an organization in Brooklyn to help black youths find decent jobs. Young black people don't have access to the right channels or they get passed over or their parents haven't prepared them well enough.

Sometimes it's really difficult to look at my parents. Why did they do what they did? Why did my mother dump me at my aunt's when I was eight, knowing I was being teased and was horribly unhappy? She wanted to finish her degree and couldn't cope with raising me and holding down a job too. Okay, but what does that tell an eight-year-old?

I remember getting a letter from my father. "Please forgive me," and all that. I showed it to my mother. "He's probably in some rehab clinic." I said, "Okay." Not that it left me cold, but what was I supposed to do? Once you've built a wall around yourself, you can't let this kind of stuff in, or else everything will collapse. I've never really dissed him out loud, but maybe I should. Of all his children, I'm the one with the most issues with him; I feel the most resistance. Amina is the most conciliatory. She's the one who always tracked him down, the one who keeps contact with me and my siblings. I know

Khalil and Sabreeyah are close to my father. I like him. He's smart. And I like smart people. But it's difficult to carry on a coherent conversation. If he were sitting here right now, his thoughts would be out there, with all the hubbub and the lights. We've talked. Like that time before I went to Brazil on vacation and he told me he'd been there, and some other stuff. It was what I'd call real contact. There's an attraction but it's so difficult to really get close.

I remember once returning from a trip to Jamaica. I was so excited, wanted to share my adventures and stories with my mother. It was 1996. The first thing my mom said when I got home was: "There's something I have to tell you." A somber face. I thought: Oh no, what now? "Your father's in the hospital." That was when Jalal stabbed him in the neck in Paris. It was pretty serious. But all I can think of was: How am I supposed to react? It wasn't like it ruined my vacation, but ... why'd she have to spoil my moment?'

NEW YORK CITY, 1986

Mood Indigo

He phoned his sister in Connecticut from the New York City bus station.

'Sandra?'

'Who's calling?'

His entire body shivered; he had to concentrate to control his chattering teeth and speak normally.

'Jerome?'

Help me.

'Where are you?'

'Port Authority.'

'Stay where you are.'

'I'm sorry.'

'I'll be there in two hours, okay? I'll find you.'

He nodded. Help me, Sandra.

'Jerome?'

Help me.

'Jerome?'

Twice she drove right past him. Until she caught a glimpse of something vaguely familiar leaning against the glass entrance door to the Port Authority. Afterward, this is what surprised her the most: how her brain managed to subconsciously connect that stinking, filthy pile of misery with her older brother. She was proud of this proof that a blood bond is stronger than anything.

Sandra watches television. The children are in bed.

'Want some ice cream?' she asks.

No ice cream.

'I do.' She dashes into the kitchen. 'You watch.'

Watch what?

'You sure you don't want any? Vanilla ice cream? With chocolate chips?'

'Yeah, okay.'

She returns with two bowls and settles back onto the sofa. 'So what'd I miss?' She nods at the TV.

I shrug. Only now do I notice she's watching *Miami Vice*. I can't concentrate. I catch a glimpse of a few people talking animatedly with each other and then the image spatters into silver-gray fireworks.

'That was the exciting part,' Sandra says.

'Oh.'

She switches off the sound. Commercials.

'You like it?'

I feel the chill of the ice cream in my throat. The chocolate shavings stick to the roof of my mouth, melt on my tongue. We eat in silence. Until *Miami Vice* is back and Sandra turns the sound back on. She tucks her feet under her buttocks.

Evening after evening, the same ritual. The only difference is the TV program. It doesn't matter what's on. Sandra's life revolves around these small rituals. Routine. No expectations, no promises. The comfort of repetition, of the everyday bustle that sings and hums and ricochets off the mint-green walls. Have you done your homework? Can I have my allowance? Are my new jeans washed? Get to bed now. Since when don't you like oatmeal? Like a spider, she spins a web of certainties around her existence and that of her children. My arrival has not affected her small family. She wouldn't allow it. It's almost like I'm invisible, like I've always been here.

'Nettie next door is going to have a child,' she says between spoonfuls of ice cream; she tries to look at me but her eyes are glued to the screen. It's a statement, not a judgment. Nettie is still just a child herself.

'Does her mother know?' I hear myself ask.

'Uh-huh, and she said Nettie had to finish school and that she'd work shorter hours so she could help with the baby and if it's too much she'll ask her sister. I take my hat off to that woman, don't you?'

'Uh … yeah.'

The television sucks up her attention again, but our brief exchange echoes in my head. Not the content, only the familiar nasal sound of Sandra's voice, the matter-of-fact intimacy of her words—just words, it doesn't matter which ones, words designating casualness, kin-ship; soft, warm sounds that serve no other purpose than to sound like themselves, lazy jazz music on a weekday evening. And I realize that here, in this house, I don't have to remember anything. I don't have to prove anything. Just breathe calmly, watch TV, eat, wash dishes, tidy up, converse, listen, sleep.

''Night, Sandra.'

She absently raises a hand. 'Mm.'

'See you in the morning.'

'Uh-huh.'

'Redbone' (2001)

To sucking off of each other's laughter in order to survive the
sizzle of crack pipes and temporary insanity runs in our fears,
runs in our families should be more like you are the true ...
sisters of the Church and the Temples at Memphis ...

... and hands on healing ... placed on wide hips of subtle and
gracious insinuations challenging and imploring me to keep
writing poems for

    RED
        BONE
            women
                like
                    you.

NEW YORK CITY, SEPTEMBER 2011

Bill Laswell, producer

'In the late 1980s, John Singleton, the film director, wanted to use "Niggers Are Scared of Revolution" in his new film and needed to find the author. Jalal heard about it and was keen to perform in the film, so he went looking for Umar. A few weeks later he called me to say he'd tracked him down in a crack house. He asked if they could record some material in my studio. "Sure," I said, "come around sometime."

It was about three in the afternoon. Ornette Coleman was just about to leave the studio when the bell rang. Umar. In a T-shirt, no bags. It was obvious he came off the street. "Sorry I'm early," he said. "You got anything to eat?"

He shook hands with the musicians. He felt right at home. Jalal and Suliaman got there in the evening. Jalal all excited, shooting off at the mouth: "This is important. We're back, we're back." Umar kept to himself. So we started the recording session. Jalal stepped up to the microphone. But his voice was weak, whispery; his poem was unimpressive. This wasn't the performer we remembered. Then it was Umar's turn. He sounded exactly the same as twenty years earlier. Everybody in the studio woke up. The next day they left for California for the film shoots.

A few weeks later Umar phoned to apologize. "Sorry I

wasn't so good, could I come back and do it again? And better?"

"Sure," I said, "but this time with real musicians. What're you doing?"

"Now?"

"Yeah, now."

"Nothing."

"Come on over then. Buddy Miles is here too."

An hour later we recorded some new poems, really good stuff. There was a drummer from Senegal and he jammed along. And Buddy, of course. After a while I said, "Let's make a record. I shouldn't have any trouble selling it." Over the next few weeks I invited all the musicians who used my studio to come listen. I said: "This is Umar, from The Last Poets. It's important that his work gets out there, you've got to play on his new album." Everybody was enthusiastic. Bootsy Collins joined in too. And Abiodun. Umar had gone to his apartment and asked him to come.

It wasn't easy to cut a deal for *Be Bop or Be Dead*, but when it finally came through I went to see Umar. We rented a hotel room for him and after deducting my own costs I gave him the rest of the money, twenty thousand dollars. He was ... how should I put it ... humble. But happy with the money. Of course he went right out and bought a new car and a few days later was arrested on Times Square swigging from an open bottle of cognac at the wheel. That was that. But he was back. The Last Poets were back. Jalal is still sore at me for helping Umar register the rights to the name The Last Poets.'

AKRON, OHIO, SEPTEMBER 2001

Notes

Monday

Amina sounded better today. She's thinking about going back to work next week.

'Where, though?' I asked.

'They've rented another office near the WTC. They want things to get back to normal as soon as possible.'

'And you?'

'Me too,' she sighed, 'me too.'

I can barely think back on last Tuesday. As though time's just had a hole blown through it.

I finally get Queenie on the phone. The next morning, 5 a.m.

'She's here.'

'And?'

'Nothing, just shock.'

'Our child, honey,' I said.

'Our child.'

I still regret not having been closer by. But there was no bus service to New York. I could only wait and hope. All those times Amina managed to find me, and now all the lines were dead.

Queenie said, 'She walked down all those stairs, even though some voice on the PA system kept saying they should stay put. She followed her instinct. She's a survivor.'

I would never have gone to Akron if it weren't for Reggie. He'd gone to so much trouble to get me that gig. He invited all the folks from the old days. 'A kind of reunion,' he said. 'And you'll be well paid.'

I'm glad Sandra drove with me. She said she wanted to see Mama and Chris, but I know she did it for me, she knew I couldn't face bumming bus money from her. This afternoon she took Chris to the movies. He was in one of his moods. Stood there with his droopy, sad eyes, shook his head and kept mumbling, 'I have to take care of Mama, I can't leave her alone, I have to take care of Mama.' Sandra laughed, and I did too. He's a child in a giant's body.

Mama told us she's applied for assisted living, that she couldn't care for him 24/7 anymore. Not with those manic moods of his.

Chris's disappearance is still a mystery. He and Billy had been out on the town but Chris wanted to go home early and left Billy in the bar. Billy was a year younger. They both still lived at home.

'You coming?' Chris asked.

'In a while,' Billy said. When he left the bar half an hour later, some dude put a gun to his head and shot him dead. He grabbled Billy's few remaining dollars out of his pocket and vanished. Afterward we heard the guy was sore because Billy'd had a thing with his ex.

Chris disappeared a few days later. Mama went to the police station to report him missing, but there's no chance in hell that any of those white bastards ever went looking for him. He was gone for three years. Until one day Mama heard footsteps on the veranda. There was Chris, crumpled up, on the top step. He looked like a savage, Mama said, you should have seen him. But she couldn't get a word out of him. No one could. Sandra reckons he spent all that time in the woods. Built fires, hunted and fished. He was always good at that, right?

He was always good at that.

When I look at Chris, it's like looking at myself. Only with him everything is so uselessly big. His hands, his feet, his torso, his head. Like he'd just kept growing in those three years, no one to hold him back. You can tell he's awkward with his body when we're in Mama's living room. He can hardly sit still, his limbs jitter and stir like they have a life of their own.

When we were kids Chris used to drive me crazy, he followed me everywhere and wanted to be just like me. But he disappeared before I did, I have to hand it to him. Poor Chris.

Everything here is memory, even the way the sky turns pink and orange in the late afternoon, how the light contrasts with the neighbors' white shingle house. I have this vague feeling that these memories can somehow protect me.

Queenie said, 'It's a good thing you're at your mother's. She's had the fright of her life.'

We spent all afternoon together. I lay on the sofa watching TV and she fussed in the kitchen. Later she sat out on the veranda. It's still nice out, late summer weather, but the leaves are already turning. Every morning it's misty.

Tuesday

Called Dun. I could hardly get a word in edgewise, he rattled on about the attacks and Amina and America and the CIA and how convenient this all is for those Republican motherfuckers. He read me his poem 'Reign of Terror' in a single breath, but all I heard was panic and fury set to rhyme. It sounded good but I had a hard time connecting those terrible television images with his stream of words. There was something missing. I saw only black. When he was finished I heard him panting.

'What do you think?' he asked.

'Powerful.'

'Do you think I can use it in the show?'

'Sure.'

There was nothing more to say, but we didn't hang up. It was as though we both hoped to hear something in the silence, something that went beyond our awkward conversation, that would simply come bubbling up as a sort of reward for our years of togetherness, for our struggle.

After a while Dun asked, 'When are you coming?'

'Thursday.'

'We leave first thing Saturday morning.'

'Then I have two days with Amina.'

'Don't beat yourself up, Umar.'

'Yeh.'

And we hung up. I was relieved neither of us had the nerve to admit we were at a complete loss. It would have sounded so cheap, so obvious. Sometimes it's better to just shut up and wait.

Reggie came to pick me up last night in his new white Cadillac. 'I've gotta show you something,' he said. We drove straight through Akron, the radio on, the same smooth jazz Reggie always liked. Canned nightclub music. We were supposed to go to his house, but I could see Reggie was taking a detour. We drove past South High, across North Street, and passed St. Thomas Hospital. It was meant as a sentimental journey, but everything looked surprisingly small to me; Akron seemed to have shrunk in my absence. I didn't need this tour to refresh my memory—my memories led their own life. Maybe Reggie realized that; he hardly said a word during the drive. As we approached his new house he began to beam. He slid his glasses further up on his nose and stepped on the gas. 'Show those assholes a thing or two,' he said. We tore down the street and screeched to a halt in front of a huge house painted completely white. The yard was landscaped and dotted with classic lanterns. Reggie always did have a sense of style. He led me into the spacious living room with white leather sofas, a mirrored wall, glass-topped coffee tables on elegant gilded legs, showed me the four luxurious bedrooms, the new kitchen, the gleaming bathroom. He saved the basement for last. 'This is my space,' Reggie said. It was like stepping into a museum. Heavy, improvised curtains covered the high, shallow windows; an old leather sofa stood against one wall. There was a stereo and a refrigerator with an enormous television on top. The coffee table had a cloth draped over it and a vase of plastic flowers. It looked like Reggie had been in hiding all these years— this was a replica of the basement of Mammio and Daddio Bellamy's house on Bailey Court. Stunned, I stared at Reggie, my oldest and dearest friend. He had led his life, been married and divorced, seen his daughter grow up, conducted his business and earned money in his own shrewd way, bought a house in Akron's whitest neighborhood. That was his revenge.

'Hank, do you remember when we stood up on the hill waiting to see if those white motherfuckers would have the guts to fight us? You remember beaning their leader with a rock, up on Wooster? He was so busy ogling that chick he didn't see it coming. You clobbered him from behind. He bled like a pig. Remember?'

'I still remember, Reggie.'

He was living in his basement.

'You know me,' he said. 'I can be myself down here. The house is too big for a guy on his own.'

'Yeah,' I said. I thought of Sandra, how often she'd offered to buy me a mattress, or a sofa bed. But I told her to save the money. I preferred sleeping on the floor under a blanket or a coat. A mattress made me feel like I was drowning. It gave me headaches and backaches. I didn't care if the floor was carpeted or if I slept on wood planks or even bare concrete. I felt safest on the floor: I slept lighter and was on my guard.

'How 'bout a beer,' I said.

'In the fridge. Help yourself.'

At about eleven Reggie wanted to drive to Cleveland to pick up some marijuana, but I was too drunk to get into a car.

'T-t-t-tomorrow then,' Reggie said.

This morning I walked from Reggie's to Mama's. It was eight, nine o'clock, but the streets were deserted. The mist was streaked low above the fields. The sunlight wove yellow and pink threads in the mist, and the sparkle of the droplets hurt my eyes. There was no wind, so I was the only thing in motion, like I was walking through a fake landscape.

I rented a car. I tore down the highway, the urn with my father's ashes clamped between my thighs. I had treated myself to a few lines of coke and a bottle of Courvoisier. It was winter: clear blue sky and a low-lying, icy mist. Winter was in the air, I smelled it as soon as I had parked the car at the edge of the lake, got out, and inhaled. Dry, crisp air. I took the urn and the bottle of cognac with me. This was something between my father and me. This water—even in good weather it was solid gray. But you loved the water, Dad. I saw you play your trumpet at the edge of the lake. I heard it. A gentle, lazy melody, no mistakes, no cracked notes, only that husky, melancholy sound that seemed to come straight from your throat. 'Why don't you play anything?' 'I can play too, Daddy, I can play just as well as you. Listen. You taught me everything about phrasing and timing. Listen.' Jesus, what day was it? I lost all sense of time. But I knew that the pond in the woods behind our house on North Street was too small and too shallow for you. You wanted to dive, swim, splash, gasp for air. It was up to me to give you that freedom now, even though the immensity of Lake Erie scared me out of my wits. The chill that rose off it. I couldn't imagine life existing under that dark, slick surface. All those memories. And no photos. In all the photo albums in Mama's bedroom, there's not a single picture of you. I can barely recall your face. Only your soft, round afro. Your slender fingers, your gait, the slight drag in your right leg, as though you doubted every step you took. The disillusionment in your hunched shoulders and back. The urn was made of stone; it was heavy and nearly slipped out of my hands. I took a swig of cognac to warm me up. I wanted to say a few words, I really did, but I couldn't, the words spun around in my head but refused to come out. Just like when I was a kid, I hear you say. Yeah, just like when I was a kid. But you gave me the music, Sonny. No matter how hard you hit me, no matter how often you humiliated yourself and Mama, I still hear the music. I forgive you. I have no choice. I think I understand you better than anyone. Do you hear me? I followed you, I always followed you— d'you remember when you worked in Jackson's barbershop, and I stood there staring through the fogged-up window? I wanted to know what you were doing, what you felt, what you thought.

I went to the edge of lake, as close to the water as possible. I didn't want the ashes to end up on the shore. I'd saved a line of coke for this moment, washed away the sharp aftertaste with a warm swig of cognac. Here's to you, Sonny. Off you go. And I watched as the particles fluttered in the air; the dim winter sunlight made them sparkle for just a few moments, until they landed in the water. Thousands of imperceptible specks of ash floating on the dark-gray surface.

He's been dead for eleven years. At the end he slept in the back of a bread truck. While he had an apartment. In the back of a fucking bread truck.

A few days after I'd scattered his ashes I left for New York. Only then did I dare return.

'We thought you were dead,' Dun said. The implications of this remark didn't sink in right away. The chill of Lake Erie was still in my bones. What he said didn't even strike me as strange. Did I really think I could just disappear, no strings attached?

'I heard myself on the radio,' I said. 'Actually my nephew heard it. "That's Uncle Jerome!" We were in the car. Sandra was there too. You remember my sister Sandra?'

'How's she doing?'

'D'you know how strange it is to hear your own voice coming out of nowhere? What's that band's name? *A Tribe Called Quest* or something. They'd sampled my poem "Time" from The Last Poets' second album. It was like hearing the voice of a ghost, Dun, *my* ghost. I was dumbfounded.'

'I thought you were dead.'

'That's what I mean. The voice was trying to tell me something. Sandra said I had to stand up for myself, demand royalties. Without her I'd probably still be flipping burgers in that diner in Hartford. I was scared of my own words, can you believe that?'

'Sure can,' he said, avoiding eye contact. He cleared his throat. 'So you were in Hartford, huh?'

'I was everywhere, Dun, everywhere. How're you doing?'

'I'm fine. Just fine.'

'What do you think? About The Last Poets?'

'What're you talking about, The Last Poets? It's 1990, man. What have you been doing all this time?'

'They're sampling my voice, Dun, don't you understand what that means? It means they can't find the words, *real* words. Believe me. I know what I'm talking about.'

'I sold your rights.'

'You what?'

'You were dead.'

'How much?'

'Three, four thousand dollars. I'd have to look it up.'

'Shit.'

'Sorry, Omar.'

'It's Umar. Umar Bin Hassan.'

'A real Muslim, right?'

'Fuck you.'
'I'm sorry, Umar.'

Time is dancing boogalooing away all memories of the past dancing away experiences all thoughts of personal and collective manifestations dancing dancing dancing until you become a slave of rhythm.

I got high. I couldn't think of anything else than to get high. *For ever let us wave our banners: high high high.*

I wrote 'A.M.', my personal ode to America.

sweet land of Napalm and unwritten poems of soprano saxophones crying for those whose tears are stuck in reverse and the latest cable TV channel. And I hear the voice of nature whisper, the victory is yours if you want it. […] Loving … all the women in the crowd and their dreams. Miles … the warm afterglow of an African sunset. Someday my Prince will come. Someday my Prince will come. Miles turning his back on guaranteed death and low-life insinuations perpetuated by the perverted fantasies of the founding fathers of these United States of … Fuck you motherfuckahs!
Fuck
you
motherfuckahs!

Wednesday

The cell phone is a blessing. This morning Amina called.
'When are you coming, Dad?'
'Tomorrow.'

'Good.'
'I love you.'
'I love you too.'

'A.M.'
Somewhere I hear revival. Somewhere I hear bop playing ...
in the faces of Southern old men full of Northern pain.
It is Dizzy, Sonny, Jackie, Philly Joe, Kenny, Charlie,
Clifford and many many more if you listen to the laughter
of the children in the Projects and their sense of rhythm to
survive.

'A.M.'
Bad was only a test of faith. I now find strength in the
humility of this moment of peace to all ... all ... of those
who come to understand that bop is love ... and love ...
is all ... you are and ever will be.

One night I was in a crack house and the next night Dun
and I were performing in Harlem or on a university campus. Small auditoriums, anyway. Baba was there too.
Baba the peacemaker, our conscience. Without him we'd
never have made it. I was still pretty weak, sometimes I
barely had the strength to walk on stage, but every gig,
no matter how minor, was a step, a promise. When Baba's
hands glided over the congas and his imploring notes
searched their way through the auditorium, only to
boomerang back at him as though he'd put a spell on
them, his eyes shut, his softly humming, singing voice,
then I felt myself become hypnotized and had no choice
but to take the microphone; adrenaline was my drug. I
didn't care that I was totally beat afterward. Dun dragged
me to his apartment on Morningside Drive and I'd sleep
until the next afternoon. I did my best, that's all I could

do. And even though I still succumbed to my own demons, for the first time in years I entertained thoughts of a future.

In any case, I was totally unprepared for what would happen in Paris. Now that I look back on it, I can't see it as anything but the ultimate test. Maybe I was being naive, or didn't dare consider what effect a Last Poets comeback might have on Jalal's state of mind, and on ourselves. I had forgotten the promise, the responsibility that rested on our shoulders, that had always been there, ever since the very beginning when David came up with that mythical name—The Last Poets. I always felt that we were no match for the prophetic power our own words. It was never easy. We all made sacrifices for our poetry.

But that was not on my mind when Dun and Baba and I toured Europe in '96. I'd always wanted to go to Paris. I'd bought a cheap camera and tried to capture every new and intoxicating street scene in the city of light for later, for my children. It was December but somehow the weather gods were smiling on us. Every day was sunny. Paris was gilded. The reflection of the late afternoon sunlight on the yellow brick buildings, the gold leaf on the statues at the Louvre. The chirping of the birds in the Tuileries, the unexpected side streets, the grimy cafés, and the syrupy brown water of the Seine. Everything here was old. But my outlook was new and unbiased, unclouded by reality. The confrontation with the timelessness of Paris made me dizzy. And I imagined how Dexter Gordon, Charles Mingus, Eric Dolphy, and all those other guys must have felt here. Removed from their own histories. How they must have ambled dreamily through the city, liberated from the heaviness of their bodies and the close-minded vulgarity of America.

Focusing on that one woman in the metro, the finely woven fabric of her dress. Even the air smelled different here, older, like burned wood and dust and unheated houses. Paris. We did a sound check for that evening's gig. The club was called Rapperhole, a small, dark bar with a nice stage and good lighting. It was about five in the afternoon. We were going to get a bite to eat near our hotel in Montparnasse when the back door opened and in walked Jalal. Bill Laswell had told me Jalal was in France a lot, he had contact with some or other record producer, but it never crossed my mind that he would come looking for us. I nudged Dun, who was trying his best to carry on a conversation with a sound technician who didn't speak a word of English. Baba must have already gone back to the hotel.

'What?' Dun asked, irritated.

'Over there.'

Jalal stood at the back of the club, leaning quasi-nonchalantly against the black wall. Not a single sign of recognition. As though it was normal that he hung around here and we were perfect strangers, artists from another world visiting his territory. I was shocked at how old he'd become. He had always been skinny, but now his cheeks were hollow and his forehead creased. Time had not been kind to him. His beard was thinned and gray and he had heavy-framed glasses that made him look older than he was.

'Hey, yo,' he called out.

'What're you doin' here?' I asked.

'You're asking me that?' His voice was still the same: monotonously pointed and rhythmic. I felt a surge of almost childlike pleasure at seeing him. We had traveled all across America together. Okay, I'd gotten sick of his suspicious nature, his insatiable thirst for fame and

approval, his arrogance—but I had a part in those con-
flicts too. We shared so many memories.

'How you doing, man?' I said, stepping off the stage
and walking over to him. I could sense Dun holding
back, how he deliberately kept his conversation going
with the sound guy.

Jalal slid his left leg up and nestled closer to the wall.
'A tour, huh?'

'Yeah. Day after tomorrow in Amsterdam, then London.'

Jalal smiled. A dark, cryptic smile meant only for
himself. His eyes were concealed by the reflection in his
glasses.

'So you survived it,' he said.

I ignored it. 'So how are you?'

'How d'you think?'

'I dunno.'

''Course you don't know. You only know what you
want to know, isn't that right?' he said impassively but
still smiling. His muscles were so tense that he was
almost frozen. He seemed to be waiting for something; I
registered the cynicism and the iciness that stuck to his
few words, but it never occurred to me to walk away. This
was Paris. The rules were different here. Even time went
slower. Here, I had a respite from myself, from life. I
experienced a constant rush that no drug had ever given
me. I almost felt in control over myself, invulnerable.

'You murdered Suliaman,' he said.

'What?' I didn't even know Suliaman was dead. The
last time I saw him was six years ago in Los Angeles
during the filming of John Singleton's movie, where we
had a cameo as The Last Poets. Suliaman was Jalal's
shadow. Or was it the other way around? I liked Suliaman; he was relaxed, a powerful poet as long as he didn't
let himself get too whipped up by his religion. Jalal had

brought him into the group, but I always thought Suliaman stayed an outsider. For Jalal, he was a mentor and
alter ego at the same time. And now he was dead.

'You murdered him.'

'I did what?'

'His heart. He never got over the humiliation. You
sneaky little muthafucka. You use everything and everyone and always manage to stay in the clear. Isn't that
right? Closing a deal with Laswell behind my back. I
know everything, Umar Bin Hassan. Who introduced
you to Bill Laswell, huh? When Suliaman heard about
your CD, when he heard how you ran off with the legacy
of The Last Poets, like he and I didn't exist—just you and
Dun. You're a shameless whore, Umar, a traitor to Islam.
When Suliaman heard it, his heart gave out. It's your
fault.'

I was so bowled over by Jalal's tirade that I didn't notice him make his move. This whole conversation lasted
only a couple of minutes, near the back door of the Rapperhole. We were too far away for Abiodun to hear any of
it.

'I'm sorry about Suliaman,' was all I could say.

'You're sorry?' He leaned over toward me. And still I
just stood there. It all went so fast. I felt his warm breath
against my face. 'This is for Suliaman,' he whispered
in my ear. 'From now on, your voice is dead, asshole.' I
didn't notice anything at first, but when I got a glimpse
of the long needle he pulled out of my neck a fraction of
a second later, I felt a brief, sharp pain. I reflexively
brought my hand to the spot Jalal had jabbed me, right
under my Adam's apple. I looked at my hand. No blood.
Nothing. When I looked back up, Jalal was gone.

At first I felt fine, but on the train from Paris to Amsterdam a couple of days later my Adam's apple started to swell up, and I got a fever. I had told Dun about Jalal stabbing me with that needle. 'You should go to a doctor, Umar,' he said. 'Jalal knows exactly what he's doing. He's had an acupuncture clinic in Brooklyn for years, didn't you know?'

'How'm I supposed to know that?' I squeezed the words out. My throat was dry and my voice started getting thinner and weaker.

'This was premeditated, you know. You could file charges.'

I didn't respond. Just leaned up against the window and sank into the monotonous rhythm of the train. I had my own thoughts about Jalal. Dun kept looking at me.

'No, Umar, uh-uh ... put it out of your goddam head. You're better off thinking about why this happened to you.'

'Meaning ...?'

'Shh. Don't talk. Save your energy.'

'What do you mean?'

'Nothing. Drop it.'

I spent our two days in Amsterdam in my hotel room bed. I can hardly remember a thing. When I wasn't sleeping I drifted in a feverish hallucination. I was back in America, in Brooklyn, the light was blue and hazy, it refused to turn into regular daylight. The streets were wet and gave off a strange sort of light. No people out, no traffic. I was searching for something, just kept walking, Fulton St., Atlantic Ave., Bergen St. I recognized the street names but still everything struck me as strange. All the doors and windows of the houses and shops were shut, blackened, like the city was deserted or everyone was asleep. The only thing I could do was keep walking, walking, walking. If it would only become daytime and that weird blue light would go away.

In London, Dun and Baba told our taxi to drive straight to the nearest hospital. I couldn't talk anymore, was having trouble breathing. I remember seeing emergency room doctors at my bed, I heard the distant murmur of their English accents. That's all. And then I tumbled into a bottomless pit where everything was soft and black. I don't know how long I was out, but when I woke up I was high from the anesthesia and the painkillers. I was in a room with tall windows with long white curtains. I remember the curtains well. They were thin and silky, more like being in a hotel than a hospital. I imagined seeing them billow, I felt a gentle, warm breeze on my face and arms, and fell back to sleep.

'You were lucky,' Dun said when he came to visit. 'They cut you open. Your lungs were full of fluid. If we'd waited, you'd have been dead, man. You were suffocating. I told your family. Your mother, Sandra ... '

'Hggrrr ... '

'They call every day. Amina too. You've got to rest. Everything'll be okay.'

I didn't realize how close to death I was. I'd watched my father die, I felt the last puff of air escape from his alcoholic body, and still I thought death was something grotesque and dramatic, an event unlike anything else and something I would see coming for miles. Not as quiet and ordinary as Dun would have me believe. 'You were lucky.' Fuck that. My death would be something to celebrate, to provoke and embrace, once the time came.

Nor did I realize, lying in that London hospital, that I was setting a trap for myself. I neglected to see the bigger significance of that incident with Jalal. I only thought of revenge. I thought of revenge as though it were a law of nature. You fuck with me, nigger, and I'll fuck back, and good. I was an involuntary player in an age-old myth.

Once recovered and back in the States, I hung around New York. But I didn't go to my family. I hid out with an old friend; he sold me a small, handy pistol. I roamed through Brooklyn for days on end in the neighborhood of Jalal's acupuncture clinic. I was biding my time, as though I wanted to savor that blinding, all-devouring, miserable feeling that raged through my body. I didn't need to think ahead. The past did not exist. The only thing that counted was Jalal; he had put his fate in my hands. This simple fact gave me a new kind of power.

One evening I was strolling through the neighborhood when I accidently bumped into an old black man putting out his garbage. I was so lost in thought that I just didn't see him. I had reduced Brooklyn to Jalal; as far as I was concerned the rest was a ghost town. I mumbled a sort of apology but the man wouldn't accept it.

'You crazy or something?' he said.

'I said I'm sorry.'

'Never seen you around here, you got business here?'

The question took me by surprise. I gave him a blank look, that old black man with the stately face. He was wearing a brightly colored lumberjack shirt with a turtleneck underneath. He was bigger than me and his body was angular, bony, and his long arms hung loosely at his side. I guessed he was about seventy.

'You don't look like a junkie,' he said.

'Thanks.' I chuckled at his remark.

'Perry,' he said, extending his hand. 'Matthew Perry.'

'Hey Matthew,' I said. I didn't tell him my name.

Considering my plans, I figured it was better to stay anonymous. But Matthew Perry wasn't going to be put off that easily.

'What's your name?'

'Umar.'

'Umar what?'

'Just Umar.'

'Uh-huh.'

'What do you mean, "uh-huh"?'

'You look pretty lost. Where do you need to be?'

I remembered the neighborhood from when Queenie and I lived here.

'Mermaid Ave.,' I said off the top of my head. I'd always remembered the name of that street.

'You like the sea,' Matthew said.

'Eh, yeah ... '

'You can smell the seawater from here, d'you know that? If the wind blows the right way, you can smell the ocean. That's why I've always stayed.' He must have needed to chat, because he didn't let me go. I sniffed but did not smell the ocean.

'You want to come in?'

'Where?'

'Just for a drink. It's cold out here.'

'Okay.'

Matthew led the way. His apartment consisted of a small hallway, and two rooms separated by sliding doors. They were open, and in the dull light the space looked smaller than it was. The apartment was scattered with papers and books, there was an unmade single bed and a huge television set tuned to a rerun of The Cosby Show. He obviously lived alone.

'Take a seat.' He cleared some newspapers off an old rattan chair. 'What'll you have? Coffee, or something stronger? 'Fraid all I've got is gin.'

'Gin's fine.'

Matthew turned down the volume. It struck me that for the first time since being back in America I was in a normal house. The guy whose couch I was crashing on rented a room in a noisy boarding house in Harlem. I couldn't get out of there fast enough in the morning, and took the subway out to Brooklyn. I spent my European earnings in diners and bars where I didn't know anyone. I was living in a netherworld.

'What do you do here all day?' I asked.

'Nothing. Read, think, watch TV. What else does an old man on his own do?'

He handed me a glass of gin. 'And you? You're young. You're not from here.'

'Used to live here, years ago.'

'And now you've come back. What for? Love?'

'Yeah,' I said, just to get him off my back. I sunk deeper into the chair. It was nice and warm inside and I felt the fatigue wash over me. I'd hardly recovered from the operation and the flight home, and the jetlag kept me up at night. My eyelids were heavy.

'Love,' Matthew mumbled. 'I doubt that.' He chuckled to himself. 'Cheers,' he said.

'Cheers,' I replied, my eyes still half shut. I tried to resist sleep but it was like my body was weighed down with lead, like I was being slowly pulled downward. I heard my heavy, regular breathing and the sound of the TV—Matthew had turned it back up and was sitting on his bed, propped up against the wall and his legs on a pillow. I couldn't talk anymore.

When I woke up a few hours later, Matthew's room was pitch-black. The old man lay snoring on his mattress.

He'd covered himself with a blanket; the TV was off. I didn't want to disturb him so I tiptoed out of the apartment. I had no idea what time it was, maybe about 4 a.m., but it could just as well have been only midnight.

The moon was in its last quarter and spread a silvery-blue light—the same light I saw in my feverish dreams, except for now there was nothing frightening about it. It was dead quiet, only the freeway roared in the distance. I walked down the empty street and after about ten minutes I realized it wasn't a freeway I heard, but the ocean, the waves lapping gently against the Coney Island beach. I walked toward the sound, crossed a wide street and between two apartment blocks to the boardwalk. The place was deserted. The amusement park rides were dark silhouettes against the nighttime sky. They'd covered the merry-go-round with a yellow tarp. The steel construction of the roller coaster made me think of a skeleton of a huge prehistoric animal. The ocean was calm, but the sound of the waves rolling onto the shore was deafening against the silence of the night. I sat down on a bench, licked the salt off my lips. I didn't dwell on anything in particular. The nap at Matthew's place revived me, and the haze that had clouded my head since the stabbing in Paris gradually cleared. I touched my coat pocket, felt the gun. I'd off Jalal tomorrow. It was time, I'd put it off long enough.

I saw the lights of a cargo ship in the distance. The air was surprisingly mild for January. I sat on the boardwalk waiting for the blackness of the horizon to thin out. Who knows how long I sat there—I heard the lethargic squeak of the metal rolling blinds on the kiosks, workmen's footsteps, a radio. No one seemed to take any notice of me. When the sky became pink and purple and white, and the sun hung like a huge orange ball over the water, I got up and walked eastward along the board-walk. I was hungry but didn't feel like ordering a sand-wich somewhere; the idea of having to speak turned me off. I can't remember ever feeling as relaxed as that morning. I was entirely conscious of my resolution to murder Jalal but felt no trace of excitement or fear. I was empty, my body no more than a shell. I looked out to sea and breathed in the fresh, salty air. I thought of Matthew in his dingy, toasty apartment. It was as though the old man had broken my fall, woken me out of my haze. Thoughts wafted into my head and I walked and listened to the rhythm of my footsteps. I saw myself in the freez-ing cold field behind Roxy's. Heard the rough, deep tim-bre of the sax, the earthy rhythms of the bass. I waited until I was numbed enough to go into a bar, where the smell of alcohol and sweat and smoke hung like heavy perfume. I let the smoke sting my eyes, and felt the warm tears well up. I pretended to be deaf, ignoring the breathy commentary from the ugly black women: 'Ain't you got a mama, honey?' 'Poor little thing, having to polish those assholes' shoes, c'mere, c'mere.' The men's bleary-eyed expressions: a mix of loathing and pity and affection, as though they recognized their own downfall in my youth. *Get 'm, Junior, get 'm.* I've spent my life testing the limits of my existence, convinced that there was something beyond it. Ruby Lee took me to the hill behind Roxy's and I felt how the clammy mist became soft and warm on our skin, and how our naked bodies became shadows in the bluish moonlight—I fantasized the part about the light, but never mind, I could see the beauty behind her twisted smile, just one touch and everything changed before my eyes, one glance, one smile. Things can change, just like that. If you weren't scared, you'd be rewarded and you felt like you existed.

When my father died he pulled me closer and whispered: 'My Jerome, my Jerome.' Like he was giving me permission for something—his blessing.

I heard the jingle-jangle of the merry-go-round. I looked up and saw the brown and white and gold horses, still riderless, go up and down. The cotton candy stand was still closed. A few elderly Russian immigrants sat on folding chairs, chatting. There was no wind. The light was thick and orange. I slowed down, listened to the naive merry-go-round music and recalling vague memories contained in those tinny tones. At that moment I knew I'd let Jalal go. It wasn't a clear or conscious decision, just the realization that I'd lose everything if I went through with it. I kept walking. At the New York Aquarium I went into the subway and waited for the F train to take me to Manhattan.

BROOKLYN, SEPTEMBER 2001

Epilogue

'Listen, Christine.'

'What?'

'Come closer, I can't turn the music up too loud.' Sassan Gari nodded at the old leather sofa at the back of his cramped apartment. Umar Bin Hassan dozed sitting upright, his chin resting on his chest. He had taken off his cap, exposing his bald spot. He snored.

The walls in Sassan's apartment were painted aquarium-turquoise, all the windows were open, and you could see laundry flapping on the clothesline strung high across the alley. It was a fine late-summer day. Sassan was a good friend of Umar's. A young Iranian musician and composer. He was small and agile, sweeping through the apartment like a tornado, barefoot, he had put on water for tea, took a CD from the rack and stared obsessively at the blinking red and green LED lamps on his homemade mini-studio. He turned a few knobs.

'Listen.'

Thin, eerie high notes from a trumpet filled the messy apartment. Watery pink and purple swaths against a blank white canvas. In the background, metallic sounds of decay and destruction mixed with the wispy music. The deep, crisp rhythm of a tabla pulled the trumpet notes downward, kept them from blowing out the window.

'D'you hear it?'

Umar murmured something from the sofa.

'Shh ... go to sleep.'

The music slithered through the apartment like an invisible snake.

'I happened to be up on the roof Tuesday morning, taking pictures of Manhattan,' Sassan said. 'It was like you saw the spirits of the dead rise up, the air was orange and lilac. I could see it through the smoke.'

'I hear it,' Umar said.

'Just go to sleep, man.'

'That's why you were so wound up when I called.'

'Shh.'

Umar tilted his head, like he could hear better that way. 'What were we just talking about?'

'How Billie Holiday sang slower than the music.'

'D'you remember the track Dun and I cut with Pharoah Sanders? I asked him what he saw when he played. You know what he said? "Nothing ... colors, maybe." Pharoah said that. But I saw flames, he spat flames with his sax. He didn't listen to anything I said. "This Is Madness" was just sounds to him.'

'Yeah. The first time I heard The Last Poets in Iran, I didn't speak any English. Nobody spoke English. And yet I still felt the allure of the words, how the poetry played with the rhythms. Same as with the old Sufi poets.'

'When was that?'

'A few years before the revolution.'

'The revolution ... ooh ... re-vo-lu-tion.'

'We watched your revolution, but we got the guys with the long beards.'

'God Bless America.'

'You want some tea?'

'We all lost something, Sassan, but it doesn't matter anymore. Let's hear some more of that music.'

Sassan hesitated. Lost in thought, he plucked at his pointy chin. 'I played some of your first records a while ago. Good grief, how old were you guys?'

'Young enough to think we were immortal.'

'That poetry ... '

'Yeah.'

'Wait a second, the water's boiling.' Hopping over a few loose electric cords, Sassan turned off the gas, and poured the hot water in a long stream into small, colored glasses. 'Sugar?'

Umar shook his head. 'What were you going to say?'

Sassan brought the glasses to the back, set them on the table next to the sofa and climbed back behind the mixing console. 'Forgot.' The patterns of light on his laptop occupied all his attention.

'Poetry.'

'Without music I'd have gone crazy down in Texas. Of all the places in the world, my sister had to go and live in Houston.'

'D'you know that poem by Baraka? "Explainin' the Blues". *What are / these / words / to / tell / it / all? facts / acts / Do they have / their own / words?*'

'Nice.'

'So where's that music?'

'Calm down. Here. Shh. Here it is. JT on trumpet.'

The music slowly, almost imperceptibly, took control of the turquoise room. As if the air was electrically charged. Umar pressed his chin to his chest and rocked gently back and forth. Then the rhythms intensified and the trumpet became more strident and edgy, drowning out the painful sound of steel grating against steel. Sassan pushed the window further open and leaned outside. He squinted into the sunlight. The sheets on the clothesline billowed in the wind. Then the music died down, just as imperceptibly as it had begun.

Umar opened his eyes. 'You're a magician.'

'Did you hear it?'

'Sure did. But you'll have to make me a tape, okay? This poem's gonna take some concentration. The words are still faint, just a whisper. I need more time.'

'I'll give you a copy.'

'... make something beautiful out of ugliness ...'

Sassan was hunched over his mixing console. 'What'd you say?'

'That tape ready yet?'

AUTHOR'S NOTE

The Last Poets is the result of extensive conversations and interviews with most members of the group: David Nelson, Gylan Kain, Felipe Luciano, Abiodun Oyewole, Umar Bin Hassan, Don 'Babatunde' Eaton, and Anne Hurrey, the widow of the late drummer and 'heartbeat' of the group, Nilija Obabi; as well as Poets' family members, fellow poets, producers, musicians, and friends.

Jalal Mansur Nuriddin declined to share his story with me, and Suliaman El-Hadi was already deceased when I began my research.

The Last Poets is a novel. The stories these men shared with me were so vivid and full of imagination that the form of the book came about more or less by itself. And in keeping with the art of The Last Poets themselves, it had to be raw, daring, unpredictable, and jazzy. A chronicle allowing room for atmospheric impressions, poetry, and individual testimonials. The free-narrative form allowed me to zoom in on the book's main players. I have added some fictional elements, characters and scenes, and have taken the liberty to color in or otherwise embellish the description of places and events.

Christine Otten, May 2016

ACKNOWLEDGEMENTS

I extend my thanks, first and foremost, to The Last Poets themselves: Umar Bin Hassan for his unconditional friendship and support. To Gylan Kain, Felipe Luciano, David Nelson, Abiodun Oyewole, Don 'Babatunde' Eaton; and to Anne, Collette, and Ayinde Hurrey, Nilija's widow and children. This book could never have been written without their help and trust. Sincerest thanks also to the families of the Poets—Sandra Saint Claire, Barbara Owens, Queenie Mae, Amina Hassan, Khadijah Hassan-Da Silva, June Lum, Essie Mae Nelson, David Nelson 3rd, Bill Nelson, May Dawson, Obadeli, and Anita Jackson—for their hospitality, their openness, and their stories.

Thanks also to Jalal Nuriddin and Suliaman El-Hadi for their poetry and music. To the late Amiri Baraka, Bill Laswell, DXT, Clayton Reilly, Mickey Melendez, Alan Douglas, Reggie Watson, Sassan Gari, Bob Holman, Ayib Dieng, and Professor Griff and Chuck D. from Public Enemy, all of whom took the time to speak with me about their relationship with The Last Poets.

To Bill Adler who steered me in the right direction. The Detroit 'crew': Khalid El-Hakim, who opened his house to me. Tania and Monique McGee. Anthony. (Thank you, Umar, for 'sharing' your friends with me.)

Rob Schröder and William de Bruijn for their excellent documentary *Something 2 Die 4*.

Special thanks to Dr. Melvin T. Peters (Associate Professor in the Department of African-American Studies at Eastern Michigan University) for agreeing to be my American mentor for this project. Diet Verschoor for her critical eye and warm support. Emile Brugman and Ellen Schalker, who were always there with words of support, stimulating criticism, a kind gesture ... Geert Mak, who showed me that 'anything goes', which gave me the courage to discover my own literary form. Ariadne Harsta, as always. Babs Gons, my 'partner in crime'. And of course, Hans, Daniël, and Tina for their loving patience and for believing in me.

SOURCES

P. 12 'Stellar Nitolic (29)', Amiri Baraka. From the collection *Transbluesency*, Marsilio Publishers, New York, 1995.

P. 24 'A.M.', Umar Bin Hassan. From *On a Mission: Selected Poems and a History of The Last Poets* (Abiodun Oyewole and Umar Bin Hassan, with Kim Green), Henry Holt and Company, New York, 1996, and the album *Be Bop or Be Dead*, Island Records, 1993.

P. 33/35 'Sacred to the Pain', Umar Bin Hassan. From the album *Funkcronomicon*, Axiom Funk, 1995.

P. 69 'Homesick', Umar Bin Hassan. From the album *Holy Terror* (The Last Poets), Black Arc/Rykodisc, 1993.

P. 72 'Rhythm Magic', Umar Bin Hassan. From the album *Rhythm Magic* (Ayib Dieng), Subharmonic, 1996.

P. 83 'This Is Madness', Umar Bin Hassan. From *On a Mission: Selected Poems and a History of The Last Poets* (Abiodun Oyewole and Umar Bin Hassan, with Kim Green), Henry Holt and Company, 1996, and the album *This Is Madness* (The Last Poets), Douglas Records, 1971.

P. 99 'A.M.', Umar Bin Hassan. From *On a Mission: Selected Poems and a History of the Last Poets* (Abiodun Oyewole and Umar Bin Hassan, with Kim Green), Henry Holt and Company, New York, 1996, and the album *Be Bop or Be Dead*, Island Records, 1993.

P. 100 'Epic', Umar Bin Hassan. From the album *Life is Good* (Umar Bin Hassan), Stay Focused Recordings, 2002.

P. 105 'Redbone', Umar Bin Hassan. Idem.

P. 109 'Wise 2', Amiri Baraka. From the collection *Transbluesency*, Marsilio Publishers, New York, 1996.

P. 110 *6 Persons*, Amiri Baraka. From *The Fiction of LeRoi Jones/Amiri Baraka*, Lawrence Hill Books, Chicago, 2000.

P. 110 *6 Persons*, Amiri Baraka. Idem.

P. 132/133 'When the Revolution Comes', Abiodun Oyewole. From *On a Mission: Selected Poems and a History of the Last Poets* (Abiodun Oyewole and Umar Bin Hassan, with Kim Green), Henry Holt and Company, 1996, and the album *The Last Poets*, Douglas Records, 1970.

P. 154 'Bum Rush', Umar Bin Hassan. From *On a Mission: Selected Poems and a History of the Last Poets* (Abiodun Oyewole and Umar Bin Hassan, with Kim Green), Henry Holt and Company, New York, 1996, and from the album *Be Bop or Be Dead*, Island Records, 1993.

P. 161 'Love', Umar Bin Hassan. Idem.

P. 168 'Puerto Rican Rhythms', Felipe Luciano. From the album *Right On! (The Original Last Poets)*, Juggernaut Records, 1968, and the film *Right On!* by Herbert Danska, 1970.

P. 192 'Untogether People', Gylan Kain. From the album *Feel This* (Baby Kain), privately issued, 1997.

P. 195 Excerpt from a poem by Gylan Kain. Recorded live during a performance by Gylan Kain at De Binnenpret in Amsterdam, 1994, for the documentary *Book of Kain* by Ian Kerkhof, 1994.

P. 225 'Jibaro, My Pretty Nigger', Felipe Luciano. From the album *Right On! (The Original Last Poets)*, Juggernaut Records, 1968, and the film *Right On!* by Herbert Danska, 1970.

P. 237 'The Library', Felipe Luciano. Idem.

P. 261 'Hey Now', Felipe Luciano. Idem.

P. 288 'What It Is', Gylan Kain. From the album *Feel This*, privately issued, 1997.

P. 298 'Sacred to the Pain', Umar Bin Hassan. From the album *Funkcronomicon*, Axiom Funk, 1994.

P. 309/310 'Niggers Are Scared of Revolution', Umar Bin Hassan. From *On a Mission: Selected Poems and a History of the Last Poets* (Abiodun Oyewole and Umar Bin Hassan, with Kim Green), Henry Holt and Company, New York, 1996, and from the album *The Last Poets*, Douglas Records, 1970.

P. 319 'Niggers Are Scared of Revolution', Umar Bin Hassan. Idem.

P. 320/321 'Hustler's Convention', Lightnin' Rod. From the album *Hustler's Convention*, Celluloid, 1973.

P. 322 'Malcolm', Umar Bin Hassan. From *On a Mission: Selected Poems and a History of the Last Poets* (Abiodun Oyewole and Umar Bin Hassan, with Kim Green), Henry Holt and Company, New

York, 1996 and the album *Be Bop or Be Dead*, Island Records, 1993.

P. 338 'The Last Poets', David Nelson. From the album *Redemption Song*, B & B, 2001.

P. 365 'Today Is a Killer', David Nelson. From the album *Right On!* (The Original Last Poets), Juggernaut Records, 1968, and from the film *Right On!* by Herbert Danska, 1970.

P. 368 'Portrait of Dad', David Nelson, from the collection *Cracking the Pavement* (David Nelson), Baculite Publishing Company, Denver, Colorado,1989.

P. 375 'Black Women', David Nelson. From the album *Right On!* (The Original Last Poets), Juggernaut Records, 1968, and the film *Right On!* by Herbert Daska, 1970.

P. 379 'When We Are Weak', David Nelson. From the collection *Cracking the Pavement*, Baculite Publishing Company, Denver, Colorado, 1989.

P. 390 '25 Years', Abiodun Oyewole. From the album *25 Years*, Black Arc, 1994.

P. 407 'New York New York The Big Apple', Abiodun Oyewole. From *On a Mission: Selected Poems and a History of the Last Poets* (Abiodun Oyewole and Umar Bin Hassan, with Kim Green), Henry Holt and Company, New York, 1996, and the album *The Last Poets*, Douglas Records, 1970.

P. 410 'Brothers Working', Abiodun Oyewole. From the album *25 Years*, Black Arc, 1994.

P. 418 'When the Revolution Comes', Abiodun Oyewole. From *On a Mission: Selected Poems and a History of the Last Poets* (Abiodun Oyewole and Umar Bin Hassan, with Kim Green), Henry Holt and Company, New York, 1996, and the album *The Last Poets*, Douglas Records, 1970.

P. 430 'For the Millions', Abiodun Oyewole. From the album *Time Has Come* (The Last Poets), Mouth Almighty Recordings, 1997.

P. 448 'Pelourinho', Abiodun Oyewole. From the album *Holy Terror*, Rykodisc, 1993.

P. 457 'Niggers Are Scared of Revolution', Umar Bin Hassan. From *On a Mission: Selected Poems and a History of the Last Poets* (Abiodun Oyewole and Umar Bin Hassan, with Kim Green), Henry Holt and Company, New York, 1996.

P. 463/464 'Personal Things', Umar Bin Hassan. Idem, and from the album *Be Bop or Be Dead*, Island Records, 1993.

P. 469 'Illusion of Self', Umar Bin Hassan. From the album *Holy Terror*, Rykodisc, 1993.

P. 473 'Tribute', Umar Bin Hassan. From the album *Life is Good*, Stay Focused Recordings, 2001.

P. 475 'Drums', Umar Bin Hassan. From *On a Mission: Selected Poems and a History of the Last Poets* (Abiodun Oyewole and Umar Bin Hassan, with Kim Green), Henry Holt and Company, New York, 1996.

P. 477 'Vows', Umar Bin Hassan. Idem.

P. 478/479 'This Is Madness', Umar Bin Hassan. Idem, and from the album *This Is Madness*, Douglas Recordings, 1971.

P. 486 '25 Years', Umar Bin Hassan. From *On a Mission: Selected Poems and a History of the Last Poets* (Abiodun Oyewole and Umar Bin Hassan, with Kim Green), Henry Holt and Company, New York, 1996.

P. 493 'Illusion of Self', Umar Bin Hassan. From the album *Holy Terror*, Rykodisc, 1993.

P. 497 'Love', Umar Bin Hassan. From *On a Mission: Selected Poems and a History of the Last Poets* (Kim Green), Henry Holt and Company, New York, 1996, and the album *Be Bop or Be Dead*, Island Records, 1993.

P. 505 'Redbone', Umar Bin Hassan. From the album *Life is Good*, Stay Focused Recordings, 2001.

P. 517/518 'A.M.', Umar Bin Hassan. From *On a Mission: Selected Poems and a History of the Last Poets* (Abiodun Oyewole and Umar Bin Hassan, with Kim Green), Henry Holt and Company, New York, 1996, and the album *Be Bop or Be Dead*, Island Records, 1993.

On the Design

As book design is an integral part of the reading experience, we would like to acknowledge the work of those who shaped the form in which the story is housed.

Tessa van der Waals (Netherlands) is responsible for the cover design, cover typography and art direction of all World Editions books. She works in the internationally renowned tradition of Dutch Design. Her bright and powerful visual aesthetic maintains a harmony between image and typography and captures the unique atmosphere of each book. She works closely with internationally celebrated photographers, artists, and letter designers. Her work has frequently been awarded prizes for Best Dutch Book Design.

The photograph on the cover (from 1969) shows the face of Umar Bin Hassan, founding member of the Last Poets. It belongs to the collection of David Redfern, world famous music photographer of Miles Davis, Ella Fitzgerald, Jimi Hendrix, Bob Dylan, Frank Sinatra and many others. The photo has been heavily cropped to obtain a feeling of intimacy and strongly color-edited by lithographer Bert van der Horst of BFC Graphics (Netherlands).

Suzan Beijer (Netherlands) is responsible for the typography and careful interior book design of all World Editions titles.

The text on the inside covers and the press quotes are set in Circular, designed by Laurenz Brunner (Switzerland) and published by Swiss type foundry Lineto.

All World Editions books are set in the typeface Dolly, specifically designed for book typography. Dolly creates a warm page image perfect for an enjoyable reading experience. This typeface is designed by Underware, a European collective formed by Bas Jacobs (Netherlands), Akiem Helmling (Germany), and Sami Kortemäki (Finland). Underware are also the creators of the World Editions logo, which meets the design requirement that 'a strong shape can always be drawn with a toe in the sand.'